"I STILL THINK
ANNOUNCED
AND TAKEN O
THE VOTERS . . ."

Lily wanted to hear more, but their conversation shifted to political strategies. She tiptoed back to her room.

Peering into the mirror, she tried to decide if Quinn had been speaking rhetorically or if Miriam really was dead. There was no way to know for certain what had happened to Miriam Westin. All she had to do was play the role she had been hired to play.

But it wasn't that simple anymore. She was beginning to identify strongly with Miriam.

It was Miriam's face she saw in the mirror. Miriam's eyes staring back at her. Tomorrow she would slide Miriam's wedding ring on her finger.

And there was Miriam's husband. And a kiss that had seared her and left her shaking...

✿ ✿ ✿

ALSO BY MAGGIE OSBORNE

The Wives of Bowie Stone
The Seduction of Samantha Kincade
The Promise of Jenny Jones
The Best Man

Published by
WARNER BOOKS

MAGGIE OSBORNE

A Stranger's Wife

WARNER BOOKS

A Time Warner Company

WARNER BOOKS EDITION

Copyright © 1999 by Maggie Osborne
All rights reserved.

Cover design by Diane Luger
Hand lettering by David Gatti
Line art by Michael Racz
Cover illustration by Leslie Wu

Warner Books, Inc.
1271 Avenue of the Americas
New York, NY 10020

Visit our Web site at
http://warnerbooks.com

 A Time Warner Company

Printed in the United States of America

First Printing: March, 1999

10 9 8 7 6 5 4 3 2 1

A Stranger's Wife

Chapter 1

Not until Lily heard the iron gate clang shut behind her did she release the anxious breath she had been holding. Outside the high adobe walls, the air tasted cleaner, fresher, freer, just as she had believed it would.

Hurrying away from the hated gate, she scanned the barren horizon, watching heat waves shimmer above a sweep of short desert grasses broken only by the outstretched arms of giant saguaro cacti.

For five seemingly endless years, she'd been counting the minutes until she could leave this godforsaken wasteland. Now, she was finally free. Blinking at tears of relief, she thought about Rose as she had done every day since she had placed her infant daughter in the arms of her aunt before she stepped into the sheriff's wagon. She'd wondered if she would ever see Rose again or hold her baby daughter. Now, thank God, it would happen.

"Here's your satchel," the warden said, dropping a worn and faded canvas bag near the hem of her skirt.

"Is that the stage?" she asked eagerly, shading her eyes and peering toward the road.

"The stage don't come by here for another three hours."

"Oh." Well, she was used to disappointment. Turning, she spotted a bench near the hitching post. There wasn't a scrap of nearby shade, but she didn't care. She would luxuriate in the novelty of having absolutely nothing to do, would sit and daydream about going home to Missouri and her reunion with Rose. Picking up her satchel, light because she hadn't accumulated anything during the last five years, she carried it to the bench and seated herself on the hot wooden boards.

The warden contemplated the spiral of dust approaching along the road. "There's some things we got to talk about."

"All I want to hear from you is good-bye." Careful, she warned herself. He could drag her back inside the walls. Folding her hands in her lap, she lowered her head and examined his dusty boots. He wore the brown boots today, with the odd white spot near his left instep. She had spent countless hours speculating about what might have caused that white spot.

"I'd a sworn we beat that defiance outta you. Guess you still got some things to learn." Leaning to one side, he spit in the sandy dirt. "That visitor we had about six weeks ago . . . His name is Paul Kazinski."

Cutting her eyes to the left, she watched his spit drying in the October heat and remembered the man he mentioned. The visitor had spent almost an hour watching her wash sheets in the laundry yard. His attention had made her uncomfortable, and later, a dozen jealous slaps had paid her back for his interest.

"Mr. Kazinski has a proposition for you."

Now she looked up and her eyes narrowed. "I ain't interested in any propositions." That she was sitting here outside the Yuma Women's Prison proved she wasn't lucky with men. Men had been her downfall, and she didn't want anything to do with another one. She'd learned her lesson.

The warden's mouth twisted in disgust. "Don't flatter yourself. It's not that kind of proposition. If Kazinski wanted a whore, he could buy the best there is. You think he wants a broken-down jailbird in his bed? You're dreaming."

There were things she could have said. She might have reminded him that he and his stinking guards had found her attractive enough. But she sat too close to the iron gate, and the stage wouldn't arrive for three hours. She bit her lips, seethed, and said nothing.

"Are you listening, Lily? Kazinski is almost here."

The visitor who had watched her was in the conveyance speeding toward the prison? "What does he want?" she asked, sitting up straight, alarm flaring in her eyes.

"He wants to talk to you, that's all."

But that was never all. Men always wanted something more.

"Who is he and why should I talk to him?" She didn't want to waste time with Paul Kazinski or any other man. She just wanted to go home to her daughter. That's all she had thought about for five long years.

The warden tilted back on his boot heels. "They call Kazinski the Kingmaker. He's a big man in politics up in the Colorado Territory. Lately, he's been touring prisons in the West, talking about reform." Leaning, he spit again. "You owe him. If it wasn't for Paul Kazinski, your butt would still be on the other side of the wall. He pulled some strings to get you out early."

If Kazinski had arranged for her early release, then she was grateful. She was also worried. Not for a minute did she imagine that Kazinski had arranged her freedom from the goodness of his heart. Her hands twisted in her lap, and anxiety thinned her voice. "Why is he interested in me?"

"How would I know? Maybe he's so deep into reform that all he wants is to help you begin a new life." The warden's expression indicated he didn't believe this any more than Lily did. "All I know is I said you'd listen to his proposition."

It didn't surprise her that he had made a promise he expected her to keep. For the past five years Ephram Callihan had been the supreme deity in her life and in the lives of every woman behind the walls. On his whim additional food could appear on the mess plates or meals could shrink to bread and water. He decided how they would dress and how they wore their hair. They slept when he told them to and awoke on his schedule. His mood determined if and when they had a rest hour, if and when they could speak. He made the rules that governed their lives.

She had forgotten there might be men like Kazinski who could wield authority over the warden. Being reminded pleased her intensely.

"What if I refuse to talk to Mr. Kazinski?" With the King-maker's carriage in sight, a bit of her old courage asserted itself, and she felt brave enough to display a flash of defiance.

His eyes narrowed in an expression she well knew, and she jerked back from the heat and the stink of him. "You're released into Kazinski's custody, and that means he owns you. It means he can dump you back here if he wants."

Her heart stopped. "I'm going home to Missouri," she said, trying to sound firm, her gaze fixed on the approaching coach.

"You're going to do whatever Kazinski tells you to do."

The carriage skidded onto the side road leading toward the walls and the gate. "Kazinski spent some political chips to get you out. He bought and paid for you, and don't you forget it." The warden stared down at her. Then he shouted at one of the guards to bring water for Mr. Kazinski's horses, and he knocked his hat against his hip, shaking off the dust.

Damn it. She should have guessed it wasn't going to be easy. Nothing had ever come easy. Lowering her eyes, Lily clasped her fingers together and worried about what was coming. Sun pounded the frayed hat she wore, penetrating the straw and heating her scalp. Sweat trickled down her sides, drying almost as rapidly as it soaked through the mended black jacket she wore over skirts that were a slightly different shade. A hundred years ago in a different lifetime she would have fretted about meeting a Kingmaker in her present state. All traces of vanity had disappeared long ago, but she was plenty worried about meeting this man.

She didn't look up until she heard the coach stop in front of the hitching post, then it surprised her to discover a closed Rockaway and not an open gig. Heavy silk shades protected Kazinski from curious onlookers and against the heat and dust; a fine pair of matched blacks stood in the traces. The conveyance was as elegant as any Lily had seen.

The door opened before the driver could climb down to offer assistance, and an impeccably dressed man emerged. She thought he might be forty or so, younger than she had expected a Kingmaker to be. He was so immediately and completely in command of his surroundings that she didn't at first realize how ordinary his features were. He was slightly below average in height, with dark hair and eyes, and broad cheeks that made her think of peasants tilling fields. But his confidence and obvious importance, the powerful way he moved and the cool authority in his eyes made her forget about peasants and think instead of feudal lords. People would not want to cross this man, and they wouldn't forget him.

Ignoring the warden, Kazinski walked directly to the bench where she sat, and removed his hat. That simple act of unexpected politeness melted the coldness she had intended to show him, and a hot lump rose in her throat. It had been a long time since anyone had shown her a bit of courtesy.

He gazed at her for a full minute, studying her intently. "Miss Dale? My name is Paul Kazinski. I believe Mr. Callihan explained that you and I have some business to discuss."

Unnerved by his frank scrutiny, she swallowed hard and strained to detect a hint of his intentions. Nothing came to her, indicating that he was skilled at concealing his thoughts and purpose. Those were probably good traits in a Kingmaker. Shrugging, hoping to hide her nervousness and appear indifferent, she said, "I'm listening."

"It would be more comfortable to converse in private, don't you agree?" Clearly their business did not include the warden, which pleased Lily. "May I offer you a ride?"

There was no real choice about accepting his offer, and she understood that, but she hesitated, pretending there was. Not until she saw him lift a questioning eyebrow toward Callihan did she reach for her satchel and stand. "I guess I wouldn't mind a ride." At least she wouldn't be sitting here for three more hours worrying that Ephram Callihan would throw her back inside.

Immediately the driver hastened forward to take her satchel and drop the step in front of the coach door. It was hard to grasp that she would depart five years of squalor in such a splendid conveyance, difficult to wrap her mind around the contrasts. She stepped forward, then stopped and held herself rigid when she heard the warden call her name.

"You have paid your debt to society, Lily Dale, and you have a new life before you." Callihan delivered a sermon worthy of a preacher, a speech Lily suspected was designed to impress Paul Kazinski more than herself. When he finally finished, she raised her head and looked him squarely in the eyes.

"I hope you die a painful death and burn for all eternity," she said in a low, shaking voice. She'd waited five years to deliver her own speech, and she took great pleasure in watching a dark flush of fury and embarrassment turn Callihan's cheeks florid. He would have backhanded her into the next territory, she knew, except the Kingmaker stood watching.

"I have a long memory, Lily." Not taking his eyes off of her, he leaned forward and spit near her scuffed boots, spattering her hem.

"Go to hell, you bastard," she said before she shook her skirts and climbed into the carriage. She hoped someone made him pay for his brutality and for all the beatings she had endured. One thing was certain. She would die rather than return to the Yuma Women's Prison.

The interior of the carriage was dim, perhaps a degree or two cooler than the desert heat outside. But it was the upholstery she noticed first, sinking into the seat. Removing one glove, she pressed a hand against real velvet, gently stroking the nap back and forth and wishing the calluses on her palms would instantly vanish so she could better enjoy the sensation.

A sharp hiss of breath from the facing seat startled her and she jerked her head up. "Oh!"

At once she became aware of the scent of hair oil and barber's cologne and a residue of cigar smoke. If the luxurious trappings had not distracted her, she would have noticed the other passenger immediately. The man stared at her, then hastily lifted a finger to his lips. Lily frowned, then nodded, inspecting him in silence.

His features were anything but ordinary, and he wasn't dressed in business attire like Paul Kazinski. This man wore a Stetson, a leather vest over a white shirt, and handsomely tooled riding boots. Although he was younger than Kazinski and looked like a cowboy, Lily gazed into eyes the color of hard-polished pewter, and she understood he was as powerful a man as the Kingmaker. In fact, his request for silence suggested he was someone the warden might have recognized.

Although he continued to stare at her openly and rudely, he, too, removed his hat, revealing wavy dark hair sunstreaked with reddish highlights. He was tall, Lily guessed, judging by the length of his legs, broad-shouldered and lean. His face was square, strong jawed and clean-shaven; it looked like his nose had been broken at one time. His was a craggy, lived-in face that men would respect and women would find slightly dangerous and arresting.

She met his eyes and felt her face grow hot in the sudden realization that it had been a very long time since she had been with a man. Not that she wanted to be. She didn't want any more men in her life. But this man's rugged handsomeness sent a tiny frisson of electricity down her spine.

Mr. Kazinski entered the carriage then and fell heavily against the velvet upholstery. No one spoke until the coach had lurched forward and settled into a steady rate of speed.

"Well, Miss Dale, are you happy to be free?" Kazinski inspected her through the dust motes dancing between the seats.

"I ain't in no mood for polite conversation," she said, striving to give the impression that riding in a fancy coach with a Kingmaker didn't intimidate her, that she wasn't nervous and wary. "What do you want?" It puzzled her that Kazinski didn't acknowledge the second man's presence.

"For the moment, I'd like to hear your voice and how you speak." Paul Kazinski smiled, as if trying to put her at ease. As if that would happen. "Would you care for a glass of lemonade?"

Now she noticed the basket at his feet. The thought of something wet and cool made her mouth seem drier, and she couldn't recall the last time she'd tasted real lemonade, but she shook her head. She didn't want to add to her indebtedness until she knew what this was about.

"Perhaps you'll change your mind later." Leaning back on the coach seat, Kazinski opened his collar, then placed his hat on the seat between himself and his silent companion. The other man continued to scrutinize Lily through narrowed grey eyes, making her acutely conscious of every small movement she made. "I believe you grew up on a farm in Missouri?"

"So?" As far as she knew, it wasn't a crime to grow up in Missouri.

"If you would, Miss Dale, please elaborate on your answers." Because for some strange reason they wanted to hear her speak. "How did you happen to come to the New Mexico Territory?"

"I expect you know." The second man kept staring like she had two heads or something. Fidgeting, she shifted on the seat. "I think your cowboy friend might be ill." His face seemed paler beneath his tanned jaw, and although he pressed his hands flat against his thighs, she noticed a tremble in his fingers.

"He's not ill. I'd like to hear your story in your own words," Kazinski said.

She wasn't naive enough to suppose he'd arranged her release without knowing her history, but she owed him her freedom. If he wanted to hear her story now, she supposed she was obliged to tell it. "When I was eighteen I ran off with a man just home from the war. We drifted west." It felt like a hundred years ago, something that had happened to a different person. She might have been reciting a story she had read or recalling a half-forgotten nightmare. "When that man went bad and went off to prison, I found another. Cy wasn't much good either. When he couldn't find work, he got into trouble just like Albie did."

"And you along with him?"

"Eventually." An expectant silence told her that he wouldn't be satisfied with less than the whole sorry tale. "This last incident . . . well, Cy decided to rob one of the gambling halls in Tombstone, but his partner got sick."

Then had come the talk, talk, talk that she hated. Cy wouldn't wait for Charlie to recover from the fever, he said he could manage the job alone if Lily would help. All she had to do was dress like a man and hold a gun in her hand. Make it appear like she was covering him. He would never ask this of her again. He was only doing it for her, so he would have money to buy her and Rose some nice things, money to move on to another town. Eventually their luck would turn, but he had to do this one thing first, and she had to help him. Talk, talk, talk, until she was worn to a frazzle.

She shook her head, marveling that she had been stupid enough to finally agree. "Everything went wrong. The men in the hall jumped Cy, and in the melee the gun I was holding discharged. At the trial they said I tried to kill Mr.

Small, but I didn't even realize the pistol had fired. I just ... if Mr. Small had died, they would have hanged me. They did hang Cy."

"How old are you, Miss Dale?" Kazinski might have been discussing the weather for all the emotion in his tone. Her story and how she had ended in a women's prison didn't touch him.

"I turned twenty-eight last month."

But she probably looked older. Five years of harsh summers and bitter desert winters had wreaked havoc with her complexion. Her hair was dry and lackluster, her eyes dull and tired. The lye soap used in the laundry had reddened her hands and chapped them raw. Finally, gaunt cheeks and a thin frame probably added years to her appearance. Lowering her head, she clenched her teeth and blinked hard, remembering once upon a time when she had cared about how she looked.

"You also have a daughter, is that correct?"

Drawing a breath, she turned to the subject dearest to her heart, feeling the usual painful twist of joy and sorrow. "Rose was three months old when I went to prison. She's with my aunt in St. Joe, Missouri." Lifting her head, she leveled a warning look on the Kingmaker. "Whatever you're selling, mister, I ain't buying. I've been waiting five years to see my baby girl, and there ain't nothing going to keep me away from her. So I'm telling you right now. Whatever you want from me, the answer's no. I ain't got no time to waste."

Finally, the unidentified man spoke. "Her voice is husky. It isn't an exact match. We couldn't hope for that, but it's close." He hadn't looked away from her since she entered the carriage. Reaching into his vest pocket, he withdrew a gold heart-shaped locket and tossed it in her lap. "Does this woman look familiar to you?"

Starting to lose patience, Lily lifted the locket, tested the weight of real gold in her palm, and wished they would get to the point of all this. With a sigh she opened the small clasp and glanced at a miniature portrait inside.

Her eyes widened, and she covered her mouth with her fingers. "Well, son of a bitch!" She couldn't believe what she was seeing. Someone had painted a portrait of her. The artist had painted her heavier than she was and all gussied up, but it was her.

"She sees it, too," Kazinski said, leaning against the upholstery with a satisfied smile.

"It's uncanny," the second man said, his gaze fixed on her face. "You're enough like her that you could be twins."

Then it wasn't a portrait of her, but of someone else. Astonished, Lily lifted the locket to the light at the edges of the shade so she could examine the miniature in detail.

The woman's hair had more yellow in it than Lily's sunbleached shade, but her hairline dipped into a widow's peak just as hers did. The eyebrows were straight and feathery, like hers, but the eyes were the most remarkable similarity. The woman's thick-lashed eyes were a shade of lavender-blue that Lily had never seen except in a mirror. If she gained thirty pounds and arranged her hair differently, she could easily be mistaken for this woman.

The peculiarity of it raised goose bumps on her arms. With a light shiver, she tossed the locket back to the second man, who watched her intently.

"Who is she?" she asked uneasily, shocked to discover there was someone else in the world who resembled her so exactly.

Paul Kazinski shifted to face his companion. "It's up to you. We can go forward, or end it right here."

It surprised her that after ignoring him, Kazinski now deferred to the cowboy. But this was no ordinary cowboy. He wore ruby-and-gold cuff links, and a ruby set in his belt buckle. His shirt was woven from fine Irish linen, and she suspected that his boots had cost more money than she'd seen in her lifetime.

He considered her for a long moment, staring until she felt her cheeks flush and she looked away. Then he leaned forward. "My name is Quinn Westin, and the woman in the portrait is my wife. Forgive me for staring, but looking at you is like looking at Miriam. The resemblance is stunning and shocking."

His voice didn't fit Lily's idea of a cowboy either. He spoke with authority, in a full-throated baritone that vibrated with power and energy and a hint of anger.

"It's her eyes," Kazinski agreed, studying Lily intently. "That's what gave me the idea."

There it was, Lily thought, uneasily. Men hadn't changed during the last five years. They still used women to further their interests, and as sure as the sun would set tonight, Mr. Kazinski's idea involved using her in some way. Now the talk, talk, talk would begin in earnest.

But these men were too polished to begin with something as obvious as reminding her that she wouldn't be out of prison if it weren't for them. First, they would attempt to convince her that whatever they wanted was in her best interest. That's how men induced women to ruin their lives.

"I'd rather have a whiskey, but if all you have is lemonade, I'll take some now," she said in a weary voice, leaning against the seat back and closing her eyes. "Then you gents can tell me how you want to use me and why I should be grateful to let you do it." She cut a glance across both of them. "But if what you want involves a delay in me going home, then I ain't going to agree."

No one spoke until Mr. Kazinski placed a crystal tumbler in her hand and she had raised it to her lips. The sweet-and-sour lemonade slipped down her throat like ambrosia, and she had to struggle not to gulp the treat and beg for more.

Kazinski cleared his throat and opened his tie, preparing for the talk, talk, talk. "It's true that we wish to use you, Miss Dale, but not as callously as you appear to assume. We wish to hire your services."

There was the first dangled benefit. Undoubtedly they knew that she had just enough money to get to Missouri and not a penny more.

"I ain't interested, mind you, but what kind of services are you looking to hire?" she asked suspiciously. She doubted they would have gone to all the trouble to arrange her freedom if they wanted to hire a housekeeper or a washwoman.

Mr. Kazinski rested his elbows on his knees and leaned forward, his dark eyes intent on her face. "Do you recognize Mr. Westin's name?"

"Should I?" She glanced at Quinn Westin who continued to regard her with a slightly stunned expression.

"Mr. Westin hopes to be the first elected governor of Colorado after the territory joins the union next May. The election will be held in April, six months from now, and Mr. Westin's campaign is well under way. His chances of winning the governor's race appear excellent."

"I don't know anything about politics except that politicians are always making speeches." She thought of politicians as old men dressed in frock coats and top hats. Not hard-angled cowboys in their mid to late thirties. She tried to imagine Quinn Westin striding across a bunting-draped podium, speaking to an enthralled audience. Maybe the Kingmaker would insist that he dress differently for such an occasion. Or maybe she had the wrong idea about politics.

Regardless, she could imagine him capturing a crowd's attention with his rich confident voice and intense eyes. From the moment she had first noticed him, his powerful presence had slightly overwhelmed her.

"So what does Mr. Westin's ambitions have to do with me?"

"A candidate for governor must lead a circumspect life, Miss Dale. There can be no whiff of scandal or impropriety, do you understand? At this stage of the game, a candidate must be like Caesar's wife, above suspicion. He must be cleaner than clean, the most noble beast in the jungle. After the election . . ." Kazinski shrugged. "But right now and during the next six months, unpleasant rumors or malicious gossip could destroy the promise of a brilliant political career."

Her uneasiness increasing, Lily lowered the lemonade glass, waiting to learn what lay at the heart of this discussion and how it could possibly apply to her.

"My wife has disappeared," Quinn Westin stated quietly, watching her as if unable to look away.

"I'm sure you grasp the difficulty," Kazinski interjected. "How do we explain Mrs. Westin's untimely disappearance?"

"Well, gents, this is merely a suggestion," Lily commented, raising an eyebrow, "but have you considered saying Mrs. Westin has disappeared?"

The cowboy's expression didn't change, but Kazinski gave her a chilly smile. "Such an announcement would give rise to damaging speculation which ultimately would destroy all the effort that's gone into positioning Mr. Westin as a viable candidate."

"If it's that important, then you should find your wife," she said to Westin. "Where did she go?"

"That isn't your concern." Dark brows came together, and she watched his hands curl into fists.

Suddenly, Lily grasped their intentions, an idea so startling that she almost dropped the crystal glass. "Good Lord. Are you suggesting that I . . ."

"Of course that's what we're suggesting, Miss Dale. We want to hire you to impersonate Mrs. Westin."

She stared in disbelief. "That's crazy. I ain't going to do something lunatic like that. I'm going home."

Kazinski waved aside her protest. "We only require seven months of your time. Once Mr. Westin has won the election, we'll release an announcement stating the sad news that Mrs. Westin's consumption has returned, and she must leave at once for Santa Fe to recuperate. Shortly thereafter, we'll announce that she succumbed to the disease."

"Seven months? Never!"

"For appearances' sake, we'd prefer that you remain in position for a month after the election."

"No!" She shook her head hard enough that her hat tilted to one side. "When I went to prison, my Rose was a baby. She's five years old now, and she doesn't remember her mama." Her voice shook with emotion. "You'll have to find someone else because I won't wait another seven months to be with my baby!"

"Yes, you will, Miss Dale." Kazinski's dark eyes went flat. "First of all, there *is* no one else, not with your eyes. Secondly, perhaps this is the moment to mention that you have a provisional pardon. Do you understand what that means? It means we can return you to the Yuma Women's Prison at our discretion. Think about that, Miss Dale."

"You sons a bitches," she said softly, striking the upholstered seat with a gloved fist.

Quinn Westin turned his face toward the window, but Kazinski met her furious stare head-on.

"Would you rather wait seven months to be reunited with your daughter . . . or serve out the remainder of your term and wait another five years?"

Fighting to control the helplessness and fury burning in her chest, Lily made herself think. Anger wouldn't help, it never did, but reason might. "This plan ain't going to work," she said finally, struggling to keep her voice even.

"And why is that?" Kazinski inquired, as if he were genuinely interested in her opinion.

"I look like your wife," she admitted to Westin. "But we ain't the same person. No one will believe I'm her."

"It will take some work on your part," Quinn agreed. He was still frowning, and squinted at her through narrowed eyes. "But I'm starting to think it's possible."

Kazinski nodded. "With your hair arranged differently and decent clothing . . . when the sun damage fades and some attention is paid to your skin . . . Right now you're as thin as a candlewick. Once you gain a little weight, the resemblance will be even more amazing. And we'll work on your speech and mannerisms. At the moment, the public believes Mrs. Westin is in seclusion battling consumption. People expect changes after a long, debilitating illness."

"I can read and write, and I speak fairly well because the aunt who raised me is a schoolteacher. But I ain't what you would call educated." She gazed at both of them, anger burning in her eyes. How could they imagine she would be willing to give up seven months of her life to further a stranger's ambitions? "I worked on a farm while I was growing up, building fences, hoeing fields, doing whatever had to be done." Her eyes went flat. "I'm a long way from being a lady." Pulling off her gloves, she showed them her hands, callused, fiery red, and chapped raw.

"These hands have never known leisure. They're work hands, and they look it. I swear, I like my whiskey, and I smoke cigars when I can get one. And finally . . . a women's prison ain't no finishing school. I was beaten monthly. Twice I had broken bones. I was starved, isolated, whipped, worked until I was sick. You have to be tough to survive that, and I'm tough."

The two men listened in silence, their faces expressionless.

"Now, you tell me," she said, knowing the answer. "Is my background similar to Mrs. Westin's? Do I sound like a woman who could convincingly impersonate the wife of a candidate for governor?"

Folding her arms across her chest, she sat back and waited for them to concede that she was right. Once they did, she'd do some talk, talk, talk of her own and try her damnedest to convince them to let her continue on to Missouri instead of returning her to prison and Ephram Callihan, God rot his soul.

It was Westin who spoke first. "You're correct. Miriam's background is nothing like yours. My wife was the daughter of a prominent judge. She grew up in comfort, attended by servants. She was tutored at home, sent on a grand tour of Europe before her debut."

"There you are," she said with a short, satisfied nod.

Kazinski's eyes narrowed. "Let's talk a bit more about

you. You've lied to us," he stated coldly. "Cy Gardener was not your legal husband."

"I considered myself married," she said with a shrug. "That's what counts." If he hoped to embarrass her, he'd guessed wrong. Marriage was a state of mind, not a piece of paper. She didn't need a preacher man saying words over her to feel married.

"You claim that Mr. Small was shot accidentally, but five witnesses testified that you shot him deliberately."

"That's not how it happened. I ain't much, but I ain't a killer."

He held up a hand. "Deception is a way of life for you, Miss Dale. Your proclivity for deceit and dissembling is what we wish to hire. If your testimony at your trial is any judge, you're capable of mounting a fine performance."

"If that's meant as a compliment, it ain't swaying me none."

"You've demonstrated an ability to adapt and do what you must in order to survive. And I suspect you learn quickly. I'm sure you can master the art of pouring tea, can adequately preside as Mr. Westin's hostess, and do whatever else we require. Moreover, may I remind you that you have a strong motivation to succeed."

"I do what you want or you send me back to prison," she said bitterly, hating them. They didn't care about her or Rose. All they cared about was getting what they wanted and winning an election.

"Let's focus on what you have to gain," Kazinski said smoothly. "We are prepared to pay you two hundred dollars a month from now until the inauguration. That's fourteen hundred dollars . . . a fortune to someone like you. We'll allow you to keep the expensive clothing and jewelry you'll require to impersonate Mrs. Westin. And when you leave, you'll be furnished with transportation to Europe, and we agree to buy you a small house on the Continent. You'll benefit handsomely merely for doing what comes naturally, deceiving those around you."

Stunned into speechlessness, Lily stared at both of them. "That's a generous offer," she said finally. An amazing offer. "If it wasn't for Rose, I'd sure have to think about this. But I don't want your money. I want my daughter." Leaning forward, she gave them a look that she hoped was as hard as theirs. "So I'm turning down this proposition, and I'm begging you to let me go home."

"You'll be reunited with your daughter eventually," Kazinski said with an impatient gesture. "We just want a few months of your time."

Biting her lips and struggling not to scream, she swung her gaze to Quinn Westin. "Why is Mr. Kazinski explaining this, and not you? Ain't you the one with the missing wife?"

"The impersonation was Paul's idea. Frankly, I was against it until I saw you," Westin said shortly. "Paul has explained our offer because it's his job to handle details."

"And I'm just a detail?" She could read the handwriting on the wall. They were not going to let her go.

"You're the most important detail," Westin replied. "Without you, my campaign is in jeopardy." His rugged face settled into lines of granite. "I've come too far to let that happen."

Abruptly it occurred to her that if she pretended to be his wife, then she would have to live with this man. Suddenly she was very conscious of him, aware of his size and leathery scent and brooding grey eyes. Although he hadn't spoken much, and he held himself very still, she was acutely aware of an angry inner energy that simmered on the verge of explosion.

Ducking her head, she touched her fingertips to her eyelids and pressed at hopeless tears gathering beneath her lashes. They had her neatly boxed between a threat and extravagant promises.

"Well, Miss Dale?" Kazinski crossed an ankle over his knee and withdrew a cigar from his vest pocket. "You've had a moment to rethink your refusal. What is your decision?"

"You know damned well that I don't have a choice."

"Of course you do." But the Kingmaker was too experienced at his game to state her choices aloud. Acquiesce or return to prison. "Frankly, this is a wonderful opportunity for you. We're offering you seven months of luxury. Gowns, jewelry, balls, soirées . . ." He let his voice trail, giving her a moment to imagine a fairy-tale world she had never experienced. "When it's over, you'll have money, a house, and a secure future with your daughter, none of which you have any hope of obtaining now."

Feeling as if she were drowning, she glanced up at Westin. For a long moment they held each other's gaze, then Lily looked down at the crystal glass she still clasped in her hand.

There was no choice, and she knew it. But at the end of seven months, she would finally and truly be free, and then she could go to Rose. If she had to, she thought, wanting to weep, she supposed she could make herself wait another seven months to see her baby. And it appeared that she had to.

"You knew from the beginning that I would agree to whatever you wanted rather than return to that hellhole," she whispered. She didn't dare look at either of them for fear they would see the hatred in her eyes and find an additional way to punish her.

"Excellent," Kazinski said. "You won't regret your decision."

Her decision? She almost laughed. Silk-lined walls were no less a prison than adobe.

When she could control her expression, she looked up at Westin, waiting for him to say something, but he didn't. He leaned back on the coach seat, an ankle crossed over his knee, gazing at her with a stony frown.

A light shiver traveled down her spine. It had been a long time since a man had studied her so intently or had looked at her as if trying to probe beyond her exterior.

She watched his jaw tighten and release, tighten and release. And she wondered what had happened to his wife. Where was Miriam Westin? And just why had she disappeared?

Chapter 2

"Now that you've seen her, talked to her, what do you think?"

"I think we're sinking deeper into quicksand." Before lighting an after-dinner cigar, Quinn rolled up his sleeves and opened his collar. Undoubtedly the heat was worse inside the house, where Lily Dale had remained. Perhaps she had retired to her room and stripped out of her heavy black prison clothing. An unwanted thought leapt into his mind as he narrowed his gaze on the low dunes rolling away from the house Paul had borrowed for their use tonight. Hating himself for wondering, he tried to guess if her hips and breasts could be as remarkably similar to Miriam's as her face.

Paul leaned back in a porch chair and crossed his ankles on top of the railing. "We can scrap the plan at any point before we publicly announce that Miriam has recovered from her illness. Until that moment, we're not irrevocably committed." He smoked in silence for several minutes. "Nothing has changed, Quinn. The reasons for replacing Miriam with a ringer remain valid. First, voters prefer a family man. Second, everyone knows you have a wife. Eventually you either have to produce Miriam or explain her absence. Do we really want anyone to learn what happened to her?"

Quinn swore and fixed his eyes on the deepening darkness. "It would be a hell of a lot easier and cleaner simply to announce that Miriam did not recover from her illness. We arrange a funeral and go on from there."

"A sympathy vote might work in any election but this one. The first year of statehood will require a great many social events, and the candidate with a social wife will have an edge. That means we have to produce Miriam. If you bury Miriam before the election, you also bury your political chances. Without her, the party will drop you like a hot potato," he finished flatly.

Quinn turned the glass of whiskey between his fingers, then flexed his shoulders in a futile effort to ease the tension squeezing his spine. "Her table manners are atrocious. She stole the leftover bread and hid it in her pocket."

Lily Dale looked enough like Miriam to be her twin, but the two women had not inhabited the same world. The profound differences between them appalled and fascinated him.

"Stealing food is a habit that will pass." Paul rolled his cigar between his thumb and forefinger, studying the ash. "We have two months, Quinn, no more. After that, if we don't produce Miriam, your wife's continued absence will begin to raise questions and hurt your candidacy."

Quinn didn't see how she could be ready in two months. "She'll deceive people from a distance, but the minute she speaks . . ." He shook his head and pulled a hand down his jaw.

" 'Ain't' is the biggest problem and easily eliminated."

"Her personality is nothing like Miriam's."

Toward the end, Miriam had become silent and remote, but she had never been tough. Suspicion and boldness had not formed part of her character. And she had been too much the lady to express anger or outright opposition. In contrast, Lily had studied him throughout dinner with a burning gaze that revealed all too clearly her deep resentment and anger.

"Lily isn't a lady, and she never will be," Paul commented, releasing a stream of smoke into the still, hot air. "But she's smart enough to recognize eventually the opportunity she's being offered, and clever enough to make it succeed for her and for us." He paused. "This will work. People change. If someone mentions that Miriam doesn't seem like herself, you nod and agree that tragedy and illness have changed her. Mention that she's stronger in some ways, still confused and vulnerable in other areas." He shrugged. "I'm convinced we can be successful."

"If the impersonation is ever exposed, we're both ruined," Quinn said, watching fireflies dance past the porch.

"Then we have to make sure that doesn't happen."

Until today, Paul's idea had been an interesting abstraction, but Lily Dale had suddenly become real when Quinn saw her snatch the supper rolls and stuff them into her pocket. She was a woman fresh out of prison with opinions and viewpoints colored by that experience. He couldn't guess how her life experiences would impact on the success of the deception, and it worried him. He could imagine countless possibilities for disaster.

There was something else that he hadn't had time to consider thoroughly when Paul first proposed this plan. He and Lily Dale would be living together privately as well as publicly.

Frowning, he shifted in the porch chair. Already he could see that she would be beautiful once the damage of the last five years began to fade. Living with her would be difficult and dangerous; he sensed that, too, because he was drawn to her, attracted by this strange new Miriam who did not acquiesce easily, Miriam with defiance and fire in those stunning lavender eyes. Miriam who was suddenly an interesting stranger.

"Lily will emerge from the prison mentality very rapidly. She'll understand that we aren't going to punish her by withholding food. She'll grasp that we won't beat her or mistreat her, and the defensiveness and defiance will disappear." Paul studied him with a thoughtful gaze. "The key to success is you. If you treat her exactly as you treated Miriam, any small doubts about Lily will fade."

Could he do that? Accept a stranger as his wife? Bitterness twisted his lips. Of course he could. At the end, Miriam had been a stranger. "How do you plan to accomplish the miracle of transformation?"

"Clothing will create an immediate improvement. Senora Alvarez is taking her measurements now. We'll telegraph the information to a seamstress in Santa Fe and another in Denver. The Santa Fe seamstress will have a small traveling wardrobe ready for Lily when we arrive. The Denver seamstress will begin at once to alter Miriam's clothing. She's already been informed that Miriam lost significant weight during her illness."

An expression of distaste pinched his face. "Must she wear Miriam's clothing?"

"Of course she must."

"It's going to take more than a new wardrobe to make a lady out of Lily Dale."

"Agreed." For the next half hour Paul detailed the steps necessary to transform Lily into a credible semblance of Miriam. "Finally, I'll use every minute of our travel time to tutor her in etiquette and deportment. She'll have approximately four weeks to acquire some polish."

Quinn's smile didn't reach his eyes. "You're a man of unsuspected talents."

"I've been studying the subject," Paul said with a laugh. Standing, he placed his hands against the small of his back and stretched. "You're going to miss learning the etiquette of calling cards and how to manage the train of your ball gown."

"We need to talk about that," Quinn said after his grin faded. "Perhaps I should stay with you and Lily instead of returning to Denver." He wasn't entirely sold on this idea. It might be wise to stay so he could cancel the impersonation if it appeared to him that it couldn't succeed.

Paul shook his head. "I want her focused on learning to be a lady, and frankly you'll only be a distraction. More importantly, you know you need to be in Denver. Do I need to remind you that you have two upcoming speeches, you're on the committee drafting the new state constitution, there will be a hundred decisions to make in order to finish the rebuilding of your house, and there's your law firm to attend to. You'll have plenty of time to get acquainted with her later."

"Most likely I'll go directly to the ranch. I can handle my obligations from there."

Paul shrugged and glanced at his pocket watch. "Speaking of speeches, I'll have the corrected versions ready before we part company in Santa Fe."

Quinn remained on the porch after Paul went inside. Insects bumped against the lighted window behind him. The desert cacti had retreated to dark silhouettes that resembled men with their arms raised in surrender.

He smoked in the darkness and contemplated the upcoming year and everything he hoped to accomplish. As the first governor of a newly created state, he would be faced with fascinating challenges. He would be the man who set Colorado's direction and guided the new state through its infancy. If he did his job wisely and well, he'd earn a small place in history.

It all hinged on winning the election. And for that, regardless of how he felt about it, he needed Lily Dale. But he didn't need her through the inauguration as Paul insisted. Once he won the vote, Lily became expendable. The sooner he was rid of her, the better.

Rubbing his neck, he stared into his empty whiskey glass. Lately it had become a game to try to pinpoint exactly when and how things had started to go wrong, and then to follow the chain to the present moment. Would Lily Dale improve his luck, or would she be the worst mistake yet? Swearing beneath his breath, he stood abruptly and entered the house, intending to refill his glass from the decanter in the library before he returned to the cooler air on the porch.

He didn't bother to light a lamp. Enough light fell through the library door to illuminate the decanters atop a cart near a wall of books. He filled his whiskey glass, replaced the decanter, and turned. That's when he saw her.

For one ghostly moment, he believed he was looking at Miriam, and he sucked in a sharp breath. She stood behind a high-backed chair as if she'd heard him approach and tried to hide.

Damn it. She knew he'd seen her, now he had to talk to her.

"I ain't snooping. I came in here looking for a drink, same as you," she said quickly, sounding sullen and defensive.

The shadows were too deep at the edges of the room for Quinn to see her clearly, and he was glad. He swallowed a long drink of whiskey then glanced toward the door. "I have what I came for . . . good night, Miss Dale."

"I'd like permission to speak to you."

"You don't need permission to speak." This glimpse of her life made his chest tighten. "It's cooler outside. Shall we?"

When she stepped into the bar of light, he noticed she still wore the shabby mismatched suit provided by the prison, but she'd brushed out her hair and tied it at the neck. From there, it hung to her waist like a golden cord. Although the long strands were dull and dry, he was unaccustomed to seeing a woman with her hair down, and he found the sight annoyingly provocative.

Turning away from her, he reached for the decanter. "I'll pour you a glass of whiskey."

"Thank you." A long pause suggested that she wasn't accustomed to observing polite amenities.

But her voice reminded him of Miriam's when Miriam was coming down with a cold, husky and low-pitched. However, Miriam's voice had possessed a tentative quality that Lily's didn't. Lips pressed in a tight line, he carried their drinks to the porch and set them on the table between two chairs.

When she reached for the glass, passing her hand through the light from the window, he noticed ragged, torn fingernails.

"That is so good," she said with a sigh. Tilting her head, she gazed up at the stars. "We used to describe tastes and smells—it was a game we played occasionally to pass the time. I thought I remembered the taste of good whiskey, but I didn't." She hesitated. "I suppose I should ask if your wife liked whiskey?"

"No." Miriam had considered even the smell of whiskey unpleasant.

"Too bad for Miriam," she said after a moment of silence. "I guess she didn't smoke either."

The image was so ludicrous that he almost laughed. Then he realized she was eyeing him with an expectant expression. "Are you saying you want a cigar?"

"I wouldn't refuse if one was offered."

He reminded himself that she was not Miriam, and therefore her request should not surprise him. Removing a cigar from the silver case in his jacket pocket, he clipped and lit it before he passed it to her. She inhaled deeply, then released a stream of smoke with a small sound of pleasure.

"Who does this house belong to?"

"The name of the owners doesn't matter," he said, unwilling to impart information that she didn't need to know. "The important issue is privacy. Right now, you wouldn't be mistaken for Miriam. That will change by the time you leave Santa Fe. After Santa Fe, you and Paul will stay in hotels. If you're remembered, it won't matter then. In the press release, it will be mentioned that Paul fetched you back to Denver."

"Where will you be? Won't you be with us?" Her lavender eyes studied him above the rim of her glass as she took another sip, but she dropped her gaze when he looked at her.

"I'll leave you and Paul in Santa Fe and take the stage straight through to Denver. You'll follow in the private coach at a more comfortable pace. Paul needs time to teach you the things you need to know."

She nodded and her lips tightened. "So which of you is the boss? Do I take orders from you or from Mr. Kazinski?"

It was an interesting query. It also wasn't the real question. "Either Paul or myself can scrap this plan at any time. That's what you're asking, isn't it?"

"I want to know which of you bastards can send me back to prison. Who do I have to please?"

"You have to learn a role and play it well enough to convince people who knew her that you're Miriam. If you do that, you'll please us both," he said sharply. At this moment, watching her draw on the cigar, he held serious doubts as to the possibility of success.

"Next question. What am I supposed to call you?"

"In public, you'll refer to me as your husband, Mr. Westin." His tongue formed the words with repugnance. "You may call me Quinn in private."

For the moment at least, it appeared her questions were answered. Although it didn't seem to trouble her to smoke and sip her whiskey in silence, her simmering resentment made him uncomfortable.

"Have you been to Denver?" His inclination was to leave her and go inside, but he would have to live with this woman. Surely they could find something to say to each other.

"No."

"The city's growing rapidly. At last count the population had reached about eighteen thousand." When she didn't comment, he ground his teeth, then continued talking. "Denver sprang up near the confluence of Cherry Creek and the South Platte River. The most distinguishing features are the mountains west of town."

He couldn't tell if she was interested or even if she was listening. She kept her face turned away from him, gazing out at the starlit desert, watching their cigar smoke slowly dissipate.

"Are you always this quiet?" If so, then he'd finally discovered something she had in common with Miriam.

"We were punished for talking without permission."

"Prison reform is part of my campaign platform. Someday I'd like to hear about your prison experiences."

"Well, you ain't going to. I don't want to think about that time ever again."

Trying to talk to her was like attempting to push a boulder up a steep hill. "As you wish." Frowning at the darkness, he searched for a new topic. "Did you have an attorney at your trial?"

"Why do you care?"

He had already noticed that she looked for traps in every question. "I'm an attorney," he explained, speaking through his teeth. "I'm interested in trials."

When she turned to stare at him, the light from the window lit her cheekbone and the tip of her chin, sharpening the gaunt contours, calling his attention to how painfully thin she was. For an instant he experienced a disorienting conviction that he was looking at Miriam after a long and wasting illness.

Her stunning resemblance to his wife kept him off-balance, made him believe he knew this woman when he didn't.

"You don't look like a lawyer," she said at length. "You look like a cowboy."

Her comment made him smile and relax a little. "I own a ranch outside Denver. Presently I'm winding down my affairs at the firm. Once I win the election, I'll close the firm's doors."

"Oh. Well Cy and I had a lawyer all right, but it didn't do any good. He was in the judge's pocket."

He disliked assumptions of that sort and was tempted to say so, but decided against provoking her. "I'm sorry your husband was hanged," he said instead, noticing that she crossed her legs at the knee instead of at the ankle. Paul had his work cut out for him.

A soft sigh dropped her shoulders. "Cy wasn't any good. He deserted from the army. Lied when the truth was better. Stole things he didn't even have a use for. It didn't bother him to shoot a man in the back." She hesitated, then her chin came up. "But he did one good thing. He gave me Rose."

"There's something I want to say. You may not believe this, but I deeply regret the necessity to interfere with your plans."

"Then don't do it," she said bluntly.

Standing, he walked to the porch rail and pushed his hands into his back pockets. "If I don't produce Miriam soon, the party will select another candidate."

"That's supposed to matter to me? I don't give a damn if you get elected." Her eyes flashed as brightly as the fireflies darting through the desert night. "Your goal of becoming governor ain't no more important than my goal of finding my daughter again. So don't tell me you're sorry about putting yourself first, and don't hint that you ain't got a choice. You sure as hell do, and you've chosen to step on me!"

He flipped his cigar over the porch rail and silently cursed. "Circumstances force people to do things they might not otherwise do," he said after a minute.

"Circumstances?" Her laugh was short and harsh. "Maybe for you it's circumstances. For me, it's always been men who have forced me to do things I don't want to do. You men always find a way to twist wrong into right."

Standing abruptly, she dropped her cigar on the porch floor

and ground it under her heel. "I'll get my mind turned around to this because I'm the one without a choice. I'll put your needs before mine, and I'll make the impersonation succeed because I ain't going back to prison. But don't you ever forget. Even when I'm pretending to look at you with the adoring eyes of a wife . . . inside I'm hating you and Kazinski. When this is over, I'm going to spit on you both!"

Turning on her heel, she walked into the house, slamming the screen door behind her.

He stood at the porch rail for another minute, fighting an urge to smile, and wondering if she realized how puny her threat was or how vulnerable her bravado made her appear.

Long after the lights were extinguished and the house fell silent behind him, Quinn remained on the porch, his fingers tented beneath his chin, thinking about Lily Dale.

He would have only one chance to be Colorado's first governor, whereas she would eventually be reunited with her child regardless of how the election turned out.

After thinking about it, he dropped his head and massaged the bridge of his nose with his thumb and forefinger. Disgusted with himself, he conceded that he was capable of justifying whatever he felt he needed to do. Miriam was proof of that.

After a hurried breakfast, they left the house and walked to the waiting Rockaway.

"Stop," Paul Kazinski said sharply. "A lady never enters a conveyance unassisted. Wait for the driver or your escort to hand you inside."

Feeling foolish, as if somehow she should have known this, Lily reluctantly accepted his arm only to be corrected again once she was inside the coach.

"A lady always takes the forward-facing seat. If you're riding with other women, the oldest or most honored and respected lady takes the forward-facing position."

After changing seats, she smoothed her heavy black skirts with an irritable swipe and made herself as comfortable as possible for the long day's ride. It was cooler today, but still hot.

"Never cross your legs at the knee. Always at the ankle," Paul instructed as the coach rattled away from the house.

Slowly Lily uncrossed her legs, and her lips tightened. Paul Kazinski had maintained a steady flow of criticism from the instant she appeared for breakfast. She couldn't just sit down. She had to wait to be seated. She held her fork wrong. She ate too fast. She made slurping noises while drinking her coffee.

She hadn't felt shame often in her life, but their expressions as they watched her eat had made her feel about one step above a brutish animal. The irony was that her friends in prison had believed she had good manners and teased her about how daintily she held her knife and fork and cup.

Frowning, she looked down at her hands. Even walking to the coach had earned criticism. Her stride was too long. She hadn't opened the parasol Paul had given her. Although the distance from porch to coach was only a few feet, she should have donned her gloves and hat.

Lily was quick, and a lot was at stake. She would learn what she had to and swiftly, but so far the rules seemed foolish and ridiculously inconvenient.

"Do you mind if we smoke?" Quinn inquired politely, patting his leather vest for the silver cigar case. This morning he was clean-shaven and smelled of barber's soap. He didn't stare as openly as he had yesterday, but she could tell that her uncanny resemblance to his wife intrigued him and perhaps repelled him a little. When his hard gaze settled on her, he frowned as if he hadn't yet decided how to react to her.

Lily hadn't made up her mind on that point either. She was determined not to let another troublemaking man into her life, yet here she was with two of them. And when Quinn's stormy eyes met hers, she felt as if she were drowning in grey heat, and her stomach did a slow roll and her throat flamed hot.

Irritated by her unwanted reaction to him, she turned her face to the window. "Smoking don't bother me. I'd like a cigar, too."

Horror widened Paul's dark eyes. "Never! Ladies do not smoke cigars. Or drink whiskey," he added firmly.

Five years in prison had conditioned her not to object to a man's instructions. The punishment for disobedience was severe. Therefore, her first instinct was to accept his decree without a whimper. But she was free now, even if her freedom was conditional, and she had promised herself that once she regained her liberty, she would never again meekly accept a man's word as law.

"I'm willing to be a lady in public, but in private I should be allowed a few pleasures," she insisted stubbornly. She didn't have much hope that they would agree and issued the statement simply to test their reaction.

Actually, the pleasures she had already experienced left her feeling almost giddy. She had gone to bed with a full stomach for the first time in years, and the sheets had been clean and sweet-smelling, the mattress and pillow soft and downy. She hadn't had to share her bathwater with four other women, and the soap had been smooth on her skin and rose-scented. She had slept in a private room and, amazingly, her morning coffee had been served on a bed tray by a servant who pretended not to notice the yellowed, much-mended state of her nightgown. Best of all, her world was no longer defined by high, stuccoed walls. Anytime she wanted to, she could look outside and see the horizon.

"Your pleasures will not include smoking or whiskey," Paul stated sharply in a voice that left no room for negotiation.

Prompted by resentment, she impulsively decided to try an experiment. "If I can't have a cigar, then yes, I sure as hell do mind if you smoke," she said to Quinn, a challenge blazing in her eyes.

He paused in the act of clipping the end of a cigar. Then his face settled into craggy lines and he replaced the cigar inside its case. "As you wish," he agreed in an expressionless voice.

His submission astonished her as much as the small hint of amusement flickering at the back of his eyes. She didn't figure out why he agreed until the end of the day. If Quinn and Paul expected her to behave like a lady, then they had to treat her as one. Interesting. Spirits rising, Lily decided a lady wasn't as defenseless as she had assumed. She'd found one small weapon among the mannerly dos and don'ts, perhaps there were more.

Like the house Paul had borrowed for their first night on the road, the second house they stayed in was also isolated from any nearby town or neighbors. Both houses were larger and more luxurious than any Lily could have imagined. Until now, she had never seen an indoor water closet or stayed in a home that employed servants.

"In this instance, ignorance works to your advantage,"

Paul commented, taking a seat in the courtyard after dinner. "You're striking the right tone with the servants. Coolly polite, a little distant."

Intimidated half to death would have been a better description, and intimidation accounted for her behavior. The servants totally cowed her. Their smirks of superiority plainly stated they knew she was no lady.

As if to refute Paul's offhand compliment, Senora Menendez stepped into the courtyard and asked Lily if she wanted coffee served outside. The Senora's expression remained bland, but her dark eyes resented deferring to someone dressed so shabbily.

The simple question paralyzed her. She had no idea if the men wanted coffee, and wasn't comfortable making a decision for them. She wasn't accustomed to being waited on, and didn't blame the Senora for resenting an ex-convict issuing orders. She imagined the servants took one look at her and knew she'd been behind bars only days ago. Feeling her cheeks heat, she cast a wild glance of indecision toward Quinn. He examined her expression, then gave Senora Menendez a lazy smile of easy charm.

"Bring us a bottle of whiskey and three glasses, *por favor.*"

Paul's head snapped up. "Bring two glasses and coffee for the lady."

"*Three* glasses, and no coffee," Quinn repeated firmly.

Paul waited until Senora Menendez had withdrawn. "No one knows better than you that Miriam never drank hard liquor."

"Lily is not Miriam." Quinn studied her a moment, then returned his gaze to Paul. "Lily applied herself today and made excellent progress, but let's not lose sight of our expectations. We expect her to impersonate Miriam, not become Miriam."

"At present, it's important that she totally submerge herself in her role," Paul stated angrily.

"Which she has done for the last ten hours."

"All it takes is one slip at a crucial moment, and everything comes crashing down around us," Paul warned. He gave Quinn a long look. "Everything," he repeated firmly.

Lily observed the sharp exchange with fascinated interest. Both men were authoritative and powerful, unaccustomed to being countermanded. Today she'd learned they had been friends long before Quinn decided to toss his hat into the political ring. Had friendship not been involved, Lily suspected the Kingmaker would have claimed final authority on every decision, large and small. Instead, they occasionally clashed, and she sensed their friendship complicated a professional association.

After she accepted a glass of whiskey from Senora Menendez's tray, she murmured a silent word of appreciation that Quinn was not a man who backed down easily. Catching his eye in the dying rays of sunset, she lifted her glass in a salute of gratitude. He held her gaze for a long moment, then nodded.

Although it annoyed her to focus on such things, she had decided the Stetson and string tie suited him. In the past, she had believed there must be something soft about men rich enough to wear rubies in their cuffs, men who decided to be politicians, men who rode in private coaches and lived in luxurious houses.

Two days of near constant exposure to Quinn Westin had altered her opinion. There was nothing soft in his flinty grey eyes, or in the ruggedly strong lines of his lips and jaw. His ambition was as diamond-hard as his hands, shored by ruthless determination. And beneath that surface polish, she suspected he was tougher than the outlaw types she'd known in her past. Already she knew that nothing would stand between Quinn Westin and whatever he wanted.

Therefore, it surprised her that he had interceded on her behalf.

The next morning when they entered the coach for another long day of travel and etiquette and deportment lessons, Lily gazed into his eyes and felt her pulsebeat quicken. He was one good-looking son of a bitch. He made her remember things she had vowed to forget.

"I guess you can smoke if you want to," she said, striving for an offhand tone.

"You *may* smoke," Paul said, correcting her automatically. "Can means you are able to smoke, may means you have permission to smoke."

Lily ground her teeth and narrowed her eyes. Miriam had learned these stupid rules. Damn it, so could she.

When she glanced at Quinn, he was clipping a cigar with a half smile on his lips. The breeze from the coach window teased his hair into an appealing rumpled look, and already he had loosened his collar and arranged his long legs as best he could in the limited space. She inhaled the scent she was beginning to associate with him, the pleasant tang of hair oil and shaving soap and leather.

Lily watched him light the cigar and felt a stirring in the bottom of her stomach. His hands were darkly tanned, slender and sure. The nails were cut square across and were scrupulously clean. Irritated, she stared down at her mended gloves.

He was darkly handsome, powerful and wealthy, and she secretly enjoyed the intense interest he focused on her. And he'd shown her a small kindness last night when he allowed her a glass of whiskey. Given these facts, she supposed it wasn't too surprising that she might feel drawn to him.

Once again she thought about Miriam as she supposed she would be doing from now on. Why on earth would Miriam run away from a man like Quinn Westin? Lily would have wagered everything she owned that he was every woman's secret dream, not just hers.

On the other hand, a man willing to replace his wife with an impostor was a man driven by cold ambition to the exclusion of all else. A man capable of ruthlessness. As a husband, such a man might well have been a nightmare rather than a dream.

Feeling the heat inside the closed coach, she fanned her face and watched him tilt his head back and release a perfect smoke ring. "Are you trying to find Miriam?" she asked curiously. "Have you hired someone to search for her?"

He coughed, waved at the smoke, and swore.

Chapter 3

"The issue isn't whether you should have lied to her," Paul insisted a week later, urging his horse up beside the mustang Quinn rode. "The issue is idealism versus reality. Damn it, Quinn. That's where you and I continue to butt heads."

"Reality begins with someone's idealistic dream," Quinn said stubbornly, leaning over the saddle to stroke the neck of his horse. He was a big man and preferred a larger mount, but the little mustang had given him a good ride, and he'd needed a hard run. Most of the tension bunching his shoulder muscles had eased the minute he swung into the saddle.

Paul thumbed back his hat and wiped a sleeve across his forehead. "Here's the reality you've created. Lily is now puzzled as to why we aren't searching for Miriam. A simple lie would have diverted her curiosity and questions."

Quinn's lips twisted, and he frowned at the desert landscape. "Is there such a thing as a simple lie?" He no longer believed there was.

Lies required more lies. They piled one on top of the other until the weight crushed a man's integrity.

"The world is a hell of a long way from being ideal," Paul said irritably. "In this instance, we don't want Lily getting too curious about Miriam's disappearance. Surely you agree."

Of course he did. But there was something about Lily that made him believe men had lied to her all of her life. He didn't want to be like the other men in her life, and he hadn't wanted to add another lie to the burden he already carried.

They rode past a cluster of tall cacti, turning back toward the house and stable. "There's another thing. I've strongly disagreed with your insistence that Lily be allowed whiskey and a cigar at the end of the day. But after thinking about it, I believe I understand what you're doing."

"What am I doing?" Quinn asked, stretching his neck against his hand. Once he returned to Denver, he'd go directly to the ranch and work out the kinks of travel with a few days of riding and ranching. Some satisfying labor and a day or two of solitude might help him sort out the troubling emotions aroused by Lily Dale. She disturbed him on half a dozen levels.

"You're making yourself sympathetic in her eyes, building a relationship. That's good. Lily needs to feel comfortable with you if she's going to succeed at being your wife."

His head snapped up, and he felt his shoulders tighten with returning tension. "Lily and I are never going to be comfortable with each other." They couldn't be. He needed her to win the election, and he hated having to depend on her for his success. She hated him for keeping her from her daughter. The mustang responded to his tightening thighs and danced away from Paul's mount. "She doesn't see either of us as sympathetic. She detests us both for interfering with her life."

Paul's scowl deepened. "Don't start thinking of Lily as Mother of the Year. She isn't," he said coldly. "So don't waste any sympathy on her. In the overall scheme of things, these seven months will be a brief interlude in her life. And in yours."

Paul's steady regard made Quinn realize how angry he sounded, and he loosened his grip on the reins, made himself rock back in the saddle and let his shoulders relax.

He had spent four years positioning himself for this run at the governorship. To get where he was now, he had compromised nearly everything he believed in, had done things it was better not to recall. Forcing Lily to impersonate Miriam was merely the latest link in a chain of decisions he would live with for the rest of his life. Knowing most people didn't think politicians had a conscience brought a humorless smile to his lips.

However, he hadn't anticipated how disturbing Lily would be. Hadn't believed he could forget for a moment that she wasn't his wife. But occasionally he gazed at her face and his chest burned with rage and resentment, betrayal and guilt, emotions he had believed were laid to rest.

Two weeks had made a remarkable alteration in Lily's appearance. As her face and body began to fill out, as her tan faded, her resemblance to Miriam became more pronounced. Two days ago, she had borrowed the locket containing Miriam's likeness, and this morning she'd appeared for breakfast wearing her hair in the style Miriam had worn for the portrait sitting. Quinn had stared at her and felt a sickening lurch in his stomach.

"She's making astonishing progress," he said in a thick voice, touching his heels to the mustang's flanks. He was tempted to make an offer for the little horse, but knew he

wouldn't. It was simply less upsetting to think about horse-
flesh than to think about Lily Dale.

Paul leaned back in his saddle. "We have a long way to
go."

"If you stopped right now, you've already wrought a
miracle."

Her table manners had improved one hundred percent.
She had slowed her speech, her gait, her gestures. She no
longer looked baffled that he and Paul rose when she entered a room or stood when she did. She was still tentative
with servants, but she was improving. Now it was Lily
who instructed the housekeeper to serve their after-dinner
whiskey, and last night she had sent a dish back to the
kitchen with the instruction that it be reheated. Unless corrected, she still crossed her legs at the knee, and she swore
when she was frustrated or irritated, but she was learning
her role more swiftly than Quinn would have believed possible.

"She's defiant, but she's also clever, and she learns fast,"
Paul conceded, as they rode into the corral. Two Mexican
boys walked forward to take their horses. "The problem is
we're trying to make a silk purse out of a sow's ear," Paul
continued, walking toward the house. "Inside, she is who
she is." He frowned. "That worries me. Gentility was in-
grained in Miriam. She didn't have to remind herself
which fork to use or strain to remember not to say ain't. By
the time Lily's lessons are well learned and the results habitual, we'll be through with her."

If Quinn's future hadn't been on the line, playing Pyg-
malion might have proven an interesting experiment. It
was fascinating to observe Lily's evolution, the swift

changes occurring hour by hour. But she was becoming Miriam, and watching it happen was profoundly troubling.

"May we join you?" he inquired in an expressionless tone, climbing the steps to the house. She sat on the porch, smoking and enjoying her nightly glass of whiskey, mysterious in her strangeness, disturbing in her familiarity.

"Please do," she said with cool politeness, managing to mimic a grande dame while ignoring her bare feet and opened collar. During the day, she worked at being a lady with grim determination, but on her own time she made a point of reverting to behavior that reminded them she was only playing a role. Lily would never be a lady. She didn't want to be.

"If you'll excuse me," Paul said, throwing a scowl of disapproval toward her crossed legs and the bare toes peeking out of her hem, "tonight is my last chance to edit Quinn's speech notes."

This was another point of contention straining their friendship. Quinn wasn't accustomed to having his thoughts or words edited, and he didn't like it. "We should review the notes together," he stated, wanting to minimize changes. He also sought an excuse to avoid joining Lily on the porch.

"I'd prefer to organize my thoughts before we discuss any changes. We'll give Lily a respite tomorrow and talk during the drive to Santa Fe."

"What are your speeches about?" Lily asked after Paul had gone inside.

"Are you really interested?" He couldn't imagine that she was. After pouring a glass of whiskey from the bottle on the table between them, he leaned back in the porch chair.

"I doubt it. But tell me anyway, then I'll decide."

Her honesty made him smile. "The most important speech is an address to the territorial legislature targeting the challenges of statehood and what I hope to accomplish as governor."

"The challenges of statehood," she repeated, inspecting the end of her cigar. "That doesn't sound too interesting."

"I hope the legislature doesn't share your conclusion," he said, suppressing a laugh.

She glanced at him. "Did you always want to be a politician?"

"To be successful, society must live by rules. Long ago I decided if someone is going to make rules I must live by, then I want to be the man who's making those rules. Politicians are rule makers. So yes. I've been moving toward politics most of my life, preparing myself for this campaign."

"There are too many rules already. Why do you want to make more?"

Glancing at her bare feet, he tried to recall if Miriam's feet had been short and slender with a defined arch. That he couldn't remember raised an annoying twinge of guilt. "I also believe I'm the best choice for Colorado's first governor."

"Is that so?" Tilting her head, she gave him a curious look. "Why do you think you're the best man for the job?"

"Mining and ranching are Colorado's future. My family made their fortune in the Utah silver mines, and I oversee the family's ranching interests. Both endeavors can devastate the land if they're not managed well." Powerful convictions prompted him to say more, but regulation and reform had not been subjects that interested Miriam, and he doubted they would interest Lily. Patting his vest pockets, he withdrew a cigar and lit it, then looked down at her bare toes.

When she saw him frowning at her feet, she pulled her legs up under her skirt and hugged her knees close to her chest. Even in the privacy of her bedroom, Miriam would never have adopted such a posture. His instinct was to correct her, but he bit off the words. For the plan to succeed, she had to become Miriam. But for him to remain sane, he had to remember that she was Lily Dale.

"I never heard of a lawyer who's also a rancher," she commented, reaching for her whiskey glass.

"In my time I've worked in the mines, sat behind a banker's desk, and I spent a year on Wall Street," he said, smiling at the memory. "My father wanted his sons to be at least passing-familiar with most of the family's business interests. In fact, I only practiced courtroom law for about two years. Long enough to discover I don't have the temperament for litigation."

Rubbing the bridge of his nose, he remembered a brawl on the steps of the Denver courthouse. By the time the sheriff arrived, Quinn's nose had been broken and was gushing blood, and the other attorney had two black eyes and three caved-in ribs. "I don't like losing," he said. "At present the firm handles corporate matters and seldom has to litigate."

"I already figured out that you want things to go your way even if you have to force people to do what you want them to do."

Her tone irritated him, and he felt the anger rising in his chest. Suddenly he needed to punish her for having Miriam's heart-shaped face and blond hair and lavender-blue eyes. "Rules are necessary. Otherwise, everyone would have children out of wedlock, rob gambling halls, and shoot bystanders who are trying to protect their property."

She stared at him, her eyes narrowed and combative. "It was wrong to rob the gambling hall. Cy paid for that mistake at the end of a rope, and I paid with five years of my life. I understand those kinds of rules, and I'm sorry I tried to steal money that didn't belong to me. The rules I hate are those made by someone who thinks he knows how I should live better than I do. What the hell does it matter if I was married or not when I had my Rose? Is it anyone else's business if I want to live with a man outside of marriage? And who made the rule that men can swear and smoke and drink whiskey, but women can't? Who in the hell decided there was a right and a wrong way to eat your supper or get into a carriage? Most of society's rules are stupid."

Oddly, he enjoyed hearing her opinions enough to raise a skeptical eyebrow and give her another prod. "You don't care that Rose is a bastard? That you'll be a pariah in your community in Missouri?

"Oh hell no," she said with a shrug. "Why should I care what anyone thinks?"

He rolled the sweet heat of cigar smoke over his tongue and exhaled slowly. "Most people do."

Her laugh was light with genuine amusement. "Not me. I ain't, I mean I'm not, going to live my life to please other people." She stopped and the corners of her full lips turned down. "Present company excepted, of course. I understand well enough that I have to live by your rules or go back to prison."

"Your insistence that Paul and I are the enemy is starting to wear thin," he said coolly, sitting up straight. "We're not your enemies."

She shifted to face him, and quick anger blazed in the lavender eyes he knew so well. "The hell you're not!"

Seeing unfamiliar anger in familiar eyes both fascinated him and disturbed his balance. Miriam's weapons had been tears, silence, and a deep quiet sorrow when he disappointed her. If she'd been able and willing to express anger in a straightforward manner, would things have gone so wrong between them?

"You haven't thought your situation through," he said, bringing himself back to the present. "Use your head, Lily. One day you'll thank God that Paul Kazinski found you."

Flinging herself back in the chair, she made a sound of derision that set his teeth on edge. "That will never happen! I'll thank God when I've seen the last of you ruthless bastards."

"Is that right? Well, darlin', let me show you two possible futures," he said, speaking between his teeth. "In the first, you leave here right now and go home to Missouri to your daughter. How do you plan to take care of Rose? Where will you live, and how will you support her? Have you thought about that?"

"I've thought about nothing else for five years!"

"And?"

"I'm sure Aunt Edna will let us live at the farm," she said finally, returning his stare with a defiant expression. But he identified a sudden leap of anxiety in her eyes.

He nodded. "Let's say you're correct. Your aunt permits you to hand off your responsibilities to her and you live on her farm." Sparks kindled in her stare and she would have exploded, but he raised a hand. "So Rose will grow up as you did. Slopping hogs, carrying heavy buckets, building fences, chopping wood, cleaning the henhouse. Working dawn to dusk. Is that correct?"

"I'll carry my own weight," she said angrily. "I won't be a burden on Aunt Edna."

"There isn't much extra cash on a farm. Rose won't have pretty, little-girl dresses or ribbons for her hair. There won't be a spare nickel to press into her hand when the fair comes to the county. She'll be needed at the farm, so she won't go to school. She'll be tutored at home like you were. She'll feel different from other children, apart from them because her childhood will be spent earning her keep."

The combativeness drained out of her shoulders, and she lifted a shaking hand to her forehead. "How did you know it was like that?"

"You say you don't care about the circumstances of your daughter's birth, but maybe Rose will care. Maybe it will hurt when she hears someone refer to her as a bastard. Maybe she'll feel shamed. Regardless, she'll have a hard life on your aunt's farm, and one day as sure as sunrise she'll run off with the first man who glibly tells her that she's pretty and promises her something better than working from dawn to dusk. Maybe she'll choose as unwisely as you did and end up like you did, watching the years go by through the bars on her cell."

"Stop! Just shut the hell up!" She started to rise, but he reached out and gripped her wrist, feeling the small bones beneath her warm skin.

"Or . . ." Pushing her back into the chair, he leaned to gaze into eyes that stared hatred at him. "Rose can grow up in Europe, surrounded by culture and gentility, raised by a beautiful mother who can support her and who will fit into society. And you will, Lily. When these seven months end, you'll have the polish to pass yourself off as quality. And what you're learning one hard step at a time, Rose will absorb without effort simply by emulating you. She'll never do a minute's hard labor, and you'll have the funds to educate her. She'll be a genteel young lady with pretty dresses and pretty manners and a chance to marry well."

She shook off his grip. "You're twisting things around with your lawyer's tongue!" But she didn't walk away. She sat poised on the edge of her chair, frowning and listening.

"What you're doing here is earning Rose an opportunity to enjoy a better life than you ever had, and you're also earning a second chance for yourself. It comes down to this. What do you want for Rose? The same hard life you've experienced? Or something better."

"I wanted a baby so bad," she whispered, rubbing her temples and closing her eyes. Long lashes fanned across her cheekbones like inky crescents. "I never had anything of my own. Never had anybody to love me back. The first time I held her, and knew she was mine and part of me, I thought I would burst. I didn't think I could hold that much joy inside without it shaking me apart." She dug her fingers into her scalp. "Of course I want pretty dresses for her, and ribbons and an education and all the other things I never had."

"Then stop fighting us, and start looking at the next seven months as something you're doing to provide Rose a secure future."

Quinn tossed off his drink and fell backward in his chair, scowling into his empty glass. Before this journey began, days had passed when he didn't think of Miriam. From now on, he would see her every day, would hear ghostly echos of painful conversations. Biting down on his back teeth, he raised his face toward the darkness.

"I just wanted her. I wanted her bad. I figured I'd find a way to raise her."

"You can keep fighting and hating us, begrudging everything we ask you to learn and do," he said wearily, wanting to end this conversation. "Or you can seize this opportunity, learn everything you can, and use the knowledge to build a comfortable life for yourself and your daughter."

She was silent so long that it startled him when she broke into his thoughts. "Why aren't you searching for your wife?"

"I've already explained that it would be a pointless waste of time and money."

"But why?" After lowering her feet to the porch floor, she shifted in her chair to study his expression. "I don't understand that."

The intimate glimpse of her bare feet made him look away and clench his teeth. He didn't want to know that her second toes were slightly longer than the first.

"Miriam will never be found."

"But how can you be so certain?"

Standing, he crossed the porch and gripped the railing. "Lily, this isn't a subject for discussion." That statement and his sharp tone would have ended any conversation with Miriam.

"But suppose your wife returns," she persisted. "You've painted a rosy picture about how this impersonation is going to help me and Rose. So what happens to me if Miriam comes back?"

"She won't return. We will not discuss this further."

"If you think exposing Miriam's disappearance would raise a scandal, consider what will happen if suddenly there are two Mrs. Westins. Now that would be a scandal!"

He pulled a hand through his hair and silently cursed. There was a lot to be said for obedient women. "It will never happen. Miriam is not coming back."

"Damn it, how can you be so positive that she won't?"

He took a moment to collect himself before he turned to face her. "You're right. I can't be positive. If Miriam reappears, Paul and I will deal with the problem."

She stared up at him. "When you say Miriam disappeared, what does that mean? Was she kidnapped? Did she vanish into thin air? Did she run away? Was she afraid of something?"

"Lily, I mean it. Don't pursue this," he warned.

She threw out her hands. "How am I supposed to impersonate Miriam when I don't know the most important thing about her? Why she's missing."

"Paul will tell you what you need to know." His shoulders ached with the strain of being with her, of talking to Miriam who was not Miriam. The slanted eyes, the slightly pouty mouth, the widow's peak . . . but not Miriam. "Just do the job you were hired to do and leave the rest alone."

When she stood, he realized suddenly that she was shorter than Miriam. In her bare feet, she could easily have stood beneath his chin. Staring hard, he searched for other differences, needing to find them. She was argumentative and confrontational. Quick-minded and direct. She was strong and tough and barefooted. Thinner, fuller-breasted. His eyes lingered on the full curve of her ill-fitting jacket, and he felt his stomach muscles contract.

"I think you know what happened to Miriam," she said

slowly, watching his expression intently. "But you don't want me to know."

He pulled a hand down his jaw before he poured another whiskey and tossed it back. "Why would you assume that?"

"It's either that, or you don't give a damn about what happened to her or where she is." Lifting her hem up from her toes, she walked away from him. At the door to the house, she paused to look over her shoulder. "You convinced me that this job will give me and Rose a decent life, and now I want to impersonate your missing wife because I want something good for Rose. But maybe you'll regret changing my thinking. Because if you don't keep your promises to me and Rose, if you don't live up to your side of this bargain, then I'll destroy you, and I can do it, too. All I have to do is tell the newspapers that you forced me to impersonate Miriam so you could win the election."

"Don't threaten me, Lily," he warned, holding her gaze.

"Or what? I'll disappear like Miriam did?" She gave him a long stare. "I just want you to know that if Miriam comes back, you still owe me everything you promised. And I want you to know that you ain't sending me back to prison without me paying you back. You've got something to make me do what you want, and I've got something to make you keep your promises to me and Rose." She gave him another hard look, then slammed the door behind her.

Quinn sat down, tented his fingers beneath his chin, and considered her last words. It didn't really surprise him that she'd figured out that she could destroy him. She was intelligent, and she was accustomed to searching out ways to protect herself. Unfortunately, he didn't immediately see how he could protect himself if she chose to expose the impersonation. For the duration of his term in office, Lily Dale would be a bomb primed to detonate anytime she chose to light the fuse. In fact, she would be a threat long after his term ended. His reputation and his place in Colorado's history books would not be secure while she was alive.

There were a couple of ways around this problem. First, he could abandon the impersonation and send Lily packing. Arguing against this solution was the fact that she would take his hopes and ambitions along with her. In that event, the compromises, the lies and deceptions, everything he had done to reach this point would have been for nothing.

Tossing back his head, he drained his glass in a single long swallow, then lowered his hand. It had all begun with Miriam. Just thinking her name gave him a punishing headache.

A sharp sting followed by a warm gush made him look down, and he discovered he had crushed the whiskey glass. Broken glass reflected slivers of moonlight.

Swearing, he pulled a shard of glass from his thumb, then shook out his handkerchief and wiped blood from his fingers.

He had come too far to quit. He would produce a wife for the voters, and he would win the election. He would deal with Lily's threats if and when it became necessary.

Leaving the porch, he walked out onto the desert floor, listening to the scurry of night creatures moving in the chaparral and low brush. All he could do was go forward.

An hour later he paused in the still darkness outside Lily's door, listened for a minute, then clenched his fists and continued down the corridor.

* * *

High, thin haze filtered the sunlight, and it was cooler today, but still hot enough inside the closed coach that Lily's shirtwaist stuck to her skin. She had two jackets and two skirts, but only one shirtwaist, which she washed out every night along with her smallclothes and thick cotton stockings. When she received the new traveling wardrobe that Paul had mentioned, she intended to burn every garment she owned, every shabby reminder of prison. Thinking about it improved her spirits.

Leaning her head back on the coach cushions, hovering at the edge of dozing in the heat, she half listened as the men argued various points Quinn wanted to make in his speeches.

Watching Quinn through half-closed eyes, Lily enjoyed the play of light and shadow through his wavy dark hair, and noticed a few strands of grey at his temples. He was one of those men who would become more handsome and ruggedly distinguished as the years went by.

She'd been awake half the night, reviewing their conversation on the porch, thinking about everything he had said.

If Quinn's ambitions hadn't kept her from Rose, she wouldn't have thought twice about his plan to replace Miriam with a ringer. If she was honest with herself, she had to admit she understood doing what a person had to do. Life didn't hand out prizes simply because someone wanted one. You had to fight for what you wanted, and Quinn was fighting.

She also understood that her uncanny resemblance to Miriam was an anomaly unlikely to be repeated. There weren't an abundance of women who looked enough like

Quinn's wife to be her twin. If there had to be an impersonator, it had to be Lily.

While deciding that Quinn would be surprised if he knew how well she grasped his situation, she fell asleep and didn't wake until he tapped her on the knee to call her for lunch.

She awakened at once, her knee tingling, and frowned at his fingers withdrawing from her skirt. Then she lifted her hands to smooth her hair, embarrassed that he'd observed her sleeping. "Did you get your speeches fixed?" she asked, watching Paul search for napkins and plates in the lunch basket.

"My speeches didn't need to be fixed, as you put it," Quinn snapped, his mouth tight.

Paul spoke to her, but his reply was directed to Quinn. "It's better to focus tightly on one or two issues than to propose sweeping changes."

Lily decided it might be smart to come down on Quinn's side. She was uncomfortable about the way they had parted last night. She lifted an eyebrow at Paul, "No sweeping changes according to who?"

"Whom," he corrected automatically.

"Whom. Is there some kind of political gospel that says a Kingmaker's ideas are better than the candidate's?" She was hot, and tired of the endless days rattling around in a bouncing coach, in no mood to attempt tact even when she noticed Quinn's frown.

"This isn't your area," Paul said, glancing up as he handed her a fried chicken leg. "We may ask you to attend some rallies or speeches, but we don't expect you to take an active interest in politics."

"I'm definitely not interested in politics," she stated

firmly. "I'm just asking why the candidate"—she nodded at Quinn, who was staring at her—"can't say what he wants to in his own speeches."

Paul nodded approval as she started to tuck her napkin into her collar, then draped it across her lap instead. "It takes money to get a candidate elected. Quinn's backers have the right to expect him to support their views."

She tilted her head and considered the candidate in question. "You're rich. Why don't you use your own money to finance your campaign? Then you can say whatever you want to."

Quinn smiled in an attempt at patience, but his gaze informed her that she was trespassing in territory where she wasn't wanted. "That isn't how it's done. Don't concern yourself with this, Lily."

Perspiration pasted tendrils of rumpled hair to his temples, and he had removed his jacket and opened his collar, with her permission, of course. He held his long legs carefully away from her skirts, and looked as cramped and uncomfortable as she was.

"I'm trying to take your side," she pointed out, "as a way of saying I regret some of the things I said last night."

"Any unpleasantness is already forgotten," he said with a polite shrug.

"What's this about?" Paul looked back and forth between them.

"I got my dander up," Lily said slowly, watching Quinn. "Maybe it doesn't seem like it, but I got some pride left."

"Have some pride left," Paul corrected.

"Damn it, Paul, I'm trying to say something," she snapped. This was one of those moments when the constant barrage of criticism and correction made her feel crazy inside.

"Then say it correctly."

She regretted trying to say anything at all. Why should she care about getting along with Quinn Westin? She didn't have to like him to pretend to be his wife, and he didn't have to like her. A year from now, he would be just another name on the list of men who had forced her to do something she didn't want to do. *Even*, she thought sourly, *if that something ultimately benefits me and Rose.*

If he resented her threat, well, she didn't like being threatened either. Tit for tat. After finishing her noon meal, she folded her arms across her chest, glared, and didn't speak another word.

In midafternoon they drove into Santa Fe, a boomtown with a strong Spanish flavor. Mexican music drifted from open-fronted cantinas, and there were as many sombreros as cowboy hats and gentlemen's felts. Freight wagons and immigrant trains jammed the narrow dirt streets, and dust capped the town like a lid, holding in the noise and heat.

Avoiding the crowded main street, the coach driver took them directly to a house a few blocks off the plaza. As Lily now expected, the tile-and-stucco house was secluded by thick adobe walls. Inside, the rooms were refreshingly cool and fragrant with the scent of roasting chilis.

Unpinning her hat, she stretched her neck against her fingertips and sighed. Riding in a coach all day was nothing like the hard labor she'd been accustomed to, but it was tiring nonetheless. The constant jostling was gradually pounding her bones to powder. She was glad they would spend a few days here before continuing the journey.

"Take the luggage to our quarters," she timidly instructed Carlos, the servant who had welcomed them inside. "And please send a bath to my room."

Wherever they stopped, an initial confusion arose among the servants as to her position, and this time was no exception. Carlos stole a sidelong glance at her scuffed boots, her mismatched and travel-worn clothing, and his eyebrows lifted.

Cheeks burning, she turned away and watched in the hall mirror while Paul took Carlos aside. The servant's expression altered to one of surprise that was so comical Lily would have laughed if his hasty apology hadn't also made her feel the sting of pretending to be something she wasn't.

Paul knocked his hat against his thigh to shake loose the day's accumulation of dust. "A seamstress is waiting in your room. She'll make final adjustments to the wardrobe you'll find there. Tonight we'll dress for dinner so you can begin managing a train."

The promise of a bath and fresh, clean clothing drove the weariness from her mind, and she felt a burst of renewed energy. She couldn't remember the last time she'd had a new dress or clothing that wasn't prison issue.

When she saw the array of finery draped across every available surface in her room, her knees gave out, and Lily collapsed into the nearest chair, overwhelmed. In her wildest dreams she had never expected so many beautiful new things. There were gowns and dresses, petticoats and stockings and boots and slippers. Hats and gloves and brooches and hair ornaments. Day dresses and walking suits and traveling ensembles.

"You're so thin!" the seamstress groaned, wringing her hands in dismay. "The corsets won't fit." She threw up her hands and spoke in a rattling burst of Spanish. "Well," she said, holding up a jacket and eyeing it critically. "Have your bath, and we'll begin."

With trembling fingers, Lily stroked a nightgown folded on the table beside her. The material was so soft that touching it raised tears of wonder to her eyes. Her world had been filled with hard people, hard objects, and hard choices. She had never known such softness existed.

When she entered the parlor, Quinn rose to his feet, and knots ran up his jaw. Her resemblance to Miriam jolted him each time he saw her, but tonight his shock was deepened by her complete transformation. It was impossible to believe that this was the same bedraggled woman he had met outside the women's prison.

Tonight her hair was piled high in a crown of ashy blond curls; wispy tendrils had escaped jet-trimmed combs and floated around her long throat. Puffed sleeves ran to her wrists, flowed into a beaded bodice that molded her breasts like a second skin. Purple satin draped her hips and hugged a narrow line to the floor.

High color burned on her cheekbones. "I've never owned a dress like this. I never dreamed that I would." Her fingertips brushed against her thighs, nervously stroking the smooth satin.

Walking around her, Paul judged the fit and drape of the gown. "You wear both gloves, not just one," he said absently. "The bodice is too revealing. It's almost scandalous." Pulling a pad from inside his jacket, he jotted some notes.

The fitted gown revealed her body as the shapeless prison clothing had not. She was small, still too slender, but her figure was perfectly proportioned. Quinn had been married long enough to know the coveted hourglass shape could be achieved through the use of a tightly laced corset, but he was also experienced enough to notice that Lily wasn't wearing a corset.

She seemed to be waiting for him to say something, but he couldn't speak. Turning his back, he swallowed hard, then walked to the drink cart beside a fireplace that smelled of chaparral even when not in use. "Miriam preferred sherry before dinner," he said in a thick voice.

Lily took the stemmed glass he handed her, careful not to touch his fingers. Crimson still burned on her cheeks, and she was clearly nervous. Quinn glanced at the fading arrow of tanned skin that pointed toward her cleavage and felt his thighs tense and his stomach harden.

"We need to discuss precedence," Paul announced, straightening his dinner jacket. "When there is an extra man, the hostess enters the dining room with a gentleman on each arm."

Lily nodded, but her eyes remained on Quinn. He didn't know what the hell she wanted from him. Did she want him to tell her that she was beautiful? Yes, damn it, she was beautiful. Did she want him to say that she looked so much like Miriam that he had to fight to remember that she wasn't?

Staring at her, he saw Miriam as she had been when he first met her. Slender, unsure, shyly seeking his approval.

But there the similarity ended. The trickster who had fashioned Lily in Miriam's image had subtly altered the original creation. He had thinned Lily's nose and widened her lips. Had lengthened her throat and filled out her bosom. He had nipped in her waist and flared her hips into a smooth, erotic curve. Considered alone, the differences were slight, but the overall effect was not. She was sensually provocative, arousing in a way that Miriam had never been.

"For God's sake, will you stop running your hands over your thighs?" he said harshly.

Paul frowned, and Lily's color deepened. "I was just touching the satin," she explained in a low voice, jerking her hands to her waist. "Why are you so pissy tonight?"

"Cross, not pissy," Paul said, looking at Quinn.

"You're behaving like a doxy in a brothel."

Paul's frown deepened. "I wouldn't state it that strongly." He turned to Lily. "It's true that a lady does not touch her body except at the waist when she folds her hands." He studied her a moment. "Walk to the door, turn and walk back."

For an instant Quinn believed she would refuse. Her chin lifted, and anger flared in her eyes. Then she sighed and did as Paul had requested, her train jerking along behind her. At the turn, she almost stumbled, glared down at the train twisted around her ankles, and swore.

"No, no," Paul said, setting down his sherry glass. "Like this. Float forward. Glide." He moved across the room. "And turn like this, to the right. If you pause after the turn, the train is gracefully displayed beside you. If you continue walking, it straightens out behind. Watch, I'll show you again."

A sparkle sprang into her eyes. Her lips twitched, and she sucked in her cheeks. Then she collapsed against the wall in gales of tension-releasing laughter. "You look so . . . the way you're holding your hands and mincing along, like . . ."

Paul glared, then grinned. And he, too, gave a shout of laughter. "I'll admit, train management isn't my long suit."

That set them off again, and they laughed until they were holding their sides. When they caught their breath, they smiled at each other.

Angry without knowing the reason, Quinn set his sherry glass down hard. "We've had our half hour of polite chat and unbridled hysteria. The first course should be on the table."

Lily looked up at him, the smile disappearing from her lips. When he stiffly extended his arm, she accepted it with a show of reluctance, then waited for Paul to step to her other side.

Moving gingerly rather than gracefully, her stride constrained by the narrow skirt, she let them escort her into the dining room. The tremble in her fingertips signaled that she wasn't comfortable in formal attire and probably wouldn't be for a while yet.

In the early years of marriage, when he and Miriam had still talked of trivial things, Miriam would have smiled and said the dress wore Lily.

Tugging at the stiff collar strangling his throat, Quinn silently swore. He looked at Lily and saw an echo of Miriam. He tried to remember Miriam's voice, but heard Lily's husky laugh. He felt as if he were losing his mind.

Chapter 4

Lily climbed out of bed, eager to hold the satin gown and reassure herself that she hadn't dreamed her fairy princess evening. In the past there had been times when she'd felt pretty, but until last night she had never felt beautiful. The experience had been exhilarating and nerve-wracking, and ultimately crushing.

Reverently, she stroked her palm over the gown spread across her lap and winced at the memory of Quinn saying that she reminded him of a brothel doxy.

Although she doubted he would ever approve of her, she had looked to him for validation last night. But Quinn was a man who respected society's rules, and she was an unconventional woman who had borne a child out of wedlock and had assisted in a robbery. She reminded him of a brothel doxy.

She was a fool to hope that he might find something to admire about her or that he might learn to like her a little. Frowning, she tried to figure out why his acceptance mattered so much. Maybe it was because she'd never known a man like Quinn Westin, wealthy, powerful, educated, and handsome enough to stir her even when she didn't want to be stirred. A man so confident and sure of himself that he believed he was the best man to govern a whole state.

When he narrowed those stormy pewter eyes and looked at her, really looked at her, her mouth dried and her skin felt as if flames raced along the surface.

Jumping up and forcing herself to think of other things, Lily folded away her soft new nightgown, then rolled on dark silk stockings, careful not to snag them, and donned undergarments trimmed with lace as filmy as cobwebs.

What Paul referred to as a make-do traveling wardrobe represented more clothing than Lily had owned in her life, and of finer quality than she had known existed. She also hadn't suspected that ladies changed clothes several times a day, but the seamstress had indicated an at-home dress was different from a receiving dress which would not be worn to dinner.

Standing in front of a cheval glass, she taped herself into a black-cashmere walking suit with black-silk pleats beneath the overskirt, then peered over her shoulder to admire the drape of a stylish silk puff and bow that curved over a light bustle. Both the jacket and overskirt were richly embroidered in a black-and-maroon design, the maroon repeating in the plumes on her hat, and again on the buttons that ran down a crisp white shirtwaist.

Resisting an urge to stroke the amazing softness of the cashmere, she turned and blinked at her reflection in disbelief.

Fine clothing had worked wonders, transforming her into a woman who looked as if she had a dozen servants at her command. She could not believe her eyes.

Quinn was right. Stepping into Miriam's life would change her forever. Already she had learned most of the mannerly behaviors that set genteel society apart from people like her. Before this was over, she would know how

to dress, how to speak, how to pass herself off as a real
lady.

With a tiny shock she realized it was indeed time to stop
resenting the threat that had brought her here, and time to
apply herself and learn everything she could for her future
advantage.

Because she wanted this life. She wanted it badly.

Peering into the mirror, she let her fingertips caress the
fine cashmere and lovely embroidery, and a powerful
yearning welled up inside, making her chest ache.

Now that she'd felt satin and cashmere next to her skin,
she never again wanted to wear homespun. Or shoes with
holes in the soles. Or mended gloves. Or heavy shapeless
stockings. She wanted beautiful, soft clothing with a longing so achingly deep that she trembled with the wanting.

Extending shaking hands, she stared at the returning
whiteness and smooth backs. She couldn't remember having clean, neatly trimmed fingernails until now. Never,
never, never again did she want to look at her hands and
see rough, chapped skin and dirty fingernails. Or calluses
as hard as horn.

Oh yes, she thought, closing her eyes and swaying. She
wanted Miriam's life the same way she wanted air in her
lungs.

Disturbed by the intensity of confusing new feelings, Lily
gave her head a shake, then caught up a small, beaded purse
and slipped out of the house into the morning coolness.

Drawing a deep breath and collecting herself, she
looked about to make certain she was unobserved before
she walked out of the gate then rushed along the adobe privacy wall and dashed around the corner, not slowing her
pace until she was certain no one had followed.

There she paused, inhaled deeply, and pretended to adjust her parasol while she let herself fully experience a moment she had dreamed of for five excruciatingly long years, the glorious unfettered weightlessness of freedom.

Miraculously, she could go where whimsy directed. There was no one to stop her. No hard-eyed guards with carbines cradled in their arms. No Ephram Callihan to take away her supper or order her to work harder or raise his fist to her. There was no one to tell her to stand here or go there. And best of all, she was alone.

Although Santa Fe's streets and walkways were beginning to fill with traffic and pedestrians, she felt wonderfully alone. No one was watching, judging, criticizing, or crowding, pushing, or infringing on her small space.

An overwhelming joy made her dizzy with pleasure and gratitude, and she feared she might faint to the ground and soil her beautiful new ensemble. She was free. Oh God, she was free. When the dizziness passed she laughed out loud and spun in a happy, unladylike circle. Then, smiling broadly, she unfurled her parasol, tilted it against the sun, and sallied forth to explore her newly restored liberty without a care in the world.

During the next two hours, she happily wandered where fancy took her, fascinated by everything she saw. When she discovered a stone church that claimed to be the oldest in the Americas, she stepped inside and lit a candle for Rose. "We have to wait a little longer, but I'm doing this for us. I'll come for you the instant I can."

The waiting wasn't hard for Rose because Rose and Aunt Edna didn't know Lily had been released from prison. They believed she was still in Yuma. And her friends in Yuma believed she was now in Missouri.

It occurred to her suddenly that if something happened to her, she would never be missed. For an instant the realization alarmed her, then she decided it had to be that way for the impersonation to be successful.

After a brief hesitation, she decided to light a candle for Miriam Westin, too.

"I'm going to learn all I can about you," she murmured, watching the flame flicker uncertainly, as if it might sputter out. "And I promise not to forget that my change of fortune came about because of your possible misfortune. I'll learn what I must, and I'll try not to bring shame on your name."

Eventually, she wandered back to the plaza where Indian and Mexican vendors sold pottery, food, silver and turquoise trinkets, and items they hoped would appeal to the broad mix of people spilling into Santa Fe off the trail.

Aware that admiring eyes followed the stylishly draped sway of her bustle, and thrilled by the realization, she strolled around the plaza as she imagined a lady might do, trying to glide. After inspecting the vendors' wares, she decided that she would use some of her go-home money to buy Rose a small trinket and send it to her.

Leaning to examine an array of silver chains displayed on an Indian blanket, she pursed her lips and tried to choose which of the chains Rose would like best.

That's when an appalling realization struck her like a poisoned arrow. In prison she had constructed a fantasy of Rose that made her believe she knew her daughter. But she didn't. She knew nothing about Rose. During her incarceration, Aunt Edna had written only two letters and both had been frustratingly empty of details. Perhaps Aunt Edna had hoped to spare her pain by not mentioning Rose. In any case, Edna had written about the farm and the weather and her quilting group, and ended by briefly mentioning, "Rose is healthy and a good worker."

Swaying on her feet, Lily blinked and swallowed hard. She didn't know the color or texture of her daughter's hair, didn't know if Rose had inherited her lavender-blue eyes or Cy's dark gaze. She had no idea if Edna had made Rose a corn-husk doll as she'd done for Lily when Lily was a child, or if Rose was timid or outgoing, quick or slow.

When her vision cleared, she discovered she was staring at a plainly dressed woman and child, their sunbonnets suggesting they came from one of the immigrant trains. The little girl hung on to the woman's skirt and gazed at Lily with large round eyes. When the child saw Lily watching, she smiled, then pressed her face against her mother's hip.

"Oh dear God." With one glance, she knew more about another woman's daughter than she knew about her own.

Bitter tears blinded her, and she spun in a swirl of silk pleats, rushing away from the mother and child and headlong into the solid body of a man.

"I . . . I'm sorry, excuse me."

"Lily?" When she dashed the tears from her eyes and looked up, Quinn was holding her by the shoulders, scowling down at her. "Where in the hell have you been? We've been looking for you for over an hour." Then he saw the tears in her eyes. "What's happened? Are you all right?" The scowl became threatening as he scanned the crowds around them, seeking the source of her distress. "Did someone offend you?"

Squeezing her eyes shut, she pressed her fingertips to her forehead and shook her head. "It's nothing like that. I just . . . is there a place to sit?"

Taking her arm, he escorted her to a table beneath a tree outside a restaurant. When a waiter hurried forward, he ordered coffee, then studied her. The scowl returned to his lips.

"Don't ever do this again. Tell someone where you're going."

"I need permission to take a walk?" Fumbling in her purse, she found a handkerchief and wiped her eyes, ignoring the tingle that burned along the arm he had held next to his body.

"For all we knew, you'd boarded a stage for Missouri. You should at least have left a note. Where have you been, for God's sake? And why didn't you take someone with you? By now you know that a woman doesn't go walking without a companion."

"You mean a guard," she snapped, slowly regaining control. When she scanned the plaza, she no longer saw the mother and little girl. But there would be other little girls. And none of them would be Rose.

A few hours ago, she had yearned to seize Miriam's life and make it her own. Now, in an emotionally confusing about-face, all she wanted to do was go home.

"There's something you need to understand," she said when she could speak, lifting her head to meet his steady grey gaze. "Right this minute I want to go home so bad it hurts my heart." Even her voice quavered with her need to go. "But I ain't," she paused and ground her teeth. "I'm not going to bolt for Missouri however much I want to. I'm going to see this through and earn a future for myself and Rose."

She reminded herself that she wasn't the type to cut and run. Quinn wasn't the only one who would do what he had to to get what he wanted.

"There's another thing," she said, staring at his hard mouth. "I don't like rules, but I have a few I live by. When I give my word, I honor the bargain. And I'm giving you my word that I'll see this through, and I'll do the best I can to convince everyone that I'm your wife."

The waiter served their coffee then, noting the richness of their dress and hovering until Quinn waved the man away with an irritated gesture. "Why were you crying?" he asked after a silence lengthened between them.

"Why should you care about a doxy's tears?"

Irritation lifted his eyebrows. "It's dangerous to assume you know what someone else is thinking."

She had hoped he would apologize for his remark. When he didn't, she let her shoulders drop and glanced toward the sound of guitar music strumming out of a cantina. A pretty Mexican whore leaned against a grinning cowboy, wiping grease from her chin as she ate a rolled tortilla and watched the people strolling in the plaza. Unlike the man sitting at Lily's table, that cowboy's expression was open and happy and easy to read.

"You don't care about anything but yourself and your all important ambition to be governor," Lily said, turning her gaze back to him. "You've made that clear."

He'd maintained a distance even in the confined space of the coach, gazing out the window with a brooding expression while Paul taught her how to speak and how to sit and all the rest. Quinn hadn't been part of the transformation process. Instead, he'd withdrawn into a solitary silence and pulled it around him, shutting out the world.

"You have no idea how much that statement sounds like something Miriam would say." Patting his vest pockets, he found a cigar and clipped the end, then leaned back as the waiter jumped forward with a light.

Lily watched the subservience he so easily commanded. As she became more familiar with Quinn and Paul and more comfortable around them, it was easy to forget they were wealthy powerful men who effortlessly conveyed that impression to those in their sphere. A tiny chill skittered down her spine. She'd do well to remember they could send her back to prison on a whim.

"Do you ever wonder where Miriam is?" she asked, recalling her promise to Miriam in the church.

A humorless smile curved his lips. "Haven't we discussed this already?"

She didn't like the feeling that he was toying with her. "Something is strange about Miriam's disappearance," she said irritably. "Do you ever think about her?"

"Oh yes," he said softly. "I think of Miriam every time I look at you." Leaning back in his chair, he crossed an ankle over his knee, scanning the people in the plaza. "Everything in my life is geared toward the election. You're damned right it's important to me, and I care about winning. That doesn't mean I don't care about my wife." He turned his head to look at her. "You and I are strangers, Lily, and we will always be strangers. There is no reason for either of us to confide in each other or discuss personal matters."

"You don't like me, do you?"

Sunlight highlighted dark flecks in his grey eyes, smoothed the lines near his mouth. She was aware that women cast sidelong glances at him as they passed the table, and a surge of jealousy brought a sharp taste to her mouth. She didn't want to feel anything for Quinn Westin, didn't want to fall into his quicksilver eyes or think about his sure hands or tall, solid body. Most of all, she didn't want to care how he felt about her and could have kicked herself for asking a stupid question.

"I'll never know you because you're trying to be someone else. That's how it has to be. I have to see Miriam when I look at you. And there's no reason for you to know me any better than an actress knows her leading man. We're strangers whose lives will intermingle for a time and then never again."

She listened carefully, then nodded. But she couldn't let it go, couldn't halt the words burning her tongue. "Do you dislike me because of who I am, or because I remind you of Miriam?"

His head came up, and his expression froze in granite. Surprised, Lily watched the color of his eyes flatten to cold slate. Apparently she had struck a sore spot.

"What in the hell are you suggesting?"

She spread her hands, intrigued by his reaction. "Perhaps I asked the wrong question," she said softly, wondering how far she could push this. "Perhaps I should have asked if you liked Miriam."

"Finish your coffee," he ordered abruptly. Pulling a gold watch from the pocket of his trousers, he consulted the time, then snapped the lid. "Paul has a full day planned for you, and I need to check the schedule for the stage to Denver."

There had been trouble in the Westin marriage, she was sure of it now. When Quinn looked at her and saw Miriam, she sensed he felt the anger and resentment that had existed between himself and his wife. It wasn't Lily he disliked as much as the memories she evoked. As he'd pointed out, he didn't know her and never would. But he had known Miriam.

Standing, Lily smoothed her gloves over her skirt, then accepted his arm with reluctance, knowing the heat of his body would shoot through her like a bolt of lightning. The instant her arm wrapped around his, she drew a quick soft breath, and they both stiffened.

Ten years ago she wouldn't have understood the push/pull between them, the moments of accord swiftly followed by small explosions of temper. And even now, though she knew better, she tried to deny the hot weakness that sapped her strength when she felt the muscles in his arm go rigid at her touch.

But she was experienced in the ways of men and women. And she could deny the electric attraction between them until the cows came home, but that didn't alter the fact that she trembled at his touch, and her mouth went dry. She didn't want this complication and would resist it, but she was drawn to him, and the attraction was powerful.

What made things confusing was that despite his aloofness and occasional coldness, she had observed Quinn watching her and had seen the heat in his eyes. Had sensed his struggle to pull away from whatever emotions she aroused in him.

People flowed around them as they stood frowning at each other. Something hard and sensual flickered at the back of Quinn's gaze, and an involuntary tremor shot down Lily's spine. Her knees shook, and she felt as if her insides were turning to liquid.

Her fingers tightened convulsively on his arm, and she licked her lips. And suddenly she wondered what their sleeping arrangements would be when they began to live together as man and wife.

* * *

"Do you believe her?" Paul asked, waving a crisply clad Mexican waiter away from their table.

"There's no reason I should," Quinn answered, finishing the last of his steak. "But I do," he added with a shrug. "At some point we have to trust that she won't cut and run at the first opportunity. She didn't today. She says she won't in the future."

They were dining at the Santa Fe Men's Club, which reminded Quinn of his club in Denver. The dining room and smoking lounge were paneled in aged cherrywood and hung with hunting scenes. Cigar smoke thickened the air, and the room buzzed with a low hum of male voices. If it hadn't been for the stuffed iguana and armadillo atop the fireplace mantel, he could have believed he was in Denver.

"Before we discuss Lily," he said, putting down his fork, "we need to address the alterations you made in my speech for the territorial legislature."

Paul lifted a hand. "I know your objections, we covered them yesterday. You'll cut your own throat if you propose regulatory measures for the mining industry."

"When's the last time you rode up to the mines? Slag piles are disfiguring the landscape." He leaned forward, his gaze focused and intense. "That dirt is coming from deep inside the mountains, Paul. Nothing will grow on it. What I'm proposing is that the mining industry clean up its mess. Bring in some topsoil and cover the slag. Otherwise, Colorado residents are going to be looking at a blighted landscape for a hundred years."

"The small operators will walk away, and you'll never find them to enforce such a regulation. The financial burden will fall on the big operators. That means you'd be imposing additional costs on the very men who are financing your campaign. The silver barons will never support this measure, Quinn. Or you, if you propose it."

"The cost is small compared to long-term benefits."

"Small? Hiring a platoon of day laborers to dig topsoil, then haul it up the side of a mountain? The silver barons will insist that future Coloradoans repair the damage if they don't want to look at slag piles. Quinn, the name of the game is profit, and you know this. You threaten the mining industry's profits at your peril."

Leaning back in his chair, Quinn raked a hand through his hair, tousling the dark waves. Frustration made his shoulders ache.

"There are days when I ask myself why in the hell I'm running for office. For every goal I want to accomplish, you have four reasons why it can't or shouldn't be attempted."

"That's politics, my friend," Paul said, smiling. "I've been at this longer than you, long enough to know whose toes not to step on. You don't trample the men whose money will get you elected."

He leaned back as the waiter removed their platters. "Maybe Lily's suggestion had merit. Perhaps I should use my own money and run as an independent."

Paul ordered brandies, then leaned forward and folded his hands on the white-damask table linen. "Only a political innocent would suggest such an expensive way to lose an election. Understand that I agree with many of your ideas, and in a perfect world I'd help you fight for them. But I absolutely guarantee you'll lose this election by a landslide if you enrage the mining industry by proposing regulations that will slice profits. Or if you offend the religious community by espousing divorce. Or if you throw the ranchers up in arms by demanding water controls. Or, or, or. Your ideas are farsighted and good. But this isn't the right time."

Brooding, Quinn gazed out the windows overlooking the territorial governor's residence. He knew how the game was played; he just didn't like it. First get elected, *then* introduce controversial issues. It was the misrepresentation that stuck in his craw. He would rather have been elected based on full disclosure of what he hoped to accomplish rather than win based on sidestepping real issues in order to avoid offending the money men.

"I know you're frustrated and angry. Impatient to launch an agenda you passionately believe in," Paul said, cupping his hands around the brandy snifter. He hesitated, then met Quinn's gaze. "Have you considered taking a mistress?"

The question was so unexpected that it blindsided him, and he laughed. "You're suggesting a mistress as an antidote for the frustrations of a stressful campaign?"

"Partly," Paul replied with a smile. "Actually, you're the only politician I know who doesn't have a mistress." His expression sobered. "But there's another reason. Closer to home."

"Lily," he said flatly, the amusement vanishing from his expression.

Paul nodded. "She's becoming a beautiful woman. As time goes by she's regaining her spirit. She's willful and challenging, bright and unique in many ways." He looked Quinn in the eyes. "And there's a strong attraction between you."

"For Christ's sake, Paul. Are you suggesting that I make Lily my mistress?"

"Not at all. Exactly the opposite, in fact. Once we finish polishing her, there are going to be moments when you forget that she is not Miriam. There may be a temptation to . . ." He lifted his shoulders and spread his hands. "And that can't happen. If you form an attachment for her, it will only be that much harder to get rid of her."

Paul wasn't saying anything he hadn't already realized. Lily was indeed becoming more beautiful by the day. Her hair had regained a healthy shine, her body was filling out. Her skin seemed smoother and paler. When he'd located her in the plaza earlier today, for one moment he'd simply seen her as a desirable woman and had wanted her.

She possessed an innate sensuality that Miriam had lacked, and it surrounded her like an exotic perfume. It was there in the way she moved, the way she needed to touch things, the way she drew the tip of her tongue across her upper lip. As her confidence grew and as she became more comfortable with her new persona, she would draw men the way pollen drew bees.

"You'll see her every day. You'll behave as if devoted to each other. You'll sleep in the room next to hers. She's going to be a powerful temptation, Quinn. Made worse by the fact that anyone can see she's fascinated by you. To Lily, you're an interesting puzzle. She doesn't understand your ambitions or your way of thinking. You're a man who wouldn't have noticed her a few weeks ago, and now your future depends on her. You're unknown to each other, yet familiar. This mix could be a strong aphrodisiac. And that worries the hell out of me. I need you focused on the campaign."

Was Paul's assessment true? It was difficult to judge objectively, as Miriam kept getting in the way.

"Lily would make a delightful mistress," Paul continued, a frown drawing his brow. "She's ideal for that purpose in many respects. I doubt she would bore you. She wouldn't be as expensive to maintain as some. She wouldn't demand marriage."

He had realized these things, too.

"But forming a sexual alliance with her would be unwise in the extreme. She would be more time-consuming than a mistress housed elsewhere or a woman who presents no danger of emotional involvement. When the time comes, you need to be able to get rid of Lily as easily as you rid yourself of Miriam."

Quinn stared, and his voice sank to a rough timbre. "You can't possibly believe that it was easy to dispose of Miriam."

"What I'm saying is a mistress would be a relaxing diversion during the campaign, and she would alleviate the stress of sleeping next door to Lily. Think about it, Quinn."

"I'll think about it," he conceded after a lengthy silence. "But I have neither the time nor the inclination to create another complication."

They carried their brandy into the smoking lounge and joined two senators from the New Mexico territorial legislature, where Paul set the next block in the foundation of deception that would culminate in Lily's impersonation.

He introduced Quinn as the man most likely to be Colorado's first elected governor, and managed to mention they were in New Mexico to fetch Mrs. Westin home from a convalescence for consumption. There was some good-natured competitiveness about New Mexico air versus Colorado air as a curative for consumption, but no one asked uncomfortable questions.

Quinn discovered he'd half expected one of the men to become suspicious and demand details. Which sanitarium? Can you prove your wife was actually there? It didn't happen.

Leaning against the mantel, he told himself the story would get easier with repetition. And reminded himself that liars could not afford the luxury of a conscience.

When they left the club near midnight and stepped into the chilly night, he watched Paul climb into a waiting carriage, then decided he'd prefer to walk back to the rented house.

Scanning the shadows, half-looking for trouble and half-hoping he'd find it, he walked down the middle of the dark street scowling and thinking about the campaign, his frustrations, the compromises, the lies . . . and Lily.

This morning when she'd wrapped her hand around his arm, he had looked down into those incredible violet eyes, and he'd wanted her. Instantly, powerfully.

Miriam had never aroused such an instantaneous response. Yet he didn't know if he reacted to Lily or to a new and fascinating Miriam whom he had never seen before.

"Damn it to hell!" Thrusting his hands deep in his pockets, he kicked at a horse apple and considered returning to the plaza, finding a rowdy cantina, and starting a fight.

In the morning, he left the house early and waited for the stage at the depot instead of having breakfast where he would have to speak to Lily.

The stage was an hour out of Santa Fe before the irony of last night's conversation struck him. Paul had urged him to take a mistress, and had suggested he choose any woman except the woman who looked like his wife, was posing as his wife, and with whom he would be living as man and wife. His "wife" was not to be touched.

Yet she was the woman he couldn't get out of his mind.

Chapter 5

The week in Santa Fe stretched into ten days, and Lily spent them practicing from dawn until nearly midnight. Beginning immediately after breakfast, she and Paul simulated tea parties, luncheons, small suppers, large dinner parties, receiving lines. She reviewed the language of cards, deciphering folded edges and titles, and she pretended to call on ladies of varying social rank and receive calls from them. She practiced introductions, and the proper wording of invitations and responses. She memorized the specific duties of household servants and how to manage a staff. Clothing changes occurred several times a day until she gradually became comfortable with trains and bustles.

She soaked up knowledge like a dry towel sponging up a spill. A hairdresser taught her to arrange her hair in flattering styles, the local chemist brought her lotions and creams, the seamstress discussed fashion and accessories.

As she had to unlearn the habits of a lifetime, some tasks were more difficult to master than others, like table etiquette, her nemesis. So many of the rules seemed utterly ridiculous.

Removing her elbows from the table, she gazed across a flower centerpiece at Paul and sighed. "Who would have imagined there was such a silly thing as a finger bowl? Or that I would know about it and how and when to use it."

"You almost received a perfect score tonight," Paul said, smiling at her. "Truly, Lily, your progress is remarkable. That is, unless you have your knees crossed beneath the table."

"I don't." The corset pinching the waist of her dinner gown curved over the tops of her hips and dipped low enough in front that she sat too stiffly to cross her legs with any comfort.

Without deliberately having to recall how to do it, she signaled Carlos to pull back her chair. Then Paul offered his arm to escort her to the parlor, where, by mutual agreement, she could become Lily again. The first thing she did was kick off the violet-satin heels that matched her gown and prop her feet on a low stool. Wiggling her toes with pleasure, she sprawled backward in an upholstered chair.

Paul packed his pipe and lit it, puffed a satisfactory glow into the bowl, then regarded her through a curl of cherry-scented smoke. "I've had some books delivered to your room. From now on, I want you to read every night for at least an hour. And I want you to make it a habit to peruse the newspapers every morning."

"Etiquette books?" she asked with a groan.

"Also books by Mark Twain, Thomas Hardy, Jules Verne. You'll hear these authors discussed or referred to, and it will be expected that you've read them. Throughout the next months I'll continue to provide you with reading material, some educational and some merely entertaining."

"I haven't read a book in fifteen years." Crushing her curls against the top of the chair, she frowned at the ceiling. "Am I going to be successful at this? Occasionally I get shaky inside and start thinking this is ridiculous. What the hell difference does it make if my chair is eight inches from the table or ten inches? Did Miriam believe this nonsense was important?" she asked, lowering her head enough to see him standing by the fireplace. A small fire burned in the grate, chasing the chill from the evening.

"I doubt Miriam ever questioned her upbringing. There's a great difference between absorbing something automatically and unlearning old behaviors and adopting new ways."

"Did you know Miriam well?" Lily asked curiously. She expected him to evade the question, and of course he did.

"Damn it, Paul. When are we going to actually talk about Miriam?"

"It will be easier to remember not to swear if you excise swearing completely." He ignored her perpetual complaint. "Tomorrow, when we leave Santa Fe, I'll begin calling you Miriam, and I'll register you as Mrs. Westin at the hotels we stay in along the way."

The moment had to come, of course, but it startled her. "Miriam," she said aloud, rolling the name on her tongue. It didn't yet apply to her, but it would. The strangeness of answering to another person's name gave her a peculiar feeling. She released a slow breath.

"That's the fourth or fifth time you've sighed. Are you tired? Bored?"

"Am I being rude?" So sighing wasn't allowed either. She now understood that whatever felt natural was certain to be considered bad manners. "Have you heard from Quinn?" she asked, wishing Paul hadn't disposed of all the cigars in the house. She also wished that the mention of Quinn's name didn't bring a rush of warm color to her cheeks. The truth was, she missed the tension and underlying excitement of the friction between them.

"I received a telegram this morning. The speech to the legislature went well. He'll await our arrival at his ranch."

"Did he say anything about me?" The question was an embarrassing blunder, and she wished she could recall the words. To cover the revealing lapse, she quickly added, "Speaking of rude, Quinn didn't even say good-bye."

"He didn't say good-bye to Carlos either, or to the cook or charwoman," Paul stated bluntly. "You're an employee, Lily."

Paul had an annoying way of lulling her into believing they were becoming friends, then putting her in her place with a painful jolt.

"Quinn has an obligation to pretend, too, doesn't he?" she snapped, sitting up straight. The color in her cheeks deepened. "Or did he also treat Miriam like an employee? If so, no wonder she ran away."

She waited to see if he would confirm or deny that Miriam had run away, but his expression revealed nothing.

"Quinn will play his role when the time comes," Paul said mildly, offering her a liqueur before he took the chair facing her. He puffed on his pipe, studying the spots of crimson high on her cheekbones.

"You're walking a fine line, Lily. On the one hand you must submerge yourself in Miriam's life so totally that you seem to become her. On the other hand, you can't become Miriam so completely that you forget her life is not your life. Don't ever forget. At the end of this, you walk away."

"I know that," she said, unable to identify why she felt frustrated and her chest ached. "But pretending to be Quinn's wife would be easier if he were more cordial."

"The situation is difficult," Paul agreed, choosing his words slowly and fixing his dark eyes on her face. "You're a dead ringer for Miriam. You'll be wearing her clothing, living in her home, moving through her life. There are going to be moments when Quinn forgets you're not his wife, and that will lend authenticity to the deception. But I don't want you to forget it, too, or this situation will end badly."

Lily threw out her hands. "Now there's a perfect example of the conflicting messages you're sending. One minute you're telling me to become Miriam, the next minute you're telling me to remember that I'm not. How in the devil do I manage to do both things at once?"

"The truth?" She identified a flicker of sympathy in his gaze. "I don't know. You're a clever woman, Lily. I hope you'll figure it out." He leaned forward, cradling his pipe in his palm. "I know you don't always believe this, but I like you. I don't want to see this experience hurt or damage you, but it will if you forget who you are."

"Is that a threat? If I don't follow instructions exactly, you'll send me back to prison?"

She had promised herself she would never forget that Paul and Quinn were powerful, ruthless men using her to accomplish their own goals. But she did forget. It was difficult to regard a man as ruthless when he was benignly explaining the difference between an at-home gown and one worn to receive.

"It's a warning intended for your benefit."

Warnings were threats in a blunted form and she knew it. So did he. Paul could be direct, but he could also be subtle.

"Sometimes you talk, talk, talk, and the words pile on top of one another like bricks hiding a dark cellar," she said, staring at him. "If you're not threatening me with prison, then how can impersonating Miriam harm me?"

"At the end of your employment, you leave," he said evenly, meeting her eyes. "There is no possibility, none whatsoever, that your impersonation of Miriam will continue beyond the date we've given you. Don't become so attached to your role that you can't walk away from it."

"That won't happen," she said with an irritated wave. "I'm counting the days until I can be with my daughter!"

"Really? I wonder." He lifted an eyebrow. "You wouldn't be the first woman to trade an illegitimate child for the luxury of fine clothing, jewels, and a mansion filled with servants."

"You're wrong," she insisted, sounding defensive and swallowing a sudden sour taste of guilt. He'd spotted her hunger for the life she was moving toward. The truth was she wanted it all, her daughter *and* Miriam Westin's fairy-tale life.

"Besides, we're beyond threats, aren't we?" he asked, looking down at the pipe he held in his palm. "All I'm saying is take time for yourself, make time to be yourself. Privately, of course," he added with a thin smile. "Keep Rose in front of your mind. She's something that is uniquely yours, not Miriam's."

Lily dropped her head and plucked at her gown. "Did I tell you that I considered writing to Rose? She'd be thrilled to receive an actual letter." A sigh lifted her shoulders. "But I decided not to. Six months would seem even longer to a five-year-old than it seems to me. I'll wait until the election is over before I tell her that I'm coming home."

She glanced up in time to notice something hard and cold at the back of Paul's eyes, a sharp-edged flash, gone before she could be certain of what she'd seen.

"That's a wise decision," he said smoothly. "The fewer

people who know where you are, the less possibility of being unmasked. You don't intend to instigate a correspondence with your prison friends, do you?" His tone was mild, but something in his expression told her this was an important question.

"No," she said slowly. "It's understood that continuing any prison friendships might jeopardize a fresh start. If Alice or Ida or Crazy Jane walked in the door right now, we'd pretend not to recognize each other."

She thought of them often and missed them. Not a day passed that she didn't wish she had a woman friend to talk to, someone to show her new lovely clothes to. But it would never be Alice, Ida, or Crazy Jane. Those friendships had ended the instant she walked out of the prison gates. It was better that way for all of them.

"Excellent." Leaning to the ashtray, he tamped out his pipe. "Well. We have a long coach ride tomorrow. Are you packed?"

When she recalled this part of the conversation later, she experienced an uneasy sense that it had been a mistake to reveal that she had not written to Aunt Edna or Rose, and wouldn't contact anyone she knew.

Perturbed, she thought about that for a moment, then convinced herself she was being foolish to hear a little bell of alarm. There was no reason to be concerned.

Any residue of uneasiness sank beneath the greater nervousness of considering tomorrow when she would pass herself off as Mrs. Quinn Westin for the first time. The trail of Miriam's reemergence began here, along the drive from Santa Fe to Denver. Little would be expected from her initially; all she had to do was answer to Miriam's name for the benefit of a few hotel employees.

Nevertheless, it felt as if she were taking an irrevocable step. Idly, she rubbed at the goose bumps rising on her arms and wondered where Miriam was tonight.

For the first few days Lily felt like an impostor when Paul addressed her as Miriam, or referred to her as Mrs. Westin when they checked into a hotel at the finish of the day. By the end of the week, however, her new name began to feel as if it belonged to her. Still, it would be peculiar and a little bizarre when Quinn called her by his missing wife's name.

She fought thinking about Quinn and didn't like it when she lost the battle. Unfortunately, it seemed he popped into her mind at every idle moment. And she anticipated their reunion with a secret eagerness that she knew could only lead to disappointment.

"You're sighing again," Paul commented, looking up from the notes he was arranging in his lap. "Actually, Miriam sighed frequently, too. Frankly, I've always considered sighing an unattractive quality."

Not bothering to answer, Lily pulled aside the curtains and gazed out the coach window, inspecting the mountains. A few of the peaks were sprinkled with snow, which didn't surprise her as the weather had steadily gotten colder as they traveled north. Wools and cashmere were comfortably welcome now. Today she had added a cape over a dark navy traveling ensemble.

"You said we'll reach Denver soon?"

"Probably the day after tomorrow," Paul confirmed. "We'll go directly to the ranch, where you can rest for a week. I doubt you've fully recovered your strength. I'll release an announcement that you've returned from Santa Fe and will continue your convalescence at home. The following week you and your husband will move into the mansion."

These were the statements that continued to startle her, when he spoke as if the fiction were real. It always gave her a tiny shock. In keeping with the deception, he'd become very solicitous, as if she were actually recovering from consumption. Yesterday, she had pretended to have a coughing fit, just to test him, and he'd rushed across the hotel lobby with the appearance of genuine anxiety.

"The mansion," she repeated, trying to imagine a house so grand it could be referred to as a mansion. And hoping to hell that she remembered the servants' names and how to address them. Hoping she had improved to the extent that they didn't see through her. "You mentioned that Quinn had the house rebuilt. Is that to accommodate state dinners and balls?"

Paul glanced at her. "That's one of the reasons."

"Surely you aren't adding *more* information, are you?" she asked after watching him struggle against the rocking of the coach to add scribbled notes to the cards.

Every day they went through the note cards which were filled with details about people Miriam knew. Lily had hoped the cards would reveal a glimpse of the real Miriam, but Miriam remained frustratingly elusive. "Miriam had a lot of friends," she said, frowning at the thick card collection.

Paul frowned. "*You* have a lot of acquaintances," he corrected. "But you're too timid to form intimate friendships easily."

Like a starving man falling on crumbs, Lily pounced on any information about Miriam and wrung every drop of conjecture from each reference.

If Miriam was shy, then she would not push herself forward in social situations, would not meet a stranger's gaze. Entertaining might cause her great anxiety, and repaying calls had probably been a task she dreaded. It also occurred to Lily that shy people seldom expressed their opinions.

"I'm not very shy," she said slowly, wondering if she could successfully pretend to be.

Paul glanced up from his lap desk with a laugh. "So I've noticed."

"But I think I see how to give that impression." Pursing her lips, she considered. "If I pretend every person I meet is a prison guard, I'll remember not to look into anyone's eyes directly, and not to speak until spoken to. If Miriam is timid, then I'm guessing she's also a quiet person?"

"That's my impression, yes." Leaning forward, he handed her the stack of cards. "Read through the new notations, then we'll review the information again."

It wasn't necessary to remind her how important it was to learn everything she could about the people listed on the cards. If a revealing mistake occurred, it would happen here. And the consequences would be disastrous for Quinn.

"We can't possibly know everything we need to know about Miriam's relationships with these people."

"About *your* relationships," he corrected.

"I'm certain to make a mistake. It's inevitable."

"You should have been hanged, Lily," he said flatly. "You managed to slip and slide through a trial for your life. I think you can slip and slide through conversations with these people."

Once again the subtle suggestion of a threat hung in his voice and in his expression. She stared at him, then down at the cards spread across her lap. Each person's name represented enormous potential for error. "I wish I had the faith in my abilities that you do," she said with another sigh.

Suddenly the plan of impersonating Miriam seemed doomed to fail. And perhaps dangerous. If she blundered, would they punish her by sending her back to Yuma and Ephram Callihan?

The Westin ranch comprised twenty thousand acres beginning a half a day's ride north of Denver. The land rolled and dipped like the waves and troughs of a fertile green sea in summer, and reminded Quinn of a rumpled white blanket in winter. Every year the hands cleared more sage and converted more land into grassy pasture. Water was abundant.

This was the place he most liked to be, he thought, drawing up on the reins and crossing his arms atop the pommel. Here life seemed simple, reduced to fundamental issues of survival. Nature favored the predator, and that was a truth he understood. One was either a predator or a victim, no middle ground existed.

He watched a bushy-tailed fox devour a rabbit, then raised his eyes to the jagged skyline of snowcapped mountains scraping the western sky. The Great American Desert fell away toward the east. Denver lay behind him, and farm communities were springing up north of his property. One day the ranch would be squeezed by Denverites and farmers, moving toward each other.

But that problem was for the future. There were more immediate problems to consider. A few weeks at the ranch had honed his muscles and restored his spirits, but Lily Dale was never far from his thoughts.

In the crisp November air of late afternoon, with his

horse beneath him and the land around him, hiring a convict to impersonate Miriam seemed an absurd idea. He didn't trust his memory of Lily's astonishing resemblance to his wife, believed he must surely have deceived himself into imagining similarities that couldn't exist.

Frowning, he shifted in the saddle to observe a small herd of Texas longhorns as they ambled through the lengthening shadows toward a shallow creek that crossed this section of land. The longhorns were crafty, mean-tempered animals, and lately he'd been considering an experimental program of crossbreeding. He thought it possible to blend the steely endurance of longhorns with the milder temperaments of more domesticated breeds.

That thought returned him to Lily as so many thoughts did. Could Lily Dale be domesticated to the point of deceiving people who knew his wife? Today, he doubted it. Not a woman who snatched bread from the table and hid it in her pocket.

Still frowning, he shaded his eyes from the sun sinking toward craggy peaks.

For the past five years the Westin Ranch had trailed two thousand steers to the railheads in Kansas and from there to the beef markets in Chicago. When he became governor, his primary market would be closer to home. The party bosses had promised a guaranteed market in Denver for as many cattle as he wanted to sell. This was a perquisite of the job. To Quinn it smelled like graft.

Lowering his head, he rubbed the bridge of his nose. There were so many things he wanted to change about government and how it operated. But none of his ideas stood a chance of becoming reality unless he won the election.

His thoughts circled back to Lily Dale.

That his future and perhaps the future of an entire state depended on an unwed mother fresh out of prison made him grimace and shake his head. When he considered how easily she could destroy him, the cords rose like wire along his throat.

Jerking on the reins, he turned his buckskin back toward the ranch house and urged the horse into a full gallop, letting a twilight breeze cool his face.

Within the hour the deception would begin in earnest.

The men knew very little about Miriam, as she had seldom visited the ranch, preferring the house in town. But Smokey Bill, his foreman, had met her last year. Quinn couldn't part with Smokey Bill, but he had replaced the house servants. He had decided to test Lily with Smokey Bill, and afterward he would make his final decision as to whether the deception would go forward.

He would know soon enough, he thought, riding up to the barn as Paul's coach circled the drive in front of the house. Handing the buckskin's reins to one of the hands, he drew a breath, straightened his shoulders, and walked forward with a stony expression.

But he stopped in his tracks when the driver opened the coach door. First Paul emerged then turned to hand Lily down. No, not Lily. He was to call her Miriam now.

When he saw her, he sucked a sharp breath through his teeth. She wore a grey jacket and skirt, a feathered black hat atop piles of ashy blond curls. Her figure was fuller, rounder, her skin lotion-smooth and pale in the fading light. Unlike the last time he had seen her, she wore her traveling ensemble, it didn't wear her.

Quinn stared. This wasn't—could not be—the woman he had first seen outside the Yuma Women's Prison. She also could not be Miriam, although he had to struggle against the conviction that he was staring at his wife.

Forcing himself to step forward, a scowl on his face, he tried to recall how he would have greeted Miriam after an absence. It surprised him to discover that he couldn't remember.

When she spotted him, a delighted smile lit her face, and his chest tightened painfully. It had been years since Miriam had smiled at him like that. If she ever had.

"Quinn!" Stepping forward, she placed her gloved hands lightly on his leather jacket and lifted her face.

Placing his hands on her shoulders, he gazed into eyes as deep as the violet heart of a pansy. He didn't see Lily in her expression, nor did he see Miriam. This was a hybrid creature, partly one thing and partly another, a beautiful chimera.

Releasing a breath, he forced himself to speak her name. "Miriam." He would have kissed her; therefore, he should do so now for the benefit of any ranch hands who might be watching.

Her skirts wrapped around his boots, followed by a curve of warmth as she leaned into him. For the first time in his life, he felt awkward with a woman, unbalanced by her closeness and the scent of forget-me-nots, Miriam's favorite perfume. His hands tightened on her waist.

He intended to hold her away from him, but her momentum carried her forward, and he found himself pulling her hard against his hips instead. Eyes flaring, she paused in the act of lifting her cheek and turned slightly to cast him an uncertain look. The unexpected movement brought her lips within inches of his.

It was an invitation no red-blooded man could resist. He hesitated for the span of a heartbeat, then kissed her on the mouth, feeling a tremor of shock ripple down her body. She stiffened slightly, and her hands curled into fists on his chest.

A public kiss should have been light and impersonal, and that's what he intended. But his mind exploded when his lips covered hers. It had been a long time since he'd held a soft, vibrant woman in his arms, a long time since a kiss had set him on fire with sudden intense desire.

His embrace tightened, and his body radiated sudden heat and urgency. The feel of her hips pressed to his, the taste of her mouth, her hands on his chest, he felt her in his blood.

When he made himself release her, he was breathing rapidly, stunned by the forces unleashed by a single kiss. She raised a hand to her lips and looked at him with wide eyes, her breasts rising and falling beneath her cape.

His mind reeled. What the hell had happened? He hadn't had such a powerful reaction to a woman since he was a moonstruck adolescent.

Dimly, he was aware of Paul studying his reaction, stepping forward to shake his hand, a frown drawing his eyebrows. Then he heard Smokey Bill behind him.

"Welcome to the Flying W, Mrs. Westin."

Lily gave her head a light shake and arranged a smile on trembling lips. "It's a pleasure to be here, Mr. Johnson."

Quinn's boots felt rooted to the ground. But her hesitation was so brief that he doubted Smokey Bill had noticed. It utterly astonished him that she had not looked to Paul for prompting, had named Smokey Bill on sight. The tight knot that had gripped his chest for weeks eased, and he glanced at Paul, who was watching him with a lifted eyebrow.

"Something is different from the last time I visited," Lily said thoughtfully, looking around her. It was a clever guess, and her delivery was convincing. "That would be about a year ago, I recall. September, I think."

Smokey Bill beamed. "Yes, ma'am. We installed another well this summer, so that windmill is new." Turning, he pointed toward the source of a grinding, squealing whir. "And we enlarged the bunkhouse and the summer kitchen."

When Lily walked away from them, following Smokey Bill to the edge of the veranda to peer through the deepening darkness at the new bunkhouse, Quinn stared after her. "I wouldn't have believed this if I hadn't seen it with my own eyes," he said in a low hoarse voice.

Her gestures were not as fluttery as Miriam's, she was more controlled, and her husky voice would never match Miriam's lighter tone. But she was no longer Lily. She didn't meet Smokey Bill's admiring gaze directly, but cast him shy, sidelong glances. She glided forward with a graceful step.

Paul watched her with pride. *And why shouldn't he feel proud,* Quinn thought. *Lily is his creation. Paul had taken a lump of rough clay and polished it to resemble a diamond.*

She strolled back to them, gave them a smile, then lifted those incredible eyes to Quinn. "Please ask Curly to bring my valise inside. I'd like to rest before Jamison serves us one of his heavy beef-and-potato suppers."

She was showing off for him and clearly enjoying the disbelief in his eyes. But she kept lifting a hand to her lips, and she hadn't met his gaze for more than an instant. She, too, had responded to their kiss.

"Curly's gone, and so is Jamison," Quinn said after a minute, watching Smokey Bill jump forward to assist the coach driver with her valise. He shouldn't have kissed her.

"Oh?" She cast Paul a look of reproach. "I don't recall anyone telling me."

Her performance was for Smokey Bill's benefit, but also for his. And he was undeniably if reluctantly impressed. But this hybrid beauty was not Miriam. When Miriam had visited the ranch, she had elicited curiosity as the owner's wife, but not the look of near adoration he now read on Smokey Bill's face.

Miriam could be charming in her quiet way, but only after she knew someone well enough to overcome a natural timidity. Lily's charm, however, was immediate. Curiosity and high spirits sparkled in her glance, and she moved with unconscious sensuality. He understood she was trying to imitate timidity, but her lowered lashes appeared more coquettish than shy, her sidelong glances more flirtatious than timid.

A burning sensation flared inside Quinn's chest, and he narrowed his eyes on the swing of her bustle as she lifted her skirts and swayed up the steps of the veranda. She had been with another man. She had borne that man a child. She was wearing Quinn's name, but she was not his.

"Quinn?" Paul said for the second time. "Shall we talk here, or inside?"

Lily retired to her room as they crossed the veranda and entered the house, but a light fragrance of forget-me-nots lingered in the foyer. Quinn clenched his fists and imagined her stepping into Miriam's room, laying out her toiletries on top of Miriam's vanity. Sleeping in Miriam's bed tonight. She was not Miriam, he reminded himself, bringing his thoughts back into line.

Waving Paul toward one of the chairs facing his desk, he crossed his office and went straight to the whiskey cart. He tossed back a long swallow, letting the liquor scald down his throat, then poured a glass for Paul.

"You've accomplished a miracle," he said, sinking into the wooden chair behind his desk. He raised his glass in a salute. "I didn't believe it was possible."

Paul tossed his hat on the desk then rubbed his neck. "Don't forget the transformation is a veneer as thin as perspiration. She's just as likely to make a blunder or swear like a muleskinner." But the pride returned to his dark eyes. "I doubt such a thought has occurred to her, but she would have been a skilled actress if she'd chosen to go on the boards."

"An hour before you arrived, I was determined to call off the impersonation."

"She can pass for a lady right now." Paul packed his pipe and frowned. "But she isn't Miriam yet. That part of her instruction rests with you. At present, anyone who sees her from a distance won't question they're seeing Miriam. But she'll raise questions at close quarters. Her gestures are wrong, and she's too forthright, still too confrontational." Leaning back in his chair, he puffed on his pipe. "But the changes are astonishing. I doubt anyone noticed her between Yuma and Santa Fe. And I doubt anyone ignored her between Santa Fe and Denver."

Quinn lit a cigar and waved out the match. "Do you have any idea how unsettling this is?" he asked after a moment.

He wasn't accustomed to confusion or uncertainty; such feelings had played a very small role in his life. But he looked at Lily and reality melted and re-formed, and his mind reeled as he saw a new personality inhabiting his wife's form. Her face was familiar, but the expressions were foreign. He knew her body, but she used it differently in the way she walked and stood. Her hands moved in motions less graceful but more provocative. It was like meeting Miriam without having known her before, a Miriam that might have been but never was.

Suddenly he recalled Miriam as he had seen her last and a heavy pain sliced at the walls of his chest. Angrily, he stubbed out his cigar and tossed back the whiskey. "How long will you stay?"

"I'll return to Denver early tomorrow. I'll need a week to catch up the paperwork that's undoubtedly accumulated during my absence." He touched his collar and smiled. "And there's a certain lady I'm eager to see."

Nodding, Quinn swiveled to gaze at his late father's portrait. At this moment he envied Paul Kazinski. Paul had no need to prove himself—he'd built a solid reputation as the best behind-the-scenes man in the territories; his quick mind and an opportunistic eye had amassed a substantial fortune. Paul was untroubled by compromise, a master at finding the middle road. He did what had to be done and never looked back; past deeds would never haunt him. Perhaps most enviable, Paul had decided not to burden himself with a wife and amused himself with a series of delightful mistresses whom he discarded with ease when they displeased or began to bore him.

Quinn's office door opened and closed, and he inhaled the memory-provoking scent of forget-me-nots. When he turned in his chair, Lily had hitched up her skirts and perched herself on the edge of his desk. Leaning, she flipped open his humidor and withdrew a cigar.

"I haven't had a smoke since you left us in Santa Fe," she said, tossing Paul a defiant glance.

Her hair had regained its gloss and shine, and she wore it in an elaborate arrangement of blond curls that dropped over her right shoulder. It didn't concern her that a froth of petticoats were exposed when she crossed her legs or that she displayed several inches of trim ankles.

Quinn watched with fascination. Like a chameleon, she had changed again. The genteel lady who had emerged from the coach had become a hoyden. But he understood this, too, was a performance. She had shown him her version of a lady, exaggerating the downcast eyes and gliding steps; now she showed him an exaggerated version of herself.

She inhaled, then blew a smoke ring into the air before she looked at him, her gaze flicking to his lips. Then her eyes narrowed and she glanced at Paul.

"All right, gents. No more stalling."

"Gentlemen, not gents," Paul said automatically, frowning at her cigar.

"The time has come to talk about Miriam. I want to know who she is and what happened to her." She stared at Quinn, and the light shining up from his desk lamp illuminated her eyes and the determination stiffening her chin. "We've put this off long enough. Either we talk about Miriam now, or I'm leaving for Missouri in the morning." Leaning her head back, she blew a stream of smoke at the ceiling. "So talk, cowboy."

Chapter 6

"Keep your voice down," Paul warned sharply, glancing at the door. "Threatening to leave is unnecessary and damned annoying. The plan was always to turn you into a lady first, and then into Miriam."

"Well now's the time for the Miriam part," Lily repeated, watching the lines deepen on Quinn's craggy forehead. His mouth thinned, and his stare was as dangerously flinty as a rock cliff. He had a way of looking at her as if he saw inside, and his gaze sent a light shiver down her spine as he removed his jacket and slowly rolled up his sleeves. The muscles in his forearms swelled, and she knew he was angry.

Obviously, she disturbed him in complex ways. As he did her. When he'd kissed her, she had felt his arousal and a corresponding leap of desire that shook her to her toes. He hadn't intended to kiss her, that had been an accident. But the instant his mouth took hers, he'd wanted more. She had felt his desire in the bruising tension in his fingers and in the flare of heat that enveloped her. And Lily had wanted him, too. All her good intentions had flown out of her mind, replaced by a wave of physical sensation that weakened her knees and robbed her of breath.

For a moment she'd felt dazed, and then she'd wondered who he was kissing. Miriam? Or her? She'd been surprised how painful it was to think he might have been kissing Miriam.

One thing was certain. There was no confusion now. Quinn looked at her and saw Lily Dale, and he disliked her for making demands, for resembling his wife, and, she sensed, for arousing him.

She held his gaze while she waited for him to speak, and her stomach tightened and grew hot. Never had any man provoked such a confusing mixture of emotions. When Quinn stared at her with that electric blend of desire and anger, her neck prickled, and she felt a tiny thrill of fear, remembering this was a powerful man who could return her to prison on a whim. Confusingly, power mixed with desire also exerted a darkly seductive appeal.

"All right." His voice was as hard as his gaze. "What do you want to know?"

"Everything." Suddenly she felt foolish, perched on his desk like a bar girl. Telling herself that she had made her point, had jolted him into taking her seriously, she slid her feet to the floor and took the chair next to Paul. "Why is obtaining information about Miriam like prying a barnacle off of a rock?" she asked, leaning forward to tip an ash into the tray and wishing she hadn't lit the cigar. It didn't taste as good as she had expected. Worse, enough ladylike qualities had rubbed off on her that smoking seemed crude and distasteful.

She'd had an idea that by flaunting herself, she would force Quinn to admit the contrast between Lily Dale and the performance she'd put on for Smokey Bill. Now she suspected her flamboyant entrance had only annoyed him.

"I can't succeed in this impersonation if neither of you will talk about Miriam. How does she move? How does she behave? What was her daily routine? What made her happy or sad? What did she like or dislike?" Looking up from smoothing down her skirts, she held Quinn's gaze. "What was her marriage like?"

"I understand the necessity for this conversation, but it's repugnant to expose my wife's life to a stranger," he said, speaking between his teeth.

Anger choked her. "Listen. I'm going to be the best friend Miriam Westin ever had. I'm going to do my damnedest to represent her well and not embarrass her. When she returns, she'll have nothing to apologize for. And that ain't going to be easy." Deliberately she said "ain't" in another attempt to remind him of how far she had come. Lifting her hands, she waved the cigar and hoped he noticed that her fingernails were clean and no longer ragged. "I can't succeed without knowing more about her."

"She's right, Quinn." Paul frowned at both of them. "It's time."

Leaning back in his chair, Quinn gripped his whiskey glass against his stomach, his jaw working. Lily could almost see sparks of resentment flashing off his lanky body, and she knew she caused them. Anger was the barrier he erected against whatever he felt when he looked at her.

"I gave you the impression that Miriam had led a comfortable and sheltered life, and that's true. But Miriam's early life was not easy or happy. Her mother died when Miriam was ten. Five years later her sister Susan died at the age of twelve. Her brother was killed in the war, and the man she was engaged to marry never returned. Her father died five years ago. Miriam spent most of her life in mourning."

"Good Lord," Lily said, blinking. "Everyone she loved fell over dead." For the first time in years, she thought of her own family. Drunken Indians had killed her parents, and she'd had a sister who died young of diphtheria. She, too, had grown up motherless and missing a cherished sister.

Miriam began to take shape in her mind. Miriam had been a deeply sad person. "Go on."

Quinn's brooding gaze dropped to a portrait of a forbidding-looking man who shared Quinn's strong jaw and pewter eyes. "When I met Miriam, she was twenty-two and living with her father." He fell silent, then dragged a hand through his hair. "Judge Alton was an influential man, a powerful political figure."

Lily listened carefully, then straightened abruptly. "You bastard," she said softly. She saw it now. "You married Miriam to further your political career, didn't you!" Her mouth twisted. She hadn't begun to suspect how ruthless he could be.

He stared at her, no apology in his gaze. "Ambition was part of the reason, yes. But Miriam was also a beautiful woman." His eyes traveled over her face, and Lily knew he was seeing the woman he had married. "And I was ideal-istic enough to believe I could make her happy."

"Did you?" Lily demanded.

He returned his gaze to the portrait of the man who must be his father. "I doubt it," he snapped.

"Well, that's not too surprising. It couldn't have made her happy to know you married her to gain her father's po-litical support. Did she know it?" Lily asked, her eyes blaz-ing. Of course Miriam had known. She must have felt as used as Lily did.

He shrugged and took his time lighting a cigar. "People marry for many reasons. Miriam was an innocent, but she wasn't stupid."

"Then why did she marry you?" Lily asked rudely. Right now, she didn't like Quinn Westin.

"Her father wanted the match," Quinn answered, his words falling like chips of ice. "Miriam had waited for a man who didn't return from the war. She was approaching spinsterhood, and after the war suitors were few and far between. At the time I came along, the judge was already ill and anxious to see his daughter married and settled."

But what had Miriam wanted? Had she been content to live in her father's home and care for him? Or had she dreamed of a home of her own? Had she wanted to marry Quinn, or had she married him because the match would make her father happy?

"How old is Miriam now?"

"Two years older than you. She's thirty."

With every unwilling word Quinn uttered, Miriam's ghost gradually took on flesh and form. Lily could imagine her. A pretty woman, sad, quiet, and shy, an obedient daughter who wanted to please the only remaining member of her family.

She considered Quinn as objectively as she could and decided he was handsome and compelling even when he was scowling in anger. Had Miriam thought so? Had she found it easy or hard to love him? Had he made her heart pound and her skin flush? Had she welcomed his touch, yearned for his kisses, or had she dreaded the times he came to her?

Paul stood abruptly and returned his whiskey glass to the drink cart. He glanced at Quinn. "If you'll excuse me, I have some reading to finish before supper."

His tact surprised Lily. But of course he knew this story.

Quinn waited until the door closed, then continued speaking in a flat voice. "Miriam wanted children. I'm sure you'll understand that. Unfortunately, her constitution was never strong, and pregnancy was difficult for her. She suffered four miscarriages before she carried a baby to term."

Lily's mouth dropped, and she straightened with a jerk of astonishment. "You have a child?" she asked when she could speak. She could not believe they hadn't told her. The omission was shocking.

He walked to the drink cart and turned his back to her. "Miriam delivered a daughter eight months ago. She named the child Susan in memory of her sister."

Lily sputtered. "You have a daughter? And you never mentioned her?" It was an outrage that he hadn't so much as hinted at a child. That neither of them had mentioned that Lily would have to deceive a child. Placing her hands on the arms of the chair, she prepared to rise. She would not do this.

After setting a whiskey glass on the desk in front of her, Quinn stubbed out the cigar she'd left forgotten and smoldering in the ashtray, then returned to his chair.

"In May the house in town caught fire. Susan died in the blaze."

"Good God." Bits of information fell on her like stones dropping from the sky, battering her sensibilities. She fell backward in the chair. "And Miriam?" she asked after catching a breath, staring at his expressionless face. "Did Miriam die, too? Is that what happened to her?"

"Miriam suffered minor burns and a serious burn on her leg." Unable to remain seated, he rose and stood at the window, sipping his whiskey and frowning out at the dark range. Leaving Lily to work out the implications.

"Oh my God," she whispered, her fingers flying to her lips.

The air rushed out of her lungs and she slumped, blinking hard. Miriam had lived, but her baby had died. She would have blamed herself, would have tortured herself by replaying the fire in her mind, desperately trying to re-arrange the outcome.

A moist lump rose in Lily's throat, and tears glittered in her eyes. She knew about torturing oneself with if onlys. If only she hadn't listened to Cy. If only she hadn't agreed to accompany him to the gambling hall. If only she had done this differently or that, she would be with Rose right now.

Not a day of her incarceration had passed that she hadn't run the conversations with Cy through her mind, trying to make them end differently so she could be with her baby. A thousand times she had imagined herself saying no, or turning away at the door of the gambling hall and refusing to step inside. Imagined herself not pulling the trigger.

Miriam would have tormented herself in the same way, only it would have been worse because her baby had died. There would never be a second chance to save her child, there would be no reunion at some date in the future.

"Oh my God," she whispered again, pressing her fingertips to her eyelids. Her chest ached, and her heart went out to Miriam Westin. "She blamed herself for Susan's death."

"Miriam saved herself but not her baby," he said harshly, his voice a low, gravelly rumble. "Of course she blamed herself."

"And you blamed her, too." She heard it in his coldness, in the odd lack of expression in the telling.

"The fire was swift and intense. No one could have saved Susan. Her nursemaid died that night, too, as did one of the upstairs maids. Frankly, it's a miracle that Miriam escaped."

She wiped her eyes, surprised that she'd guessed wrong. If not blame, then what was she hearing in his voice? "Where were you? Did you try to save your daughter from the fire?"

"I was out when the blaze started. By the time I arrived, the interior was an inferno."

Did he blame himself for not being there? Was that what she was hearing? Lily wished she could see more than his profile. She drew a deep breath. They had to finish this. "How long after the fire did Miriam disappear?"

"Almost immediately." He rubbed his forehead, concealing his eyes from his reflection in the window glass.

Lily swallowed the last of her whiskey, hoping the liquor would steady her. "Quinn, you have to find her." She gazed at him, wishing he'd look at her. "Wherever Miriam is, she's hurting, and she needs you."

His laugh was shocking. The sound was harsh, almost cruel. "Believe me, Miriam is happier where she is than she ever was with me."

She stared at the Irish linen molding his broad shoulders and following the ridge of his spine, and clenched her fists. "How in the hell can you be so cold?" she asked in a low furious voice. "Your daughter died five months ago, and your wife has run away. She did run away, didn't she? That's what happened."

"Oh yes," he said, lowering his hand from his face and staring out the window. "Miriam ran far, far away."

Suddenly he turned and hurled his whiskey glass at the wall. The crystal exploded in a shower of glass with a sound like shot, and Lily jumped, her heart pounding.

"Don't tell me that Miriam needs me because she doesn't. Don't suggest that she wants to be found, because that will never happen." A silvery fire burned at the bottom of his eyes. "If you have any more questions about the fire or about Miriam's disappearance, ask them now—because we will never again discuss this."

The intensity of his fury pushed her back into her chair, although she didn't understand it. Either his grief had taken the form of rage, or there was something he still wasn't telling her. She suspected the latter since he hardly seemed like a man in mourning.

"You and Paul always speak of Miriam in the past tense," she said after he turned back to the window. He tightened his jaw, and his fists opened and closed at his sides. "Do you believe she's dead? Could despair have driven her to take her own life?"

She didn't think he would answer, but finally he said, "Miriam is alive."

The revelations had come too fast, were too shocking, for Lily to think of the questions she would later wish she had asked. She couldn't move beyond imagining Miriam's despair and grief and self-blame.

Lifting a hand, she watched it fall back to her lap. "Where is Susan buried?" At the moment, it was the only question she could think to ask.

"In the Prospect Hill Cemetery."

She tried to think of something else, frustratingly aware that a hundred questions would crowd her mind an hour from now. "Was Miriam really suffering from consumption?"

"Her health was delicate, but I doubt she was consumptive."

A rap sounded at the door, and Paul leaned his head inside Quinn's office. He looked at the shattered glass on the floor, then lifted his eyes. "Supper is on the table. Would you prefer to have it served here?"

Quinn withdrew his pocket watch, snapped it open, and glanced at the time before he tucked the watch back in his pocket. "Are there any other questions?"

Lily gazed at him, feeling limp. The anger had faded from his expression, and he looked as tired and drained as she was. It occurred to her that he had known this conversation was coming, and had dreaded it. "I have dozens of questions, but I can't think . . . I'm just . . ."

"If there's anything more about the fire or that night, ask now."

She pushed a wave of hair off her forehead and tried to focus her thoughts. "Where were you that night?"

"I was with Paul."

"How did the fire start?"

"The cause was never verified."

His answers were clipped, unelaborated, resented. Every instinct suggested there was more than he had revealed, but she couldn't guess what it might be and didn't know the right questions to ask. Frustrated and suddenly angry, she rounded on Kazinski.

"Why didn't you tell me about Susan?"

"Would knowing that Miriam lost a child have changed anything?" He opened the door wider as if to allow the tension in the room to escape.

"She lost five children. Susan and four miscarriages!" How had Miriam borne the losses in her life? Lily knew how it felt to lose people she cared about, and she could identify with Miriam's pain. But not the depth of it. Miriam's losses had continued year after year. Just as she began to recover from one blow, another had fallen.

But one small mystery was solved. Now she knew why the clothing they had provided was all in dark shades. Miriam would only now be entering the second phase of mourning.

Standing, Lily cut a slow stare across both men, and her lip curled in disgust. "The two of you make me sick." Her stomach had begun to churn when she heard about the fire, and it hadn't stopped. "You have ice in your veins. No compassion, no pity, no sympathy. All you think about is yourselves."

Right now, she had a sad suspicion that Miriam was more real to her, a stranger, than she had been to her husband and Paul.

Lifting her skirts, she strode toward the door. "Get out of my way. I don't want to sit at the same table with either of you. Tell someone to bring a supper tray to my room!"

"Wait." Paul caught her arm. "Quinn? We have to give her the rings sometime. It might as well be now."

Quinn swore and thrust a hand through his hair, then he threw open a drawer. He withdrew a small box, held it for a minute, then tossed it to Paul as if the box had burned his palm.

"What is this?" Lily asked, taking the box. But she knew.

"Those are Miriam's wedding rings," Quinn growled, sitting heavily in his desk chair. Lifting a hand, he rubbed the bridge of his nose.

"Are these replicas?"

Paul said yes, and Quinn said no. After giving them both a scathing glance of contempt, she pushed past Paul and strode to her room, slamming the door with enough force to knock a picture off the corridor wall.

Someone had lit the lamps and laid a small fire in the grate. After warming her hands, Lily sank to the edge of the bed and opened the box. Carefully, she withdrew Miriam's rings and held them on her palm. The betrothal ring featured a diamond nestled between two gold roses that locked into a third rose on the wedding band. Extending the wedding band to the lamp, she strained to read the inscription inside the band. Q.W. to M.A., 6/10/67.

Sighing, she dropped backward on the bed and closed her eyes. Quinn was right. A woman who left her wedding rings behind did not want to be pursued or found. Miriam had no intention of returning.

She roused herself when a smiling cowboy brought a supper tray to her room. He introduced himself, but it was a name she didn't recognize.

"Put the tray there," she instructed listlessly, pointing to a small table near the vanity. She shouldn't have requested a tray, her appetite had fled.

After the cowboy departed, she wandered around the room, opening bureau drawers, looking inside the armoire. But there was nothing of Miriam here.

The ranch house was furnished to suit a man's preference and comfort, there was no evidence of a woman's softer touch. No effort had been made to conform to style or to coordinate colors or furnishings. This was a man's house, from the heads of trophy animals to the leather chairs to the rustic tables and simple draperies.

Miriam had left no imprint here, telling Lily that Quinn and his wife liked different things. Miriam had not shared his interest in ranching, had not cared enough for his company to accompany him to the ranch. Or perhaps he had not invited her, which amounted to the same thing.

After inspecting a utilitarian pitcher and washbasin, she wandered back to the table and her supper tray. Beefsteak and fried potatoes, beans, greens, and a slab of apple pie. Sitting down, she nibbled at the beans as more questions began to come.

Exactly how had Miriam managed to run away?

Paul had explained that ladies did not discuss or handle money. When Lily shopped, she'd been instructed to direct shopkeepers to send an invoice to her husband. She would have a carriage and driver at her disposal, so she would not require coins to hire transportation. In fact, a lady had no need of actual money.

So, how had Miriam financed her escape? She would need money to buy a ticket to somewhere else, money to replace the clothing she had left behind, money to feed herself and pay for lodging, money to establish herself in a fresh start.

The question nagged her enough that she decided to ask Quinn if Miriam had access to money of her own. Perhaps an inheritance from her father?

After smoothing her hair, she walked down the corridor to the dining room, stopping outside the door when she heard Quinn laugh. Following the turmoil of talking about Miriam, the sound of his laughter set her teeth on edge. It seemed wrong.

On the other hand, she told herself, trying to be fair, while the information about Miriam and Susan was new to her, it had been five months since the fire, almost that long since Miriam's disappearance. He'd had time to adjust and come to terms with his altered circumstances.

Shamelessly, she eavesdropped as Quinn brought Paul up to date on events that had occurred during his absence, and referred to political topics obviously discussed earlier. When she heard their chairs scrape back, Lily turned to flee, but stopped when she heard Paul's next question.

"Has anyone inquired about Miriam?"

"The inquiries were easily handled," she heard Quinn answer. The scent of cigar smoke drifted into the corridor, and she heard the clink of glasses, pictured them pouring brandy. "I still think we should have announced Miriam's death and taken our chances with the voters."

For an instant Lily stood rooted to the floor, then she edged nearer to the doorway.

"You know my advice. But if you absolutely cannot accept Lily, then I'll get rid of her." Something about Paul's tone made the hair stand up on the back of her neck. "But it would be a mistake. She's going to be successful. You saw how easily she managed Smokey Bill."

"Damn it, Paul. It's like seeing a ghost."

"And it's going to get worse as she adopts Miriam's mannerisms. I don't know what to tell you, Quinn, except you have to deal with the resemblance. You need her to win this election."

"Will she pass Helene Van Heusen's inspection?"

During the ensuing silence, Lily's mind raced. Helene Van Heusen. Miriam's close friend. A friend Quinn and Paul both objected to because Helene's husband ranked high in the opposing political party. That Miriam had insisted on continuing the friendship revealed a flash of spunk that surprised Lily.

"I'm guessing Helene will spot the personality differences at once," Paul conceded. "But the resemblance is so stunning it will never occur to her that this isn't Miriam.

She'll try to explain the differences some other way. The best solution is to limit contact."

Lily waited to hear more, but their conversation shifted to Helene's husband and political strategies. After a time, she tiptoed away from the door and crept back to her room.

Peering into the mirror as she brushed out her hair, she tried to decide if Quinn had been speaking rhetorically or if Miriam really was dead. Earlier he had insisted Miriam was alive, but Lily didn't trust either Quinn or Paul when it came to Miriam. There was no way to know for certain what had happened to Miriam Westin, so she told herself— once again—that Miriam's fate was none of her business. All she had to do was play the role she had been hired to play.

But it wasn't that simple anymore. She was beginning to identify strongly with Miriam.

It was Miriam's face she saw in the mirror. Miriam's eyes stared back at her. Tomorrow she would slide Miriam's wedding rings on her finger.

And there was Miriam's husband. And a kiss that had seared her inside and left her shaking.

Turning, she spun away from the face in the mirror.

Chapter 7

Surprisingly, Quinn found Lily at the corral when he arrived at the stables to saddle up for his morning ride. It hadn't occurred to him that she would be a horsewoman.

"That's stating it too strongly," she said with a smile, lifting her face to the cool sunshine. She wore a sliver of a hat that trailed gauzy wisps behind her but didn't protect her face, and she'd forgotten to bring a parasol. "I'm not a horsewoman, but I did grow up on a farm, and I like horses and riding. Although this is the first time I've ridden a lady's saddle."

She rode well, sitting relaxed in the saddle, her touch light on the reins. Quinn pulled down the brim of his hat and turned the buckskin's head toward a copse of bare-branched cottonwoods. He couldn't shake the notion that he was looking at Miriam when he glanced at Lily. More accurately, looking at Lily was like observing a shadow that didn't conform to the movement casting the shadow. He didn't subscribe to the current vogue of spiritualism, but there was something otherworldly and almost eerie about her similarity to his wife. And jolting when she did or said things that Miriam would never have done or said, startling when her expression or gesture was eerily exact.

"Miriam didn't ride," he commented. When Lily arched

a pale eyebrow in his direction, he shrugged. "I bought the saddle years ago before I knew she had no interest."

"She disliked the ranch, didn't she?"

Paul had correctly assessed Lily's quick mind. Already she had assimilated the information Quinn had provided only last night and let her shoulders drop slightly, conveying an overall suggestion of sadness. He hadn't realized that Miriam didn't hold her shoulders back, that she'd had a drooping carriage. But he saw it now in Lily's altered posture.

"The ranch is too rustic for Miriam's taste," he said, studying her from the corner of his eyes. The possibility that she would uncover things better left buried concerned him greatly now that he grasped her talent for nuance.

"Miriam would have been offended by the animal heads mounted on the walls," she continued in a musing tone. "Am I correct?"

She was picking up information she needed in order to be successful, but it startled him that she intuited Miriam's likes and dislikes so readily. Curiosity prompted his own question. "Do the trophy heads upset you, too?"

Lily adjusted her leg in the saddle brace and ran a gloved hand over her riding skirt. "People have to eat. If a set of trophy antlers comes with the meat . . ." She shrugged.

A practical woman. But then, he supposed she would have to be to survive the life she'd led. "Like many women, Miriam didn't care to be reminded where her dinner came from."

"If she'd wrung the necks of a few hundred chickens, like I have, or prepared hams for smoking, or butchered a cow or stuffed sausages, she would have learned to be less squeamish." Looking back at the house, she added, "Miriam may not have liked the ranch, but I like it very much."

"So do I," he said quietly, pride in his voice. He'd had the building stones and roof tiles imported from Italy, and the design was an adaptation of a farmhouse he'd once stayed in outside Milan. "You might consider Italy," he suggested after he'd explained the house's origin. "The climate is mild, and the people are warm and friendly."

"I haven't had time to think about where I'll go when this is over."

They rode toward the cottonwoods, and occasionally Quinn's boot brushed the hem of her riding skirt. It would have been less jarring on his nerves to move away from her, but harder to converse. To his surprise, he found her easy to talk to.

"I think I'll see how this saddle rides and discover if I can stay on it." Leaning forward, she patted her horse's neck, then made a low, clicking sound and touched her crop to the mare's flank. The horse accelerated to a trot, and then, at her urging, broke into a canter.

Quinn watched with a smile. As Paul had predicted, her confidence was growing. Only a self-assured woman would urge an unknown horse into a canter while riding an unfamiliar saddle.

Touching his heels to the buckskin's belly, he followed, admiring her form, and reined up beside her. "That could have been a foolhardy experiment," he said, studying her flushed face. Her lavender eyes sparkled with pleasure. "She might have tossed you."

"Oh hell, I've been tossed before." Tilting her head, she gave him a measuring look. "Want to race back to the barn?" His expression must have reflected his astonishment because she laughed. "I was only joshing."

Their horses stood side by side in a meadow cleared of

sage and sunflowers. Autumn leaves fluttered along the fence line, riding the tail of a cool breeze. Sunshine stitched the heavens to the earth. On a fine autumn morning like this, there was no place Quinn would rather have been than riding his land with an interesting woman at his side. And she was interesting.

The black riding habit suited her admirably, making her throat seem paler by comparison, providing a stylish contrast to the abundance of blond hair. Today she wore her hair pulled back in a thick knot on her neck, a plainer style than Miriam had ever worn and flattering in its elegant simplicity. The first time he'd seen her, her hair had reminded him of straw. Now he thought of corn silk.

A few weeks of nutritious food, rest, and fashionable clothing had transformed her into a beauty.

"Quinn, for heaven's sakes. You don't need to look so angry. I wouldn't have raced. I know it isn't something Miriam would do." She lifted a hand to shade her eyes. "And Miriam wouldn't have forgotten her parasol either. How did your nose get broken?"

He was watching the sunlight glowing like a halo around her wheat-colored hair, lighting her face, and the change of subject was so abrupt that it took a moment to realize she had asked a question.

"We should go back," she said when he remained silent. "I shouldn't be out in the sun, and Cookie will have breakfast on the side table by now." Tilting her head, she gazed at him. "Seriously, what happened to your nose?"

He told her the story on the way to the barn, then she told him about breaking her arm when she was a child. He fixed his gaze on the cowboys drinking coffee near the corral and clenched his teeth. He was far too interested in her and needed to reestablish a distance. He didn't want to know that she'd climbed trees as a girl. Or had wrung the necks of chickens. Or could ride a horse with grace or foolhardy bravery. She had asked questions when he explained his broken nose, but he didn't inquire what she was doing in the neighbor's apple tree, or how old she had been when she fell and busted her arm.

Ideally, she should only be an employee, an insubstantial shadow hired to impersonate his wife. But he was beginning to understand that Lily was too strong a personality to remain in any shadow. As her confidence returned, so did her stubbornness, defiance, and a vibrant, sparkling spirit. Miriam had been quiet and unobtrusive, like a fine aged wine. But Lily was like champagne, bright, bubbling, irrepressible.

And she would only become more so as time carried her further from Yuma and her prison experience.

They didn't speak between the corral and the house and said little during breakfast, but Quinn was acutely aware of every careful movement she made, every bite she swallowed. He watched the way she handled her napkin and utensils, observed the practiced grace with which she now held her coffee cup.

"I'm not going to steal the muffins," she said in that low, husky voice. Amusement danced in her eyes. "Those days are behind me."

"I apologize for staring," he said, letting his gaze travel to her lips, then back to her eyes. "You've changed a great deal since I saw you last." Looking at her now, it was hard to picture her even as she'd been last night, flouncing into his office and perching on his desk top in a show of ankles and petticoats. Part of her fascination was her mercurial ability to be one thing one minute and something else a minute later.

Of all meals, breakfast was the most intimate. A man didn't share breakfast with an unknown female. If a woman sat across from him, it was a woman whom he knew well, a woman he most likely had slept with. Frowning, he studied her, knowing they would share many breakfasts before her term of employment ended, breakfasts like this one where an awareness of unacknowledged sexual tension sizzled between them. He didn't recall ever being this alert to every small nuance of a woman's voice or movements.

She had removed her hat and gloves and riding jacket, and he carefully held his gaze above the high-necked shirtwaist that curved over her breasts. But he was aware of the rise and fall of each breath to the extent that he silently swore and tried to recall when he had last been with a woman. It had been too long. Hell, maybe Paul was right, maybe he should consider a mistress.

To bring his thoughts back to reality, he made himself inspect her left hand and the rings flashing when she moved her hand through the sunlight.

His jaw clenched and he recalled the day he had purchased Miriam's rings. He'd been rushed, due in court and running behind schedule, consulting his pocket watch every few minutes. When the jeweler offered a suggestion, he'd accepted it with only a cursory glance at the sketch he was shown. Later, Miriam had praised him for making such a thoughtful selection. Even in the beginning he hadn't done right by her.

He set down his coffee cup as Paul strode into the dining room dressed for traveling.

"It's acceptable to dine informally at the ranch," he said to Lily by way of greeting, "but in town you would wear a morning dress to the breakfast table." He nodded to Quinn, then filled a plate from the buffet laid out along the sideboard.

"I believe we're about to receive a hundred instructions," Lily said with a sigh. But she surprised him by giving Paul a fond smile as he took a seat at the table.

Paul returned her smile, and Quinn felt a sudden and unreasonable barb of jealousy. "You and Quinn are to work on mannerisms this week. And you're to review the prints for the house in town so the layout will be familiar. Continue going over the cards describing people you know, and continue practicing any areas where you feel shaky or unsure. Pass the butter, please. Are you reading every evening?"

"I like Mark Twain," Lily said, handing him the butter dish. "Thomas Hardy is slower and harder."

"Something both of you need to remember is that servants have big ears. And all servants are gossips. Once you leave the ranch, you should assume that someone is always listening and conduct yourselves accordingly."

"No one is listening here?" Lily asked, glancing over her shoulder at the dining-room door.

"The housekeeper is Spanish and speaks no English," Quinn explained. "Cookie spends most of the day in the summer kitchen and will until the end of the month." He met her thick-lashed eyes. "For the most part, we'll have the house to ourselves. That's why Paul and I decided this week would be spent here rather than in town."

"From now on," Paul said, "you must call her Miriam. If you call her Lily even once, anyone who finds the new

Miriam puzzling will be pointed toward figuring out the truth."

Quinn doubted he would address Lily by name. Referring to her as Miriam was a final capitulation that he was not prepared to make.

"Use this week to practice relating to each other as if you have been married for several years. From now on," Paul said to Lily, "your past does not exist, and you should make no reference to it. Any reference should be to Miriam's past."

She blinked. "I won't be able to talk!"

Paul laughed. "Yes, you will. You can invent whatever you like about the sanitarium you've supposedly been in, as long as it sounds reasonable. Take your cue from whatever others say to you. You're quick, you'll come up with responses vague enough to steer you away from trouble."

Drumming her fingers lightly on the table linen, she looked back and forth between them. "And what do I say if someone refers to the fire or Susan's death?"

Quinn set down his coffee cup and felt his stomach tighten. "No one will mention Susan or the fire," he said firmly.

Frown lines appeared between her eyes. "It irritates the hell out of me when you make sweeping statements like that. You can't possibly know what one of Miriam's," she hesitated, then swallowed and drew a deep breath, "what one of my friends will say to me in private. They very well might refer to the fire or—my—daughter's death." The last words made her cheeks pale.

She was thinking of her own daughter, Quinn guessed. The last time Lily had seen her baby, Rose had been three months old, the same age as Susan at the time of the fire.

Lily's wound was older, but similar enough to Miriam's that she would be convincing if anyone was rude or tactless enough to make a reference to that night.

"Paul and I have made it clear to—your—acquaintances and friends that—you—cannot bear any reference to the fire or Susan's death. The only person who might breech that request is Helene Van Heusen. All you need to do is looked distressed and murmur that you don't wish to speak of the incident."

"Excellent," Paul said, smiling at them. "That's exactly the way you should speak to each other. As if you're really Miriam. Don't drop the pretense, even in private."

Lily had been relaxed and companionable during their ride and through breakfast. Now her gaze hardened, and she shoved her plate away. Her lips thinned, and her jaw tightened. Her narrowed eyes reminded him of the moment when she had discovered etiquette could also be wielded as a weapon.

"The loss of our daughter devastated me," she said, staring at him. "Why didn't it devastate you? How can you mention Susan's death so unemotionally?"

He was right to be concerned. She wouldn't be content until she had pried open Pandora's Box. "You know the reasons," he said, staring back at her. If she had hoped to force revelations by addressing him as if she were actually Miriam, she was mistaken.

Paul also understood what she was trying to do. He pulled his chair next to Lily's and took her hand, glancing down at the rings on her finger. "I suppose it was inevitable that you would become fascinated with the woman we've hired you to portray. But there are lines that you are not permitted to cross."

"I hate it when you take that threatening tone," Lily said, pulling her hand out of his grasp.

"Do you understand what I'm saying?"

"Oh yes." She flicked a glance at Quinn. "The two of you don't want me to know the real Miriam or what happened to her."

"The private side of my relationship with my wife is none of your concern," Quinn stated flatly. "And you don't need to know my feelings about Susan in order to play your role convincingly."

"What we want from you is a surface performance, Lily. You know what happened to Miriam. She disappeared. She ran away. As for learning about the 'real' Miriam, if you mean her private nature, Quinn is correct. Restrain your curiosity because that isn't your concern." He pushed his chair back in place. "With apologies to my friend Quinn, I assure you that Miriam was not an especially interesting person. There's no mystery about her, nothing to hide, nothing to explain. Miriam was an ordinary woman who led an ordinary life."

Lily returned his smile in kind. Her lips curved, but her gaze was hard and wary. "I'm starting to like you, Paul, but I wouldn't believe you if you swore the sun set in the west."

"You can believe me on this point," Paul warned. "You know where the line is. Don't cross it."

She placed her napkin beside her plate and hesitated just enough to allow Quinn to rise and pull back her chair. At the door of the dining room she looked back at them. "Do all politicians lie, or is it only you two?"

Her fighting spirit might have made Quinn smile if their circumstances had been different. And though it worried him, he also admired her for refusing to surrender. He also understood why she had received more than her share of prison beatings.

"Good-bye, Miriam," Paul said fondly, smiling at her. "I'll see you again next week when you return to the mansion."

She glared, then her mouth relaxed into a genuine smile and she threw out her hands. "You're a sly scoundrel, Paul Kazinski."

"That's what I get paid to be."

"Notice that I didn't call you a lying son of a bitch."

Paul laughed. "I noticed. And I applaud your progress."

"You enjoy her, don't you?" Quinn asked after Lily's footsteps had receded down the hallway. He poured another cup of coffee and added fresh cream.

"Actually, I do."

Leaning back in his chair, Quinn lit a cigar and studied Paul through the haze of blue smoke. "Did you enjoy Miriam's company?" he asked curiously.

"Frankly, I've never thought about it."

It was the answer a friend could be expected to make, tactfully vague, less embarrassing than a blunt no or an expression of indifference. Quinn might have answered the same if Paul had inquired if he enjoyed Effie Mallory's company. Paul's mistress was a beautiful young woman with absolutely no opinions to clutter her brain and nothing interesting to say.

"Looking at Lily doesn't evoke private memories for me as it undoubtedly does for you," Paul said, blotting his lips with his napkin. "I see her objectively in a way I never saw Miriam until near the end. Then, frankly, I saw Miriam only as a political liability that needed to be handled and quickly."

It was a sad admission and one he deeply regretted, but Quinn privately conceded that he had viewed his wife in much the same way. He remembered telling Paul shortly before his wedding that it didn't matter whom he married, not really, because all women were basically alike. They were cut from the same pattern. All ladies embroidered, read the fashionable literature, sang a little, played the piano a little, devoted hours to fashion and their appearance, organized their lives around social events. Their conversation was as predictable as the seasons. Aside from appearance, women in his class impressed Quinn as largely interchangeable.

Looking back, he wondered if Miriam had been unique or merely another version of a familiar pattern as he had assumed. If they had talked more, had spent more time together— if he had encouraged her to state her opinions freely, if he had shared more of his life with her—would he have discovered some of the qualities that made Lily so fascinating?

These thoughts pointed him in a direction he did not want to go. He couldn't turn back the clock and conduct his marriage differently, so there was no point in pondering the might-have-beens. Miriam was gone. And God help him, he hadn't known her well enough to miss her. When he thought of her, his strongest emotions were guilt, injured pride, and deep anger.

The week flew past. Lily practiced everything she had learned, went over and over the cards describing people and relationships, learned Miriam's mannerisms and tried to make them habit, reviewed her etiquette books.

Finally, she pored over the blueprints of the rebuilt mansion, memorizing the layout of the rooms, trying to visualize the furnishings as Quinn described them.

Having never lived with servants, everything to do with staff interested and worried her.

Leaning over the prints spread across Quinn's office desk, she studied the narrow staircases that climbed three floors at both ends of the house, flanking a central staircase that she and Quinn would use. The two extra staircases were provided to spare the lady or gentleman of the house the indignity of passing a servant carrying a pile of laundry or whatever. Servant and master kept to their own spheres.

"It seems so silly," she murmured. She tapped one of the servant's staircases with her fingertip, but her gaze rested on the connecting bedrooms on the second floor. She told herself that finding confirmation of separate bedrooms was a relief.

"As you can see, the third floor is given over to the servants' quarters," Quinn said, gazing down at the prints. He stood near enough that Lily inhaled the combined scents of cigar smoke, hair oil, shaving soap. "At present there are more rooms than servants, but that will change after I win the election. I'll require additional staff then, and rooms have been provided to meet that requirement."

His ruby cuff links winked in the sunlight as he moved a hard brown hand across the prints and through the light falling across his desk.

"You've mentioned that it would be bad form for the mistress of the house to visit the cook's domain." Apparently real ladies did not step foot in their own kitchens except on rare occasions. "Does the same protocol apply to the servants' quarters?"

"It's your house and strictly speaking, you're entitled to access all areas." He continued to study the prints. "In practice, a thoughtful mistress respects her staff's privacy and seldom visits the servants' quarters unless there's a good reason. Illness, for example." His grey eyes lifted, more charcoal than pewter today. "All the servants have been given Saturday night off. You'll be free to explore every part of the house. If you care to examine the servants' rooms at that time, you're welcome to do so."

"I think I should see everything, don't you?"

"As you wish."

By now Lily recognized his "as you wish" signaled a concession he didn't welcome. "I won't go into their rooms, I'll just peek inside the doors." Leaning over the prints, her shoulder almost touching his, she studied the layout of the third floor. "This area looks more like a small flat than a single room."

"It is. Mr. and Mrs. Blalock live here." He tapped the area she'd referred to. "Blalock has been with me for years. He was my first valet and served as butler after I married. When his eyesight began to fail, he retired from house duty and now oversees exterior maintenance and the gardens."

"And Mrs. Blalock?" Lily inquired, easing away from him. She remembered Quinn mentioning that he'd hired a completely new staff except for the Blalocks and Mr. Morely the carriage driver, who were the only servants left who had known Miriam.

"Mary Blalock came with Miriam from Judge Alton's household," Quinn explained, stepping away from the desk and reaching for the coffeepot. Lily nodded when he lifted an eyebrow, then took the cup he offered her, careful not to brush his fingers. "Mary and James were married about a year after Mary joined the household."

Lily carried her coffee to the window and gazed out at the distant mountain peaks. Frost had glazed the range this morning, and it would have been uncomfortably cold in Quinn's office if he hadn't lit a fire in the corner stove. Not that long ago she had been sweating in the Arizona heat, trying to remember a day like this when the air lay chilly against her cheeks and the last of the autumn leaves fluttered from the trees like falling jewels. A day when the tang of woodsmoke leaking from the stove door reminded one that winter was on the way. Years had passed since Lily last caught a snowflake on her tongue, or peeked through a frost-laced window.

"Mary Blalock worries me," she said, dropping her gaze from the mountains to the men forking hay near the corral. "If she came from the judge's household, then she must know me—" Lily paused, wondering if she would get used to this, "know me well."

She felt Quinn stiffen behind her and knew without looking that he grimaced. They were gradually becoming accustomed to Lily referring to herself as Miriam, but this was the hardest part of the deception for both of them. So far, he had not addressed her by his wife's name.

"It's going to be an early winter," he said from directly behind her. Lily jumped slightly. She hadn't heard him cross the room. "Already there's a lot of snow on the peaks."

The clean outdoor scent of him filled her nostrils along with the other scents that were uniquely his; and she felt the heat of his body radiating along her shoulders and spine. He was tall and whiplash-slender, but like everything else about him, his appearance was deceptive. She'd seen him lift a saddle to his horse's back as if the saddle were weightless. Powerful muscles filled out his frame.

If she leaned backward, she could rest against his chest. Her head would fit beneath his chin. A powerful longing overwhelmed her, and she badly wanted to collapse against him and be held and assured that she could do what she had to.

Pressing her lips together, she turned suddenly and returned to the desk, then cleared her throat. Because her fingers were trembling slightly, she set down her coffee cup. "Will I see much of Mary Blalock?"

Quinn leaned against the wall next to the window, his eyes narrowed and his voice deep. "Her eyesight is failing and her legs pain her. She seldom leaves the flat, as the stairs are difficult for her to manage."

"Then she has no household duties?" She knew the answer, but needed to throw words into a silence that quivered with the strangely electric push/pull that existed between them.

"No." Quinn's gaze traveled down the dark bodice that molded her body to the waist, then he straightened abruptly and pulled out his pocket watch. "I have some things to go over with Smokey Bill. If we're finished here . . . ?"

To give her hands something to do, Lily rolled up the blueprints. "I need to review the cards again and pack. What time will we leave tomorrow?"

"We'll have an early supper and depart immediately after."

"Well. I'll just . . ." She waved a hand at the door and took a step toward it.

Their situation was artificial enough that they didn't meet or part company without Lily feeling uncomfortably awkward. Especially now, knowing that the day after tomorrow the impersonation would begin in earnest and she would be put to the test.

"Quinn . . . I know you have a lot riding on my success." She licked her lips and looked down at her hands. "I'm going to do everything in my power to convince people that I'm Miriam."

"Thank you." For a moment she thought he would say more, but he didn't.

"Honestly, do you think I can be successful?"

When she raised her head, he was staring at her. His eyes were so changeable and such an unusual color that they dominated his face. The grey could be hard and cold, a stony wall, then alter to the quicksilver of curiosity or the warmth of ashy coals in a grate. And sometimes, like now, his gaze turned a smoldering smoky color that made Lily's stomach tighten and made her skin feel hot.

But he didn't answer her question. Lifting her skirts, she fled from the room, not sure what she was fleeing.

They had established a pattern during their week together at the ranch. They rode in the morning, worked together during the day to perfect Lily's performance, then Quinn took his supper in his office and Lily had a tray in her room. Afterward, she prepared for bed, brushed her hair and braided it for sleep, then read a little.

Tonight she couldn't sleep. After tossing and turning, her mind humming with people she needed to remember, with Miriam's habits and mannerisms, with the jitters of stage fright, she finally threw back the quilts, wrapped herself in a warm shawl, and stood beside the window.

A square of light illuminated a patch of frosty brown grass outside Quinn's office window. Hugging the shawl around her shoulders, Lily imagined him sitting at his desk, a glass of whiskey beside him, reading through the dispatches that arrived daily from Denver.

When his silhouette appeared in the center of the square of lighted ground, she caught a quick soft breath and drew back from the window even though her room was dark, and he couldn't know she was watching.

What was he thinking as he gazed out at the cold night? Was he as worried as she about her success? Did he regret forcing her to impersonate his wife? Was he having second thoughts? Or was his mind still focused on the papers strewn across his desk?

When she and her prison friends listed the things they wanted to do immediately after they were released, several of the women had said they wanted to be with a man, wanted to be held and caressed and loved. They had missed men more than anything else.

That hadn't been the case with Lily. The day the sheriff clapped her in irons, she had vowed to turn her back on men forever. Men had been nothing but trouble in her life.

But she stood in the chilly darkness, watching a man's silhouette, and her skin burned, and her legs trembled.

Chapter 8

Quinn mentioned that he wanted to avoid attracting attention; therefore, he'd instructed his carriage driver to avoid the boulevards lit by newly installed gas lamps, but Lily glimpsed the lamps from cross streets and marveled that man had conquered the night. And she noticed the glow of gas lighting from the windows of many of the houses that grew larger as they turned onto Fourteenth Street.

The evening was frosty and dark, and she couldn't see as much as she wanted to, but she had an impression that Denver was a sizable city spread across low hills. The gaslights and newly planted cottonwood and elm trees proudly stated the Queen City of the Plains was here to stay and thriving.

"The house in town is located between city hall and the site for the new state capital," Quinn explained from the facing seat. All Lily could see was the glowing tip of his cigar, his face was lost in ebony shadows. "Cherry Creek is about four blocks from here."

In this section, the homes were two- and three-storied stately brick mansions decorated with iron grillwork and stone insets. Each was surrounded by enough ground to accommodate a carriage house and private stables. Lily stared at the mansions with wide eyes.

When Quinn's carriage slowed then turned onto a gravel drive that circled before an imposing three-story larger than any private residence Lily had ever seen, she licked her lips and fell back against the squabs, raising a hand to her forehead.

"I ain't never been this nervous in my whole life," she whispered. Immediately she realized she had said "ain't" and silently cursed. "My hands are shaking."

"It's only a house, and we have it to ourselves tonight. No one will be in except Paul." Quinn flipped his cigar out of the carriage window, and she heard the rustle of his clothing as he sat up straight and collected his hat and gloves.

Tonight was the first time Lily had seen him dressed in anything other than cowboy attire. He'd made the journey to Denver in what he called his city clothes, a dark suit and waistcoat, snowy shirt, and a low hat. For the first time he resembled her idea of a politician, sleekly tailored, somber, and imposing. And so handsome that she welcomed the darkness as it added to her nervousness to look at him.

Rubbing her hands together, she gazed out the carriage window as they rocked to a halt, peering at the light sparkling through leaded-glass panes set in a massive front door. "I wish we could stay at the ranch."

What she really wished was that she were home in Missouri. She didn't belong in a palatial mansion, wouldn't know how to conduct herself. She would give the game away by getting lost in a place this size, or she'd break some priceless bibelot or spill coffee or whiskey on a carpet worth a king's ransom. No, not whiskey; her whiskey-drinking days were over. From now on she would sip sherry, which she didn't like, or tea, which always tasted like water to someone who preferred stronger libations.

The front door opened as Quinn grasped her trembling fingers and handed her out of the carriage, and Paul stepped onto a wide brick porch. "Welcome home, Mrs. Westin."

"Thank you, Mr. Kazinski." Her voice quavered on a husky whisper. While Quinn and Paul shook hands, she peered behind them into the foyer. Light falling from a brass-and-crystal chandelier reflected on marble flooring. She glimpsed velvet flocked wallpaper and a tall vase containing an enormous spray of yellow chrysanthemums. Three prison cells would easily have fit into the foyer.

While Paul directed the unloading of their luggage, Quinn offered his arm and escorted her inside. Now she saw the central staircase, gracefully curving to a gallery above them. She was so awed that she didn't think about clasping Quinn's arm or realize that she clung to him.

"When you return from an outing, Cranston will take your parasol," Quinn said, looking down into her face. "You can remove your hat and gloves here or in your room if you prefer."

"Cranston is the butler," she reminded herself, wetting her lips and glancing at a gilt-framed mirror. Beneath it was a small table holding a brass card tray. She tried to imagine herself tossing her gloves on the table, then leaning to the mirror to unpin her hat and hand it to Cranston before she examined the cards.

"I can't do this. I don't belong here." The blueprints had not given her a real perspective of size, had not foretold the intimidating opulence of the Westins' home.

Quinn placed his hand on her waist, the first time he had voluntarily touched her. Lily felt the sudden scald of his palm and sucked in a small sharp breath. Part of her wanted him to touch her, but not now. Right now the tingling distraction of his hand on her waist only added to her confusion.

"We'll chase the chill with a snifter of brandy, then you can explore." Brandy was not on the list of drinks that Miriam preferred. He was making an exception tonight.

The pressure of his fingers directed her toward one of the doors opening off the foyer. Frantically, she tried to visualize the blueprints of the house, but her mind had gone blank, wiped clean by size, space, and too many sensations to grasp all at once. She had expected a comfortable home, but she hadn't anticipated that the house would be enormous or so lavishly decorated and furnished. Trembling with nerves, she gripped Quinn's arm and pressed close to him.

She felt him stiffen, and he gazed down at her. "You're shaking."

"I've never been in a place like this. Never imagined I would be." And tomorrow it would be her responsibility to direct the servants and manage this house that felt like a palace.

"It's just a house," Quinn repeated. He guided her into a hallway and from there through double doors into a beautifully appointed room that had been labeled the family's parlor on the prints. A cheerful fire burned in the fireplace faced with tiles of imported, dark blue marble. A flower-patterned carpet covered the floor, repeating the burgundy and navy of comfortable-looking chairs and footstools.

It was a lovely, intimate room filled with so many wall hangings and table decorations and shelves and plants that Lily felt she could spend the entire evening here and still not examine each item thoroughly. Her heart sank. One evening would not be enough to familiarize herself with everything in the house.

While Quinn poured brandy from a cart near a small bookcase, she stood stock-still, staring around her, afraid to move or touch anything.

Accepting the snifter he offered, she took a long swallow and waited for the brandy to hit her stomach with an explosion of warmth. "Is all of this new?" she murmured, lifting a limp hand and noticing she still wore her gloves. "Or did you rescue some of it from the fire?"

"The fire occurred while we were still moving into the house and many items were in storage. Clothing, wall hangings, decorative items, several furniture pieces." He shrugged. "The rest is new. The rooms were redone as closely as possible to what they were before the fire." Moving to stand in front of the fireplace, he placed a hand on the mantel and gazed into the flames. "Miriam wanted the house restored as she had planned it." Lily heard a clock chime somewhere; otherwise, deep silence filled the house. "Obviously any personal items you see were either in storage or saved. Mostly odds and ends."

Now she noticed the collection of photographs covering a round table. Choosing one at random, she tried to focus on the figures smiling back at her. "Who are these people?" She didn't seem able to speak above a whisper.

Quinn came up behind her, bringing the scent of bay rum and his hair pomade, and leaned over her shoulder. Lily felt a tremor shoot down her spine and fought an absurd urge to turn, throw herself into his arms, and burst into tears. "That's Miriam, of course. And her brother Richard, and the judge."

"Mistakes like that will be costly," Paul warned, entering the room and going directly to the drink cart. "You should have recognized yourself in that photograph and known the men were your father and brother. And Quinn, you wouldn't say 'that's Miriam,'" he added. "You'd say, 'that's you.'"

Quinn stepped away from her, and she cast a pleading look at Paul, searching for reassurance in his broad ordinary face. "I'm scared to death."

"Of a house?" He smiled and patted her hand.

"You might as well send me back to Yuma. I'll never convince anyone that I belong here." She carefully replaced the photograph and set down the snifter of brandy before she spilled it. "You told me not to forget who I am. Right now I'm Lily Dale, and I feel like I'm trespassing, like I should be knocking at the servants' entrance instead of coming in the front door. Look at all of these things." She heard her voice becoming shrill. "There are more items in this room than my Aunt Edna had in her whole house!"

Quinn and Paul exchanged a glance, then Quinn gently placed his large strong hands on her shoulders and turned her to face the mirror above the mantel. "No servant ever looked like that," he said, meeting her eyes in the glass. "Look at yourself. No one seeing you now could possibly mistake you for a servant."

The fashionable hat and expensive ensemble she wore helped some. She could admit her exterior might fool people. But inside she was still Lily Dale, an ex-convict and a nobody. A woman who knew her place, and this wasn't it.

"You selected the items in this house, Miriam," Paul said in a soothing voice, trying to coax her into her role. "This is your home."

Whirling out from under Quinn's hands, she spun to face them both. "I didn't select any of these things! Hell, the carpet I'm standing on cost more money than I ever saw in my life! This is like visiting a palace and waiting for the queen to arrive. And we all know who that would be, don't we?" She covered her eyes with shaking hands, then glared at them, knowing they didn't understand. She didn't understand either, except the house overwhelmed her. This was Miriam's house, the house where Susan had died, and it was profoundly intimidating and disturbing. "I just . . . oh just leave me alone."

Running into the hallway, she turned right and passed two doors before she stopped and placed a hand on her pounding heart and tried to collect herself and recall the blueprints.

One of the doors was a coat closet, and she should have known that when she stumbled over the umbrella recepta-cle that stood beside it. She would figure out the others.

Gulping a deep breath, she angrily told herself that she could do this, that she'd been crazy to suggest to Paul that he send her back to Yuma. A home like this was a fairy-tale palace, and she would live here for several months. It wasn't frightening, so why was she so deeply disturbed? This house was a dream come true; living in it was a chance of a lifetime.

She just wished she didn't expect Miriam to appear at any minute and accuse Lily of intruding, trespassing in her house.

Exploring with no plan in mind, she found the dining room, which was large and stiffly formal, then walked through a smaller, charming breakfast room before she peeked into the butler's pantry. She touched nothing, kept her skirts carefully away from brushing against things. Farther along she located the kitchen and spent thirty min-utes examining sinks, ovens, and gleaming utensils, know-ing she very likely would not come here again. The ballroom chandeliers had been lit, so she could view the polished floor, the orchestra platform, but the huge room didn't particularly interest her as she knew it wouldn't be used during her tenure, not while Miriam was still in mourning for her daughter.

The last room she entered on the ground floor was the formal drawing room, labeled the receiving room on the prints. As in all the rooms she'd seen so far, the gas lamps had been lit and hissed softly against the walls. A welcoming fire burned in the grate.

The receiving room was intended to be impressive, and it was. Patterned silk covered the walls and ceiling, the furnishings and accoutrements had the look of imported antiques. Or so she guessed. Lily wouldn't have recognized a European antique if it danced across the room and curtsied.

But she hardly noticed the luxurious furnishings. Her gaze flew to a large silver-framed portrait above a long, low table. Her knees gave out, and she collapsed onto a brocade ottoman, staring up at the portrait.

It was she. Not Miriam, her. To be certain, she removed the gold locket from around her neck and beneath her bodice and clicked it open with shaking hands, comparing the miniature inside to the portrait on the wall. She had never worn that elaborate white dress, had never posed for a portrait, but the woman faintly smiling with sad lavender eyes was her. The shock of it took her breath away.

"Yes, it's you," Quinn said from the doorway. She wondered how long he'd been watching her. "The painting has been altered."

She felt so dazed that the only thing she could think to ask was, "Did someone rescue it from the fire?"

"The portrait wasn't here that night, it had been sent out to be reframed. When I returned to Denver, I had the artist retouch his work to accommodate the changes that occurred during your recent illness. He thinned the nose, widened the lips, altered the hair color a little, enhanced the bustline, and made a few other small adjustments."

The eeriness of discovering a portrait of herself that she had never posed for sent a chill down Lily's spine. Fascinated and repelled, she stared at herself, fighting an absurd attempt to remember sitting for the artist. Giving her head a shake, she forcibly redirected her thoughts and fought to see traces of Miriam in the painting.

"Something just . . ." Frowning, she gazed down at the locket in her hand. "In the miniature, she's heavy, but—" Puzzled, she peered up at the portrait.

Quinn leaned against the silk wall covering and pushed his hands in his pockets, watching her. "The large portrait was painted two years ago. The miniature is more recent." The lines vertically cutting his cheeks deepened. "The miniature was made to commemorate Susan's birth."

Lily closed her eyes. "Oh." Miriam had still been heavy from her pregnancy. Lily had assumed that Miriam was much heavier than she was; however, the larger portrait portrayed her as nearly as slender as Lily. Now Lily understood why Paul and Quinn had so quickly seen the resemblance between herself and Miriam. They were accustomed to seeing Miriam without the additional weight.

Quinn took the locket from her hand and dropped it into his pocket. "I forgot you still had this." His expression hardened.

"The locket was a gift, wasn't it," she asked absently, staring at the large portrait that was her, yet not quite her.

"What makes you think that?" Quinn inquired.

"The inscription." Etched inside the locket were the words, To M. with love. "I think I understand why you altered the large portrait," she said slowly, gazing around the room. "This is where I'll receive callers." Her mind raced, working it out. "Callers will have seen the portrait before. They may have doubts about me, but they can see with their own eyes that I'm the woman in a painting they are familiar with."

Quinn nodded.

Standing, she faced him across the ottoman, blinking in disbelief. "What kind of man would alter a painting of a wife he may never see again?" she whispered. He fascinated her, attracted her, she felt alive and on fire in his presence, but there were moments when she intensely disliked him. "How could you do that?"

"Because he wants to ensure your success," Paul said crisply, striding into the room. "Because he wants to be governor of Colorado. Because he's the best man for that job. Because I urged him to do it. Because it's a damned clever idea. How many reasons do you want?"

"You're both despicable!" Furious, she pointed a finger toward the portrait. "Can you imagine how Miriam would feel if she walked in right now and saw that you'd changed her likeness? Can you even imagine how much that would hurt?" When Quinn opened his mouth, she thrust a palm toward him. "Don't tell me that Miriam isn't coming back. I knew that when I put on her wedding rings. But she could, damn it. I'll tell you something else, cowboy. I don't blame her for running away. A man who could so coldly alter his wife's image couldn't have been much of a husband!"

They stared hard at each other, her face white, his flushed with dark anger. "Are you finished?" he snapped.

Paul stepped up beside her and gripped her arm. "We'll inspect the rooms on the second floor now," he said tightly.

"Then, I understand you wish to view the servants' quarters." At the door, he looked back. "Quinn? I left my satchel in the family parlor. Inside, you'll find some papers that require your signature."

At the top of the central staircase, Lily paused to look down into the foyer, pushing at the fingers of her gloves. "I behaved badly, didn't I? But everything is starting to blur," she said softly. "You can't guess how confusing that is." Her emotions were running amuck. Closing her eyes, she touched her fingertips to her forehead. "It's like he did it to me. Altered my portrait. And those feelings are all mixed up with seeing a likeness of myself wearing a gown I've never worn, sitting in a chair I don't recognize, thinking about something terribly sad that I can't quite remember."

"Lily . . ."

She opened her eyes. "How can any man be that cold and ruthlessly ambitious? He gives her a locket commemorating the birth of their daughter, but he seems untouched by Susan's death." She slapped at her dark skirt. "*He* isn't wearing mourning."

"You know the mourning period is much shorter for men—"

"He says he wants to protect Miriam's privacy, then defaces her portrait. Is that how he protects her memory?"

Paul gripped her shoulders and gave her a shake. "Stop it, Lily."

"Lily? I'm not Miriam now?" Her voice sounded thin and skated along the edges of hysteria. "But I'm not Lily anymore either."

"Get hold of yourself. You're talking nonsense."

"I know," she said, sagging against the gallery railing. "I'm so angry right now. But I don't know why."

Or maybe she did know. Quinn had awakened desires she had believed—had hoped—were dead. To justify what she was feeling, she wanted to admire and respect him. But she kept slamming against the stone wall of his ambition and the lengths he would go to get what he wanted. And embedded in the wall of his ambition was Miriam's imprint.

"I feel so sorry for her," she said quietly. When she looked at Paul, she saw worry in the frown lines between his dark eyes.

"We talked about this, remember? About the need to balance who you are against who you're pretending to be."

"Tonight that's hard to do," she said, gazing at a bronze figurine atop a gracefully curving wall table.

Once she had been grateful to own an extra set of petticoats and a clean hanky. She'd slept on straw-filled ticking until she ran away from the farm. Had used an outdoor privy all of her life. She had never dreamed that one day she would be standing in a palace, wearing real pearls in her ears, and wedding rings on her finger. Seeing a portrait of herself dressed in white lace like a princess, or a sacrificial lamb. She had gone from half-starved hard labor in an Arizona prison to a sumptuous mansion and soft, elegant clothing. From the low-bred habits of a lifetime to fancy speech and refined mannerisms. The changes had happened too swiftly for her mind to accommodate them easily.

"I'm trying," she said to Paul. Lifting her head, she bit her lips and straightened her shoulders. "I don't want to see Quinn's bedroom, and I'll see my own later, but show me the rest of the house."

She looked into a half dozen guest rooms, the second-floor water closet, and Miriam's morning room. Miriam's desk interested her, but closer inspection could wait for a later time.

Touring the third floor was a decision she regretted. Standing in the doorways, looking into the servants' private quarters reminded her of the prison matron's inspections and how much she had resented the intrusion into her private space.

"Did they know I'd be looking at their rooms?" Each of the rooms was exceptionally tidy and oddly impersonal, as if the inhabitants had tucked away all personal items.

"The house has been rebuilt, their mistress is seeing it for the first time. They were all given tonight off," Paul said with a shrug. "I'm sure they understood an inspection was probable." They walked along a corridor narrower than those in the main house. Paul opened doors, Lily glanced inside and they moved on. "This is James and Mary Blalock's apartment."

"We can skip it," Lily said wearily. She'd seen enough. All she wanted to do was curl into a ball in the middle of bed and think about tonight and everything she had seen.

"We're here, and the opportunity may not come again," Paul said, opening the door. "A locked door on a servant's room is a privilege earned by tenure and loyalty. This door would ordinarily be locked, as the Blalocks have earned that privilege."

The Blalocks' apartment was as tidy as the other rooms, but had a homey feel to it, and not all personal items had been tucked away. Hand-tatted lace doilies protected the arms of comfortably worn furniture, a collection of flower paperweights were displayed where the sun falling from a row of windows would show them to advantage. Mary Blalock's kitchen was small but well organized; Lily didn't look into their bedrooms.

"This apartment is larger than my Aunt Edna's house," Lily said with a sigh.

It was clear that Quinn thought a lot of James Blalock to have created the roomy apartment for him and his wife. This was the very type of thing that made Quinn so confusing. Just when Lily decided he was cold and uncaring, she ran into evidence that he could be considerate and thoughtful.

They walked down the servants' staircase and emerged on the second floor, not far from Miriam's bedroom door. "Do you live here, too?" Lily asked. "Or is that a stupid question?"

Paul didn't laugh often but he did now. "I know it must seem as if Quinn and I are inseparable, and it will continue that way until after the election. But no, my house is a few blocks to the east."

"Is your house this grand?" she asked curiously.

"I live alone, and I'm a behind-the-scenes man, remember? It wouldn't do to attract too much attention. My home is comfortable for my needs, but modest."

"I'd probably like it better than this," she said, finally pulling off her gloves. Miriam's rings caught the light from the lamp mounted on the wall near her bedroom door.

"You're an interesting woman," Paul said, studying her face. "Most women dream of being the mistress of a home like this."

"It's too much," Lily said simply. "Two people don't need this much space."

Then she remembered that Miriam had longed to fill her house with babies, and she ducked her head, feeling an ache behind her chest. Quinn had not replaced the nursery. There was no reminder that a child had ever lived in this house or ever would in the future.

Chapter 9

Miriam had chosen rose-colored velvet draperies and rose-and-green striped wallpaper, the color and pattern of which repeated in a ruffled satin bedcover. A strand of blond hair was caught in the bristles of a silver-backed brush atop the vanity. She had worn the wrappers hanging in the armoire and touched the stopper of the perfume bottle to her ears and bosom. Lily inhaled the sweetness of forget-me-nots, then replaced a heart-shaped bottle on the vanity, feeling like an interloper.

The room was too crowded with fringes and ruffles and flowers and stripes for Lily's comfort. Opening the windows a few inches, she inhaled deeply, drawing frigid night air into her lungs while she tried to picture Quinn in a room this suffocatingly feminine.

His masculinity and smoldering virility would crash up against the feminine defense of satin and ruffles, flowers and lace.

She gazed at a fringed canopy arching over the bed, then turned aside and unpinned her hat. In looking for a place to put it, she discovered a small room set aside just for clothing, which surprised and delighted her.

Stepping inside, she inspected racks of dresses and gowns and ensembles. Rows of hats, boots, glove boxes, and a special chest for jewelry and hair ornaments. Were these the new things Quinn had ordered? Or Miriam's clothing? She'd explore more tomorrow. Right now she was exhausted, her mind whirling with confusing impressions. She placed her hat on a shelf with a row of others, hung up her traveling suit, and found her nightgown in the luggage Paul or the driver had placed in her room.

Her room. She thought about that as she stood before the vanity and brushed out her hair with Miriam's brush. This would never be her room or her hairbrush or her perfume or her bed. It would never be her home. She was a trespasser, a shadowy impostor who would leave nothing of herself inside these walls.

Lowering the brush, she peered into the mirror, needing to see Lily Dale. She had never looked this beautiful, had never imagined that she could. Yet she wasn't vain about her appearance as she once had been. The knowledge that another person looked exactly like her was humbling. She was not unique, as she had always believed. Biting her lip and blinking at tears, she stared into the mirror and saw a stranger frowning back at her.

She would never be the old Lily again. It was impossible. The person she was evolving into would never be satisfied with straw-filled ticking or coarse homespun or chunky thick cups and plates. She would never step into the sun without opening a parasol to protect her face. Would never make noise when she drank her morning coffee, or hold her fork in her left hand. Would never again use the word ain't or approve of those who did. She couldn't unlearn the refinements that were becoming habit.

Dropping the brush, she lowered her head and massaged the headache throbbing behind her temples. She was three people, Miriam, Lily, and the blended person she was becoming. And oh Lord, it was confusing and upsetting. Nothing made sense anymore.

After Paul departed, Quinn walked through the house turning off lights, banking the fires in the grates, trying to see his home through Lily's eyes. The rooms seemed ostentatious, extravagantly overdone. He had thought so when Miriam furnished the house originally, and he thought so now. The ranch house was too spartan, but this house was too grandiose. He and Miriam had never found a middle ground or a way to be comfortable in each other's spheres.

Before he turned off the lamps in the receiving room, he poured another whiskey and stared up at the portrait that had upset Lily. After the election, he would have the damned thing destroyed.

Jaw working, he stared at the painting and thrust his hands into his pockets. He'd forgotten about the locket. That was something he should never have kept. Should never have shown to Lily or anyone. He should have taken one of the tintypes to Arizona, not the locket. He didn't know why he'd kept it, except the locket fed his anger. Anger was easier to handle than the other emotions Miriam evoked.

When he couldn't put it off any longer, he went upstairs and entered his bedroom, instantly aware of a bar of light beneath the door that separated his room from Miriam's. Lily's.

He had intended to read the material Paul left for him, but he couldn't concentrate, kept glancing up from his chair toward the light beneath her door. When the light went out, he hesitated, swore under his breath, then gave in to impulse.

The instant he opened the connecting door, light from his room fell across her bed. She bolted upright and clutched the coverlet to the lacy white nightgown molding her breasts. "What are you . . ."

"There's something I want to say." He took a swallow from the glass of whiskey he'd been replenishing all evening. A long golden braid fell over her shoulder, and her face gleamed with the lotions that had restored her complexion. He noticed she wore gloves, also filled with lotion he guessed. Her lavender eyes flared wide. With outrage? Fear? He couldn't tell.

"You want me to hound Miriam and try to bring her back. You're offended that I don't beat my breast and tear my hair when talking about her, offended that I had her portrait altered." He gazed down at the whiskey then frowned at her. "Why in the hell should I chase after a woman who left me? Why should I revere her portrait or her memory?" He guessed he was intoxicated, suspected he would regret this intrusion in the morning. "What you forget is that Miriam made a choice, and she didn't choose me." His fingers tightened around the glass. "You've placed Miriam on some kind of pedestal, and you think I should, too. Why is that, Lily? Why should I honor the memory of a woman who didn't honor me?"

"You're drunk."

"A little."

She sat up straighter, pulling the coverlet to her throat. "I have to know this. Did you love her?"

He hadn't expected that question and tried to consider it honestly. "I don't know," he said finally. "I cared for her. I care for her now. You said I was probably a poor husband, and you're right. Whatever I felt for Miriam, it wasn't enough." He rubbed his forehead, telling himself to shut up, return to his room and end this. Instead he leaned against the doorjamb and swallowed the last drops of whiskey. "Her father was a politician, he'd been a lawyer. I thought she understood the demands of those professions, how much time they required. I didn't intentionally set out to neglect or ignore her. It never occurred to me that she might be vulnerable or lonely. Looking back, she probably was."

She listened intently, her lavender eyes wide. And good God, she was lovely. He stared at her and imagined himself opening that gleaming braid and filling his hands with spun gold, spreading a halo over her pillow. Imagined her thick-lashed eyes going violet and dazed with desire. He needed to leave her before he did something profoundly foolish and ungentlemanly.

"It irritates me that you think I'm some kind of unfeeling brute," he murmured, wondering if he imagined the tremble along her lower lip. He didn't imagine the dampness on his palms or the tension in his loins. "There's no reason why I should care what you think, but I do."

Her breast rose on a sudden intake of breath, and his stomach twisted in knots. The powerful female scents of lotions and creams reached him, dizzying in the images they evoked. But it was Lily that ignited a fever in his blood, watching him with wide eyes and parted lips.

"By now it should be obvious that Miriam and I were mismatched. I can't think of a single damned thing we enjoyed in common. I wanted her to be something she wasn't, she wanted me to be something I wasn't. When the end came, we were living separate lives, strangers inhabiting the same house."

"Even after Susan's birth?"

"Especially after Susan's birth."

What in the hell was he doing? Kicking open doors that he and Paul had decided must remain locked. He truly did not know why her opinion mattered, or why it stung that she saw him as a different man than he wanted to believe he was.

"Go to bed, Quinn," she said after a long minute. "We'll talk again in the morning."

He doubted it. This kind of conversation required darkness and quantities of whiskey. "There's another thing," he said, leaning against the jamb to steady himself. "I've lied to you. You're correct about that. And I may need to lie to you in the future. But I'm trying like hell to keep the lies to a minimum. You have to understand there are things you can't know, don't need to know."

"Are you suggesting that I should be grateful that you only lie to me when you feel it's necessary? And how often is that?" she asked softly. Her voice seemed huskier than usual, curling from the long arch of her throat like an invitation. "I need to trust you, Quinn. I need to trust that you won't send me back to prison on a whim. That you'll keep your promises when this is over." Her fingers twitched on the coverlet. "How can I trust you when you admit you've lied?"

Because he had no convincing answer, he sidestepped the question. "You've never lied?"

Color rose in her throat and cheeks, and he experienced a glimpse of how she would look in the throes of passion. Crimson staining her pale skin, her face gleaming, her lashes lowered, and her lips slightly parted. Silently he cursed the sudden powerful stirring between his legs. Lathered in lotion, her hair braided and her hands in damp gloves, she wasn't attempting to be seductive, but God in heaven he wanted her.

"I've lied," she said evenly. "But not to you." A faint smile hovered at the corners of her lips. "Well, maybe a little. But not about anything important."

They were absolutely alone in the house, a circumstance that would not happen again. She was a woman for whom rules held no meaning, a woman who would not let convention stand in the way of what she wanted. A vibrant, desirable woman. And he was a man aching with loneliness. Neither of them had experienced lovemaking in a very long time. Would it be so wrong to seek comfort in each other's arms?

He took a step toward her, but her voice stopped him.

"Is it me, Quinn?" she asked in that husky voice that swirled in his mind like smoke. "Or are you seeing Miriam now?"

He almost laughed. Miriam had never looked at him like that, her eyes challenging and unafraid, the heat of desire warming lavender depths. Miriam had never scalded his mind with feverish desire or made his hands tremble to look at her. He had never visualized Miriam bathed in salty sweat, arching her naked body to meet him.

But her words poured over him like a shower of ice water. Standing straight, trying to remember how much he'd had to drink tonight, he pulled his shoulders back and released a low breath.

"It's late," he said hoarsely. "Good night."

It wasn't until he was lying in his own bed, hands folded

behind his head, staring up at the ceiling, that he realized how close he had come to placing an appalling complication on their situation. Worse, she had tracked his thoughts perfectly. She had known he wanted her and what he was thinking when he took that step toward her bed.

But she had not objected or ordered him out of her room. Her only question was if it was Miriam he saw or her. If he let himself dwell on the implications, he would go crazy, he thought, lowering his eyes to her door.

He burned for her.

In the morning Lily met her new ladies' maid, Elizabeth, who opened the draperies, laid a wrapper across the end of the bed, and inquired which dress she wished to wear this morning. Sitting up in bed, Lily removed the lotion-filled gloves and discreetly inspected Elizabeth's small neat figure clad in a black dress and white cap and apron.

She drew on Miriam's wrapper, inhaling the scent of forget-me-nots before Cranston appeared, bringing a tray with her morning chocolate and two cranberry muffins. Quinn stepped through the connecting door in time to answer Cranston's knock. He wore a green dressing gown, and his dark hair was charmingly tousled. Although Lily suspected he suffered from a morning-after headache, he made an heroic effort to show no indication of discomfort. Last night's visit might never have happened.

"This is Cranston, our new butler," Quinn said pleasantly, taking the tray. He placed the tray across Lily's lap, looked into her eyes, then leaned to lightly kiss her forehead, his lips warm and dry.

The deception now began in earnest.

"Welcome home, madam. It's a pleasure to meet you."

She certainly was not at her best, hardly awake and rattled by Quinn's kiss. Hoping to hide the color on her cheeks, she lifted a hand to pat her hair and discover if her braid had unraveled during the night. That Cranston would meet her while she was still in bed revealed his importance to the household and his intimacy with master and mistress.

Cranston was about fifty she guessed, white-haired and puffed with dignity, wearing crisp white linen with dark grey trousers and a black waistcoat.

"With your permission, madam, I'd like to suggest that we bring the staff to your office after breakfast. The presentations won't take long." Keen dark eyes examined her, and Lily supposed he was looking for lingering signs of illness in her face. "Afterward, if I might have an hour of your time, we'll review the household routine and make any necessary adjustments to suit your preference."

Lily flicked an uncertain glance toward Quinn, who stood gazing out her window, then she licked her lips and nodded. "Shall we say ten o'clock?"

"As you wish, madam."

After Cranston withdrew, she took a sip of the chocolate, lifting the cup with both hands lest nervousness cause a spill.

"Remember," Quinn said in a low voice. "Of all the people you will meet today, only the Blalocks have met—you—before."

Idly she touched her forehead, half-expecting to find an impression of his kiss branded on her skin. She wanted to talk about last night, wanted to ask a dozen questions, but she ground her teeth together and swore she wouldn't mention the incident unless he did.

"Are you feeling well this morning?" he asked politely, looking out the window, his hands deep in the pockets of his dressing gown.

"Yes, thank you." The intimacy of the moment, her in bed and neither of them dressed, made them awkward with each other. Lily's throat closed, and she put down the muffin, knowing she couldn't swallow. "Will this be our morning routine?"

"Occasionally."

At once she understood. His presence in her room when Cranston arrived was intended to impart an impression of normalcy between man and wife, meant to suggest they were comfortable seeing each other in a state of undress. Undoubtedly there would be mornings when he entered her room before Elizabeth appeared, creating an assumption that they had slept in the same bed. Heat flooded Lily's cheeks and stomach, and she closed her eyes, thrusting shaking hands beneath the coverlet.

"Will you be with me when I meet the rest of the staff?" she asked, frantically needing to turn her thoughts away from the crisp dark hair at the collar of his gown, away from the hands he used so expressively, away from grey eyes that smoldered as if a fire burned behind them.

"If you like," he said, fixing his gaze on something outside the windows. "But my presence would be unusual. You've dealt with staff people all of your life." He paused and his jaw clenched. "This situation is different for you only in that all the servants are new."

Did he suppose that someone listened at the door? Perhaps someone did; she didn't know the habits of servants. But they were into the game now, and would play at deceit even in private. Setting aside the tray, her appetite gone,

Lily nodded slowly. "I'll manage." What did one say to a pretend husband? "What will you do today?"

"I'll be at the firm."

"Oh." He continually surprised her. "I thought you no longer practiced law." A hand flew to her lips, and her eyes widened. Silently she cursed herself. If anyone was listening, she'd just revealed that she didn't know diddle about her husband's daily life.

"You mean litigation, of course, and I no longer argue in court. I'm doing corporate work, and I'm involved in the legalities of establishing a new state." Turning from the window, he glanced at the collar of her wrapper, then at her face. "As we've discussed, after I win the election I'll close the firm."

"I'm sorry." She mouthed the words silently and rolled her eyes, irritated with herself. Aloud, she added, "I believe I'll spend most of the day resting in my room." Familiarizing herself with the clothing in the closet and in the drawers. "I haven't recovered my strength yet."

Quinn moved around the bed toward the door to his room. "Today's edition of the *News* will carry an announcement of your return from Santa Fe. Are you well enough to receive this week?"

"I'll resume my usual Friday at-homes," she said. As they had discussed. "I hope you'll honor the ladies with your presence this week."

"It would be my pleasure."

At the door, he paused to look back, and she was conscious of her sleep-raveled braid and lotion-shiny face. The hard speculative look in his eyes also made her aware that they could remove wrapper and dressing gown and be naked in less than two minutes. Scarlet scalded her throat, and she lowered her face, plucking at the stripes on the coverlet.

Lily hated herself for thinking such things, didn't want to hear the blood drumming in her ears when he came near her. It was as if her body had awakened from a long slumber and yearned toward the man who had awakened her. No matter that she didn't entirely trust him, that sometimes she disliked him. He looked at her with those smoky eyes, and a volcano erupted in her stomach, spilling molten lava down the inside of her thighs.

When the door closed behind him, she fell backward on the bed and threw an arm over her eyes, moaning softly, waiting for the tingle to subside from her lower abdomen.

Meeting the household staff went more smoothly than she had imagined. James and Mary Blalock appeared near the end of the presentations, and even that meeting went well, Lily thought.

Mary had stared at her, then gripped her husband's arm as if she might faint. For one awful moment Lily had been certain that Mary would denounce her, then Mary had collected herself and stammered, "You're so thin! And your voice . . . you're catching a cold."

Lily had pulled up what she recalled from Paul's cards. "Perhaps you could send down some of your wonderful chicken soup to help me recover."

The reminder of days gone by had brought tears to Mary Blalock's eyes, and her husband led her away soon after. The moment the door closed behind them, Lily sagged against her chair in relief, only now letting herself admit how much she had dreaded meeting someone who had known Miriam well. She felt as if she had passed the first crucial test.

The morning's second test came when Cranston arrived to review the household routine. Paul would have been proud of her slipping and sliding. When Cranston assumed that she would set the menus each day, she managed to convey the deep weariness of someone recovering from a serious illness, and she'd maneuvered Cranston into suggesting that she approve the cook's menus rather than compose them herself. When he inquired what she wanted served at her first Friday at-home, she asked that the cook submit two tea menus and she would choose which she preferred.

There was a bit of the martinet in Cranston, and Lily used his desire to control "his" household to disguise her ignorance. At the finish of their interview they beamed at each other, well pleased to discover they were of one accord. Cranston wished to manage every small detail of his household, and Lily wished to let him.

After Cranston departed, she opened every drawer of Miriam's desk, again feeling like a trespasser, though there was nothing interesting to discover. She found a crystal inkwell and malachite pen, engraved stationery, a box of calling cards. Any personal items such as letters or notes or the diary Lily had hoped to find had been removed or lost in the fire. The only trace of Miriam in her little office was the dainty wallpaper and furnishings.

Feeling an odd mixture of triumph over her dealings with the servants and disappointment that Miriam remained elusive, Lily curled into a corner of an upholstered window seat and gazed through bare tree branches at the distant mountains. Clouds as grey as Quinn's eyes slowly blotted the white-capped peaks, and Lily guessed there would be snow by late afternoon.

Drawing her legs up under her skirts, she clasped her arms around her upraised knees and watched the clouds.

There were so many questions, and so few real answers.

She didn't think she had placed Miriam on a pedestal as Quinn had suggested, but it was true that the more she learned about Miriam, the more she identified with her. There were curious parallels in their lives.

They each had lost a sister they adored. Both had buried their parents. They had each yearned for a child, had each borne a daughter, then lost her and blamed themselves. And there was Quinn. Had they both loved the same man?

Lily shook her head and sat up straight. What sort of nonsense was she thinking? She could understand wanting Quinn, and heaven knew she did, oh she did, but she must never allow her fascination to turn to love. That would only lead to pain when she had to leave.

That thought circled her back to Miriam, and Quinn's comments last night. On reflection, Quinn was correct. Unless this was one of the incidents where he was lying to her.

Lily had assumed early on that a beloved wife had disappeared, and she hadn't understood Quinn's seeming indifference. But if the marriage had been troubled, and Miriam had chosen to leave Quinn, several small mysteries were explained.

Wounded pride would answer why he wasn't searching for Miriam. It made sense that he wouldn't want a woman who didn't want him. If it hadn't been for the upcoming election, he might have thought good riddance.

But now Lily had a glimpse of the reasons behind his anger. Miriam had chosen a disastrous time to leave her husband. She must have known that her presence and the appearance of a stable marriage were important to Quinn's campaign. She had timed her disappearance to hit back at him.

But for what reason? Lily frowned, watching the clouds gather above the mountains. In her world, a neglectful husband was not reason to run away. In prison she had met women whose husbands had beaten them, almost killed them, but running away had not entered their minds. She doubted society women were all that different. Besides, she had already recognized that men and women lived in different spheres in Quinn's world. Men attended to business while women structured their lives around home, fashion, and social events. It could be argued that neglect was built into genteel marriages on both sides, with each partner busily pursuing solitary goals and pleasures.

Therefore, could there be a deeper, darker reason that had driven Miriam away? One thing was certain. Lily would never learn that reason from Quinn or Paul.

Resting her chin on top of her raised knees, moodily watching the billowing storm clouds approach, she decided the only way to answer the questions was to find Miriam.

The problem was where to begin.

Chapter 10

Quinn's day was crowded with appointments, meetings, messengers coming and going, and continual interruptions that he welcomed as he found it difficult to concentrate. His thoughts strayed from conversations and paperwork and winged toward the mansion on Fourteenth Street. Was Lily managing the meetings with the servants? Handling Cranston? While Quinn rushed across town to a strategy meeting at party headquarters, had Lily been boarding a stage bound for Missouri?

Resting his elbows on his desk top, he dropped his head and massaged the bridge of his nose, ignoring the lingering headache from last night's whiskey.

He had to trust that Lily would keep her word and go the distance. Had to trust that Paul was correct when he said she was ready and capable of deceiving those whom she must.

Trusting her was not a comfortable situation, and he'd never before been in a position where he had to rely so heavily on an unknown factor. Wealth bought independence and the freedom of self-reliance; he wasn't accustomed to needing someone this completely or feeling a loss of control. He chafed under the necessity of staking his future on a woman as ethereal as a ghost.

"Mr. Westin? Here are the reports you requested."

He glanced up as Walter Robin, his secretary, entered his private office. Reed-thin and meticulously turned out, Walter was grimly efficient, hard-edged with ambition. After Quinn won the election, Walter would become a force to reckon with. Walter would decide who had access to the new governor and who did not. He didn't know it, but his future also depended on Lily's success at deceit.

If Lily ran off, if the impersonation failed, or if Miriam was discovered, a great many people would be adversely affected. The scandal would reverberate against party leaders who knew nothing of Quinn's situation and hadn't had a voice in deciding the solution. Paul's career would tumble backward. Walter and others like him would see hopes and plans disintegrate. The men Quinn had privately solicited for posts in his government would regret aligning themselves with his cause.

And what would he do if his dream vanished in scandal?

He hadn't let himself consider losing the election or ending in a salacious scandal. He didn't want to think about it now.

Looking up, he frowned as a snowflake tumbled past his view of the courthouse.

No, he would not give in and go home to see if Lily was still there. He had to trust her, that was essential.

Trusting her was difficult but far easier than dealing with his obsession for her. She burned like a fever in his mind, a flaming Lorelei beckoning him to ruin.

Lily had not enjoyed much leisure in her life, and felt as if she ought to be doing something productive instead of spending the afternoon trying on clothing.

Brightly colored ensembles were hung at the back of

the closet, covered with protective cloth sacks. Deep-mourning outfits had been neatly separated from lighter-colored, second-stage mourning.

Lily tried on two of the second-stage mourning suits and discovered they had been altered to fit her perfectly. It was boredom that prompted her to try on one of the light blue ensembles at the back of the closet. That and curiosity to know if she and Miriam shared the same figure dimensions.

At the end of thirty minutes she had discovered that her bosom was larger than Miriam's and her waist a shade smaller. The hemline informed her that Miriam had been about an inch taller.

It wasn't until she was removing the blue walking suit that she noticed a pocket and absently checked it. Inside she found a monogrammed handkerchief and a wadded slip of paper. She read the message on the paper, frowned, then tucked the slip of paper in the pocket of her wrapper to consider later. At the moment she was cold.

She was perfectly capable of laying a fire and would have preferred to do so rather than deal with servants. But that wasn't how things were done in Miriam's world. Pressing her lips together, Lily rang for the housemaid, then glanced at the snow beginning to collect on the windowsill before she sat in a chair near the bed and picked up one of the books that Paul had recommended.

The housemaid's name was Daisy, and she curtsied when she entered the room, apologizing for the dusty smudges on her apron. Lily murmured a polite response. Pretending to be absorbed in her book, she sneaked peeks at Daisy over the edge of the pages, wondering if Daisy resented doing a chore the lady of the house could have performed herself.

When she had a cheerful fire crackling in the grate,

Daisy bobbed another curtsy and bustled away. Alone again, Lily tossed aside her book and studied the door separating her room from Quinn's. Curiosity blotted all sensible thoughts of restraint. She shouldn't. But she would.

But before she tiptoed to the door, she made an effort to stop herself. A bedroom was a private domain. If she stepped inside there would be no question but that she was trespassing.

She couldn't help herself. Heart beating against her ribs, she opened the door, telling herself that she wouldn't go inside, knowing that she would.

For some reason she had expected Quinn's room would be as spare and plain as the ranch, but it wasn't. His bedroom was heavily masculine, but beautifully appointed. Wallpaper, draperies, and bedspread were done in various combinations of brown, navy, and cream. The desk, scattered tables, bed, and bureau looked to Lily like more European antiques.

For a long moment she stood in the center of the room, listening to her heart pound, and inhaling his scent. Bay rum, shaving soap, a faint trace of smoke, and something else she couldn't describe except to say that it was him. An undertone of something powerfully male and slightly earthy.

After glancing toward the corridor door, afraid someone would enter unexpectedly and catch her, but unable to leave, she tiptoed around his room, running her fingers lingeringly over the razor and brush near his shaving basin and pitcher. Clutching the collar of her wrapper close to her throat, she gazed into the mirror he gazed into. Stroked the towel he used to dry his face. Touching his things sent a tiny thrill down her spine.

Moving slowly, she examined the pictures on the walls,

sun-drenched villas perched on sea cliffs, village scenes that again looked European to Lily. As she had expected pictures of horses or ranch scenes, his choices surprised her. She was seeing yet another face of a complex man.

Next she examined his desk, the only untidy item in the room. Books, files, stationery were jumbled across the surface. Leaning and twisting her neck, she read enough on a scribbled page to guess he was working on a draft of another speech. After studying his bold slashing handwriting, she skimmed a finger along his pen, touched his crystal inkwell.

Knowing she shouldn't do it, yet unable to resist, she hesitated, then slid open one of the desk drawers and stared down at a pistol. Most men owned guns, and it didn't surprise her to discover that Quinn owned one, probably several, but it surprised her to learn that he kept a gun in his bedroom.

Continuing her inspection, she peeked into his closet, noting formal dress separated from business attire, only a few items reminiscent of the ranch. Rows of top hats and homburgs, boxes of socks and gloves.

Finally she moved to stand beside his bed and felt her palms grow damp. Stretching out trembling fingers, she lightly stroked the spread covering his pillow. Her heart felt as if it would fly out of her chest, and she spun and fled back to her own room, closing the door firmly behind her and leaning against it as if to hold it shut.

When her breathing returned to normal, she opened her window and rubbed some of the snow from the windowsill beneath her nose, hoping to chase away Quinn's scent, but she imagined she could smell him on her fingertips. Dropping her head, she covered her face in her hands.

What was happening to her?

When she could think again, she gave her head a violent

shake, thrust her hands into the pockets of the wrapper, and
stared out at the falling snow. It was a relief to find the tiny
slip of wadded paper, to have something to think about instead of Quinn.

Returning to the chair beside her bed, she smoothed the
small wadded slip open on top of the book she'd been
reading.

Same time. Same place. M.

Here was Miriam, real and tangible. Tilting the slip to
the light, she studied Miriam's handwriting. The pen
strokes were plain, without flourish, impressing her as almost masculine. Considering Miriam's preference for ruffles, fringes, and frippery, Lily would have expected
curlicues and embellishments.

Same time. Same place. Leaning her head against the
top of the chair, she tried to decipher the meaning of the
message. A reminder not to forget an appointment? But
surely Miriam wouldn't sign a reminder to herself. And
why would a person remind herself of an appointment if
the time and place were the same as always? If Lily had
written herself a reminder of an established appointment,
she would have jotted something like: Quinn. Tuesday.

Most likely the note was not a reminder. Then what was it?
Frowning, she ran her fingertip over the wrinkled creases. A
note Miriam had intended for someone else? Who?

She wouldn't have needed to give Quinn a note, since
she saw him several times a day. And the message didn't
appear to apply to a servant. It was not written on a full
page of stationery, so Miriam had not intended to mail it.
If she had planned to hand the note to someone, why not
deliver the message verbally?

The puzzle intrigued her.

Watching snow melting down the windowpanes, she considered the message and wondered if perhaps the note could have been an instruction to the driver of Miriam's carriage, telling him when and where to find her. Same time. Same place.

But no, she realized, a message to an employee would have been signed Mrs. Westin. Sighing, she decided the note was not going to give up its secrets.

Instinct suggested the message was private. Instinct also warned her not to mention the note to Quinn or Paul until she figured out the meaning. Which she wondered if she could do.

Although Lily was tempted to keep this tiny sample of Miriam's handwriting, she dropped the note on the fire and watched it burn before she yawned. The warmth in the room and the cozy hiss of snow against the panes made her feel drowsy.

The remainder of the afternoon opened before her with nothing to do, a luxury she had dreamed of when she was in prison. Wishing her friends could see her now, she decided to take a nap, an almost sinful indulgence she hadn't enjoyed since childhood.

Before she drifted into a doze, a half smile played around her lips. There were restrictions attached to being a lady, and she doubted she would ever achieve true refinement, but she loved this life. Wanted it for herself and Rose.

In her dream Quinn came to her. This time he didn't stop but took the next step and the next. He loomed over her, tall, hard, and rampantly naked, his grey eyes burning in the darkness before he threw back the coverlet and slid into bed beside her. His skin was hot and his hands wild on her writhing body.

When Lily awoke, she was damp with perspiration and breathing hard.

Paul dined with them in the formal dining room, watching Lily from the corners of his eyes as Cranston glided around the table serving and removing dishes.

"Did you enjoy your first day at home?" he asked politely.

"Very much," she answered from her seat at the foot of the long table. From now on, conversations would be layered with tiers of meaning. She understood that Paul was inquiring about her meeting with the servants. Smiling, she signaled Cranston to remove the entree. "I spent most of the day resting." By omitting any reference to the servants, she informed both men that the meetings had gone well.

Quinn blotted his lips and looked down the table, his gaze lingering on the dark lace bodice of her dinner gown. "The doctors said you would gradually regain your strength. You mustn't overdo." Briefly his glance flicked to Cranston, then he added, "darling."

"The announcement of your return mentioned that you intend to resume your at-homes on Friday," Paul commented as if he'd had nothing to do with placing the release. "Are you certain your health is up to entertaining?" His dark eyes told her that he was asking if she was prepared.

"I've missed my friends," she murmured, informing him that she was as ready as she would ever be.

Quinn leaned back in his chair as Cranston removed his plate. "It was good to come home and find you here." He was relieved to discover she hadn't bolted.

"I'm finished with long journeys for now," Lily said, lifting her chin. How many times must she assure him that she wouldn't run home to Missouri? When, if ever, would he trust that she intended to wrest every drop of knowledge out of this experience? Maybe when she began to trust him, which she doubted would ever happen. There were too many secrets. After a small hesitation, she, too, added the word darling and curved her lips into a smile for Cranston's benefit. Quinn raised one dark eyebrow and held her gaze until she felt the heat rise in her throat and looked away, wondering guiltily if he knew that she'd been in his bedroom.

An awkward silence descended. And why shouldn't it, Lily thought wildly. What did they have to say to one another, three people pretending to be something they were not? Suddenly, she felt a crazy urge to announce to Cranston that she was not Miriam Westin and Quinn was not her devoted husband and Paul was not a concerned friend but her creator. They were playing a high-stakes game, and Cranston was part of an audience that would grow as the days and weeks passed.

Inhaling deeply, she fought to collect herself. There was nothing intimidating about the long table or the candles and flowers and silver serving lids. Trying to think like Miriam, she reminded herself that she had grown up with heavy silver and gold-rimmed china. She had dined in rooms as opulent as this during her grand tour of Europe. She had hosted hundreds of dinner parties, and she was prepared for this small one.

Concentrating, she recalled a topic from a list she had compiled earlier. "I read that President Grant vetoed a bill that would have protected the buffalo from extinction. Do you gentlemen have an opinion about buffalo?"

Paul gazed at her. "Why, Miriam, I don't believe I've ever heard you express interest in a political issue."

It was a mild reprimand and a reminder that Miriam vehemently disliked anything political.

"Oh my," Lily said, blinking innocently and raising a hand to the lace at her throat. "Was that a political question? I was only thinking of the poor buffalo, that's all."

A gleam of approval shone in Paul's dark eyes. She'd made a successful recovery. "I agree with the president's decision. There's no quicker or surer way to solve the Indian problem than by destroying their food supply."

Lily arched an incredulous eyebrow. "Is that your solution to the Indian problem as you put it? Starve them all to death?" A tiny cold knot formed inside her chest. Tonight Paul looked relaxed and benign. It was easy to forget that the Kingmaker's job was to solve problems quickly, absolutely, and ruthlessly if necessary.

Candlelight flashed along the blade of his knife when he spread his hands in a shrug. "A dead Indian is a problem solved."

Quinn stared. "Killing doesn't always solve a problem," he said quietly. "Sometimes death is merely the beginning of an entirely new set of problems."

"A new set of problems," Paul agreed pleasantly. "But the old problem is solved, isn't it?"

Another short silence opened, then Quinn said, "Exterminating the buffalo is a short-term solution with far-ranging consequences for the Indians and the buffalo."

Lily's thoughts drifted as they argued national policy through the pie and cheese. She didn't actively detest politics as Miriam apparently had, but neither did she find the discussion particularly interesting.

She was free to gaze down the table and realize that Quinn was slowly overtaking her every thought, waking and sleeping. When she remembered this afternoon's passionate dream, her fingers trembled, and she licked her lips, blinking hard. In her dream, he had been as intense as he was now, but focused on her. She told herself to look away from him, but she couldn't.

Helplessly, she watched him punctuate his statements with emphatic gestures and liquid expressions, his face mobile in the candlelight. Early in their relationship she had thought Quinn closed and difficult to read, and certainly he could be. But when he forgot himself in conversation or deep thought, his expressions were as eloquent as his words.

Irritation and anger deepened the craggy lines mapping his forehead and fanning from the corner of his eyes. His lips widened when he smiled or made a point. Knots forming along his jaw signaled impatience or frustration. His eyes narrowed and turned a charcoal color when strong emotion accompanied his words. His hands, slender, strong, and confident, moved aggressively, pointing, gesturing, raking through his dark hair.

She was beginning to know this man who had crawled inside her mind.

"I'm sorry, did you . . . ?" Rousing herself, she realized that Quinn and Paul were looking at her expectantly.

Cranston had cleared the table. At this point it had been Miriam's habit to withdraw to the family parlor and wait for the gentlemen to finish their cigars and join her for coffee. But Cranston did not know Miriam's habits.

Impulsively, Lily decided to create a habit of her own by remaining with the men. Lifting her chin and daring them to object, she smiled, aware that Cranston hovered nearby in the butler's pantry.

"By all means enjoy your cigars, gentlemen. As you know—darling—I don't object to the scent of smoke." In fact, she hoped they would blow a little smoke in her direction. She touched the small silver bell in front of her. "Cranston, please serve the gentlemen's brandy, and I'll have a tiny taste myself. You may serve coffee in the parlor in twenty minutes."

Even to her own ears, she sounded firmly confident. The day had indeed been successful. She couldn't resist grinning at Paul's scowl and feeling pleased when Quinn laughed. She wished she could celebrate by joining them when they lit their cigars.

"Well," Quinn said in a lazy voice, his silvery eyes settling on her lips, "did either of us convince you one way or another regarding the buffalo?" Despite his attention to her mouth, a challenge flickered in his gaze, as if he were asking her to choose sides between himself and Paul.

The old Lily would have used his question as a springboard to put forth her own opinions. But a lady's obligation was to support her husband. "You made some good points," she said to Paul, summoning a tact that did not come naturally. "But I believe my husband's argument was most convincing."

A rush of color stained her cheeks when she said "my husband." But her tongue didn't stumble.

She glanced at Quinn, and their eyes locked and held. And she felt as if she were drowning in a swirling grey pool. Holding her gaze, his speculative eyes narrowed on her face, he tilted his head back and exhaled toward the ceiling. Heat flamed through Lily's body, and she was aware of her pulse beating hard at the hollow of her throat.

Why was it that one man could look at a woman and it was just a look, nothing more, whereas another man could narrow his concentration to a woman's mouth and the hard hot flame in his eyes unleashed an earthquake deep inside her?

Wetting her lips, aware that her nerves raced along the surface of her skin, Lily placed her napkin on the table. "I've changed my mind. I believe I'll wait in the parlor."

Paul rose to assist her, and she thanked him, her eyes on Quinn. He rocked back in his chair, studying her with a slow gaze that traveled from the mass of blond curls Elizabeth had dressed high on her crown to the pulse between her collarbones to her breast and then to her waist. "We'll join you shortly," he said in a thick voice that flowed through her mind like dark honey.

Crushing his cigar between his fingers, Quinn watched the provocative sway of her bustle as she exited the dining room. Before she glided out of sight, she glanced over her shoulder and met his eyes for the span of a heartbeat.

"Christ," Paul muttered as he strode toward the butler's pantry. After firmly closing the heavy door against eavesdroppers, he returned to the table, inhaled deeply, then blew out a stream of cigar smoke in a short angry burst. "You're playing a dangerous game," he snapped. "I swear, if you don't find a mistress soon, I'll find one for you."

"You're in charge of the campaign, not my personal life." Leaning forward, Quinn tipped the ash off his cigar.

"Everything in Lily's background tells you that she's an opportunist," Paul said, his voice low and sharp. "She's seen the ranch, she's taken a good look at this house, and she sees money and a life she wants." His eyes hardened to brown stones. "Right now she's thinking this arrangement doesn't have to end at the inauguration. She's thinking she can continue playing Miriam indefinitely. And the road to that goal leads to your bed. Seducing you is how she hopes to get what she wants."

"Lily's thoughts are as impossible to guess as Miriam's were. Neither of us knows what she's thinking." He took offense at Paul's implication that Lily was attempting to seduce him. The sexual tension between them had ignited long before Lily had seen evidence of his wealth, and before she knew what kind of life Miriam had led.

"Getting defensive doesn't alter the fact that you'll create an enormous problem if you take Lily as a mistress rather than choosing a more suitable woman." Tilting back in his chair, Paul stared at the ceiling for a long moment before he looked at Quinn. "The lines are already blurred, don't make it worse. Pull back. She's not what you think she is, Quinn. She's not Miriam as you wish Miriam had been."

Anger flashed in his eyes. "Don't presume to tell me what I think."

"We've been friends for fifteen years. If I don't know what you're thinking, no one does."

"What I'm thinking is this conversation has gone too far," he said coldly, stubbing out his cigar. Standing, he shot his cuffs and touched the studs running down his shirtfront. "Shall we join my wife? We've kept the lady waiting long enough."

Paul stared at him. "She's not your wife, Quinn."

"It was you who insisted we play the game in private as well as publicly." Quinn let his gaze go flat. "Don't overstep, Paul. You manage the campaign, and I'll manage my wife."

*   *   *

After Paul said his good-byes, Lily set down her coffee cup and watched Quinn pace before the parlor fireplace. Something had changed between the time she left the dining room and the men's arrival for coffee. They'd both been angry, but too aware of the people in the house to discuss their differences and carry their disagreement to a resolution.

"Quinn?" He glanced at her, then turned to lean against the mantel, glaring into the fireplace. "I'd like to go for a walk. Would you accompany me?"

"Now?" Frowning, he withdrew his pocket watch and flipped open the gold lid. "It's late."

"All the time I was in the desert, I dreamed of snow."

"Shall I fetch madam's cloak and muff?" Cranston inquired, gliding past her to collect the silver coffee service.

Lily jumped. She hadn't heard him enter the parlor, hadn't guessed he was nearby. Paul was correct. It was crucial to maintain the deception even when she believed she and Quinn were alone and having a private conversation.

"Please do," she said, looking at Quinn but speaking to Cranston. No gentleman would permit his wife to walk alone at this time of night. She knew she pressed the issue and was forcing him to agree.

"Bring my jacket, hat, and walking stick," he said to Cranston.

On the porch, Lily raised the hood of her cloak to cover her hair and inhaled deeply. The snow had stopped, leaving the air moist and sharply cold. It was the kind of white night she had dreamed of when she lay on her thin cot longing for home.

Quinn helped her down the steps, holding her arm close to his body, and she felt the contrast between his warmth and the cold air on her cheeks, was aware of his long legs brushing her cloak and skirts. "Can you tell me what you and Paul are arguing about? Is it politics?" Or did their disagreement have something to do with her?

"Paul believes I should take a mistress."

She gasped softly and stumbled over her hem. Jealousy, sudden and acid, surged into her throat. She couldn't bear to think of him making love to another woman. "Will you take his advice?" she asked finally, ducking her head.

"I'm considering it." His arm tensed beneath her gloved fingertips.

A wave of dizziness blurred the walkway. She imagined him bending a shadowy woman into a kiss, saw his hands hot on the woman's body, his mouth on her breasts. She couldn't bear it.

Worse, if he was considering a mistress, then he was rejecting her. Keeping her head down, she tugged the edges of the hood forward to hide her flaming face.

Halting beneath the snow-laden branches of a young elm, Quinn turned her to face him and raised her chin, forcing her to look at him. His hand burned like a brand on her skin.

"I think about you all the time," he said in a low, hoarse voice. "It's like you've possessed me." They stood close enough that the vapor from their lips mingled, and she could see his eyes were so dark they looked almost black in the snowy light. "If something doesn't change, you know where this will end, Lily. I won't be able to help myself."

They stared at each other. "Would that be so terrible?" she whispered, hungering for him, aching for him.

His fingers tightened painfully on her arms. "Our time together will be short. I don't want this to end with you feeling more used than you already do. I don't want that on my conscience, too."

Would she feel that she had been used and then discarded? She had found a way to view the impersonation where she no longer felt forced, but saw her circumstance as an opportunity for herself and Rose. If she and Quinn surrendered to the magnetic tides pulling at them, would she feel that he had callously used her to satisfy a selfish hunger? Or would she remember that she had wanted him so intensely that her blood bubbled when he touched her? That he looked at her, and her knees crumpled? Would she remember a snowy night when she had trembled on the brink of offering herself to him?

"Is that the only reason?" she asked in a low, husky voice, searching his eyes. "You fear that I'll feel used?"

When he didn't answer immediately, her heart sank, and she understood he was waging a familiar interior war. To lie or tell her the truth.

"Paul believes you're an opportunist looking for a way to extend your term of employment indefinitely."

"He thinks I'm trying to use you?" Lily asked incredulously. Stung, she sucked in a breath and her chin lifted. "Is that what you believe?"

"I don't know," he said slowly, his eyes locked to hers. "I do know that taking you to bed could create enormous problems and complications."

"So you'd rather take a mistress," she said jerking away from him. "Fine, you do that." Walking quickly she moved away from him, kicking at the snow. "Let's talk about Miriam," she said abruptly, flinging the words over her shoulder.

Thinking about Miriam grounded her, reminded her that Quinn saw his wife when he looked at her with those smoldering eyes. It was Miriam he saw in Miriam's room, in

Miriam's bed. Miriam he saw at the end of the table, wearing Miriam's clothes and Miriam's earrings and perfume.

But it was Lily whom he rejected as causing too many problems and complications.

"Miriam," he repeated in an expressionless tone.

Furious that they thought she was an adventuress, she raised her hem and strode along the row of elm trees. How dare they? She hadn't come to them; they had forced her into this situation. She struck back at him the only way she knew how, by throwing Miriam at him.

"I know Miriam didn't support your decision to run for governor. How strong was her objection?" He pretended indifference to Miriam's disappearance, but Lily had grasped this was not true. There were painful unresolved issues between Quinn and his wife. He didn't like to think about Miriam, would have preferred not to talk about her.

"Miriam hoped I would become a judge like her father," he said shortly, catching up to her. "Politics bored her, and she shrank from the social obligations that would be required of a governor's wife."

"Then she didn't support your candidacy." Right now she detested Miriam and would have given the earth not to look like her. "Wouldn't Miriam's lack of support make her a political liability?" She felt his gaze swing to her and his attention sharpen.

"Yes." Although the answer came reluctantly, his tone sharpened like cracking ice.

Turning in a swirl of skirts, she faced him. "Then she disappeared at a convenient time, didn't she?"

"What are you suggesting?" His angry expression hardened into a cold tight mask.

"I ain't—" She stamped her foot in frustration. "I'm not suggesting anything. I'm merely stating the obvious."

He studied her for a long, searching moment before he caught her arm and turned back toward the mansion. Stumbling along beside him, Lily tried to recall exactly what she had said that made him so coldly furious. Whatever it was, she was glad she'd said it.

"I won't see much of you during the next few days," he announced as they approached the gas lanterns flanking the porch. "I have a full week scheduled. I'll leave the house before you wake, and won't return until after you're asleep. Please inform Cranston that I'll dine at my club."

"As you wish," she snapped.

They entered the house in chilly silence. As Lily had expected, talking about Miriam had cooled them both. He didn't look at her. She no longer trembled at the nearness of him.

But nothing had really changed. They had banked the fires, not extinguished them. When he looked at her before they parted at the bottom of the stairs, she realized he knew it, too.

Chapter 11

By Friday, Lily's nerves were frazzled. She had changed her mind a dozen times about what she would wear for her first at-home before finally deciding on a dove grey velvet trimmed in black and cream. She instructed Elizabeth to dress her hair to match the style Miriam had worn in the portrait Lily would sit beneath, and she chose the same small pearl earrings that Miriam had worn in the painting.

After much anxious indecision, she finally selected a menu featuring tea cakes with fancy French names, and toast points with marmalade. Cranston seemed content with her choice, so she told herself that she was, too. But he'd thrown her off-balance when he inquired which china she wished to use. Stumbling over her tongue, she had suggested the flowered set. Considering that the rooms where Miriam had spent her time were papered and carpeted with flowers, Lily assumed she must have purchased at least one set of flower-patterned china as well. When Cranston nodded, she knew she had guessed correctly, and her shoulders sagged in relief.

Every afternoon and evening she settled into her small household office and reviewed Paul's cards until they were crumpled and ragged and her mind reeled with names and details. It was Mrs. Brown whose daughter had recently married a Spanish count, not Mrs. Black's daughter. Mrs. Smith who was organizing the Christmas ball, not Mrs. Smyth.

Now the day of her at-home had arrived, and she was edgy and nervous, utterly convinced that she couldn't possibly succeed.

"Damn," she muttered, pacing across the formal parlor where she would receive her guests. She would call Helene Van Heusen by her first name along with a handful of others, but most of the callers were to be addressed by their married names. With luck, she would remember which were which. But she didn't feel lucky.

She was convinced the ladies would take one look at her and immediately suspect she was not Miriam. The moment she spoke they would know for certain.

Someone would denounce her. Newspaper headlines would proclaim the scandal. Quinn would be ruined, his candidacy in shambles. Paul would send her back to Yuma in chains.

"Stop pacing," Quinn said, entering the room. "You've done this a hundred times."

Glaring, she bit off a shout of frustration. She was almost certain to pour scalding tea on someone's hand rather than into her cup, or spill her own tea in her lap. She could imagine herself calling a dear friend of Miriam's by the wrong name, or politely asking a widow how her husband was feeling.

"I can't do this," she said, sinking into a chair. The wrong chair. Jumping to her feet, she flung herself into the chair beneath the altered portrait. "I'm not up to it. I'm rushing things. This was a mistake."

"Nonsense," Quinn said, taking a chair across from her. Amusement twinkled in his eyes. "You've always been nervous before a social event."

By now she knew Miriam's habits well enough to know that Miriam would not have paced or flung herself from chair to chair. Miriam would have borne up with sad sweetness, betraying her nervousness by quieter means than Lily. Perhaps watery eyes or a trembling lower lip.

Wringing her hands, she scowled at Quinn. "How can you be so calm?" Despite her best intentions, she was about to destroy his dreams, she just knew it.

Today the audience widened, and it would be a critical audience. Her callers would study her with all-seeing eyes, searching for lingering signs of illness and melancholy. They would notice every detail of her second-stage mourning gown and recall the fire and the death of her daughter, closely examining her behavior for signs of recovery or continuing grief.

Susan. Lord, in her nervousness she had forgotten why she was wearing mourning. In fact, as Susan hadn't been her daughter, Lily seldom thought of Susan at all. Guilt tightened her throat. Days passed when she was too occupied to think of Rose either.

"Do you ever think about Susan?" she blurted. "Miss her?"

Quinn looked down, adjusting the ruby stud in his cuff. "Not often."

His blunt honesty shocked her. "This is one of those times when I wish you'd lied," she said with a sigh. "Someone should remember poor little Susan." And poor little Rose. "She was your daughter, too."

"You look lovely," Quinn said, giving her one of those

long slow looks that made her feel crazy with wanting him. Today he wore a dark coat over a silver waistcoat and grey trousers, and he'd had his hair trimmed. The ladies would thrill to his charm and rugged good looks. As she did, she thought with another sigh.

"You're in a good mood," she commented sourly. "Apparently it's lifted your spirits to spend a week without me." She hated to admit it, but she'd missed him. Life without Quinn was pallid and uninteresting, the days long and bland. She'd actually pressed her ear to the connecting door between their bedrooms to hear him moving around, and had tried to think of excuses to rap on the door and talk to him.

"I spent a couple of days at the ranch. Getting out of the city rejuvenates me."

She had been correct. There were a few nights when he hadn't returned to the mansion. "How fortunate for you. I haven't been out of this house since I arrived except for one short walk." Which she didn't care to recall, especially not now when she needed to think like, act like, and become Miriam.

Five minutes later, at three o'clock on the dot, Cranston wheeled the tea wagon into the parlor and Lily felt her blood pressure surge. After fiddling with the items on the wagon, Cranston cocked an ear toward the front of the house. "There's the bell. I believe your guests are beginning to arrive, madam."

Lily's heart slammed against her rib cage, fluttered hard, and dived to her toes. She fanned her face wildly and prayed for the strength to stand when Cranston ushered the ladies into the parlor. "Damn, damn, damn. I can't do this. They'll know."

"Cranston will announce each guest by name," Quinn reminded her in a low voice, standing behind her chair. His fingers touched her shoulder, and she shuddered lightly as a hot tingle shot through her body. "Remember, none of your guests have any reason to suspect you're not who you pretend to be."

"But what if I make a mistake?" she whispered, her eyes fixed on the door. She couldn't have dreaded this more if she'd been expecting a lynch mob.

"If you make a mistake, my political career will be destroyed, a lesser man will become the first governor of Colorado, and the history of the western half of the United States will be irrevocably altered."

Gasping, she twisted around to look at him in horror. When she saw his smile and realized he was teasing her, Lily burst into semihysterical laughter. His gaze softened and astonishingly, he winked at her.

"Thank you," she said when she could speak. Some of the tension had fled from her shoulders and throat.

Quinn was standing behind her, his hand on her shoulder, and she was smiling up at him when Cranston announced her first two guests. When Lily realized the tableau they presented, she wondered if he'd arranged it deliberately.

It didn't matter. Feeling better, she drew a breath, stood, and pasted a smile on her lips. Frantically, she struggled to recall the information on Paul's cards, was certain it had all gone out of her head. Silently cursing a blue streak, she stepped forward and extended her hands, hoping coherent words would fall out of her mouth when she parted her lips.

"Mrs. Brown, I'm happy to see you again. I'm so sorry

to have missed Electra's wedding. I've heard the ceremony was lovely. And Augusta," she said, turning a wobbly smile on her second guest. "How stunning you look."

Glancing at the door, she noticed Quinn greeting the next arrivals, chatting and leading them toward her. Panic flared in her eyes as she hadn't heard Cranston's announcement. But Quinn smoothly referred to each of the three ladies by name and in less than a minute she had placed them.

During the next twenty minutes, Lily was too busy to fret, too occupied greeting guests and pouring tea to be drawn into any potentially disastrous conversations.

What she had failed to realize when she worried about her debut as Miriam was the number of callers prevented any but the most superficial of conversations. As she went about her duties as hostess, the ladies crowding the parlor talked among themselves. Occasionally she noticed someone looking from her to the portrait with a slightly puzzled expression, but to her relief and amazement, most of the women didn't appear to question that she was Miriam Westin.

The true test arrived when Cranston announced Helene Van Heusen. If Lily passed the inspection of Miriam's intimate friend, she might finally relax a little.

Stiffening her spine and squaring her shoulders, she swiftly reviewed everything she knew about Helene. A formidable and dominating woman. Active in social clubs. No children. Her husband was Paul's counterpart in the opposing party, a man who was grooming a candidate to run against Quinn in the upcoming election.

Lily could certainly understand why Quinn had objected to the puzzling friendship between Miriam and Helene Van

Heusen. What she didn't understand was why Miriam had defied her husband to continue an unsuitable and unwise association.

A brief silence befell the group when Helene appeared in the doorway, and the significance was not lost on Lily. Her lady callers did not care for the imperious woman who scarcely deigned to notice them.

Helene sailed across the parlor, her gloved hands outstretched. "No, no, dear, don't rise, you've been ill and you look it. You're much too thin." Cool black eyes settled on the woman seated beside Lily. "I can only stay a moment, so I'm sure you won't mind finding another chair, will you, dear? How thoughtful of you." She slid into the chair Mrs. Alderson silently vacated and peered into Lily's face. "You look lovely, but the changes are evident. And no wonder after all you've been through. It's to be expected," she said, patting Lily's hand.

"Helene, you haven't changed a bit," she said carefully.

"Your voice! What happened to your voice? You sound like a different person!"

The sudden silence in the room informed her that Helene wasn't the only person to notice and wonder. But Lily had anticipated this question and prepared a response. "It was the violent coughing," she explained softly, letting her shoulders slump. "The doctors fear I've permanently damaged my vocal cords."

Quinn had been listening and followed her lead. From his position near the fireplace, he added, "The doctors doubt Miriam will regain the same tonal consistency as before her illness. Most likely she'll always sound as husky as she does now."

Tonal consistency? The reference sounded like nonsense

to Lily, but the ladies nodded solemnly and murmured sounds of sympathy.

Mimicking Miriam's fluttery gestures, Lily raised a hand to her throat and gave her head a resigned shake, using the moment to examine Helene Van Heusen in greater detail.

Wings of white hair flowed back from Helene's powdered face, twisting into an intricate chignon that formed a base for a hat trimmed more elaborately than others in the room. Lily guessed that even in her youth Helene had not been beautiful, but she was striking. Fine black eyes dominated a strong face and determined chin, eyes that saw everything and passed instant judgment.

"I do hope your stubborn husband informed you that I did everything but threaten at gunpoint in an effort to learn the address of the sanitarium where you were staying. Mr. Westin is solely to blame for your friends being unable to write you any notes of encouragement."

"I wasn't permitted to receive mail." Lily patted her chest as if she were still ill. "I was so terribly weak, and my attention wandered. I couldn't have responded."

"The doctors prohibited any excitement or stimulation," Quinn explained, returning to stand behind her.

Lily could not see his expression, but she saw Helene's eyes go flat and harden. "I'm surprised to see you," Helene said rudely. "I'm afraid you've wasted your time. Your performance as a devoted husband is lost on us, as no one here can vote." There was no mistaking the dislike in her tone and expression. "You could have spared yourself an inconvenience and stayed at your office."

Even to Lily, Helene's bluntness was startling. She sucked in a sharp breath and heard the other women do the same. Only the rustling of skirts and the quiet clink of cups descending to saucers broke an abrupt and uncomfortable silence.

Quinn's hand dropped to Lily's shoulder. "Had I put work before my wife, I would have missed the pleasure of enjoying Denver's most charming ladies." Quinn's words lengthened into a lazy drawl, and Lily could picture him smiling at the guests.

It was then that she noticed Helene gripped her wrist as if she and Quinn engaged a subtle tug of war with Lily as the prize.

Helene's laugh was harsh. "More to the point, you hope these charming ladies will influence their husbands to vote for a man willing to give up an afternoon to support his wife on her return to society. I doubt I'm the only one to see through such a transparent ploy."

Quinn's fingers pressed hard against Lily's shoulder, betraying his anger, but his voice was light. "If our lovely guests should choose to mention what a swell fellow I am, I wouldn't be dismayed."

The ladies balancing teacups on their knees smiled or chuckled, and the moment passed. Conversation resumed, and Quinn moved away from Lily's chair, responding to Cranston's appearance in the doorway.

Speechless, Lily stared at Helene. She had no idea what to say to the woman.

"I can understand that you wouldn't wish to communicate with—" Helene waved a hand, indicating Lily's other guests—"but to deny *me* access to my dear little friend. Well! Such arrogance is not to be borne." Her eyes narrowed on Lily's dress. "Really, Miriam, you're too old-fashioned. I don't wish to be indelicate, but these days no one does a full year of mourning for a child."

Genuine shock widened Lily's eyes, and she pulled away from Helene's grip. All of her guests had skimmed a glance over her gown and she had read sympathy in their expressions, but none had alluded to Susan's death. Certainly she had not expected Miriam's intimate friend to do so.

"Now don't look so stricken," Helene said, waving an impatient hand. "You're young, you'll have other children. You must pull yourself together and get on with life. Sometimes I think you enjoy sadness and melancholy, honestly I do." She flicked her fingers at Lily's gown. "Put away those drab things, buy a wardrobe in gay colors, and enjoy the holiday season."

"Forgive me for interrupting," Quinn said coolly, appearing at her side. Leaning, he murmured in her ear. "Walter Robin is in the library with some papers that must be signed at once. I'll return in five minutes."

Lily nodded, and smiled woodenly at her other guests before Helene tugged her arm and leaned closer.

"I didn't dare risk a word with *him* in the room." Her voice dropped to a whisper. "Our mutual friend has been distraught. You simply vanished after the fire, and Quinn refused all entreaties as to your address. There was nothing I could do for either of you."

Frowning, Lily drew back. "Our mutual friend?"

"Darling, it's good to be cautious, but no one is listening. Need I mention that our friend is desperate to see you?"

Helene's whispered words and her tone of urgency were so singularly peculiar and unexpected that Lily had no idea how to respond. This was the very thing she had feared. A reference to something or someone in Miriam's life that Quinn and Paul knew nothing about.

"I'm eager to see our friend, too," she said slowly, cautiously. "But I haven't fully regained my strength . . ."

Helene's sharp eyes probed her face. "You look the picture of health, my dear. Or are you wearing rouge? Never mind, we don't have time for that. Shall I tell M that you'll see him soon?"

She went still inside, but not before a tiny gasp passed her lips. "Our friend" was a man. And suddenly the mystery of the note she had found in Miriam's pocket was solved. The message had not been written *by* Miriam, but *to* her. Lily's gaze swung to Quinn as he strode into the room and stopped at the tea wagon for toast and marmalade.

My God. Lily blinked hard. Surely she must be assigning a mistaken implication to Helene's words. What sane woman would betray Quinn? No one, she told herself firmly, certainly not shy, sweet, obedient Miriam. She was reading more into Helene's whisperings than was present. There must be an innocent explanation.

"Quick," Helene said in a low voice, her gaze following Quinn's movements. "What shall I tell our friend? He'll be in Denver next week, and of course he's hoping for a message from you."

"I . . ." She, too, watched Quinn moving about the room and chatting with the women, some of whom prepared to depart. "Helene, I have a raging headache. I simply cannot think right now."

"Then I shall help you as always. Come to me next Thursday. I'll have a message for you I'm sure. M will be disappointed not to have a note from you, but I'll tell him contact will be reestablished soon." Helene's gaze swept to the clock on the mantel and she rose, pulling Lily to her feet. "It's been lovely, dear, utterly lovely. I'm so happy to have you back with us and looking well. Do think about everything I've said," she ended, her black eyes piercing with meaning.

"You may be certain that I will."

"So nice to see . . . in a rush, you know . . . perhaps next time . . ." Helene moved through the room like a ship under sail, managing to speak to everyone and no one and pointedly ignore Quinn.

Lily sank back into her chair, staring at the door. She felt as if she had been run over by a coal wagon. If she felt this way, how must Miriam have felt after a collision with Helene? Miriam would not have stood a chance; Helene would have flattened any resistance as easily as rolling out pie dough.

"Are you tired, darling?"

Quinn's hand on her elbow sent a flood of electricity through her system and jolted her from a deep distraction. The room was empty. She'd smiled and chatted and said good-bye, all without being fully aware, her thoughts picking at the conversation with Helene. Lily darted a glance toward the mantel, surprised to discover it was already five o'clock and Cranston was stacking dishes and cups on the tea wagon.

"A little," she murmured, glancing up at Quinn. Concern had deepened the lines in his craggy face. "But I'm fine. Really."

"I thought we'd take a short drive before dinner."

"I'd like that." Did he wish to speak privately, or had he remembered her remark about not being out of the house? "Cranston?"

"I'll fetch your cloak and muff, madam. Shall I instruct Elizabeth to bring a hat and gloves?"

"The grey set, please." The room was still fragrant with the mingled scents of perfume, tea cakes, and tea. "Do you think it was a success?" she asked Quinn, twisting Miriam's rings around her finger, frowning up at the altered portrait.

Today she saw Miriam's sad eyes, not her own, and she experienced a depressing twist of guilt. It should have been Miriam entertaining her friends, not Lily. Miriam presiding over the tea service and accepting the looks of sympathy and words of welcome home.

Where are you? she thought, staring at the portrait.

"The afternoon was a rousing success," Quinn commented near her ear as he took her cloak from Cranston and draped it around her shoulders.

His warm breath against her ear made her feel dizzy, and she swayed slightly, her eyelids fluttering. Suddenly she felt drained and wished she could rest against him for a moment and let herself fully realize the ordeal was over. No one had denounced her. Disaster had not struck. And next week's at-home would be easier.

"I may even learn to enjoy entertaining," she said after Quinn handed her into the carriage and tucked a thick lap robe over her skirts.

Quinn laughed and sat beside her. "Is this the same woman who looked as though she might faint before her guests came through the door?"

She smiled. "I've never fainted in my life."

Suddenly her spirits soared. By God, she had done it. Lily Dale, ex-convict and woman of a million bad habits, had presided over a real tea service and poured before the critical eyes of real ladies, and she'd done so gracefully and flawlessly.

"I did it!" she said, her eyes sparkling with triumph. "Quinn, I did it. I'll tell you who would faint if he knew about today. That bastard Ephram Callihan." Raising her hands, she pressed her gloves to her cheeks. "I can't believe it. I did it, I did it! And no one suspected a thing."

Grinning, he patted his pockets and withdrew his silver cigar case. "May I?"

She nodded. "My days of leisure are over. According to Paul I now must pay calls on everyone who attended my at-home. I liked Mrs. Alderson very much. Do you know her? Apparently we belong to the same Ladies Aid Society. She said if I decide to come out of mourning, she'd like me to help the ladies put together holiday baskets for the poor." Euphoria loosened her tongue and she was babbling, but she wanted to talk about every detail.

"It's dark and we're alone. Would you like a cigar?"

Glancing out the carriage window, she noticed lamplighters climbing ladders propped against the streetlamps. Earlier, fresh snow had collected on the branches of young elms. "Where are we going?"

"I instructed Morely to drive past my firm and the courthouse. And there's a row of nearby shops that might interest you. It occurs to me that you haven't seen the city." He lit a cigar and handed it to her.

Lily inhaled the smoke, sighed with pleasure, and thought about leaning back, smoking and relaxing. But somehow a cigar didn't mesh with her present image of herself as a society hostess. "I'd like a puff of yours," she said slowly, exercising restraint, "but not one of my own, thank you."

As they passed a sputtering streetlamp, she saw his eyebrow rise. "As you wish."

She drew on the cigar, tasting him and the sweet flavor of smoke, then she handed the cigar back to him. Leaning to the window, she peered outside. Lights were coming on inside the houses they passed, shining out on snowy lawns and glazed driveways. She heard the muffled clop of horse's hooves against the snow-packed street. "It's a lovely night. This was a wonderful idea."

"Lily, we need to talk about Helene Van Heusen."

In an instant her euphoria vanished. "Helene insisted that I call on her next Thursday," she said after a minute. Studying his face in the shadows, she struggled with duty versus inclination. She wasn't sure if she should mention Helene's comments about M. Intuition said no.

"I forbid you to call on her."

Oh? Her hackles rose, and she stiffened. For one terrible instant she was back in the Yuma prison where men decided what she could or could not do and punished infractions with beatings.

This was Denver; not Yuma. And this was Quinn; not Ephram Callihan. "Is that wise?" she asked when her hands had steadied. "Helene is Miriam's close friend. And you did invite her to the at-home."

"Strictly speaking no one was invited. An announcement was placed in the newspaper that you had returned from Santa Fe and would resume your regular Friday at-homes." He shrugged slightly, his shoulder rubbing against hers. "I had hoped Helene would not attend. She won't attend next week if you don't repay the call."

But she wouldn't learn about M unless she called on Helene.

Glimpsing Quinn's stern expression in the glow of a streetlamp, she decided not to mention Miriam's secret. At least not yet.

"Frederick Van Heusen is a vital spoke in the opposing party's wheel, Lily. If my opponent beats me at the polls, he will have Van Heusen to thank." He studied the ash glowing on the end of his cigar, then looked at her. "Helene began to seek Miriam out shortly after I declared my candidacy last year. Do you understand what I'm saying?"

"You believe Helene has an ulterior motive. Her interest in Miriam extends beyond simple friendship."

He nodded. "Consider how much you know about my plans for the campaign. Miriam knew more."

Her brows lifted. "Quinn, I don't know anything about politics, and I doubt Miriam did. You've said yourself that she disliked political discussion."

"Miriam couldn't avoid political talk any more than you can. She heard it at the supper table, heard it at social gatherings. She heard Paul and me discussing strategy, she presided over a refreshment table when the party leaders met at our home. If you doubt the extent of her knowledge, ask yourself how much you know about my plans. You've heard parts of my speeches before I delivered them. You too have listened to Paul and me discuss policies and strategy. You possess more information than you realize."

"Are you suggesting that Miriam offered Helene information helpful to the opposing party?" she asked incredulously.

He was silent long enough that she guessed his suspicions. "I doubt Miriam did so deliberately," he said finally. "I also doubt Helene would have found it difficult to extract information helpful to Van Heusen's cause."

Lily frowned, trying to understand. "That explains Helene's interest in Miriam. But it doesn't explain why Miriam would disregard your objections and pursue the friendship. Did you ask why she was so insistent? To the point of disobedience?" She didn't say disloyalty, but that's what she was thinking. And she didn't point out that disobedience ran against her perception of Miriam Westin's character.

"Miriam refused to discuss her attachment to Helene."

Lily's intuition flared and she bit her lip to keep silent. Helene Van Heusen was the conduit to the mysterious M. That was why Miriam had gone against her nature, defied her husband, and refused to give up the association. Whoever M was, he was important to Miriam.

Gazing out the carriage window as they rolled past the courthouse, she thought about the note she had found in Miriam's pocket. Same time. Same place. And she remembered Helene taking her hands when they greeted each other. It would have been very easy to pass a tiny wadded slip of paper.

In fact, it wasn't unimaginable that Helene had manipulated Miriam into a compromising situation that could drown Quinn in scandal and bring him to grief.

"Quinn . . ." But no man wanted to hear that his wife was seeing another man. And Lily didn't know if that was indeed the explanation.

There could be innocent reasons for the note and for Helene's secrecy and involvement. Perhaps M was an artist and Miriam had commissioned a new portrait as a gift for Quinn. Same time, same place could refer to a sitting. Perhaps Helene was helping Miriam arrange the sittings. M certainly might be desperate if he were depending on a fee, then Miriam left abruptly for Santa Fe without a word. He would be anxious to see her again and resume work on the painting.

But this explanation felt far-fetched and unlikely. Nevertheless, the wadded note and Helene's whisperings *could* be innocent.

Lily intended to find out. She owed Miriam better than to leap to a shameful conclusion. She would reserve judgment until she knew the truth.

There was something else she'd been thinking about almost constantly and wanted to know. Needed to know.

"Quinn?" Turning to face him in the dark interior of the carriage, she hesitated, then blurted the question.

"Did you decide to take a mistress?"

Chapter 12

Smiling, Quinn handed Lily his cigar and watched her inhale deeply before she reluctantly gave it back to him. He could never anticipate her, enjoyed it that she could surprise him.

"A wife never asks her husband if he's taken a mistress," he said lightly. "The answer is either a lie, or the wife believes it is. You might keep that caution in mind for future reference."

"Why?" she asked, tilting her head back, pursing her lips, and exhaling a stream of smoke. "I'm never going to get married."

He knew the minute she realized he hadn't answered her question. She arched an eyebrow, then frowned at the lap robe, pulling at it with gloved fingers.

"There's no reason you shouldn't marry. You're still young, beautiful, an interesting woman." He'd watched her today, and she had sparkled even though she tried to mimic Miriam's sadness and frequent sighs. Next to her, the other women had seemed bland and ordinary, like common ivy surrounding an exotic dahlia.

It mystified him that Lily could have the same pale coloring and delicate bone structure as Miriam, yet impart such a different impression. Her eyes sparkled and flashed, her rosy mouth smiled, frowned, expressed a dozen different emotions. Vivacious and mercurial, she attracted people and attention without effort. Miriam had preferred to fade into the background and observe, but this woman would never be overlooked.

"I grew up hearing my Aunt Edna insist that she'd never known a minute's freedom until my Uncle Ross died. She said marriage was a hopeless trap and advised against it."

"That's a discouraging thing to tell a young girl," Quinn commented, drawing on his cigar.

"I figure some marriages are like prison. Trouble is, no woman knows in advance if hers will be like that." Her head lifted, and she looked at him. "When I heard the prison gates slam shut behind me, I understood about feeling hopeless and trapped, and I don't want to feel that way again. I'm not going to take the risk that I'll end up married and trapped. I want to be able to walk away if a man does me wrong." She smiled. "I guess you wouldn't understand that, you being a man who lives by the rules."

Lily Dale was every man's fantasy of the perfect mistress. An exciting woman with modest wants and no interest in marriage. "Cy Gardener did you wrong, and you didn't walk away."

She waved a hand and nodded. "I learned a lesson there. I was thinking about leaving him, I just didn't do it soon enough. Next time I'll know when to cut and run."

The light scent of forget-me-nots filled the carriage, mingled with the woman scents of sachet, lotions, and creams. Her thigh and shoulder rested against his, warm against the cold that turned her cheeks pink and her lips red.

Jealousy, savage and hot, constricted his chest as he listened to her talk about the man who had led her into harm's way. He didn't want another man to look at her, let alone touch her or make love to her. Didn't want to imagine her gloriously naked, opening her arms to any man who wasn't him.

Fevered images swirled through his thoughts. Lily wouldn't keep her nightgown on, wouldn't insist on total darkness. She wouldn't silently endure with her face turned to the side.

He knew how it would be with her. God knew he'd imagined it often enough. She would bring vibrancy and excitement to a man's bed. The inhibitions she pretended during daylight hours would vanish in the darkness. Her need to touch and stroke and discover would drive a man wild.

Cursing under his breath, he flipped his cigar into the snowy night, then lowered his head and rubbed his eyebrows. He had hoped a week away from her would cool the fever in his blood, but seeing her again had ignited the fire in his stomach and mind.

"Quinn?"

When he glanced up, she was watching with a frown between those magnificent eyes that tonight reminded him of violets.

"Is something wrong?"

History's famous courtesans must have had bedroom voices like hers, rich and husky, ripe with image and invitation.

Like a dam bursting, his restraint shattered, and he reached for her, pulling her roughly against his chest. A low sound rumbled in his throat when he felt the soft heat of her body electric and taut against him. Her eyes flared in surprise and then in understanding, and her gaze dropped to his mouth. Her lips parted, and the air seemed to rush out of her body. She leaned into him and lifted her face.

His lips covered hers, hard and possessive, and his arousal was instant and powerful. The taste of her inflamed his senses as he explored her mouth with his tongue, finding echoes of tea and cakes, smoke and sweetness. Anger and laughter, passion and appetite. These images flashed through a mind burning with an urgent need to conquer and take. He wanted to tear the clothing from her lush body and bury his lips between her breasts, wanted to taste her skin and inhale the musky scent of desire.

When he released her, she eased back in his arms, her eyes wide and dazed, her breath ragged. She touched the fingertips of her gloves to her lips, and he felt her trembling. "My God," she murmured, staring at him.

Then she clasped his face and lunged forward, and this time she kissed him.

There was no aphrodisiac on earth as potent to a man as knowing the woman he desired also desired him. Quinn's mind exploded. Throwing off the lap robe, he roughly pulled her on top of him, pressing her against the length of his body. Mouth locked to hers, he shoved aside the edges of her cloak and found the fullness of her breast.

Moaning, she drew her knees up on the seat and straddled him, rocking against his body, and she threw her head back to receive the feverish kisses he rained down her throat. Flying fingers knocked his hat to the floor, and she gripped his hair. He shoved at the tangle of skirts, cloak and robe, and twisted until she lay beneath him and he could run his hand along the curve of her leg, seeking that erotic bare strip of pale skin above her stocking.

Blinded by passion, his mind reeling with the dark intoxication of frantic, demanding kisses, he didn't realize the carriage had halted until a persistent knocking penetrated their gasps and small urgent moans of pleasure.

They froze and stared into each other's eyes. Lily's hat was knocked askew and several long gleaming curls had come unbound and dropped near the half-opened bodice of her gown. Her lips were swollen and her gaze disoriented.

"What?" he shouted, his gaze locked to hers. It had to be Morely. Curse the man. His timing could not have been worse, damn him.

Morely cleared his throat, the sound carrying in the quiet cold night. "Ah, we're home, sir."

Lily's eyes widened and a hand flew to her lips. A twinkle appeared in her gaze, and then she laughed, pushing him to the floor between the seats.

He pulled himself onto the facing seat and frowned down. His shirt was open to the waist. God only knew where the studs were. His gloves had vanished along with Lily's in the pile between the seats that contained the lap robe, her cloak, his hat, gloves, and studs, hairpins, and one of her stockings. Falling back on the seat, he watched Lily hastily attempting to restore order to her appearance.

Then he, too, laughed and shook his head at the ludicrous picture they presented, and he wondered how much Morely had overheard before the knocking at the carriage door had intruded on their absorption in each other.

"A moment, if you please," he said, leaning out the window. Morely gazed at him without expression, then walked away in the direction of the horses. Cranston's silhouette hovered behind the glass framing the front door.

"What on earth will Cranston think when he sees us?"

Lily murmured, shoving hair up beneath her hat. "This isn't going to work, I'm missing too many hairpins. Lord, I know I was wearing gloves when I left the house."

He buttoned his waistcoat, then found her cloak and her stocking, which she shoved into a cloak pocket. His hat was near the bottom of the pile and crushed beyond redemption.

"How do I look?" she asked, leaning into the light and gazing at him with twinkling eyes and a laugh on her swollen mouth.

"Like a brazen hussy who's been doing what you've been doing," he said, grinning. "How do I look?"

She inspected his open shirt and crushed hat and returned his grin. "Like a bounder who's been doing what you've been doing." After leaning over to slide on her shoe, she straightened her shoulders and drew a breath. "Well. This is the best we can manage." A long curl of gold sagged then tumbled down her back. "Let's go scandalize Cranston."

Cranston opened the door as they climbed the porch steps. His eyebrows soared; otherwise, he did not betray any surprise or curiosity regarding their disheveled appearance.

"Mr. Kazinski is in the family parlor, sir."

Lily removed her hand from Quinn's arm. "Damn." When Cranston's eyes widened, she made a fluttery gesture, then hurried toward the staircase, waving at Quinn to follow. "Please inform Mr. Kazinski that we'll join him after we've freshened up."

Laughing, his eyes on her bottom, Quinn followed her upstairs.

* * *

Throughout dinner they discussed her first at-home, and Lily watched Paul relax as he understood that the afternoon had gone well. Satisfaction and triumph gleamed in his dark eyes, and well it should. She understood that she was his creation, knew her success was directly due to his instruction and coaching.

"Don't let it go to your head, my dear," he said over coffee in the family parlor. "If you become too confident, you're sure to err and revert to old bad habits." A frown pointedly directed her attention to the fact that she had kicked off her slippers and sat sprawled in an unladylike posture, her bare feet crossed on a velvet ottoman.

As if this reprimand were not enough to remind her that she was not a lady born and bred, he smiled pleasantly, and added, "Will you favor us with a song, Miriam?"

She rolled her eyes toward the piano. "Not tonight. It's been a long and exciting day." She flicked a hooded glance at Quinn. "I'm too tired to play." Plus, she didn't know how.

But Paul had painted an image in her mind. Miriam sitting gracefully at the piano, playing and singing while the gentlemen enjoyed their coffee. Miriam was cultured; Lily was not.

Her eyes narrowed speculatively as she wondered who was the real target of Paul's reminder? Herself? Or Quinn?

She hadn't forgotten that Paul believed she was an adventuress seeking to ensnare Quinn with her body. Quinn hadn't forgotten either. Both had made a point to be cool and distant to each other during dinner. A performance within a performance for Paul's benefit.

As the conversation shifted to politics, she sipped her coffee and stole quick peeks at Quinn. He'd changed his shirt and combed his hair back, revealing strands of grey near his temples. If she'd had to make a choice, she would have said she preferred his cowboy attire, as it made him more accessible. Business and formal attire accentuated the authority and power in his features. However he dressed, her heartbeat accelerated when she gazed at him.

They would become lovers.

Accepting the inevitability sent a tremor thrilling down her spine, and her cheeks flushed. Her coffee cup rattled slightly between trembling fingers as she set it on the marble-topped table beside her chair.

"If you gentlemen will excuse me," she said, standing. "I believe I'll retire early and prepare for bed."

"How risqué, Miriam, to mention the word bed," Paul said, also rising to his feet. The instructions and reminders continued.

Quinn relaxed near the fireplace, his arm on the mantel. A flash of heat burned in his eyes before he controlled his expression. "Good night, darling. Sleep well."

"I'm afraid I'm too excited by the day's events to sleep immediately," she said, trying not to smile.

"Shall I have something hot sent to your room?" Quinn inquired. "Milk? Something else?"

"Perhaps something else." She let her gaze travel down his body. "But not immediately." She turned her smile to Paul. "I need time to prepare myself for, ah, sleeping."

Instincts flaring, Paul looked back and forth between them, and his lips thinned. His habitual frown appeared as if he were trying to decide if meanings flowed beneath meanings.

Trying not to laugh, Lily wiggled her fingers at him, then picked up her shoes and left the gentlemen to a political discussion which she guessed would be brief tonight.

Upstairs, she sent Elizabeth away, then hung away her gown, washed thoroughly, brushed out her hair and let it hang loose down her back. She perfumed her arms and throat, then slipped her nightgown over her head and climbed into bed to wait.

Tonight, she did not let herself wonder who Quinn saw when he looked at her. Tonight it was enough that she knew who she saw when she looked at him.

Would she regret welcoming him into her bed? Perhaps. But she wouldn't borrow trouble by worrying about it now.

It was later than she'd expected by the time she heard Quinn enter his bedroom. Quickly she laid aside the book she'd been reading, lowered the wick in the lamp near her bed, and pulled a long curl forward on her breast. When the connecting door opened, Lily placed a hand over her pounding heart and struggled to breathe slowly.

He wasn't wearing his dressing gown as she had expected. Nor was his expression what she had hoped to see. He leaned in the doorway, holding a glass of whiskey, staring at her with a contemplative frown.

Fighting a swamp of disappointment and feeling slightly foolish, Lily stiffened against the pillows. "Was it Paul?" she asked softly. "Did he remind you that I'm scheming to wed you secretly? That I'll demand marriage in exchange for not exposing this deception and ruining your candidacy? Or does he think I hope to extract more money by luring you into my bed?"

"I want you more than I've ever wanted another woman," he said in a low, tight voice. "And not because you look like Miriam. You don't sound like her, move like her, taste like her."

"But you've changed your mind." Hoping her disappointment wasn't flaming on her face, she buttoned the buttons she had earlier opened down the front of her nightgown.

"No." When she looked up quickly, he came farther into the room and sat on the end of her bed. Extending his arm, he offered her the whiskey glass, and Lily took it.

"Paul and I didn't discuss you after you left. But talking about the future reminded me of what's at stake. Every step I've taken for the last few years has been calculated to bring me closer to the governor's seat. I've worked for the party. I've cultivated the men who make the decisions. I've made myself visible to voters. I made certain I was appointed to the committee drawing up the state's charter, I've given speeches, kissed babies, shaken hands."

"I know that," she said, letting the whiskey burn down the back of her throat. "And you'll continue to do those things."

"What you need to understand is that *nothing* is going to stand in my way, Lily. Not Miriam. Not you."

"Then you believe Paul," she whispered, smoothing her hand across the counterpane. She had removed Miriam's wedding rings, thinking the sight might upset him.

"You should know by now that Paul and I seldom agree on any issue. But I don't reject his opinions out of hand. If there is any possibility, however vague, that you're thinking our passion for each other will change anything . . . it won't happen."

His blunt words and harsh tone made her draw back against the pillows and anger flared in her eyes. "I've known from the beginning that ambition is your God," she snapped. The statement was something Miriam might have said, and Lily wished she hadn't said it.

"My marriage is over, Lily, but I have a wife. I couldn't marry you if I wanted to. If making our arrangement permanent is somewhere in the back of your mind, it's not possible."

"Damn it, Quinn." She tossed back the rest of the whiskey, then sighed. "I'm not asking for marriage. I haven't talked about it, threatened it, or even brought up the subject. It's hard for you to understand a woman who doesn't want to get married, but you're looking at one." Because the weight of his body depressing the mattress disturbed her, she threw back the covers and swung her bare feet out of bed. Striding past him, she went to the vanity and briskly dragged a brush through her hair before she began plaiting it into the braid she wore for sleeping.

"You say that now," he said, turning on the bed, "but there's something between us, and walking away will be difficult."

"Will it? You'll have your governorship to console you and keep you too busy to think about me, and I'll have Rose to go to." Pride was speaking. They both knew he was right. Every day filled them with each other, heightened the tensions between two people who had not known physical pleasure in a very long time, who were powerfully drawn to each other.

"If you can accept that our association will be temporary, then . . ."

"You've stopped worrying that I might feel used?"

"Why are you angry? I haven't said anything you didn't know. As for you feeling used—Lily, this whole damned thing is about using you and your resemblance to Miriam," he said flatly. "How far are you willing to let it go?"

She had considered that question. Perhaps they were two lonely people using each other. Raising her arms, she coiled the braid around her head and jabbed the hairpins securely in place. "I don't want you to take a mistress."

Her reply must have surprised him because he laughed, the sound short and humorless. "That's what we're discussing, isn't it? And you've come right to the point."

"Does Paul know your decision?" She knew the suggestion that he required Paul's approval would annoy him. But it annoyed her that he made a liaison sound like a business arrangement.

"If we've agreed to proceed—and if you believe Paul should be told, then I'll inform him."

Lily stared at herself in the mirror. Nothing had changed. She still wanted him. She felt his eyes on her and knew he still wanted her. Marriage was not an option, and she didn't intend to blackmail him or raise any difficulties when it came time for her to leave. "Tonight you sound like a lawyer," she said, holding her gaze on the mirror. "Laying down rules."

"You've made it clear that you don't care about the outcome of the election, and I don't expect you to. But I do. I want it very clear from the beginning that winning the election comes first. In this instance, that means honoring the terms of your employment."

"I understand the rules, and I accept them. I always have because there was never a choice." She threw the hairbrush across the room and watched it bounce off a chair, then she faced him, hands on hips, her face burning. "I'll be your mistress."

"Excellent!"

"I don't want Paul involved in this."

It occurred to her that they were shouting, and she hoped their angry voices didn't carry to the third floor, where the servants were presumably sleeping. Or listening.

"But nothing is going to happen tonight," she said, lowering her voice to a hiss. Whirling, she leaned to the vanity, dipped her fingers into a jar, and slathered cream on her face. When he laughed, she scowled at him. "I have to do this to protect my skin."

"It isn't that," he said, shaking his head and pulling a hand down his jaw. "If you only knew how many times I've heard 'not tonight' in this room."

Rising, he walked forward, drew her lightly against his body, and kissed her on the lips. "What is that stuff?" he asked, wiping his mouth. "It tastes like lard."

"For all I know, it is lard."

"Soon, Lily," he said, narrowing his eyes on hers. And now she saw the hard burn of desire.

Her mouth dried and the back of her knees felt hot. "Yes."

At the connecting door, he looked back. "Two things. Buy some new perfume and throw away every bottle of forget-me-nots. And come out of mourning. Marietta Teasdale is your seamstress. Contact her and order a new wardrobe. I don't care what you order or what it costs, as long as the colors are bright. Do it immediately."

After his door closed, Lily sank to the bench seat before the vanity mirror. She had just agreed to become her husband's mistress. Except he wasn't really her husband any more than she was the person everyone thought she was.

And the deception had taken on another layer, widening to deceive Paul as well.

Climbing back into bed, she reviewed the details of this long, nerve-wracking day. But a question kept intruding on her restless thoughts.

When would Quinn come to her? When would they begin?

They breakfasted together on Monday morning, Quinn in business attire and Lily wearing a simple morning gown. When she noticed he wasn't reading his newspaper but gazing at her above the pages, she smiled. "What are you thinking?" she asked.

"Do you need to ask?"

They studied each other down the length of the table, and Lily swallowed hard, feeling a rush of crimson climb her throat. If Cranston hadn't appeared to refill their coffee cups, she might have teased him with a provocative remark of her own.

"What are you doing today?" Quinn asked, folding away his paper and consulting his pocket watch.

"I'm going out," she said, after murmuring a word of thanks to Cranston. "I'll repay a few calls. Do a little shopping."

She was looking forward to venturing out on her own. Yesterday she had asked Quinn if she required a companion for today's errands, and he had explained that Morely, the carriage driver, would fulfill that function. He had also explained that she didn't need the addresses of the ladies she would call on as they were the same ladies she always called on. Morely was not a new employee, he knew Miriam's regular schedule, knew which of her friends and acquaintances received on Monday, Tuesday, et cetera.

Quinn put away his pocket watch, hastily finished his coffee, then kissed the top of her head, touched her shoulder, and departed for his firm.

Following a routine that was gradually becoming habitual, Lily took up the newspaper he had left behind and browsed through the pages over another cup of coffee. Then Elizabeth called for her bath, and afterward dressed her hair and assisted with buttons and tapes, sashes and the buttonhooks to fasten her boots. Once dressed, she met Cranston in her household office, where they decided the menus for the day and discussed any household matters he wished to bring to her attention. After Cranston left, she reviewed the cards of the ladies on whom she would be calling, then she instructed Elizabeth to fetch her hat, gloves, and cloak, and summon Morely and the carriage.

"The usual Monday places, Miz Westin?" Morely asked, dropping the step before the carriage door.

"Yes, please," she said after he'd handed her inside and given her the lap robe. "And sometime today I want to stop by Frederick's Fabric Shop," she added, having gotten the name from Quinn.

Morely gave her a long look, rather sad, rather sweet, and she suddenly understood that the old man was infatuated with her. His rheumy eyes held a puppy-dog look of slavish adoration.

"I'm glad to see you home and looking well, ma'am."

"I'm glad to be home," she said, smiling at him.

Miriam had run away from so many people who had cared about her. Lily thought of the women who had attended her at-home and the genuine concern in their eyes, and Mary Blalock, who had sent her a pie from the third floor yesterday, and now Morely.

Usually Lily wondered where Miriam had gone. This morning she wondered why Miriam had fled.

It was too fine a morning to give herself a headache by worrying about Miriam. Today she would have her first real view of the city in daylight, and she planned to enjoy the sights.

Sliding close to the window, she peered out at a sky as blue as summer lupines. Winter lawns emerged from melting snow, and she couldn't lean too close to the window, as the horses kicked up slush and clods of mud.

In daylight she had a clear view of the mountains rimming the western horizon and could orient herself. Thus it surprised her when Morely drove south on Fourteenth Street, then turned east then south again on Broadway past the construction on the new state capitol building and away from the city.

Here the ground was gently rolling, blanketed by fields of melting snow. Traffic thinned and within twenty minutes they were well into the country and had the muddy road to themselves.

Where on earth was Morely taking her? Here and there Lily spotted farmhouses, and in the distance a collection of small houses that her Aunt Edna would have referred to as shanties. Surely none of the ladies who had called on Friday lived in such ramshackle homes. But that appeared to be the direction Morely was heading.

Less than a mile from the shanties, the carriage halted and Lily waited wide-eyed to see what would happen next.

Morely opened the door and extended his hand. Hesitantly, she took it and stepped to the ground, lifting her skirts away from the mud.

"I'll return in an hour, ma'am," Morely said, touching two fingers to his cap.

Speechless, she watched him drive away.

Shading her eyes from the winter sun, she slowly looked around. Morely had left her in the middle of the country without another soul in sight.

This lonely site was one of Miriam's usual Monday visits?

Chapter 13

Lily could see for miles in either direction. No traffic moved along the road other than Morely heading back toward the city. After the shock of being abandoned in the middle of nowhere diminished, Lily took stock of her situation.

Rescue was unlikely; she was stuck here for the next hour. Thankfully, she had dressed warmly, but she suspected she would begin to feel the cold before Morely returned for her. Unhappily contemplating the muddy road, she considered walking to keep her circulation flowing, but the prospect of ruining her boots and hems was distinctly unappealing.

Same time, same place.

The message popped into her mind. Straightening, she took another slow look at her surroundings. Morely had brought Miriam to this same place on Mondays.

If Lily had correctly deduced that the message in Miriam's pocket was to Miriam and not from her, then Miriam must have come to this place on a regular basis to meet M when M sent a message that he was available.

Therefore, Morely knew part of Miriam's secret. He knew the time and the place. Further, Morely must not have told Quinn, she decided, or Quinn would have put a stop to this part of the "usual Monday visits."

Interested now, she examined her surroundings, focusing on a thicket of winter-bare willows meandering along a curving line that led north toward Denver. The thick line of willows and occasional cottonwoods suggested a creek.

Lifting her hem away from the mud, she approached the willows and discovered a graveled path and a weathered sign identifying the City Ditch that supplied Denver's residential water systems.

On Mondays Miriam paid a call on the City Ditch?

Intrigued, Lily examined the gravel path. As most of the snow had melted, she couldn't tell if others had recently come this way. But she doubted a tryst was scheduled for today, anyway. Nevertheless, she was here, and paths were meant to be followed. She chose north and set off through the bare-branched willows. At least the path was not muddy.

Before she'd gone too far, she realized the area would be lovely in summer. The sound of water running in the ditch was pleasant, the path well maintained. Here and there she spotted remnants of wildflowers that would rejuvenate in the spring. The willows would leaf out then, and the shrubs were tall enough that a woman her size would be concealed from the sight of anyone traveling along the road. Even now, Lily doubted a traveler would notice her. The branches were bare but thick, and she wore a dark grey cloak almost the same color as the exposed trunks and branches of the willows.

If Miriam had walked this path in summer, she would have appeared to vanish minutes after Morely helped her alight from the carriage. It occurred to Lily that Miriam Westin was adept at disappearing.

Eventually she discovered a bench seat placed beneath a

large overhanging cottonwood and sat down to catch her breath. This was the same time, and the same place where Miriam had met M. Lily felt certain of it.

So much for her theory of M as a starving artist and Miriam sitting for a new portrait. A woman did not meet a man in a secluded place of concealment to discuss innocent matters.

Frowning and resisting the obvious conclusion, she watched a boy rolling a hoop along the path, coming toward her.

"Mrs. Ollie!" Catching the hoop, he ran forward with a broad smile. "Did you bring peppermints today?"

He was eight or nine years old, wearing mended knickers and a jacket with patches sewn over the elbows. The bill of his cap had begun to fray. But he was clean, and his clothing, though patched and mended, was made of warm wool. He leaned on the iron arm of the bench and gazed at her from blue eyes brimming with expectation.

This boy believed he knew her. But . . . Mrs. Ollie?

"Not peppermints," Lily said, remembering the mints in her purse. "Something else." Opening the drawstrings, she pushed aside her handkerchief and comb, found two mints and gave them to the boy, waiting to see what would happen next.

He popped both into his mouth then sat down beside her. "I ain't seen you since spring. I thought maybe you died."

Did he know about the fire then? "As you can see, I didn't," Lily said carefully, feeling her way. She wanted to ask his name, but of course she couldn't.

"You said you'd bring the baby next time and let me see."

She looked down at her gloved hands. "I would have kept my promise, but . . . . the baby died." Her mind raced

over a dozen questions. Had this boy seen Miriam pregnant? Or had he met her after Susan's birth, and she'd mentioned having an infant?

"Oh." He leaned forward and examined the rim of his
hoop, not knowing what to say. Lily didn't either. "Mr.
Ollie said you was sick. Is that why you sound different?"

"I was very ill for a long time." A dozen questions
whirled through her mind, and it frustrated her that she
didn't know how to ask them without revealing that she
wasn't who he thought she was. "You've seen Mr. Ollie,
then," she said finally, watching his face.

"Not in a long time."

"When did you see him last?"

The boy shrugged. "I only seen him once since that time
you was crying." He slid a sideways look at her as if it still
troubled him to remember her tears. "He was in awful shape.
You know, after he got the stuffing whacked outta him."

Lily cleared her throat and bit her lips against the questions begging to be asked. "He looked awful," she repeated, her expression encouraging him to elaborate.

"His arm was in the sling, and his face was all smashed
up. Pa got beat that bad once, down at Slawson's tavern.
Ma thought sure as Sunday he was going to die. Did Mr.
Ollie die?"

"No."

"Mr. Ollie said the man who done it to him would pay
and pay good. Did he get him back?"

"You'll have to ask him about that." Smiling at the
freckles fading across his nose, she tried to think how to request a description of Mr. Ollie. When she couldn't con-
ceive of a way to explain such a question, she decided a
description wouldn't have helped anyway.

"When will he come?" The boy peered down the path.

"Mr. Ollie won't be here today. Shouldn't you be in school?"

He grinned. "If Ma knew I'd cut, she'd tan my hide. You smell good." Turning red, he looked down at his boots, then jumped to his feet. "Well. I gotta go."

She wanted him to stay, wanted to ply him with questions. "It was nice to see you again."

"I wish you wasn't so sad all the time. And I'm sorry your baby died," he said solemnly. "You ain't gonna cry, are you?"

"Not today."

"That's because Mr. Ollie ain't here. I'm glad Mr. Ollie got beat up because he makes you cry." His face turned fiery red, and he ran down the path, spinning his hoop in front of him.

Lily watched until the path curved and the boy was swallowed by the willows, then she closed her eyes. Miriam had met a man here. The boy believed the man was her husband and he'd made her cry.

Although the possibility of a lover had occurred to Lily, she simply had not believed it could be true. The shock of discovering "Mr. and Mrs. Ollie" stunned her.

Had Quinn suspected that Miriam's affections had turned elsewhere? She remembered him telling her how often he had heard "not tonight" in Miriam's bedroom. A sigh dropped her shoulders. She hoped he had never learned of Mr. Ollie.

But Helene Van Heusen knew. Helene, whose husband was Quinn's political enemy. A chill skittered down her back.

"Good Lord."

By using Helene as a go-between, Miriam and Mr. Ollie had taken a terrible risk. If Helene ever mentioned to her husband that Quinn Westin's wife was seeing another man, Lily knew as certainly as she knew anything that Helene's husband would use the information to create a scandal guaranteed to destroy Quinn's political future. It's what Paul would have done if the situation were reversed.

There was no doubt in her mind that Helene had shared the information with her husband, none at all. But Lily had learned enough about political strategy to understand that timing was critical. The Van Heusens would await the perfect, most damaging moment, probably near the election, to use Miriam's affair to ruin Quinn.

Lily raised a hand to her forehead. "Oh Miriam, whatever were you thinking?" Not only had Miriam betrayed her husband, but she had placed everything he cared about in jeopardy.

Had she hated her husband that much? Or had she been swept into a passion so overwhelming that she couldn't see the devastating consequences?

Lily's head snapped up, and she blinked at the pebbles along the path. Was it possible that Miriam had eloped with her lover? Could that be the explanation for her disappearance?

Lily was feverishly considering that possibility when Morely returned for her. But no. There was a new message from M via Helene. Miriam had not eloped.

Later, as Mrs. Alderson poured tea, Lily wondered if Quinn knew about M. As he didn't know about the recent contact, could he believe that Miriam had eloped with her lover? That would explain why he wasn't searching for his wife better than any of the reasons he had given her. While the Misses Peppers chatted about fashion and parties, Lily considered the possibility that M and Mr. Ollie were different men. Could Miriam have had two lovers?

That thought left her reeling, and she could hardly focus as she examined bolts of material at Frederick's Fabric Shop. No, Miriam absolutely could not have had two lovers. M and Mr. Ollie were the same person. But one thing was very clear. Miriam Westin had led a dangerous secret life.

And there were people who knew bits and pieces of Miriam's secret. Morely knew. Helene knew. The boy on the path knew. Any one of them could have exposed her, ruined her reputation, destroyed her marriage, and ended her husband's political career.

Now Lily knew.

The question she returned to again and again was: Had Quinn known? Had he discovered that his wife was involved in an affair with the explosive potential to cause a scandal that would destroy his dreams?

Icy fingers ran down her spine as she remembered Quinn saying that nothing would stand in his way, not Miriam and not her.

Someone had beaten Mr. Ollie so violently that the boy beside the ditch had asked if Mr. Ollie had died.

Miriam had conveniently disappeared at about the same time as Quinn's candidacy swung into full forward progress.

Lily didn't like the direction of her thoughts, but couldn't alter the progression.

Coincidence or not, the Miriam problem, as Paul would have phrased it, had been solved when Miriam vanished. At that point, the liaison with M ended. And without

Miriam, an explosive scandal deflated to salacious gossip if her affair became known.

But the political powers had insisted on a married candidate who could be sold to the voters as a family man, and thus a new Miriam problem surfaced. At least until Paul had found Lily in a prison laundry yard.

Distracted, Lily handed Cranston her cloak and dropped her hat and gloves on the hall table.

"Hot tea is waiting in the family parlor, madam."

"What? Oh, yes. Thank you."

Lily didn't like the troubling denouement her thoughts tumbled toward. Quinn was a civilized, good man. She should be ashamed of herself for allowing her imagination to run away with her like this.

Still, if Quinn had learned of Miriam's indiscretion, it didn't seem too far-fetched to imagine him beating Mr. Ollie to a pulp, then ordering Miriam out of his house and his life. If the end had come that way, it seemed enormously cruel even in these circumstances to cast a woman into the street without her clothing, her rings, her personal belongings. Yet Miriam had left everything behind.

She backed up her imagination and visualized another ending in which Quinn set aside injured pride long enough to provide Miriam a home and an income in some faraway place.

Long hours of speculation had given Lily a raging headache, and she swore she would not think about this anymore today. Entering the family parlor, she walked toward the waiting tea cart with a sigh of gratitude. Her own thoughts had chilled her.

She hadn't taken three steps when the door clicked shut behind her and a hand closed over her wrist.

Quinn spun her to face him, and she stumbled as he pulled her forward. In one fluid motion, he caught and leaned her against the wall. Heart pounding, eyes wide, Lily looked into his face and saw desire blazing like embers deep within his gray eyes. Her stomach tightened, and her knees went weak.

Stepping forward, he pressed against her and she gasped when she felt the hard evidence of his arousal even through her skirts. Leaning, he spoke near her ear, warm breath bathing her cheek.

"I think of you every minute. Today I saw you in every woman, heard your voice a dozen times."

The scent and heat of him radiated against her, enveloped her, and drew her, making her part of him. Rocking her hips up to his, she raised a trembling hand and stroked the beginning roughness of new whiskers along his jaw. His skin was firm and warm and electrifying. A tremor of intense longing thrilled through her body, and Lily thought she would faint.

Pinning her to the wall with his body, he ran his hands up her arms, along the arch of her throat, then tilted her mouth to his. When he kissed her, his lips were dry and hot, and he tasted of tea and smoke and earth and air and a hard male spice taste that she could not identify.

All thought swirled out of her mind, replaced by waves of physical sensation as he moved against her, slowly, deliberately, his mouth, his body, his hands.

There was something wildly erotic in her helplessness and inability to move. Pinioned between the wall and the solid, hard press of his body, she could only submit to deep kisses that ravaged and plundered and left her breathless and gasping, her heart racing to beat against the fires raging inside her skin.

When he released her, they were both shaken and trembling, and struggling for breath. He trailed his fingertips down her cheek and let his hand ride the turbulent swell of her breast.

"You asked if I saw Miriam or you," he said in a hoarse voice. "I want you to believe I see you. That's why I want you out of mourning, to have your own clothing and your own scent." Leaning, he caught her lower lip between his teeth, then kissed her deeply, crushing her against him so tightly that she felt the beat of his heart thudding hard against her own. "When in the hell will your new wardrobe be ready?"

"In about three weeks," she whispered. He touched her, and her bones dissolved. He kissed her, and an earthquake began in the pit of her stomach and rocked through her body. Dampness spread on her palms and between her legs, and she quivered in readiness for him. Never had she felt such hunger for a man.

"Three weeks." A groan issued from deep in his throat, and he dropped his forehead against hers. "Christ!"

The door opened and Daisy took a step into the room, humming under her breath. When she saw them pressed against the wall, she sucked in a breath and turned a dark shade of scarlet. Her hands flew to her lips. "Oh! I'm sorry. I was just going to . . ." she gestured toward the fire burning in the grate. "I'll just . . ." Backing out of the parlor, she started to say something else, then firmly closed the door.

"In ten minutes everyone in this house will know I cornered you and was kissing you."

Lily laughed and lifted shaking hands to straighten her hair. "Is that so terrible?"

"You'd think a man could enjoy a little privacy in his own house." Taking her by the hand, he led her to the settee. "Three weeks. I suppose a new wardrobe takes time." He patted his jacket and the pockets of his waistcoat the way he did when he was searching for a cigar. "Do you mind if I . . . ?"

She shook her head. "Your cigar case is always in your inside jacket pocket." His habits were becoming known to her, knowledge she held close to her heart.

"Tea?"

"Thank you, no. I've changed my mind." Her chill had fled the instant he touched her. "I've had enough tea today to float a raft. How did your day go?"

As he talked about a speech he'd made to a civic group and about drafting another speech he would deliver next week, Lily's expression sobered and her headache returned. She did indeed know a great deal about Quinn's political convictions. Exactly as Miriam had.

"Paul will object to any mention of mining regulation," she said slowly, a little dismayed that she would know this, and by how much information she had picked up merely by sharing a dinner table with Quinn and Paul or being in the same room with them.

Quinn slammed his fist against the mantel hard enough to rattle the candlesticks. "At some point we have to stop feeding the voters pallid bromides and start serving up hard medicine."

"Unfortunately, the men who have to swallow that bitter pill are the same men who are financing your campaign."

"Good God. You sound like Paul." They looked at each other, then laughed. Taking a seat, Quinn smiled at her. "Enough politics. What did you do today?"

"The usual Monday things." Did she imagine the shadow that crossed his expression?

"I hope your Monday errands included ordering a new wardrobe."

"You'll have to sell the ranch to pay for all the materials and trimmings I purchased. I ran into Miss Teasdale at the fabric shop, and she'll call tomorrow to discuss designs and begin measurements and preliminary fittings."

"It can't happen soon enough."

Lily studied him then glanced at the door and said in a low voice, "Am I so like her that you need clothing you haven't seen before to remember that I'm not her?"

"You are so unlike her that I wonder I ever thought you were similar." He stared at her and knots appeared along his jaw. "Right now, I look at you, and it's impossible to believe anyone could mistake you for her." He shook his head and his voice roughened. "It's you I see, and you I want."

Her breath caught, and she closed her eyes, letting her head drop against the top of the settee. She wanted to believe him.

Lily's days of leisure, of lazy mornings and long afternoons with nothing to do but nap or read, were over. Marietta Teasdale arrived shortly after Lily's morning meeting with Cranston, and the fittings continued until luncheon. In the afternoon, she repaid calls, shopped for trimmings recommended by Miss Teasdale, and planned her Friday at-homes.

If the weather was fair, Daisy laundered personal items on Monday. Fresh linens and Quinn's shirts were returned and soiled items collected by a Chinese family who owned a laundry in Chink Alley. On Tuesday, wood and coal were delivered, and the iceman came on Wednesday. On Wednesdays, Quinn dined at his club and didn't return home until a few minutes after nine. The cook had Thursdays off, so that evening they had a cold supper. On Friday, Lily received. On Saturday, she ordered fresh flowers from the hothouse a block off Broadway, then Morely drove her along the boulevard, and she nodded out the carriage window to other ladies in the promenade.

In the evenings, Paul usually came for supper or for coffee in the family parlor. After thirty minutes, Lily left the men to their politics and retired to her bedroom to read or to discuss the next day's ensembles with Elizabeth.

And always there was Quinn and the heat between them. The long, smoldering looks of hunger, the appetite barely in check. Some nights, he stood in the doorway connecting their rooms and stared at her without speaking. Other nights, he sat on the end of her bed and they talked. He didn't touch her when she was in bed, and she understood. They would not have been able to stop with touching. There were nights she wanted him so much she wouldn't have cared, didn't want to wait for a silly thing like new clothing. It was Quinn who insisted.

"I'll keep my word to you," he'd said, his gaze on the nipples rising beneath her thin nightgown. "If it kills me, I'll keep my word. I want you to be very sure that it's you I see."

"Waiting may kill us both," Lily had whispered in reply.

During the first week of December she asked Morely to drive her to the Prospect Hill Cemetery above Cheesman

Park. There, kneeling in the fresh snow that covered the graves like a fleecy blanket, Lily gently placed a bouquet of hothouse roses and baby's breath against Susan's headstone and felt a lump rise in her throat.

But it was Rose she grieved for, not tiny Susan whom she had never held to her breast. Days passed when she did not think of Rose at all, then something would be said or something would happen or she saw a little girl and suddenly her stomach cramped and her heart ached and she missed Rose like an amputated limb.

Her daughter was growing up hundreds of miles away, a small stranger whom Lily wouldn't recognize if the child appeared on her doorstep. Remorse and longing brought tears to her eyes, and she had stumbled blindly back to the carriage and then had spent the remainder of the day curled in her bed longing for a faraway child whom she didn't know.

One thing she did not do as she settled into her life as Miriam Westin. She did not call on Helene Van Heusen.

Chapter 14

"Your mind wasn't on the game," Quinn commented as he and Paul stepped out of Babbit's House, one of the more elegant saloon and gambling houses crowding Blake and Larimer streets. "Usually faro is your forte."

"I'm ready for supper and some talk," Paul said shortly, tapping his top hat into place.

None of Denver's streets was paved, but this section of town near the railroad tracks received enough traffic that even the gravel had vanished, driven into the mud by wheels and hooves and boots. A constant flow of raucous revelers moved in and out of the entertainment establishments, and loud piano music poured over the swinging doors, spilling into frosty air.

Periodically, the saloons and parlor houses were raided and closed for as long as it took the proprietors or madams to pay their fines and renegotiate bribes. Petty crime ran rampant, hustlers worked the shell game on corners, and snake-oil salesmen arrived on every train.

Respectability was slowly chipping at Denver's notoriety as a raw frontier town, but not quickly enough to suit men like Quinn. Many of the silver barons had built mansions and brought their families to the hill, and a prosperous middle class had opened shops along Fifteenth Street.

However, there were still brawls in the street, and Denver's residents were no strangers to gunfire.

Once Quinn was governor, he would use his influence to elect the next mayor. He wanted an incorruptible law-and-order man, a man who shared his views of Colorado's future and Denver's role as the emerging state's capital.

"Would you prefer the club or a hotel for dinner?" he asked, pausing before the window of a gun shop to admire a collector's set of dueling pistols. "Charles Girtler was in my office today. He mentioned the club has some California strawberries. Imagine. Strawberries in December." If it wouldn't have made him feel like a moonstruck swain, he would have purchased a box of strawberries from the club to take home to Lily.

"Girtler stopped by your office?" Paul inquired.

"It was a legal matter. We didn't discuss politics."

"Then he didn't flay your hide for championing water management to the grange members?"

"It has to come, Paul. The state has to manage its resources."

Paul's lips thinned, and he thrust his hands into the pockets of his coat. "You're walking close to the line, Quinn. There's been talk. Men you don't want to offend have been asking what kind of governor you'll make if you're this hard to control now."

Anger flushed his face, and he hailed a hansom as a diversion, giving himself a moment to control his temper. "How did you answer?"

"I said I'd speak to you. Again."

Quinn stepped inside the hansom, and the cab moved toward quieter streets. He had been a brawler as a litigator, and he was a brawler still. It was his style to confront the issues head-on and fight his opponents to the resolution he wanted. Despite the growing list of concessions he'd made, compromise rubbed against the grain.

"When *do* we address the critical issues? At what point do we stop feeding audiences pap and start giving them something meaty they can sink their teeth into? When do we stop pacifying a few profit-hungry moguls and start righting wrongs and planning for genuine progress?"

"The truth?" Paul stared at him. "Maybe never. At least not during your tenure as governor."

"Then why have I compromised an integrity I was once proud of? Why all the lies, all the acts we've dismissed as necessary evils? For what purpose? If getting elected isn't about change or progress or the future, then just what the hell is it about?"

"Power. Damn it, Quinn, it's always been about power."

And there it was, the fundamental difference between himself and Paul Kazinski. When power was the objective, the end justified the means. No act was too heinous. No solution too ruthless.

Ethics and moral dilemmas were left to men like him, men for whom power was less important than accomplishment. Paul lost no sleep playing the game of when-did-it-begin-to-go-wrong. He doubted Paul lay awake nights attempting to trace back the chain of concessions and compromises and mistakes and bad decisions made for wrong reasons. It was unlikely that Paul avoided his own eyes in the mirror.

After they had been seated at a linen-draped table gleaming with heavy silver and had drinks in hand, Paul leaned forward in his chair. "You need to ask yourself if you really want to be governor."

"After everything I've done? The answer should be obvious."

"Yes, it should. That it isn't is worrying a lot of people. If you want to be governor, then you have to play the game. No one wants a maverick in the capital. The party needs to trust that they can depend on you to protect the interests of those who'll get you elected. They don't want any unpleasant surprises. Your political boat's wobbly right now. Rock it anymore, and you'll tip yourself out."

Quinn's fingers drummed on the tablecloth, and he frowned into his whiskey. He had come too far to quit. He'd find a way to live with whatever concessions he had to make until after the election. Once he'd been elected, the party could go to hell. Then he'd be his own man.

"Now we need to discuss Miriam. I've received a bit of disturbing news. I've been informed that Miriam has been spending a lot of time shopping for fabrics and trimmings. Am I correct to assume this indicates she's coming out of mourning?"

"At my request." It exasperated him that even in private, Paul strove always to refer to Lily as Miriam.

"And why, may I ask, would you decide to widen her sphere of exposure and broaden the risk of detection?" Paul inquired coldly. "And have you considered that once Miriam reenters society, problems surface that we didn't address. Handwriting, as one example."

"Lily is practicing Miriam's signature." He swallowed his whiskey and shrugged. "I'll write any obligatory acceptance or thank-you notes."

"And cause a minor scandal. Husbands do not write their wives' duty notes."

"I believe we can survive this small ripple in the etiquette pool," Quinn said, his voice equally cool. "We promised her soirees, musicales, balls. Then dressed her in mourning and broke our promise." He stared across the candles. "Do you ever grow weary of making promises you know you won't keep? I do."

"You're sleeping with her, aren't you?"

Quinn half rose from his chair. "That is none of your business. This conversation has ended."

Paul waved him down. "It's my business since I'll have to manage the inevitable problems that will arise." Frowning, he leaned back as their entrees were served. "All right," he said when the waiter departed. "You ignored my advice. You know I don't agree with this decision, but what's done is done. Now we deal with it."

"There isn't going to be a Lily problem. She understands that our association ends after the election. Nothing has changed in that regard."

Paul pulled a notebook from his jacket and placed it on the table. "It shouldn't be too difficult to find and hire a forger to write the necessary acceptance, thank-you notes, and whatever other correspondence is required. A potentially dangerous solution, but I'll handle it. It's better than having you write them for her." He made a notation. "You'll receive a flurry of last-minute invitations the instant it's known Miriam's mourning period has ended. We'll decide which parties, balls, et cetera will be the most politically productive. On the positive side, with Miriam out of mourning, we can put her on the podium with you for the dedication ceremony for the war memorial. Give you a more visible image as a family man."

He should have anticipated that no decision was simple, that there would be repercussions and a loss of control.

He was also reminded of why he and Paul had been friends for so many years. Paul would fight hard to steer a decision in the direction he wanted, but win or lose, once the decision was made, Paul didn't look back. There would be no reproaches, no I-told-you-so's or recriminations. If the decisions went bad, Paul would focus his energy on solutions.

"I'll need to review precedence with her. Go over protocol." Paul looked up from his notebook. "Can your wife dance a credible waltz?"

He had no idea. "She can learn."

A thoughtful look narrowed Paul's eyes. "If I didn't know you were too smart to be foolish, I'd say you were half in love with her."

"Oh for God's sake." Quinn pushed his plate away and leaned back. "I admire her, that's all. It requires courage to face people who may denounce you at any minute. Determination to learn all we've demanded that she learn, and willpower to make herself into something new. She's bright and resourceful. She's taken a greater interest in the household accounts than Miriam ever did, and she's more aware of costs. I've yet to hear her complain, and she's deeply appreciative of the opportunity to live graciously and well."

"As I said, I could almost believe you're half in love with her."

Love is the wrong word, he told himself irritably. *Lust would be more accurate.*

Tomorrow, Lily would don bright colors and come out of mourning. His palms grew moist, thinking about what that meant and remembering a promise he'd been waiting to keep.

*   *   *

Lily found it nearly impossible to swallow a bite of her ham and eggs. Already she had an eye on the clock, waiting for darkness and the moment when Quinn would take her by the hand and lead her upstairs. She had awakened this morning with a pounding heart and the remnants of a feverish dream lying damp on her skin. An hour later, her cheeks were still warm and flushed.

Quinn wasn't eating his breakfast either. For the last fifteen minutes, he'd held his newspaper before his face, staring at her over the pages, his smoky gaze fixed on her mouth, heavy-lidded with conjecture. With a sound that mixed amusement and frustration, he folded the paper and laid it near his coffee cup.

"There's no point going to the firm today. I can see I won't be able to concentrate on torts or contracts."

Lily's eyes widened, and her heart stopped. The color deepened on her throat and her mouth dried. "Surely we aren't going to . . . I mean, it's early and the servants will be . . ."

Slowly his gaze traveled along the contours of her face, traced the shape of her lips, lingered on the full curve of her breast. The low fire at the back of his eyes made her hand tremble around her coffee cup. "I'll instruct Morely to polish and prepare the sleigh. If you agree, we'll drive around the city and show you off in your new red cloak and fur muff, let people notice that you're no longer in mourning. Then if you like, we'll shop for Christmas gifts for the staff. In the afternoon, there's a matinee at Turner hall, an acrobatic troupe is performing I believe. Afterward, we can have dinner out or return here, whichever you prefer."

"Oh Quinn." Both hands flew to her cheeks. "What a wonderful idea!" Excitement sparkled in her eyes. The hours would pass more quickly than she had imagined. She'd be doing something other than waiting in a torment of heightened nerves. "I'll wear the toad green walking suit with the red-and-blue trim."

"Toad green?" he asked, laughing.

She made a face at him. "It looks better than it sounds." Jumping up before he could rise to assist her, she pressed her hands together and peered out the windows of the breakfast room at grey skies and low clouds. "I can't eat another bite. I'll run upstairs and get ready immediately."

Lily didn't think of herself as a neglected wife because she was not his wife, and because her own days were busy and full. But there were times when she wished they spent more time together as she enjoyed his company and the exciting physical current that pushed and pulled between them. And occasionally she felt a pang of loneliness during the evenings when she dined alone, or evenings when political matters called him away, or the nights he spent closeted in the library with Paul and other political leaders. The rare treat of having Quinn for a whole day to herself thrilled her.

Especially today. And tonight . . . But if she let herself dwell on tonight, she would explode with anticipation and nervousness.

"Let me look at you," he murmured, before they stepped into the sleigh. Holding her at arm's length, he smiled at her red cloak and the flounces of toad green that rippled past the fur trim. His eyes locked to hers, and his voice dropped to a husky whisper. "You are so beautiful."

She felt beautiful this morning. Until she'd donned the green ensemble, she hadn't realized how weary she was of blacks and browns and greys. For the rest of her life she would associate those dreary colors with Miriam, who had worn so much mourning in her life.

Today, with her red cloak swirling about her, she felt like a blazing column of fire, glowing inside and out. Her eyes sparkled, and her cheeks were pink from excitement and the crisp cold air. Today, for Quinn, she was a rainbow of color. Red and green, and blue trim, and blond wisps floating in the silver vapor that misted around her lips.

Even Morely appeared to approve her brightened appearance. He gave her a wide, gap-toothed smile along with the fur lap robe.

"I love this!" Lily said happily, leaning against Quinn's shoulder. Sleigh and harness bells harmonized in a jingling melody that made people smile as they passed. The air was cold enough to bring a shine to her eyes and turn her lips rosy. Beneath the fold of the lap robe, Quinn took her hand, and she wished it was warm enough to pull off her gloves so she could feel his skin. "I used to dream of riding in a sleigh when I was in Arizona, but I never thought it would really happen."

They traveled as far north as the gas works, then back through the streets of town, and then east to watch ice skaters gliding on the lake and the young people sledding down McGreggor Hill.

Lily couldn't resist. She was out of the sleigh the instant Morely halted to give them a view of the lake. She couldn't sit still another minute, wrapped in Quinn's warmth, their lips almost kissing when they turned to speak to one another. She needed to walk, wanted to run, needed to do something to release the tension drawn tight by the touch of his body and the thrill of his whisper in her ear.

When Quinn climbed down, she hesitated, biting her lips, then bending swiftly, she scooped up a handful of snow, formed it into a ball, took aim, and let fly. Quinn's hat sailed to the ground, and he gaped in astonishment. Grinning, she molded more snowballs and managed to pelt his shoulder and chest.

Laughing, Quinn sent a snowball flying in her direction. Within minutes others had noticed then joined them, and the air thickened into a blizzard of flying snowballs. When Quinn finally helped her back into the sleigh, they were both covered with snow and weak from laughter.

They both knew a snowball battle was something Miriam Westin would never have engaged in, would have been appalled to contemplate. They also knew they had been observed, and mild gossip would result. But today it didn't matter. Today was theirs, and the rules had melted away.

Nothing mattered but the smoldering promise in Quinn's eyes, and the mounting anticipation that pounded in every quickened heartbeat. The tension and physical awareness wound tighter with every passing hour filled with teasing glances and provocative, suggestive whispers.

Arm in arm, they strolled along Fifteenth Street, peering into shop windows. They purchased holiday gifts for the household staff and a few of Quinn's major clients. Quinn bought her a nightgown with a daring lace bodice. She bought him a silk paisley smoking jacket. He bought her French perfume that reminded Lily of a rose garden. She bought him a beaver-brimmed Stetson which he wore the rest of the day.

They lunched at the Lindall Hotel, but neither did more than sample the items on their plates. They flirted and laughed and drank too much wine. Lily rubbed her boot along his pant leg under the table, and Quinn suggestively circled his thumb on her palm.

No real lady created a spectacle of herself as Lily suspected she was doing, flirting and laughing in public. She didn't give a flying fig. Today, she was happily herself, or at least the hybrid creature she had become. After weeks of watching her p's and q's, of trying to move through her days with Miriam's sad eyes and slumped shoulders, she gave herself this one gloriously charged day as Lily.

The suspicious, almost defeated woman who had left the prison had vanished over the weeks. Her natural vivaciousness had resurfaced, accompanied by a newfound confidence that surprised and delighted her.

"You are simply astounding," Quinn murmured in a gruff voice. He hadn't looked away from her since they sat down. "Dazzling. Amazing. You're incandescent today; you blind me."

Intoxicated by wine and each other, they drove to Turner Hall for the matinee, but afterward Lily remembered none of the acrobatics or the tumbling acts. What she remembered was losing herself in the grey smoke of his eyes, watching his lips form words, thrilling to his fingers on the back of her hands, at the nape of her neck, brushing her cheek. They touched each other, unable not to, and pretended the touches were accidental. Their lips almost met when they turned to speak, and they pretended the mingling of breath was not deliberate. They heard the hoarseness of desire in each other's voices and pretended it was an effect of the cold air in the unheated hall.

When the performance ended, and the audience stood to depart, Lily's bones had turned to liquid, and she clung to

Quinn's arm lest she stumble and fall. Her heart raced, and her fingers quivered on his sleeve. The frosty outside air felt good against feverish cheeks. Lifting her face to the darkened sky, she let a light drift of snow collect on her eyelashes and drew a deep breath of cooling air.

"Open your eyes," Quinn said in a low voice.

"It's snowing."

"That's not what I want you to see." Placing his large hands on her shoulders, he turned her to face the waiting sleigh.

"Oh!" Her gloves flew to her cheeks and her eyes widened, then she laughed in delight.

While they'd been inside viewing the performance, Morely, following Quinn's instructions, had filled the sleigh with hothouse roses. Hundreds and hundreds of red and white roses covered the seats and the space between, spilled over the edges.

Whirling, Lily caught Quinn's face between her hands and kissed him deeply, her joyful gratitude impulsive and enthusiastic. Small hisses of shocked disapproval registered around her, but she hardly noticed.

Running to the sleigh, returning Morely's grin, she gathered an armful of roses and lowered her head to inhale their lush fragrance. "How will we get home? We'll crush them! The thorns . . ."

"I ordered all thorns removed. If you receive a single prick, I'll buy the greenhouse and raze it to the ground," Quinn said, smiling broadly at her pleasure.

After bowing, he handed her into the bower of roses, and the scent of crushed roses enveloped her. Before they drove away from Turner Hall, Lily threw roses to a small group of children who had appeared to stand and gape.

Now that it was dark, she snuggled against Quinn's chest, and he put his arm around her. Roses lay under their feet and beneath their bodies, atop the lap robe and spilling from the sides of the sleigh.

To Lily the world faded, and they were alone in a snowy garden. She didn't remember ever being this happy. Lifting her face into the falling snow, she tried to tell Quinn that she had never had a day like this one and what it meant to her, but his mouth smothered her words in a kiss that seared flesh and bone. Beneath the mounds of roses, his hands found the edges of her cloak and slipped inside, covering the warm swell of her breasts. A moan issued from her parted lips, and she arched to fill his palms. Dropping her own hand beneath the roses, she touched him and gasped as he did when she felt the rigid heat between his legs.

When his lips released her, Quinn crushed her against his chest. "Heaven help me. I have never in my life wanted a woman like I want you right now," he said hoarsely.

When the sleigh circled to a halt before the mansion doors, he didn't wait for Morely to let down the step or open the door. He vaulted out and did it himself. Then he lifted Lily from the nest of roses and swung her into his arms.

Circling his neck, she leaned back to gaze into his eyes, and what she saw pulled the breath from her body. A tremor raced through her limbs. "Oh Quinn," she whispered. When she realized he intended to carry her inside, she pressed her face against his neck. "What will Cranston think?"

"I don't give a damn."

The front door opened, and he strode past Cranston and up the staircase. When he reached her bedroom door, he opened the latch with his knee, then kicked the door shut behind them.

After setting her on her feet, he cupped her face between trembling hands and kissed her deeply, passionately, completely. His tongue explored, demanded, possessed. Lily's arms dropped to her sides in fainting submission, and her knees crumpled, then she wrapped her arms around his neck and lifted on tiptoe to thrust against him and return his kisses with equal passion.

Locked together, they tore at their clothing, sending it flying about the room. Breaking apart just long enough to throw aside cloak and jacket, reach for each other, part to claw at waistcoat and bodice, they came together again in feverish kisses that left her gasping and shaking. She jerked at his belt buckle and swore in frustration when her fingers fumbled. Mouth crushing hers, Quinn reached behind and stripped open the laces running down the back of her corset.

As he pushed out of his trousers, she wiggled out of whalebone and laces. His hands swept her knee-length pants over her hips and down her legs, and they toppled backward on the bed, locked in each other's arms.

Urgent, wild, frantic for each other, they rolled on the bed and then Quinn was above her and she saw his face in the dim snowy light and she wanted him, wanted him, wanted him. His hand slipped between her legs and she gasped and thought she was fainting, dying, then finally he thrust into her and she grasped his shirt collar with a sound like a sob and opened herself to the fullness of wave after wave of rocking sensation.

They came together with explosive force, too eager for each other's bodies, too impatient for gentle touches and tender caresses. Exploration would come later. Wild in their need, tormented by weeks of teasing glances and touches, by a day of deliberate provocation, of near kisses and suggestive whispers, they surrendered to sheer physical urgency and claimed each other with no thought but that of release from a need that had become desperate.

Afterward, they clung together, spent and gasping, sprawled half-on the bed and half-off.

When he could speak, Quinn lifted on his elbows and stared down at her, his eyes dark as charcoal. "My God."

Slowly Lily's world stopped spinning, and her gaze steadied on his face. His shirt was plastered to his torso as wet with perspiration as her chemise. His hair was damp and his expression softer than she had ever seen it.

Together they slid to the carpet and sat facing each other, struggling to catch a full breath.

When she could breathe, Lily stretched out her hand and gently laid her palm against his cheek. He brought her hand to his lips, and suddenly she felt like weeping. Never in her life had a man made love to her as Quinn had. As if he could not wait another second, as if she were the most desirable woman in the world. And never had she felt the sensations he had aroused with the fire and fury of his need. Her body had awakened as if from years of dreaming, as if she had been waiting for this man, this moment, to experience the full joy of total surrender and fulfillment.

Sitting on the floor in the pearlescent darkness of a snowy night, she let her fingertips explore the strong line of his jaw, the curve of a full lower lip. She touched his broken nose and traced the dark slash of his eyebrows, and marveled at this splendid man.

And she knew there would never be anyone else for her.

No other man could arouse her as Quinn had. No one else would ever summon the wildness of urgency and passion, or the feelings of tenderness she felt now.

Leaning forward, he kissed her lips, gently, his mouth warm and light. Then he rose and brought her a wrapper from the armoire and assisted her to her feet before he found his trousers and pulled them on.

"I'm going next door to my room. I'll order a basin of warm water." After lighting the gas lamp on the wall beside her vanity, he scanned the room with a smile and a wave. "Perhaps you could . . ."

"I'll sort it out," she said, laughing at the tangle of clothing strewn across the floor and chairs.

"Are you hungry?"

"Famished! But . . ." She caught sight of herself in the vanity mirror and gasped. Only one looped curl had survived intact. Her tangled hair flew about her shoulders, hung down her back. Her lips were red and swollen, and a rosy flush lay on her throat like a sunburn. "I can't possibly . . ."

Quinn smiled. "We'll have supper in my room." His eyes darkened and slid over her. "Don't change a thing. Don't brush out your hair, don't remove the rest of your clothing. I want to look across the table and see you as you are now, warm and tousled, and wild."

She didn't obey him, of course. After Cranston laid out a cold repast on the table near the window, Quinn carried the basin of warm water through the connecting door and discovered she had brushed out her hair and tied it at the nape with a lavender ribbon. And unless he guessed wrong, she had removed the perspiration-soaked chemise and her stockings.

When he untied her wrapper and eased it off her shoulders, he discovered he was correct and she was naked.

"What are you . . . ?" But her eyes turned sultry, and she smiled at him in the vanity mirror.

Watching in the glass, he slid the wrapper to the floor and exposed her naked body as he had wanted to do for weeks.

Gaslight had been created to flatter women. The warm golden glow smoothed out any small imperfections, cast intriguing shadows between her lush breasts and between her legs. Placed a shine of mystery in her eyes and gleamed softly on parted lips.

Quinn inhaled deeply, staring at her in the mirror. Her breasts were full and pink-tipped. Her waist a sweet curve flaring into smooth pale hips. When he saw the blond triangle between her legs, lush, lovely, promising enchantment and fulfillment, he groaned softly and lowered his face to her hair.

Turning her in his arms, he kissed her deeply, his hands moving to cup her buttocks and pull her roughly against him. He had intended to bathe her, but the sight of her body inflamed him.

This time, he slowed the pace of their lovemaking, controlling his compulsion to immediately gratify his own selfish urges. There were other needs equally as satisfying. The need to stroke his hands over her skin and her magnificent breasts, the need to taste the salt on her throat and the texture of her nipples and the heat between her legs. The need to inhale the musky scent of their mounting passions. The need to feel her thrash beneath him and whisper his name in a voice husky and frantic with desire.

She was as uninhibited and as unself-conscious as he

had fantasized she would be. She gazed at him with unabashed curiosity, explored as he had explored, and his throat grew full with gratitude that he had found her.

How could he let her go?

"Tell me about the paintings," she said near midnight, after they remembered the supper Cranston had delivered hours ago.

Quinn lowered a chicken leg and blotted his lips with a napkin. "I spent a year in the Italian countryside and fell in love with Italy. Someday I'd like to live there."

"You should have been a cat," she said, laughing. "You need nine lives. You want to be a rancher and a governor, maybe a lawyer, and now an Italian."

"What do you want to be?" he asked, refilling their wineglasses.

"Me? I don't know." Turning her head, she watched the snow pelting the windowpanes. "I know I can't go back to being what I was before . . ." A wave indicated his bedroom and the rooms beyond. "When I think about Rose and me living in Europe, it's a blur because I've never been there, and I can't imagine it. But I know we'll be living among strangers and a long long way from home." She turned her lavender eyes to him. "Do they celebrate Christmas in Europe?"

"Yes," he said, trying not to laugh. She was wise in so many ways, ignorant in others. He looked at her across the table, and he wanted to open the world for her, to watch her face as she saw Rome the first time, or Paris. He would have liked to show her the world's great architecture and sculpture and paintings.

"Well, you can't," she said, looking down at her hands

as he told her a little of what he was thinking. "You have a state to govern."

Firsts were magic and could never be repeated. It pained him that someone else would be with her the first time she saw the Mediterranean, and the Parthenon, the Louvre and Versailles. He didn't pretend that she would lack for male company. Her beauty and the polish she was acquiring would attract suitors like moths to a flame.

Nor was she a woman to stand in the shadows and merely observe. Lily would want to run barefoot on the shores of the Mediterranean, would insist on touching cool marble sculptures, would lean her nose up near the world's great paintings. She would never be content to drift through Europe—or life—as a shadow. For her the world was meant to be touched and tasted, heard and inhaled. Experienced rather than witnessed.

"What?" he asked when he realized she had asked a question.

"Where do you go on Wednesday nights?" When he didn't answer, she gave him a look of uncertainty. "I think I understand your schedule except for the regular appointment on Wednesday night." Her hand lifted in a gesture of apology and frustration. "I guess I'm asking . . . do you have another mistress?"

He made himself smile. "I'm flattered, but one mistress at a time is all I can handle." Changing the subject, he asked a question of his own. "Do you dance?"

Placing her elbow on the table, she propped her chin in her hand and gave him an exaggerated look of superiority. "I am the epitome of grace and dexterity on a dance floor. Women collapse in tears of envy when they observe my waltz."

He laughed. "Paul will be delighted to hear it. I believe he envisions a rushed course of dancing lessons."

She grinned at him. "I learned in prison. Before she poisoned her husband, my friend Ida was a music teacher. She taught young ladies and gentlemen to play the piano and dance."

"Your friend the poisoner," he repeated with a smile.

"Paul's going to be angry about today, isn't he?" A sigh lifted her shoulders, and she leaned away from the table. "I started a snowball fight." Lifting a hand, she ticked down her fingers, listing her transgressions. "I drank too much wine, I laughed and flirted over lunch. And, the worst, I kissed you in public."

Paul was also not going to be happy when he heard that Quinn had filled the sleigh with roses.

"There'll be some gossip," he agreed with a shrug.

"I'm sorry. I really didn't mean to create a problem. I just wanted a day without rules. A day when I could be me."

That's how he liked her best, when she was Lily, not Miriam. Lifting his wineglass, he looked past her at the snow piling on the sill. And he remembered Paul's concern that he was falling in love with this unique and enchanting woman.

Chapter 15

"I thought I heard you come in about an hour ago," Lily said, setting aside the book she'd been holding in her lap. It was Christmas Eve, and things had been going so well between them. She'd expected him earlier tonight.

"I only just arrived." Leaning over her, Quinn kissed her lightly, tenderly, his mouth lingering, then he poured them both a cup of hot spiced wine from the punch bowl near the Christmas tree.

How strange. Lily had been so certain that she'd heard him at the door that she had run upstairs to find him. She hadn't heard him moving about his bedroom, and he hadn't responded to her rap at the connecting door. Still, she'd been so positive he was home that she'd looked into every room.

"I'm sorry I wasn't here for supper, especially tonight," he said, warming himself before the fire. "In politics, there is always a crisis it seems, even on Christmas Eve. Well, shall we light the candles on the tree?"

Abruptly she noticed that his hair was not damp although heavy wet snow had been falling for the last hour. And he didn't have the fresh cold scent about him that he usually carried in from outside.

He was lying about having arrived home only minutes ago. He must have been in his bedroom and must have chosen to ignore her knock at his door.

Incidents like this jolted her and brought her up short. Each night when Quinn held her in his arms, her heart soared, and she felt as if she were part of him and always would be. She forgot there were sections of his life that remained closed to her. Forgot the dark ambitions that condoned deceit, lies, the secrets he carefully guarded. Her spirits plummeted.

"My aunt thought it was foolish to chop down a tree, drag it inside the house, then place lighted candles on the branches," she said finally, gazing at the Christmas tree. While she'd been waiting for him, her thoughts had turned toward Missouri and Christmases past.

This Christmas Aunt Edna would decorate her farmhouse with a few pine boughs and hang a wreath on the door as she did every year, Lily thought, *but there would be no tree for Rose to gaze at in wonder. No shining ornaments or lovely candles. There would be no pile of gaily wrapped packages bearing distinctive ribbons from expensive shops.*

Rose's Christmas gifts, like Lily's so many years ago, would be a pair of mittens, new wool stockings, perhaps a warm coat if her old one could not be mended again. And maybe, if there was enough money, the rare treat of an orange in December.

"It's Christmas Eve." Setting his wine aside, Quinn sat beside her and stroked her cheek with the back of his fingers. "I wanted this to be a happy Christmas for you. Did something happen today to dash your spirits?"

She wanted to say: You lied to me.

But there were other things that hurt, too. "I've been thinking about Rose off and on all day. I've never had a Christmas with her." A lump rose in her heart.

If Lily had been home, she would have insisted on a tree. It wouldn't have been as tall or as beautiful as the tree before her, wouldn't have been decorated with exquisite ornaments or expensive beeswax candles, but Rose would have had a tree. And Lily would have made sure there was a gift for her daughter that wasn't practical, something frivolous and wonderful like a china doll with gold hair or a jack-in-the-box or a book of fairy tales with colorful illustrations.

Quinn closed his eyes briefly, then stroked her fingers. "You'll be with her next year."

But next year she wouldn't be with him. She and Rose would be somewhere in Europe, and Lily would be missing Quinn as badly as she missed Rose tonight. By now she should have known that it wasn't possible to have it all. Life didn't work that way. Not for her. For every plus, there was a minus.

Frustrated, she started to tell Quinn that she wanted Rose *and* him even though she knew that dream could never be possible. But when she turned to him, the words died on her tongue. A deep weariness lay at the back of his eyes. The vertical lines creasing his craggy face from cheek to jaw were deeper, and his gaze seemed troubled and far away.

"Did your meeting go badly?" she inquired, pressing his hand. She couldn't be near him without wanting to touch him. Even stroking his fingers thrilled her. "You seem low in your mind tonight."

"It gets harder and harder to hide things from you," he replied, his smile humorless. Leaning back on the settee, he rubbed the bridge of his nose and passed a hand over his face. "I apologize. On the way home tonight, I let myself think about all that's happened this year and how many things have changed."

Lily turned her gaze toward the fire in the grate, aching inside. Last year Miriam was here. He and Miriam had lit the Christmas candles together, had sat before their tree and wished each other a merry Christmas. Miriam would have been pregnant with Susan, blissfully happy that it appeared she would finally carry a baby to term. They would have talked about the baby and the new house and a future that must have appeared smooth and filled with all good things.

Now Susan slept beneath a blanket of snow, and Miriam was gone.

Gently, Lily withdrew her hand from his. She didn't belong here, not tonight. The gifts beneath the tree were tagged with Miriam's name. Miriam had chosen the ornaments that decorated the branches. Miriam must have dreamed of this night; it should have been Susan's first Christmas. Wherever Miriam was, she, too, must be thinking of the disasters the year had wrought. And like Lily, Miriam would be thinking with anguish about a lost child. Was she also missing her husband? Regretting that she had run away? Yearning to come home?

"Suddenly I feel like crying," Lily whispered.

"Next year you'll be with Rose," Quinn repeated, his eyes on the tree. He gave his head a shake and emptied his cup of hot wine.

If his statement was intended to comfort or cheer, it didn't. While Lily longed for her daughter, the thought of being reunited with Rose also terrified her.

"It's so confusing. Tonight I long for her. But sometimes I think it would be best for Rose if I never went home again. What if I'm a bad mother?" she asked in a voice so low that Quinn had to lean to hear. Lifting her head, she looked at him with tortured eyes. "Sometimes I get so frightened. I don't know anything about children, and I haven't had a chance to learn. And what if she doesn't like me? What if she's ashamed of me?"

She hadn't forgotten the things Quinn had said the first night she'd talked to him, and she had thought a lot about the impact of her choices on Rose. She had brushed Quinn's statements aside and insisted that the rules didn't apply to her. And they hadn't, not then.

Oddly, it was Miriam who was showing her the value of rules. When Miriam broke the rules and ran away from her husband, her decision had altered the lives of many people. There was Quinn, of course, and Paul. The servants Quinn had replaced and those he had hired. Ripples extended to Helene Van Heusen and the mysterious Mr. Ollie and the boy beside the City Ditch. And Lily most of all. If not for Miriam, Lily would still be in prison.

In her case, breaking the rules had burdened Aunt Edna with another child to raise, had deprived Rose of a mother and Lily of her child. Breaking the rules meant that Rose was a bastard with an ex-convict for a mother. A mother who had never been there for her. A mother bowed with guilt and remorse. Blinking hard, Lily stared at the Christmas tree.

She and Miriam were alike in so many ways. They were even alike in the pain they had caused the people who might have loved them.

"I'm sorry she isn't here tonight," Lily said in a low voice.

Quinn placed his large warm hands on her shoulders and turned her to face him. "You'll be a good mother because you want to be. And you'll be living in Europe, where no one knows your past and where bastardy isn't the stigma that it is here. Rose won't be ashamed of you if you teach her that everyone makes mistakes and remind her that you paid dearly for yours. She will love you," he promised.

He thought she was still talking about Rose. Maybe it was better that way.

Tilting her chin, he kissed her, his mouth warm and heavy with promises for later. Then he looked into her eyes. "Now. What else is bothering you?"

"It's hard to hide things from you, too," she said with a faint smile. Drawing a breath, she nodded when he asked if she wanted more wine. "Helene Van Heusen called today."

Stiffening, he turned from the punch bowl. "Did you receive her?" he asked sharply.

"No. She brought us a gift. A plant in a pot tied with Christmas ribbon."

Quinn swore softly. "I wouldn't have thought Helene would breach etiquette to the point of calling when you haven't returned her calls. This is the second time she's left a card, isn't it?"

"Yes," Lily admitted uncomfortably.

What she didn't tell him was that Helene had also left a letter for her. In the letter Helene apologized profusely for whatever offense she had unwittingly committed that had resulted in the end of a friendship she had valued and cherished. She begged Miriam to please tell her how she had offended, so she could rectify the wrong at once. And she mentioned that she was not alone in her suffering. Another suffered as well. She implored Miriam to call on her, if not for her sake, then for the sake of a mutual friend whose concern approached despair.

Quinn returned to the settee and frowned. "Of course you didn't accept the plant."

"She left it at the door with Cranston."

"Instruct Cranston to return the damned thing tomorrow."

"That seems so rude," Lily said, slowly, watching his expression. "Is it really necessary or wise to make an enemy out of Helene?"

"We've discussed this. Helene is firmly in the enemy camp already. Her objective is to elicit information that her husband can use against me to his candidate's advantage."

His jaw tightened in an expression that Lily recognized. In fact, she had seen it mere minutes ago. His lips twitched at the corners, and he pushed a hand through his hair. Behind his eyes truth warred with fiction. This time he didn't lie, he said nothing.

Lily would return the plant as he insisted. But she also knew she would disobey him and call on Helene Van Heusen.

For weeks she had vacillated between wanting to learn more about Mr. Ollie and an instinct that warned her to let sleeping dogs lie. What purpose would it serve to learn the details of Miriam's secret? And she really didn't want to know if the relationship with Mr. Ollie had progressed beyond the meetings at the City Ditch, shrank from learning the extent of Miriam's betrayal.

It wasn't curiosity that had renewed her decision to call on Helene. It was the hint in Helene's letter that Mr. Ollie or M or whoever he was, was becoming unmanageable. Helene had raised a niggling fear that unless Lily sent a message through Helene, Mr. Ollie might attempt to approach her directly. That would be disastrous. Her impersonation of Miriam was adept enough to deceive women who had known her casually or as a social peer, but she doubted she could deceive a man who had known Miriam intimately, perhaps as a lover.

"Have we covered everything? Or is something else troubling you tonight?" Quinn asked gently, smoothing an errant curl behind her ear.

"One more thing. And Quinn, I reserved the most upsetting item for last."

Alarm darkened his eyes and his expression sobered. "What it is?"

"I must beg your forgiveness." She spread her hands, then stared down at her lap. "You haven't mentioned it, but I know this has been on your mind every waking moment exactly as it's been on mine. I can't think, I can't sleep or eat. I'm terribly distraught."

"For God's sake! What's happened?"

"Pretending it didn't occur won't change the fact that our lives are ruined." She cast him a sidelong glance. "I . . . I'm so desperately sorry that I trod on your toes when we danced at the Halversons' ball."

He stared at her.

"I know I humiliated us both. We'll now be social pariahs. And this after I swore to you that my waltz was flawless."

It was Christmas Eve. The only Christmas she would ever have with a man she was falling hopelessly in love with. When she remembered this special night a year from now, she did not want to regret that she had ruined it with depressing talk and a despairing mood.

"I've wept all day, knowing how angry and disappointed you must be. I've destroyed the slippers that offended by stamping on your toes. I wouldn't blame you if you can't find it in your heart to forgive. I can't forgive myself. My only recourse is to throw myself out of the window and end this shame."

Quinn fell backward on the settee and laughed until his eyes were moist. "Oh my darling. You are so unexpected, so . . . Come here," he said gruffly. Taking her hand, he led her to the doorway and stood her beneath the mistletoe. "Let's begin again. Good evening, Mrs. Westin."

She wrapped her arms around his waist and smiled up at him, her eyes shining with the love that flooded her heart. "Good evening, cowboy. Did you have a good day?"

"Very productive, thank you. And you?"

"Cranston and I reviewed the arrangements for tomorrow's brunch, and I checked the gifts to be certain we haven't overlooked anyone." They would entertain the servants in the formal receiving parlor. After the buffet, Lily would distribute gifts, and Quinn would give each employee an envelope containing an extra week's pay.

Leaning back in his arms, Lily warmed herself in his smile. "Everyone except the Blalocks accepted your offer of taking the day off to spend Christmas with their families." But it would be like having a day alone as they seldom saw the Blalocks in any case. Mary Blalock's arthritis made descending from the third floor difficult, and Lily had seen her only three times since arriving. James Blalock reported directly to Quinn.

"How do you want to spend our day alone?"

"I know exactly," she murmured, gazing up at the mistletoe with a sparkling flirtatious glance. "The instant everyone has left the house, I think we should run upstairs and jump into bed. We'll spend the day reading and . . ." Lifting on tiptoe, she kissed his earlobe and released warm breath in his ear. "Cook is leaving us cold ham and fresh bread and cheese. I'm sure you can find a bottle of good champagne. We won't answer the door, we won't do anything sensible. We'll eat and read and make love all day."

His gaze softened, and he pressed her hips next to his so she could feel his powerful reaction to her suggestion. "You are every man's dream of the perfect mistress," he murmured before he bent her into a passionate kiss.

It was a lovely compliment and should have made her happy.

The week between Christmas and New Year's was crowded with teas, soirees, musicales, parades, dinner parties, and culminated in a gala New Year's Eve ball. And these were the invitations they had accepted out of the flood of cream-colored envelopes that had arrived once it was known Miriam's period of mourning had ceased. They had rejected an equal number of invitations as having conflicting times or dates or because one event was less politically advantageous than another.

Lily leaned back in her office chair and handed Paul an envelope stuffed with names, addresses, and notations as to the type of note required. "Tell Mr. Smith"—she didn't know the forger's real name and didn't care to know—"most are thank-you notes. Two are acceptances. One is a letter of condolence. Mrs. Alderson's father passed on three days ago."

Paul placed the envelope inside his jacket and reached for his coffee cup. He nodded at her appointment book. "We want you on the podium for Quinn's speech Tuesday night. It will be similar to last week's event." He hesitated. "We've had time to conduct an informal straw poll, and your presence was well received."

Lily smiled. "You could look happier about it."

He considered her for a moment, then closed the door of her household office. "You scare the hell out of me," he said quietly, returning to his chair beside her. "You're as unpredictable as Quinn. In retrospect, being the first to jump to your feet and applaud was inspired. I'm sure you read the newspaper accounts."

"The charming Mrs. Westin will be a gracious and enthusiastic first lady should Westin win his bid for the statehouse," Lily quoted, pleased with herself.

"Enthusiastic is not a word that leaps to mind when one thinks of Miriam," Paul said, lowering his voice to an annoyed whisper. "And regardless of the voters' fickle approval, no true lady would have forgotten herself to the extent of being the first to stand and applaud."

Her smile faded and she sighed. "I haven't had a cigar in weeks. I can't recall the last time I had a whiskey."

"I can tell you exactly when you last disgraced yourself by kissing your husband in public," he snapped.

"And you've pointed it out at least a dozen times. What you haven't mentioned is how well I've conducted myself at the soirees, balls, and throughout the constant rounds of calling and receiving!" She glared at him. "You drive me crazy. You're always criticizing, refining, molding me into her. Then you turn around and remind me that I'm not her."

She admired Paul for his unflagging loyalty to Quinn, for his political genius, for his attention to detail and his dedication. For the rest of her life, Lily would be grateful to him for all he had taught her, usually with patience and good humor.

But she never forgot that Paul could send her back to Yuma and Ephram Callihan. He didn't mention the threat, but it was always there between them. As long as her fate rested on his whim, they could never be friends, would never be entirely comfortable with each other.

Paul's single-minded objective was to see Quinn sworn in as Colorado's first governor. He'd made it clear that he viewed Lily as a solution to one difficulty but also as a potential problem that could get worse.

"We haven't discussed your altered arrangements with Quinn."

"Must we?" she asked, keeping her voice light.

"This deception is a dangerous situation that could explode in our faces at any time," he said, speaking slowly, his eyes narrow on her face. "Because the impersonation has been successful so far, does not mean that it will continue so. What I'm saying is I'll breathe a huge sigh of relief when you are on your way to Europe. Do you understand?"

"How could I not? You've said the same thing over and over in a dozen different ways."

"And I'll continue to say it. I watched you dancing with Quinn at the New Year's ball. You were wearing your heart on your sleeve." Leaning forward, he touched her wrist. "You're making it very hard on yourself. Quinn has a wife, Lily. He'll never marry you, and you can't remain in Denver a minute longer than necessary. The risk is too great."

In a gesture that had become habit in moments like these, Lily twisted Miriam's rings around her finger. "I know all that," she said defensively. "I'm not looking for marriage, I never have. I know what I agreed to, and I'll honor my word."

Then she humiliated herself by bursting into tears.

Lily promised herself that she would call on Helene after Quinn's next speech. Then she decided to wait for a clear dry day. When she ran out of excuses, she pinned on her hat with a grim expression and instructed Morely to drive her to the Van Heusen residence, hoping she could trust him. Of course she could.

But there were disturbing hints that Quinn occasionally spoke to Morely regarding her journeys. Once or twice he had inquired about her visit to someone before she mentioned she had called on that particular lady. The reminder that dark undercurrents flowed between them hurt because she loved him.

It was no longer possible to deceive herself, she thought, brooding as the hansom drove her to Stout Street. Right or wrong, wise or foolish, she loved Quinn deeply and completely.

She loved his strong craggy face and hard-muscled body. She loved the sound of his deep gravelly voice and the rumble of his laughter. She loved the way his eyes softened when he looked at her over the pages of his morning paper, and the sound of his boots on the marble floors when he returned in the evening.

She no longer scorned his ambition; she admired his dedication to worthy goals. Now she had listened to his speeches, had heard political arguments at her own table, and she wholeheartedly applauded the aims he hoped to achieve. If the party would permit him to do so.

She loved the way he made her feel, as if she were an enchanting, desirable woman, as if her past did not matter. He made her believe that her perspective on his world interested and delighted him. And there were moments that he looked at her with sorrow deep in his eyes and she believed it would be as painful for him to say good-bye as it would be for her.

She loved him despite the secrets between them, the areas of his thoughts and life that she was forbidden to enter.

When the carriage rocked to a stop before Helene Van Heusen's stately home, Lily peered out the window, then straightened her shoulders and bolstered her resolve.

She had secrets, too.

Chapter 16

Helene Van Heusen received Lily in a room as lavishly appointed as Helene herself. Small ornamental tables crowded with bibelots nearly obscured a richly patterned Turkey rug. Billowy French silk concealed walls and ceiling, creating an illusion that one sipped tea inside an Arabian tent. Enormous velvet pillows and overstuffed furnishings completed an impression of opulent oriental indolence.

Helene gripped Lily's hands and led her to a settee covered in peacock green brocade, sinking down beside her in a rustle of elaborately draped skirts. "Oh my dear, forgive my tears of joy." If a drop of moisture clouded Helene's eyes, Lily couldn't spot it. "When the plant was returned, I feared our estrangement was complete. I've been distraught, simply distraught. First you vanished, and I thought you were dead, then I found you again, and then it appeared you were lost to me once more. In my heart, I know this is Quinn's doing, but one torments oneself. Could I—I?—possibly have offended?"

"Helene—"

"Your expression tells me everything." Her black eyes snapped beneath a fringe of white bangs. "It's *him*. Once again he's trying to keep us apart. I don't wonder that you fear and despise him. He's an overbearing brute."

Lily's eyebrows lifted. What on earth had Miriam told this woman? Or . . . could it have occurred the other way around? Was Helene placing ideas and images into Miriam's mind?

"I wouldn't say that Quinn—"

"It's outrageous. He all but keeps you locked away like a prisoner, deciding whom you may see and whom you may not. He neglects you shamefully. He's never considered your wishes. And now I hear he's forcing you to attend those boring political rallies. He's willing to sacrifice even you to the flames of his ambition. I'm so furious on your behalf, darling. But you've always known his priorities." Helene made a tsking sound, conveying sympathy and anger.

Lily observed the performance with fascination. She had met women like Helene in prison. Manipulative women with a talent for convincing others what they should think and feel. Women who seized upon small bits of information and interpreted that information to suit their own ends.

"I suppose he intends to exploit you to promote the lie that he's a family man. Will he continue to force you to appear at his speeches?"

Yes, she could glimpse how Helene had extracted information from Miriam under the guise of concern. "I really don't know," Lily replied warily.

"You poor dear, putting yourself on public display must be agony for you. May I hope for your sake that Quinn hasn't browbeaten you into sharing the dais during the debate at Turner Hall?"

"He isn't forcing me." Lily lowered her gaze and smoothed her hand across the brocade seat of the settee as she imagined Miriam might have done. "I'm learning to take an interest in politics."

"You?" Helene laughed. "My dear, I know you better than that. You've never supported Quinn's overweening ambition. And certainly you needn't play the loyal wife with me."

Lily was beginning to grasp Helene's value to her husband. Helene was attempting to shape Miriam's attitude in a direction damaging to Quinn and damaging to their marriage.

Lily would have wagered the diamond earrings she'd received from Quinn for Christmas that the Van Heusens' candidate would have his wife present when he and Quinn debated next week. If Helene couldn't prevent Miriam from being at Quinn's side, she would at least make certain that Miriam felt forced, resentful, and deeply uncomfortable.

"Well, my dear, if you are indeed taking an interest, perhaps you can settle a rumor that suggests Quinn wishes to impose restrictions on the mining industry." Not one to overlook an opportunity, Helene seized the moment to extract what she could. "I should think such a position would create dissension within his party." Raising a questioning eyebrow, she waited.

Lily arranged Miriam's sweet sad smile on her lips. "It's an interesting issue. Does your husband's candidate support mining regulation?"

"Not publicly, of course. But he—" Helene drew back and her gaze sharpened. At once she realized she had been about to offer a tidbit whereas Lily had revealed nothing. "How very odd," she commented thoughtfully. "You've changed remarkably, Miriam. You hardly seem the same person."

Careful, Lily warned herself. "I hope I've changed," she said in a small voice. "I had much time to think while I was in the sanitarium. I need to improve myself, to become stronger and less shy. I'm trying to do that." And now she took the first step toward resolving what Paul would have referred to as the Helene problem. Lifting her head, she met Helene's intent gaze. "I've thought long and hard, and I've decided to do all I can to make my marriage succeed."

Helene was held rigid by her corset, but even so she appeared to visibly stiffen. "I'm utterly astonished. You cannot possibly forgive all the wrongs Quinn has done you!" She waved a hand. "Need I remind you that he manipulated your father and forced you into a marriage you didn't want? After which he has proceeded to neglect you and treat you with insulting indifference. And Miriam"—her eyes narrowed into an intent angry stare—"he has made you suffer. How many tears have you shed? How many pillows have you drowned?"

"I fear I may have overstated my situation in the past. Or perhaps I was feeling sorry for myself. We do love each other. Quinn has many fine qualities. He—"

"Fine qualities?" Disbelief snapped in Helene's black eyes. "The only thing Quinn Westin cares about is himself and placing himself in the governor's seat. I've told you before, and I'll say it again. He doesn't care about you, Miriam. He never has, and he never will. If you die tomorrow, your husband will rejoice." She took Lily's hands. "Now don't cry," she said, although Lily's eyes were shocked but dry. "I beg you, think about Marshall, your solace and comfort. Marshall adores you. He worships the ground you walk. If you only knew how frantic he's been since Quinn disposed of you and sent you away."

M had a name now. Marshall. "Quinn didn't dispose of me," Lily said, trying to suppress the sharpness in her tone. She found it difficult to disguise her dislike and her resentment of the ugly ideas Helene was attempting to inject into Miriam's perceptions. "I was desperately ill. And distraught after the fire and . . . and Susan's death."

"And with good reason, dear. And so was Marshall. I'm sure it won't surprise you to learn that he visits poor little Susan's grave each time he comes to Denver."

An alarming picture began to emerge. Helene knew a great deal about Miriam's history, and she had preyed on Miriam's loneliness, planting ideas and opinions detrimental to Quinn and to Miriam herself. She was the conduit to Marshall, a relationship she clearly championed. Most startling, Helene had just made a disturbing implication.

The question was, did Helene really know something, or was she speculating, fishing for confirmation of suspicions?

Giving herself a moment to think, Lily fumbled with her purse. She withdrew a handkerchief and dabbed at her eyes. "How unexpected and touching." She paused. "How sweet of Marshall to be so supportive of a friend." She made a sniffing sound into her handkerchief, wishing she could see Helene's expression. "His loyalty only makes it harder to do what I must. But . . . when you next see Marshall, you must tell him that I cannot meet him again. Please explain that I've settled my differences with Quinn, and we're very happy. I hope Marshall will be glad for me."

Helene's mouth dropped open. "Miriam! You can't mean that!"

Darting a glance toward Helene, she saw astonishment, then anger, before Helene hastily regained her composure.

"If my marriage is to succeed, I cannot continue meeting Marshall privately. I know Quinn would not approve."

"Darling, I'm very confused. Why on earth would you wish to preserve a marriage that you didn't want and which has only brought you suffering? And abandon a man who has adored you for years?"

For years? Lily blinked. *Had the meetings with Marshall gone on for years?*

"Don't do this to yourself. Surely you deserve a little happiness. Is that too much to ask? After all you've been through?"

Oh Miriam, Lily thought angrily. *Were you that lonely and sad, that filled with self-pity, that easily led? Why did you let her speak to you like this?*

And Helene was definitely attempting to manipulate, her goal predictable to one with eyes to see. When the moment was ripe, the Van Heusens would expose Miriam's foolishness, and the resultant scandal would defeat Quinn at the polls.

"Helene," Lily said, choosing her words carefully, "my friendship with Marshall could so easily be misconstrued and twisted into something ugly. I've made a very dangerous mistake by agreeing to see him privately. I can only thank God that nothing grievous resulted."

"Nothing grievous?" Helene repeated, almost sputtering. "Miriam, you astonish me. Marshall and I have feared for your life! And there's Susan, and—" She waved a hand, conveying the impression that she could go on and on.

"You've been a dear friend, and I regret involving you in my small adventure. I trust you'll support my decision to repair my marriage." Lily arranged a thin smile on her lips. She was determined to win the battle of who would tell whom what to think. "Quinn has been wonderful. It's like a second honeymoon." She couldn't manage a blush, but she tried to look modestly blissful. "Perhaps you heard that he filled our sleigh with roses. It was such a lovely and romantic gesture."

"I'm speechless. I hardly know what to say." Agitated, Helene rubbed her hands together. "I must think about this."

Lily took Helene's cold hands and gave her the best fluttery Miriam smile she could manage. "When I was in the sanitarium, I realized I love my husband, and he loves me. I'm as much to blame as he for our previous difficulties, but we've put that behind us. We're deliriously happy." She hoped she wasn't laying it on too thick.

"Happy?" Helene stared at her. "He's forgiven you?" She hesitated, then added bluntly, "For having an illicit affair and bearing another man's child?"

The hesitation gave her away, telling Lily that Helene was guessing. She didn't know quite as much as she thought she did. But the question gave Lily the opportunity she had been seeking.

Jumping to her feet, she stared down at the settee with cold eyes. "How dare you! I open my heart, and in return you offer an unforgivable insult. I'm shocked and deeply offended that you would place such a scurrilous connotation on my friendship with Marshall. To suggest that Marshall was the father of . . . that we . . ." Closing her eyes, she swayed. "I truly believed you were my friend."

Helene looked astounded. She also came to her feet and attempted to grasp Lily's hands, but Lily jerked away. "My dear. Forgive me if . . . wait! Miriam, please." Color blazed on her throat. "You must admit you've said things that suggested . . . and Marshall has also hinted, so naturally I assumed . . . Miriam!"

"This insult to me, to Quinn, and to Marshall is inexcusable. I shall never forgive you!" Whirling, Lily rushed out of the silk-draped room and hurried down the walk to the waiting carriage. She instructed Morely to take her home.

Falling backward on the seat, she closed her eyes and drew several deep breaths. She doubted Helene would trouble her again, but her mind was reeling with what she had learned today.

Every detail concerning the Turner Hall debate had been examined, discussed and dissected at least a dozen times. With the election three months away, interest was heating and focusing tightly on the candidates. A mistake at this juncture would be costly.

Lily sat in on the nightly strategy sessions, remaining quietly in the background, listening as she served refreshments to Paul and the party leaders who had taken over the library.

To her surprise, her statement to Helene had been correct. Because politics were important to Quinn, politics had become important to her. She understood the issues now, and shared his frustration when the party leaders did not agree with his passionately held opinions, or insisted that Quinn avoid controversial topics. Paul and other party leaders had drafted ambiguous responses for Quinn to deliver if journalists or voters raised questions that would prompt unpopular answers if Quinn answered directly and truthfully.

She began to understand that Quinn was a man mired in deceit. When they were alone together, she saw glimpses of the real man, as he saw glimpses of the real Lily, but she never saw the complete man stripped of the murky deceptions that permeated all areas of his life.

Minutes before he had taken her arm and led her up the steps to the dais, his frown had steadied on the podium and his fists clenched. "They won't see or hear me," he had murmured angrily. "Hell, even I don't know who I am anymore."

Now Lily sat with a row of dignitaries, looking out at 170 faces, but her mind drifted from the opening speech delivered by Quinn's opponent.

No one saw or heard her either. And she no longer knew who she was.

Miriam's gestures and mannerisms were habitual now. She had conquered her initial reaction to the mansion, and although the size of the house still felt oppressive, sometimes she found herself taking an undeserved pride in the beauty of the rooms. She answered easily to Miriam's name, was living Miriam's life, doing the things Miriam had done. She uneasily protected Miriam's secrets as if they were her own.

The person who had been Lily Dale emerged less and less frequently. No one saw her. On occasion Quinn and Paul thought they glimpsed the old Lily, but they didn't because that Lily no longer existed. They saw the hybrid creature she had become. Or they saw Miriam as Miriam might have been.

Disturbed, she watched Quinn replace his opponent at the podium and begin the speech she had listened to him practice. Tall and heartachingly handsome, he addressed his audience with characteristic confidence and no hint of the fatigue she knew he felt.

Today he wore denim trousers, a leather jacket, and boots. Unlike his opponent, who had chosen a morning coat, waistcoat, and stock, Quinn had dressed like the majority of the men in the audience. Paul's strategy was to sell Quinn to the voters as the people's choice, and that identification would be achieved through subtle as well as blatant means.

The deception wasn't total. This was how Quinn dressed on weekends when he wasn't going in to his law firm. But it wasn't a true picture either. Little of that which the voters saw or heard today was genuine. Quinn was not giving the speech he wanted to give, not addressing the issues he cared passionately about. The woman who had been introduced as his wife was not his wife. It was all a web of lies and compromise.

Bending her head, Lily touched gloved fingertips to her forehead. She loved him, and she wanted him to win the election. After all he had gone through, he deserved to snatch the prize at the end. He deserved an opportunity to find himself again. Once he was free of the party's hold, once she was gone, he would have a chance to cast off the layers of deceit that disturbed him so greatly.

An enthusiastic pounding of applause startled her and she looked up to see her counterpart, the wife of Quinn's opponent, rising to her feet. The speeches had ended. Hastily Lily stood, clapping and pasting a smile on her face. One of the party minions arrived to assist her off the dais and was kind enough to bring her a chair.

Folding her hands in her lap, she sat near the exit, watching the audience crowding the dais, and took pleasure in noticing that more men seemed to rush toward Quinn than toward his opponent.

When a man halted before her, blocking her view, she waited impatiently for him to move along, remembering to demurely lower her eyes to the floor.

Her gaze settled on brown boots beneath dark trousers. And her breath hitched when she noticed an odd-shaped white stain on the left boot. Her head snapped up, and her heart stopped.

Ephram Callihan curled his lip in what passed for a smile. "Well, well, if it ain't Lily Dale, all gussied up and looking better than I ever imagined was possible."

Shaking and white-faced, Lily sprang up on trembling legs, clutching the back of the chair to support herself. She couldn't speak, couldn't breathe. For one terrible confused moment, she thought he was here to take her back to prison.

"Looks like you got yourself a sweet deal," Callihan commented, sliding a slow look from the tip of her hat down her rust-colored cashmere suit. "Diamond earrings and tassels on your boots. Yes sir, you sure have come up in the world. Got yourself a new name and a rich husband. This is some game you're working."

"You've mistaken me for someone else," Lily whispered.

"That's what I thought." He laughed. "I been looking at you for two hours and telling myself, no sir, that can't be Lily Dale. Can't be. Lily Dale ain't no lady and Lily never looked that good in her life." His eyes narrowed down on her. "But it's you all right. The eyes, the voice." Lifting a hand, he stroked one of the long blond curls lying on her shoulder. "I ain't got your game figured out just yet, but I think I see the outline." His gaze settled on the diamonds in her ears. "And there's money here. I can smell it."

"Take your hand off my wife's shoulder."

Quinn stepped between them, tucking Lily behind him. Rage simmered in his slate eyes. Any man but Ephram Callihan would have backed away from Quinn's expression and would have apologized profusely.

Callihan's smile was more of a smirk. "Just talking a little bidness with your—wife."

"Whatever you have to say to Mrs. Westin, you can say to me." The words were as sharp as a cold blade.

At once Lily understood that Quinn didn't recognize Callihan, didn't know who he was. He had no idea he was staring at the death of his dreams. Feeling sick inside, Lily gripped his arm. "Not here," she said in a low voice. If others heard what Callihan might say . . .

She was too shaken to notice where Paul came from, but he suddenly appeared beside them, his eyes as hard as dark stones. Clasping Callihan's arm, he smoothly turned him aside and two burly men fell in behind them. In less than a minute, the four men were out the door.

Quinn clasped her arms and frowned down at her. "Are you all right?"

"Yes." Her knees gave out and she collapsed onto the chair. "I don't know."

"Who in the hell was that?"

She gazed up at him, her heart in her eyes. It would destroy her if something or someone from her past was the cause of his downfall. They had worried that someone would realize she was not Miriam. They hadn't worried that anyone would recognize she was Lily Dale.

Whatever Quinn read in her expression, it was enough that he didn't press for an answer. Taking her arm, he escorted her out of Turner Hall, pausing to shake hands and accept congratulations for his speech. Lily's smile was wooden and her eyes dazed. The short journey from the hall to their carriage seemed endless.

Once they were inside the carriage and Quinn had covered her with the lap robe, he took her hand and studied her white face. "He's someone you know," he said flatly. After she revealed Callihan's identity, Quinn closed his eyes and let his head fall back on the upholstery. He swore softly.

"I'm so sorry," Lily whispered. Her teeth chattered, and she couldn't get warm. Even the tears hanging in the corners of her eyes felt like droplets of ice.

"I forget who you are and where you came from," Quinn said after a minute. "Who are you, and what was your life like, Lily Dale?"

She rested her head against his shoulder and battled the tears clogging her throat. "I'm just someone who has spent a lifetime doing things I didn't want to do. Doing what other people said I should."

"And it's still happening," he said. Putting his arms around her, he dropped his face to her hair. "This time I'm the man forcing you to do something you don't want to do."

But she was where she wanted to be. Loving him, wanting him to have his dream, had changed so many things. She no longer thought about the circumstances that had placed her in his life, the days of seething resentment were far behind her.

"Who are you, Quinn Westin, and what has your life been like?" she asked in a choked whisper.

"I used to know who I was and what I stood for, but that's not true anymore. My life isn't that different from yours. First it was my father, now it's men like Paul insisting that I do things I don't want to do." He fell silent. "It starts with one compromise or maybe one small lie, and it builds like a snowball. Then one day you look in the mirror and ask, how is it possible that I've done the things I've done? How did this happen?"

"I used to ask myself over and over if shooting Mr. Small really was an accident or something I intended to do. I don't know. I don't know how I got to a place where shooting a man was even possible."

She felt him nod, and his arms tightened around her. "Then one day a face steps out of the crowd and you're confronted with what you've done and what you've become," he said, speaking more to himself than her.

"What will happen next?" Right now, with his arms around her and his steady heartbeat beneath her cheek, it was difficult to believe their house of cards was about to fall. Her thoughts were too frozen to move beyond that image.

"I'll meet with Paul. We'll assess the threat. Discuss possible solutions." He shrugged and turned his face to the window. "We'll do whatever has to be done."

Lily nodded, but asked no questions.

Their lovemaking was tender and slow, as if tonight were the last night they would have together and every caress, every kiss and touch must be deliberate and cherished before being committed to memory.

Lily closed her eyes and arched her throat to the kisses moving toward her breasts like slow fingers of flame. Her hands moved through Quinn's silky thick hair, and she whispered his name over and over.

If there were no mansion, no beautiful clothes or jewelry, this would be enough. To lie in the arms of a man whose hands were magic, whose mouth was alternately hard and demanding, then sweet and tender. A man who knew her body more intimately than she did. A man who trembled when she touched him, who took her to heights she had never experienced.

For the rest of her life she would remember these deep snowy nights and the bliss she had found in this bed in Quinn's arms. No other man could ever make her feel as beautiful, as desirable, as necessary.

She wanted to tell him that he had awakened her body to joy and wonder, that he had taught her that lovemaking needn't be a hasty affair conducted in the dark. She wanted to tell him that a look from those smoldering grey eyes ignited fires in her stomach, that his hoarse whisper made her ache with wanting him. She wanted to tell him that his skin beneath her palm felt like warm satin, his kisses were like fiery nectar. He tasted like smoke and snow and whiskey and sometimes like apples. She wanted to tell him that she loved him and needed him like the air she breathed.

But she said nothing.

Chapter 17

Paul suggested his home as a secure location to discuss the Callihan problem. As he lived alone, there was no danger of servants or law clerks overhearing damaging information. He led Quinn and Lily into his library, where a low fire burned in the grate and a whiskey decanter waited on the long library table he used as a desk. After pouring a drink for himself and Quinn, he frowned at Lily.

"I didn't expect you. There's tea in the pantry if you don't mind fixing it yourself."

Lifting her chin, Lily helped herself to a whiskey and took a long, defiant swallow. Since she hadn't accepted anything stronger than wine in two months, tossing back a whiskey told Quinn how upset she was. And the face she made when the whiskey hit the back of her throat told him how much she had changed.

"I insisted on coming because I caused this problem."

"That isn't true," Quinn disagreed, holding a chair for her. His fingers brushed the silky coil of hair knotted beneath her hat, and the scent of roses drifted through his senses. "What have you found out?" he asked Paul, wrenching his thoughts from Lily and focusing on the problem at hand.

The snowy glow from the library window didn't reach

this end of the long, narrow room, but light cast by the wall sconces exaggerated the fatigue deepening the lines on Paul's forehead. Silently, Quinn studied his friend's face and vowed to remember that the campaign was equally exhausting and wearing on those who labored behind the scenes. As the election drew nearer, pressure mounted, and Paul's role had become more demanding.

"First," Paul said, watching Lily shake her head, sigh, then set her whiskey glass on the table and fold her hands in her lap. "Quinn's right. You aren't to blame for the current situation." A shrug shifted the shoulders of his dark jacket. "Ephram Callihan's father died shortly after the new year. He's in Denver to settle details of the estate. He's been staying with his sister's family."

Lily stared, her eyes cold. "It's hard to imagine that bastard having a family."

"It was sheer happenstance that he attended the speeches. Boredom, an interest in the politics of a neighboring territory, who knows? But it's clear he did not go to Turner Hall expecting to find you on the dais."

"So it was merely coincidence," Quinn said, thrusting a hand through his hair. Exposure had always been a threat, he'd known that, but he hadn't anticipated it would occur as a result of coincidence. He swore softly.

"Callihan's wandered close to the truth," Paul continued. "Once he convinced himself that it was indeed Lily on the dais, he set about constructing an explanation to account for her being introduced by another name and as the leading candidate's wife. He decided I found you a wife in the Yuma Women's Prison, then I invented a history for her and for you. In Callihan's guess, I created a made-to-order background for my candidate."

"By now, he will have identified the holes in that theory," Quinn said, rubbing the bridge of his nose. "A fictitious background wouldn't survive the intense scrutiny of a campaign. And if you'd wanted a wife for a candidate, you would have selected a woman with impeccable credentials."

"Exactly." Paul nodded. "You're wealthy, social, and can offer a wife a position as first lady of the new state. If any woman would serve, finding a bride would not be difficult. There's no reason to choose a woman with a distasteful and damaging past."

Quinn frowned. "Must you be so blunt?"

"He's right," Lily said softly. "You're also correct to assume that Callihan is shrewd enough to conclude he doesn't have all the pieces and to set about assembling them."

"I intend no offense, I'm merely stating the truth as Callihan will see it."

"No offense taken," she said with a shrug. But circles of crimson burned on her cheeks.

Paul removed his jacket and leaned back in his chair. "It won't take long for Callihan to discover this is not a recent marriage, and a little more investigation will produce a description of Miriam Westin. If he checks the newspaper archives, he'll learn about the fire and Miriam's departure for the New Mexico Territory. At that point, he'll begin to put it together. He'll resist the idea of Lily being a twin for Miriam, but eventually he'll arrive at that conclusion as the only answer that fits what he knows."

Lily looked at them both. "And the next question will be, where is the real Miriam? Why was it necessary or desirable to use me to impersonate her?"

As these were questions neither he nor Paul could address, Quinn didn't pick up the questions she left dangling.

He tossed back his whiskey and poured another. "Callihan wants money, of course."

Paul nodded. "The price of silence will go up when he works out more of the truth." Paul's hand curled into a fist on the tabletop and he swore. "I keep telling myself we've solved the Miriam problem, then here it comes again. Damn it!"

Walking to the window, Quinn thrust his hands in his pockets and stared out at the slushy street. "What happens if we don't submit to Callihan's blackmail? In your opinion, will anyone believe his story?"

"He's the warden of the prison where Lily was incarcerated. That will lend credibility. He can produce documents from her trial and from her time in prison, plus he can bring forth other people who knew Lily. A determined journalist could find the places we stayed in route to Denver. Lily will be remembered.

"Against that, we have Miriam's friends, who will swear that Lily is Miriam. Pride won't permit them to admit the possibility of being deceived by a woman who was in prison a few short months ago." Paul looked up. "My best guess? Our defense is weak. More people will believe Callihan. He can destroy us."

Lily looked down at her lap. "I've made mistakes. Small errors that Miriam's acquaintances will remember if my identity is questioned." Her voice sank to a whisper. "I'm so sorry, Quinn."

"You've done nothing wrong," he said, turning from the window. He could no longer remember the gaunt, suspicious woman he had first met. She had changed, softened, had become a caring, lovely woman.

And he loved her.

"You've done everything we've asked of you, learned what you had to," he said, staring at her. "You've succeeded better than I dreamed possible. Everyone who sees you believes you're Miriam."

Raising her head, she met his eyes in a long look, and he understood she wondered if he, too, saw Miriam when he looked at her. God help him, the answer was occasionally yes. Sometimes, when he was tired or distracted, he saw Miriam's fluttery gestures, Miriam's eyes and sad half smile, and for a moment she was Miriam.

But never in bed. And never when they could speak freely or when they were alone. Then she sat like Lily, talked like Lily, moved like Lily. And that's when he loved her most.

"The bottom line is that we can't permit Callihan to talk," Paul said flatly. "A scandal at this critical point would take you out of the race. Until we decide on a long-term solution, we'll have to pay whatever he demands."

"A long-term solution?" Lily repeated, turning back to Paul.

"After the election we'll be in a better position to handle the problem. We can apply pressure to the newspapers not to print any inflammatory tales. We can have Callihan run out of the state." He shrugged. "By then you'll be in Europe, and everyone here will believe Miriam is dead. If Callihan comes forward at that time, he'll be despised for attempting to sully the governor's late wife. His story will appear to be politically motivated." Paul thought for a moment then gazed at Quinn. "In fact, if Callihan goes public after Miriam's funeral, we can probably work his story for some political mileage. We tie him to the opposition and disgrace them for attacking a man who just buried his wife."

One of the talents that made Paul so effective and so valuable was his ability to consider several possible outcomes at once and develop tactics for all feasibilities.

Lily stared at them. "It always shocks me when the two of you discuss Miriam's funeral so casually. I detest that in both of you."

"She's never coming back, Lily." There were times when Quinn wished he could tell her why he knew this with absolute certainty.

"It's business," Paul said coolly.

Knowing Lily was upset, he briefly touched her shoulder before he sat beside her and drained his whiskey glass. "The obvious solution for the present is to meet Callihan's demands."

"Who pays the bastard?" she asked sharply. "You? Or the party?"

"Ordinarily the party leaders would be aware of every detail concerning their candidate."

"But not this time," Lily said softly.

"Quinn and I have been friends for many years. I know how he thinks, I know who he is. I believe Quinn is the best man to be our first governor. I've chosen to handle the Miriam problem privately to spare the party undue anxiety." What Paul didn't say was that the party might very well have selected another candidate had they been aware of the difficulties with Miriam.

That's where it had begun, with one man's ambition and another man's belief.

Quinn stared across the library table. "Do you still believe I'm the best choice? After all our disagreements?"

Paul returned his gaze. "Yes."

"And you two believe that only the people in this room know the truth about Miriam," Lily stated, frowning at them. "And now Ephram Callihan, God rot his soul."

Turning his face toward the window at the end of the room, Quinn wondered if anyone ever knew the truth about another person. Each of them believed he knew the truth about Miriam, but their truths were different.

Paul's truth was that Miriam was a bomb waiting to explode, a problem that wouldn't remain solved. Lily's truth was that Miriam had been a lady and a bereaved mother, a woman who had become part of herself. And his truth? His jaw tightened. His truth haunted the attic of his mind.

That night he learned that Lily's truth ran deeper and truer than he had let himself suspect.

"Quinn?" she called softly, rapping at the connection between their bedrooms before opening the door. Hesitating in the doorway, she clutched the collar of a blue wrapper close to her throat.

Leaning back from his desk, Quinn admired the gaslight gleaming in the loose fall of her wheat-colored hair. A heart-shaped face, pale skin, light hair, and those magnificent lavender-blue eyes imparted an impression of tender fragility. With Miriam, her appearance had matched her character. But Lily was neither delicate nor fragile. She was strong and courageous in her determination, and he thanked God for that. Yet seeing her now aroused his protective instincts. He wanted to gather her into his arms, hold her, and shield her from life's bumps and bruises. He wanted to wrap her in security and safety and happiness.

"I'm sorry to interrupt . . ."

"Come inside," he said, swiveling in his desk chair to

enjoy watching her walk toward him. It still surprised him that two women who looked identical could be so different. To the best of his recollection Miriam had never rapped at his door, had never stepped foot in his bedroom, had never sought him out at this hour of the night. She hadn't talked like Lily or moved as Lily did, in a way that made his mouth go dry with awareness of her hips and buttocks and milky thighs.

"I know you reserve Wednesday nights for yourself . . . but I need to speak to you."

His eyebrows lifted. He had lied to her about dining at his club on Wednesdays. That wasn't where he went. "Please sit down." He dropped his pen into the inkwell. "I was going through the accounts, bringing the books up-to-date. It's time to quit for tonight. Would you care for some sherry? Brandy?"

"No, thank you." She took a chair near his desk and crossed her legs at the knee, something she knew Miriam would never do. At this hour of the night, artificial constraints dropped away, and she became his Lily, the Lily that only he knew or saw. Her breasts lifted beneath the blue wrapper as she drew a deep breath. "I don't want to tell you this, and I'm dreading it, but there's something you need to know."

"Tell me what?" he asked, smiling. Frankly he welcomed whatever problem had raised the turbulence in her eyes. After dealing with knotty campaign issues, an irritating problem at the firm, and Callihan's blackmail, it would be a relief to solve a household difficulty for her.

"I don't know where to begin or how to tell you," she said in a low, husky voice. Her fingers moved over her lap, plucking at the folds of the wrapper. Matching slippers peeped from her hem, revealing toes he had kissed and sucked into his mouth.

"Begin at the beginning." When she had finished talking, he would take her to bed and lose himself between her rose-scented breasts. To hell with it being Wednesday night.

"I don't know where the beginning is," she admitted with a frown. "I'm not sure if my obsession with Miriam began that first day, or if it's something that grew as I began to live her life."

Instantly his expression sharpened. Not a household problem, then. Something more serious. Miriam again.

"Quinn, I've disobeyed you." Her chin came up, and she met his gaze directly. "I called on Helene Van Heusen. I'm telling you this because you and Paul need to realize there are people besides Ephram Callihan who know things about Miriam that could be devastating to everything you've worked for."

"Damn it!" Anger constricted his chest and choked his voice, not because she had disobeyed but because now he knew what she would say. An uncharacteristic sense of helplessness that he couldn't admit and, therefore, couldn't express emerged as anger. But there were also legitimate reasons. Carefully constructed plans were beginning to disintegrate like a rope unraveling, each strand curling into a hangman's noose.

His expression alone would have driven Miriam from the room in tears. But Lily looked up at him, gripped the arms of the chair, and held her ground.

"Miriam was having an affair," she whispered.

His teeth ground together so violently that the sound filled his head. Standing abruptly, he strode to the window and jerked back the draperies. A million icy chips glittered across a moonless sky as black as his thoughts.

"Is that what Helene claims?" he asked coldly.

"Don't shut me out, Quinn. It's true, and I think you know it. I haven't put together all the pieces, but I've thought of little else for the last few days. I think you discovered Miriam's affair, and I think you beat the hell out of the man involved."

He'd believed that business finished. But if Lily had discovered Miriam's affair, others might also. Swearing, he struggled against an urge to slam his fist through the window. "Say what you have to say."

She talked for twenty minutes, telling him about a note she had found in one of Miriam's pockets, about a trip to the City Ditch, and about calling on Helene, damn the woman. He listened, standing at the window and staring outside, until Lily made a sound, and he realized she was crying.

"Last night I remembered the locket. You said it commemorated Susan's birth." She held a handkerchief to her eyes. "But you didn't give Miriam the locket, did you? She had the locket made and intended to give it to Marshall."

"Why are you crying?" he asked harshly. He detested it that she knew his wife had preferred another man to him. No matter how she explained the tears, part of what she felt was sympathy for him and that was galling.

"One of the reasons I'm crying is because I think Miriam is dead," she whispered, looking up at him with streaming eyes. "You won't understand this, but . . . Miriam is part of me in a way I can never adequately explain. It goes deeper than just looking like her. I understand her in so many ways. I've walked in her shoes, Quinn. I'm surrounded by her belongings, I'm living her life. I know how it feels to lose people you love, to be alone in the world. And I know what it's like to feel hopeless or trapped. Or to know that you've made a terrible mistake and nothing you do will change it. I've lain in my cell bed and stared at the ceiling and thought I'd be better off dead. I think Miriam killed herself after Susan died, and that makes me cry, because she's me, and I'm her. Part of me loves her, and part of me wants to shake her until her teeth fall out. I feel the pain of her mistakes as if they were mine."

He returned to his desk chair, sat heavily, and dropped his head in his hands. It was all coming apart.

Slipping from the chair, Lily knelt on the floor beside him and laid a trembling hand on his cheek. "Quinn? I beg you. Tell me what happened."

One minute passed, then another, and finally he leaned back in his desk chair and gazed at the window, telling the story of his marriage to the darkness beyond.

"You asked me once if I'd ever loved Miriam. I can't remember how I answered. Perhaps I did in the beginning. But I always knew that Miriam's heart belonged to the man she had planned to marry after the war. She was fond of me, and we got along well enough, but she would have chosen spinsterhood if her father hadn't pressed her to marry."

He fell silent for a time, thinking about their early years together. "I believed I could win my wife's affection, and perhaps I might have if we'd had children. But Miriam's pregnancies ended in miscarriage, and she interpreted the loss of her babies as a sign that we should never have married."

She had withdrawn in silence and sadness and she had rejected his attempts to reach her. After a time, he'd stopped trying. Predictably, they'd become two strangers who shared the same house and a few social activities.

Lily laid her head in his lap, and he stroked her hair.

"I don't know when exactly, but it was probably about this time last year that Marshall Oliver reappeared in Miriam's life. He hadn't been killed in the war as Miriam had assumed. I don't know what the son of a bitch told her to explain why he never returned, but when I checked his background I discovered he married a woman he met toward the end of the war. He was too cowardly to write Miriam and tell her that he'd betrayed his promises. It was easier to let her think he was dead."

Lily looked up from his lap, her eyes wide. "Marshall is married, too?"

"He and his wife live in the eastern part of the territory on a small farm. They have three children." He brushed her lips with his fingertips, needing to touch her. "Marshall's wife has been an invalid for several years."

Her eyes narrowed with contempt. "He really is a son of a bitch!" Then her expression went blank for a moment before a wave of color blazed up from her throat, and a hand flew to her mouth. "It's true, then. I didn't want to believe it, told myself it couldn't be. But the reason you've always sounded so detached from Susan is because—"

"The child Miriam carried to term was fathered by Marshall Oliver," he confirmed in an expressionless tone.

She closed her eyes. "I didn't believe it. But Helene was right."

"Damn that woman to hell," he snarled, speaking between his teeth. "I believe Miriam confided in Helene about her grand love who didn't return from the war. And I believe the Van Heusens traced Marshall Oliver and discovered he was living within three hours of Denver." Bitterness harshened his voice. "I'll go to my grave believing the Van Heusens arranged to reunite Miriam and Marshall, then sat back and hoped something explosive would come of it that could be used to destroy my campaign."

Paul had said it best. How could he sell Quinn as the people's choice if even Quinn's own wife preferred another man to him?

"And something devastating did happen," Lily whispered, staring into his face. "Susan."

Since he and Miriam had not shared a bed for months before she became pregnant, he'd known at once that it was not his child she carried.

"It was a bitter time." Standing, he went to the cart beside the book shelf and poured two brandies. "Miriam was overjoyed by the pregnancy, but distraught about the circumstances. She had to confess the affair with Marshall, of course." That simple statement glossed a period of agony for her and a time of shattered pride and rage for him. He tossed back one of the snifters then refilled it. "I suppose she and Marshall discussed running off together. Maybe they didn't. I don't know."

Lily accepted the snifter of brandy. "They might have discussed eloping, but it couldn't have been a real possibility. Miriam would never have agreed to Marshall's leaving an invalid wife and three children," she said softly. "She simply could not have lived with buying happiness at the expense of another woman's pain. And even though she didn't agree with your decision to run for governor, I'll never believe she would have left you after you announced you were in the race. She would have known the scandal would destroy your chances. No, Quinn. Running off would not have been a genuine possibility. Too many people would have been devastated."

He stared at her. "You astonish me." Miriam had said enough for him to believe that she'd felt exactly as Lily had just described.

The hiss of gas jets was the only sound in the room, and the creak of his chair as he sat heavily.

"Quinn?" Tilting her head, she examined his face. "It was good of you not to cast Miriam off. Many men would have. But if you hadn't already declared for the governor's seat . . . would you still have tried to maintain the marriage? Would you still have forgiven Miriam and tried to accept Susan?"

Had he forgiven her? Not then. But now? He had dealt with the problems, but the healing had not begun until Lily came to him. Now he could accept his share of the blame and move on.

"When I learned about Miriam's affair, I expected her to leave me. I was angry enough that I would have helped her pack and good riddance." He paused to draw a breath. "In the end there was no choice. Miriam had no place to go."

"So you forgave her and beat the hell out of Marshall?"

"That's the gist of it." He drained the last of his brandy and set the snifter aside. "She's my wife, Lily. For better or worse, in sickness and in health. What would you have had me do? Cast her out in the streets? Whatever else she is, Miriam is an honorable woman. In ordinary circumstances, an affair would have been unthinkable to her. I think you know her character well enough to agree. But Oliver was her first and only love. It would have taken someone much stronger than Miriam to resist."

"The Van Heusens exploited her love for Marshall and in the process hurt a lot of people."

He wanted this conversation to end. Even now, pride made it difficult to face that Miriam had never loved him.

That she had merely tolerated him in her life and in her bed and had always held an essential part of herself beyond his reach.

But he understood now in a way he'd been unable to understand in the past. Now he knew what it was to love so deeply that consequences didn't matter. That obstacles seemed insignificant. Now he knew what it was to feel a passion so consuming that reason burned in its path and nothing made sense but surrender. When he looked at Lily, when he felt the magnetic forces irresistibly drawing them, he understood Miriam. She could no more have resisted her obsession than he could resist his.

"Quinn? Do you believe that Miriam is dead?"

"I don't want to think about the past right now," he said, leaning forward to take her hand. Running his thumb across her palm, resonating at the touch of her, he remembered when calluses had hardened the pads of her fingers and her hands had been red and chapped raw. It gladdened his heart to know there would never again be calluses on this woman's hands. Never again would she be forced to engage in hard labor, he thought, bringing her fingers to his lips. He would see to it.

"Oh, Quinn," she whispered. For an instant her gaze was so sad and anxious that he thought for one stunning moment that he was looking into Miriam's eyes.

"It isn't over," she said in a low voice. "Helene isn't sure who fathered Susan, but she suspects it was Marshall. She's been in contact with him. The reason Helene was so persistent about seeing me was to give me a message. Marshall insists on seeing Miriam."

Chapter 18

"Damn it! She called on Helene after you expressly forbade it?" Paul tapped the ashes out of his pipe with short angry raps against the ashtray.

The strategy meeting had broken up half an hour ago, but the library still smelled of cigar smoke and tension. Most of the party leaders supported Paul's tactic of evasion when it came to controversial issues, but a few supported Quinn's desire to put the issues on the table and run a no-holds-barred campaign. Arguments had been strenuous on both sides tonight.

Paul dropped into a chair away from the conference table and crossed his ankles on a low ottoman. "Can we speak freely?"

"Cranston has the night off." He'd dismissed the servants for the evening, and Lily had retired hours ago.

"The Miriam problem was solved. Completely. Now the Miriam problem has resurfaced, and it's beginning to look like we have a Lily problem."

Quinn sank into the chair facing the embers in the fireplace and laid his head against the back cushion. He had stayed at his desk until after midnight every night this week, had given four speeches, had put in a full day every day at the firm. Exhaustion tightened the back of his neck.

He glanced at the clock on the mantel, counting the minutes until he could go upstairs, take Lily to bed, and fall asleep in her arms.

"Lily deflected Helene's suspicions, and when she left the Van Heusens' their estrangement was complete," he said, hearing the weariness in his voice. "Helene won't be a factor in the future."

"But that son of a bitch Oliver will be." Paul swore. "If Lily had ignored Helene, Helene and Oliver would have gone away. But Lily opened a door we thought was nailed shut."

"When you discovered Lily and we put the impersonation in place, the door opened again. Did you really think Oliver would stay away after he learned that Miriam had returned?"

"Didn't you? How many beatings can the man take?"

Quinn pulled a hand down his jaw, gazing at the glow of ash and embers in the grate. "He needs Helene to tell Miriam when he'll be in Denver. With Miriam's connection to Helene severed, he has no way to contact her. There should be no problem."

"There's a problem, Quinn, don't deceive yourself." Holding up a hand, Paul ticked down his fingers. "Lily found a note, and she didn't tell us. She went to the City Ditch and talked to a kid who knows about Miriam and Oliver, and she didn't tell us. She called on Helene Van Heusen, and she didn't tell you until she felt she absolutely had to. Do you understand what I'm saying?"

"The point is, she did come forth."

"The point is, what the hell is she doing? She's prying into private matters that don't concern her and have nothing to do with the success of the impersonation. Where does it end, Quinn? How many blackmailers can we afford to pay?"

"You know Lily better than that," Quinn said sharply. He didn't like the turn this conversation was taking.

"My job is to consider every possibility and solve problems before they happen. If I can. Right now, Lily is dazzled by the big house and carriage, the fine clothes, the places to wear them. She's living a fairy tale, and she thinks she's in love with the handsome prince."

Quinn straightened and narrowed his eyes.

"What happens when you say thank you and good-bye? Is she going to be happy with a modest home and one or two servants instead of a houseful? When she has to check her account books before she orders a new gown? Or is she going to start thinking she was used and underpaid? Maybe she's already thinking that way. So she's nosing around, looking for security. The more she learns about Miriam, the better armed she is to come back at you for more money."

"I'm starting to wonder if our friendship can survive this campaign."

"Think about it. I met with Ephram Callihan yesterday, and he's figured out that Lily is impersonating Miriam. The price went up. Lily could be twice as damaging because she can quote chapter and verse on that one. She could prove her claim in five minutes simply by repeating a conversation she had with someone who believed she was Miriam. How hard would that be for a journalist to verify? Now toss Marshall Oliver into the mix. She's compiling enough information to bury you personally and professionally."

Anger tightened his throat. "Lily would never use Miriam's affair against me. If for no other reason, she wouldn't expose the affair because she wouldn't cause Oliver's wife and children that kind of embarrassment or pain. And we needn't worry about Oliver exposing the affair for the same reason."

"I believe Marshall Oliver was hired by the Van Heusens to romance Miriam, and I think he's still on the payroll. That tells you how much he cares about his family. And believe me, the Van Heusens don't care two cents about causing Oliver's family pain or embarrassment. They'll throw Oliver and his family to the wolves to take you out of the race at the most advantageous moment."

"I repeat," Quinn said coldly. "Lily totally severed the connection with Helene. Oliver has no means to get a message to her. Further, she instructed Helene to inform Oliver that their liaison is finished."

"Miriam already told him it was over, but here he is again. I believe you can thank the Van Heusens for sending Oliver back to your door. God knows what Helene is telling him. Right now, I'd wager my carriage that the Van Heusens are feverishly trying to figure out another route for Oliver to reach Miriam."

They had discussed the affair and every possible consequence throughout Miriam's pregnancy and afterward. Miriam had wept bitter tears and promised never to see Oliver again, and Quinn had beaten Oliver to within an inch of his life. He had believed the possibility of scandal was averted and all that remained was to pick up the shattered pieces of his marriage. Exhaustion tightened the muscles along his neck as he thought of dealing with this problem, this humiliation again.

"Let me ask you something, Quinn. How well do you know Lily Dale? Are you very certain that you aren't blurring the lines and transporting Miriam's character onto Lily? *Miriam* walked away from Oliver presumably to spare his family any embarrassment and pain. Does Lily think the same way? Are you sure? If personal gain were at stake, would she care about protecting the family of Miriam's lover? Lily is a rule-breaker. She puts what she wants before anything else, and the rules be damned. The rules of decent behavior say you don't injure innocent people. Does that describe Lily? Did her innocent daughter ask to be born a bastard? Did the innocent bystander, Mr. Small, request that she fire a bullet into him?"

Tenting his fingers under his chin, he stared into the fireplace. "I assume you paid Callihan."

"You can't ignore this forever. Eventually we'll have to discuss the Lily problem and talk about various bad endings." Paul glanced at the door. "Did you hear something?"

"Paul, Lily has done everything we've asked and more. She's not the same person who had a child out of wedlock or who shot a man in a gambling hall. That couldn't happen now." He paused to consider, his gaze on the embers. "As to how well I know her, I know her well enough to say with utter certainty that blackmail will never be an issue. She'll honor the bargain she made. And not because she fancies herself in love with the prince as you put it. She'll leave quietly and with no threats because that's what she agreed to. Lily Dale is a trustworthy woman. If she weren't, she could have stolen a king's ransom out of this house and left long ago."

"Believe it or not, I hope you're right."

"Lily didn't seek out Helene Van Heusen. Helene came to her with disturbing information, and ultimately she handled the situation to our advantage. I believe her when she says she didn't mention Oliver earlier because she had no way of knowing for certain if I was aware of Miriam's affair. She didn't wish to be the person who told me if I didn't know."

Standing, Paul stretched and yawned. "I just want you to be aware there are alternate interpretations. You know I like Lily, and I've come to admire her." He smiled. "But I see her with clearer eyes than you do."

"If Lily will try so hard to keep the secrets of a woman she doesn't know and will never know, I think I can trust her with my secrets," Quinn said, rising and following Paul to the door.

"You're staking a lot on that hope." Paul paused beneath the foyer chandelier and pulled on his gloves. "You know what the real Lily problem is, don't you?"

Quinn stared at him.

Paul placed his hand on Quinn's shoulder. Sympathy flickered in his eyes. "I'm sorry, but you know there's no alternative. When the time comes, you have to let her go." They shook hands, holding the grip longer than necessary.

Lily knew she shouldn't have eavesdropped. Nothing good ever came from listening at doors. She'd waited half an hour after she heard the meeting adjourn and the men leave the house, then she had gone downstairs to ask Quinn if the meeting had ended well and to learn if he'd convinced the leaders regarding the speech he wanted to give on Thursday.

Then she had overheard Paul mention her name. She'd intended to cough and announce her presence, but she didn't. And after she heard Paul refer to a Lily problem, she couldn't help herself. Careful not to make a sound, she leaned against the wall next to the library door and shamelessly eavesdropped.

And she had overheard enough to chill her. What did it mean that the Miriam problem was solved *completely*? And how could Paul think for a moment that she would ever extort money from Quinn in return for not destroying him? That hurt.

Pacing across her bedroom, she wished she had a bottle of whiskey hidden in her garter-and-stocking drawer. A strong calming jolt would sit well right now.

It also hurt that they dismissed her life as a series of selfish rule breaking, hurt because they were right. But that was then, and this was now. What they apparently didn't notice was that she had grown and changed and learned. Not a day passed that she didn't regret the recklessness of her previous life.

Opening the cedar chest at the end of her bed, she gazed down at the dolls and toys and fur mittens and earmuffs that filled the chest. Every time she went shopping, she bought something for Rose, pretending that Rose waited for her at the mansion.

The items in the chest would not erase the fact that Rose had been born out of wedlock and had no father. Lily couldn't change the past, but she would spend the rest of her life trying to atone and make it up to Rose that she had done wrong by her. And surely she had paid for wounding Mr. Small, hadn't she? Wasn't a five-year hole in her life payment enough?

Did Paul and Quinn believe she was so thickheaded that she hadn't learned the hard consequences of breaking rules? All right, it had taken her a while. But she'd learned her lesson.

After shutting the lid of the cedar chest, she sank to the side of the bed and covered her face in her hands. She had never intended to injure anyone. Not Mr. Small, not Rose. And she would never do anything to damage Quinn.

That's what hurt the most. He hadn't liked what Paul was saying, but he hadn't mounted a vigorous defense either. He'd listened to Paul paint her in shades of deepest black. She tried to convince herself that Quinn had defended her after she stole away. Surely he had.

He cared about her. She knew he did. She saw it in his eyes, felt it in his touch, heard it in his voice.

Or was it all a lie? Part of the deceit that circled around and around like a dark, whirling maelstrom that pulled them into the murk and distorted their life together. There were so many lies. Lies of misdirection, half lies, outright lies, the silent lie.

The silent lies disturbed her the most. Quinn and Paul had let her believe that Miriam was an ordinary woman who had led an ordinary life until the moment of her disappearance.

And all the while, they had known about Marshall Oliver and that Quinn's daughter was not his own. They had known about the fire in May and the anguish Miriam suffered because of it.

Several mysteries were now solved. Now Lily understood Quinn's lack of emotion when he mentioned Susan. She understood why he had made no attempt to search for Miriam. He didn't want Miriam back.

If Miriam was even alive. Quinn quietly insisted she was, but Lily's instinct was that Miriam had committed suicide after the fire and Susan's death. Her life would have been at its lowest ebb.

Miriam had been involved in a clandestine affair that would destroy her husband's political future if discovered. She had driven the final nails into a floundering marriage when she became pregnant by her lover. With her choices dwindling, she had sworn to give up the man she loved in exchange for Quinn agreeing to continue a sham of a marriage and acknowledge Marshall's child as his own. And finally, Miriam had run out of a burning building and left her infant daughter behind to die in the flames.

Stronger women than Miriam Westin had been destroyed by a series of events as agonizing as these.

And, Lily thought, pressing her palms to her eyelids, *if Miriam is dead, then Paul was certainly correct to have believed the Miriam problem was completely and finally solved.*

But why lie about it? Why insist to her that Miriam was alive?

Shaking her head, she pondered the questions until her temples throbbed. One question was answered only to generate more questions. They swirled in her mind like cold winds, sending chills down her body.

And it frightened her a little that Paul had mentioned a Lily problem. Sudden goose bumps lifted on her arms when she recalled him mentioning "various bad endings." If he sent her back to prison, she would die.

"Lily?"

Her shoulders jerked and she stared toward the sound of Quinn's low voice calling from his side of the connecting door. Then she jumped to her feet, turned off the lamp, and sprang into bed as the door quietly opened. Squeezing her eyes shut, fighting to control her breathing, she pretended to be asleep.

She heard him pause at the foot of her bed and sensed him looking at her, prayed he couldn't hear her heart pounding.

At length, she heard the door softly close, and she sat up in the darkness, vigorously rubbing at the chill that iced the back of her neck.

Bewildered, she tried to understand what she had just done. It shocked her that she had fled from him. She loved Quinn. She loved him so much that she hurt inside when she thought ahead to the moment when she would have to leave him. Loved him so deeply she knew there could never be another man in her life. She loved him with all her heart and would have forgiven him anything.

So why, for just a moment, had she been afraid of him?

Disturbed, she drew her knees up under her chin and blinked through the darkness at their connecting door, looking at the thin line of light shining on the floor.

It wasn't too late. She needed him tonight, yearned for his strong arms around her, craved the comfort his mouth and hands could give her. All she had to do was slide out of bed and rap on the door, and they would be in each other's arms.

But she didn't move.

Lily danced with a dozen men, including the handsome Russian duke in whose honor the ball was being given. But it was Quinn who made her heart race and her blood rush when he bowed before her, then took her hand and led her onto the ballroom floor.

Pausing with his fingers hot on her waist, her gloved hand clasped near his chest, he gazed down at her with soft eyes the color of polished pewter. "Is the most beautiful woman at the ball having a good time?" he asked in a husky voice. His gaze settled on her parted lips.

"It's been wonderful."

"Then why do you look so sad?"

The hotel ballroom blazed with candles and an enormous gaslit chandelier; the mingled fragrance of cologne and massive sprays of flowers perfumed every breath. Denver's finest musicians crowded the dais. Tonight every man in the ballroom seemed handsome, and the women swirled around the dance floor like jeweled flower petals spinning on a gentle breeze.

It should have been the most glorious evening of Lily's life. There had been a flattering rush to sign her dance card. She had danced with a Russian duke and with the richest silver baron in the territories. Diamonds sparkled at her ears and throat, and she wore a lavender gown the color of her eyes that was strewn with tiny, glowing seed pearls. She had never felt as beautiful or as dazzling as she did tonight.

And yet, a chill sense of unease distracted her pleasure in the evening. She gazed into Quinn's eyes as the sweet strains of a waltz rose to surround them. "Did you read the newspaper this morning?" she asked, struggling not to sound breathless. "On page five there's a report about the warden of the Yuma Women's Prison being killed in a brawl on Blake Street."

Not a flicker of an eyelash, not a twitch of a finger betrayed surprise. "I wouldn't think Ephram Callihan's sordid demise would cause you a moment's sadness or regret," he murmured. Stepping forward, he expertly turned her into the stream of dancers circling the floor.

They danced together as if destiny had created them for the waltz. Ordinarily Lily was aware of the admiring glances they garnered, overheard murmurs mentioning what a striking couple they made, Quinn so tall and dark, she so slender and blond. But tonight, the other dancers melted away, and it was as if they whirled alone on the floor, gazing into each other's eyes, holding each other with a strange yearning need that poured through the reserve they had recently experienced with each other.

When the music stopped, they stood locked together. And the forbidden words hovered on Lily's trembling lips. It would ease the pressure on her heart to tell him that she loved him. But she remembered Paul warning that she would try to ensnare him before the end. And she didn't utter the words engraved on her soul.

But it was February. The clock ticked toward the election in April. The end of their time together rushed toward them.

It wasn't until later, when she visited the ladies cloak room, that she gazed into the mirror and recalled the hard satisfied smile that had quirked Quinn's lips when she mentioned Ephram Callihan's fortuitous death.

He and Paul had found the long-term solution they sought. The Callihan problem was now conveniently solved.

As if a dam had burst, a stream of unwanted conjectures poured into her mind. Paul and Quinn talking, talking, talking, reaching a ruthless decision to solve the Callihan problem *completely.* Paul, assigning someone to establish Ephram Callihan's habits. And then arranging for an assassination in the midst of a barroom brawl.

Staring into the mirror, she watched the blood drain from her face. Her knees trembled, and if the chairs hadn't been occupied by chatting ladies, she would have stumbled to one and fallen into it.

"No," she whispered, her lips dry. "Don't think this."

But she had been speculating all day, she realized, struggling with the growing disturbance that pushed at the back of her mind.

Of all people, she had no reason to regret Ephram Callihan's death. He'd been a crude, brutal man with no conscience. She had wished him dead a thousand times.

But it hadn't happened until Callihan threatened Quinn.

A shudder passed over her bare shoulders. No. She was letting her imagination run away with her. Quinn was not a killer. He couldn't be. And neither was Paul. Ambition stopped short of murder.

Didn't it?

Lily couldn't guess how long she might have stood motionless before the mirror, considering possibilities she didn't want to think about, if Helene Van Heusen had not entered the room.

Helene halted abruptly in a swirl of rose-colored silk, and her eyes met Lily's in the glass. Then both women turned aside. Cheeks hot, Lily waited until Helene passed behind her, then she lifted her skirts and hurried out of the cloak room.

In the corridor, she paused beyond the light cast by a softly hissing wall sconce and placed a trembling hand on her bosom. What was wrong with her tonight? She was seeing intrigue in Quinn's smile and in Helene's knowing black eyes. Reading dark intent where surely none existed.

"Miriam."

Whirling, she peered into the shadowy corridor toward the source of a voice she did not recognize. But she could guess the man's identity. Even Quinn had not addressed her informally tonight.

He stepped out of a dark niche in the wall where he had obviously been waiting. Impressions flooded her thoughts as her mind raced. Tall, as blond as the curls that bounced on her own shoulder, beautiful sad eyes. His face was soft, so finely chiseled as to appear almost delicate. As he stepped toward the light, she identified a weak chin and thin lips. As a young man going to war, Marshall Oliver would have been handsome, dashing, and achingly vulnerable.

He came toward her, his eyes locked to hers, pleading, loving. Just as he reached her, the cloak- room door opened and two women emerged, patting their hair, smoothing their gowns.

Marshall bumped into her, apologized, and she felt him press something into her palm, then swiftly close her fingers. He bowed to her and to the ladies behind her, then touched the snowy stock at his throat and turned toward the staircase. After looking back at her, he descended out of sight.

When the women had passed, Lily stepped beneath the wall sconce and opened her glove, then smoothed out a folded slip of paper.

My darling dearest. I must see you. I beg you on my knees. Please. Same time, same place. With all my love, M.

Chapter 19

At the end of February Lily and Quinn drove the sleigh to the ranch for the weekend. There Quinn could escape the seemingly endless rounds of meetings and daily political crises that consumed more and more of his time and attention. With the election only nine weeks away, there was seldom an evening when he wasn't scheduled to speak, attend a series of meetings, or confer with Paul. A steady flow of people called at the mansion, and social obligations had become hectic.

"I need rest and air and sky," he told Lily shortly after they arrived at the ranch. "Plus, I think best on a horse."

"Then that's where you need to be. Go." She touched her fingertips to the circles beneath his eyes, then kissed him on the chin. "Don't fall into a snowdrift."

"You've been spending a lot of evenings alone lately. You don't mind if I desert you this afternoon, too?" He had dismissed the cook and houseboy for the weekend to provide them privacy in which to relax and speak freely.

"I'll be fine. I brought a book about furniture." When he laughed, she smiled then made a face. "I want to learn. Everyone except me can tell at a glance if a table is a Queen Anne or something French."

Wrapping herself in a wool shawl, she followed him to the veranda and watched until Quinn and his foreman, Smokey Bill Johnson, rode into an unbroken field of snow. Then she lifted her gaze toward the rocky peaks thrusting against the western sky.

It was a beautiful winter day, frosty and clear, the sky so sharply blue it hurt Lily's eyes to look up. Sunlight sparkled across the snowy fields and poured into the house.

That's what she liked best about the ranch house, the bright cheer of sunshine. In town, the mansion was oppressively dark and shadowy, necessitating lights in the corridors even during daylight hours.

The first time she had visited the ranch house, she'd thought it sparsely furnished and starkly male. Her experience had broadened since she had been here last, and now the rooms appeared even more spartan. She found herself imagining carpets over the planks, more furniture, ferns in the windows, softer wall hangings than the mounted animal heads. She wouldn't want the ranch house to be as opulent or as crammed with objets d'art as the mansion, but it could be made more homey, more welcoming.

"What are you thinking?" Extending her hands to the flames snapping in a massive stone fireplace, she frowned and lowered her head.

Quinn didn't want a woman's stamp on his ranch and certainly not hers. In the long span of a lifetime, her time with him would be very short. A year from now, he would have forgotten that she had passed through these rooms or his life. He would be in his element, governing the new state. His life would be rushed, packed with meetings, important decisions, and a calendar filled with glittering social events. He would move away from the brief memory of Lily Dale and into the history books.

A year from now the Miriam problem would be a thing of the past, and so would the Lily problem.

But she would have a Quinn problem for the rest of her life.

Every time she saw a man wearing a Stetson at a jaunty, confident angle, she would think of Quinn. When she looked into grey eyes or spotted a broken nose, she would see his face. When anyone mentioned politics or speeches or sleighing or horses or artwork, or roses, or, or, or . . . Quinn's voice would whisper in her mind. And each evening when she gazed at the empty pillow beside her, she would remember warm bodies intertwined on cold nights. Soft laughter and whispered words. Passionate kisses that drank deep of sweetness and desire.

He had awakened her from the slumber that had been her life, and when their time together was ended, he would send her back to a half-awakened state. When she reviewed this period, she would remember it as the time when she had been most alive and the happiest. Because of Quinn and the excitement and vibrancy he brought to her life.

While part of her already grieved the loss to come, part of her heart rejoiced because one of love's miracles was its ability to transform. She had begun her odyssey into Miriam Westin's life not caring if Quinn achieved his ambitions or won his dream. Now she cared as deeply as he did. She wanted him to win the election and everything he dreamed of and had worked for. Wanted him to have the chance to implement his ideas and tell the party to go to hell.

In the beginning she had also resisted the changes required of her, but now she played her role wholeheartedly, for his sake as much as for the opportunity it gave her.

Love's transforming qualities extended to Rose as well. Once Lily had thought only of her own need for a child to love her. But now she spent hours and hours planning how she might meet her daughter's expectations and hopes. It no longer mattered if Rose was all that Lily wanted her to be. What mattered was that she be everything Rose wanted and that Rose grow up knowing she was loved and cherished and accepted for who she was.

Truly, she was no longer the woman she had been. It was surprising that Ephram Callihan had recognized her, when she felt so utterly different from the woman he had known.

Her mind shuddered away from remembering Callihan, but he hadn't been far from her thoughts since she'd read of his death.

That was another of love's attributes. One could love even though . . . No, she wouldn't allow herself to voice ugly suspicions, not even within the privacy of her mind.

"Lily?"

Startled, she gripped the arms of the chair and sat forward, her eyes wide.

"It's all right," Quinn said, smiling and extending his hands to the heat of the embers. "We're alone."

His use of her name wasn't what startled her. She was astonished to discover the light had faded. Pink and orange glowed against the windows, transforming the frost on the panes to red lace. The afternoon had slipped away, lost in reverie.

"Are you hungry?" she asked, saying the first thing that came into her mind.

"There's no hurry." Bending, he kissed her lingeringly, his mouth still cold from the outside air. "Are you sure you don't mind cooking?"

"I hope I remember how," she said, smiling. "I've been spoiled since I've been with you."

Still leaning over her, he gazed deeply into her eyes before he straightened. "Have you decided where you'll go when this is over?" Kneeling, he added logs to the fire.

He must have read her mind, or perhaps they had been thinking along similar lines. "It doesn't matter."

"If you have no preference, I'd like you to consider Italy. I enjoyed my time there. I think it would suit you, too," he said, not looking at her.

"Quinn," she said softly, watching his shirt pull tight across his shoulder muscles, "it isn't necessary to remind me that I have to leave."

The fire was blazing now, but he remained kneeling, the poker resting across his knees. "We still have a couple of months, perhaps a little longer. But it feels as if our time is growing short."

Her throat tightened and she stared at the dark curls laying against his collar. "I sense that, too, but I don't know why."

"If there was any way, Lily . . . any possible way . . . but there isn't."

"I know." Moisture filmed her eyes, and her chest ached. Did he want to say the forbidden words, too? Sometimes she thought he did. Hoped he did. Most of the time it was enough to believe that he cared about her, at least a little. But sometimes she hurt inside with the need to hear him say the words. And to say them herself.

"The risk is simply too great."

"I understand. Truly. There could be another Callihan."

It seemed that he stiffened, but she couldn't be certain. Leaning forward, he prodded at the flaming logs.

"Or I could make a mistake and one of Miriam's friends or acquaintances would suddenly realize, this is not Miriam. We've been very lucky so far. But I think we both know disaster could strike at any moment." Immediately she thought of Marshall Oliver approaching her outside the hotel cloak room. For one fleeting instant, she was tempted to tell Quinn that she'd received another note from Marshall demanding to see her.

"I'll never forget you, Lily."

Slipping to the floor, she knelt beside him and placed her hands on either side of his craggy face. "Why are you saying these things now?" she whispered, looking into his smoky eyes. "Surely we don't have to say good-bye just yet."

"I'm not sure," he said in a thick voice, resting his fingertips on her throat. "It feels like events are rushing out of control. Forces coming together. I'm standing in the eye of a hurricane, with chaos spinning around me. Nothing is as I thought it would be."

"Listen to me." Pressing her hands against his cheeks, she gazed deeply into his eyes. "There is not a doubt in my mind that you will win the election. Paul's right. It will be a landslide in your favor. And Quinn? You're going to be the best damned first governor this state could possibly have. Do you hear me?" Hot tears glistened in her eyes.

He slid his fingers up to her lips. "The price is too high. No man should trade his soul for a line in the history books." His eyes closed, and his shoulders dropped. "If you knew . . ." He opened his eyes again. "You believe that Paul and I had Callihan murdered, don't you?"

She bit her lips and let her hands drop from his face. "Please. Don't ask that."

"I thought so." Wrapping his arms around her, he lowered his face to her hair and crushed her against him. "There have been so many lies between us. Once I thought it wouldn't matter, but now, tonight, I wish we could begin again, speak the hard truths and put them behind us."

Pressing her cheek to his shoulder, she inhaled the clean outdoors scent of him, felt his solid warm strength against her breasts and hips. But she noticed that he had not denied an involvement with Callihan's death. Perhaps he thought she would not believe a denial. "We could do that, Quinn. We could begin again with the truth. We could start right now."

"It's not possible to put everything that's happened behind us. I've done things I can't undo, Lily, things I can't forget and things I'll live with for a very long time." He stroked her hair, his touch a caress. "You're one of the wrongs I regret, forcing you to impersonate Miriam. And Miriam. There are so damned many things to regret."

In this odd close moment, kneeling before the hearth with sunset flames blazing against the windowpanes, he was saying what she had longed to hear, using words her mind did not comprehend but her heart understood.

"I love you, Quinn."

He stiffened and made a sound deep in his throat.

She didn't let him pull back, but held him tightly, pressing her head against his shoulder, her face hidden. "I ask nothing from you. When you tell me it's time, I'll go. I'll never trouble you again. There will be no letters, no contact. Your secrets are safe with me. But I love you, and I need to say the words. I will love you and think of you every day until I die because no one has made the impact on my life that you have. I will always be grateful for this time with you, and for the profound changes you've helped me make."

"Lily, Lily," he said hoarsely against her hair. "Lily of the dark valley of my life."

Then he stood, gathered her in his arms, and carried her to his bedroom. There, in the pink-and-lavender shadows of twilight, they made love as if it were the first time. Ardently, but tenderly, with passion and great joy in each other.

Afterward, Lily clung to him and wept hot tears on his bare shoulder without knowing why.

Marshall Oliver was becoming persistent and therefore dangerous. He'd sent Lily two notes through Morely, pleading and then demanding that she meet him at the City Ditch. His notes carried a desperate, almost threatening tone that worried her greatly. Quinn was too close to the prize for Lily to allow Miriam's past to explode in their faces. She couldn't disregard Marshall any longer.

Today, when Cranston served her midday meal, she instructed him to order the carriage, and she directed Elizabeth to lay out a heavy wool walking suit and warm boots.

Morely lifted an eyebrow when she stepped out of the door and informed him with a significant look that she would be making her usual Monday afternoon visits. He held his expression carefully blank, but Lily understood he recognized a code established long ago. What she didn't know was if Marshall Oliver would be waiting. Would he come again today after she had ignored him for the last two Mondays?

"I'll return in an hour, Miz Westin," Morely said after driving her into the countryside and handing her to the ground. His rheumy old eyes told Lily that he would keep her secrets, but he didn't approve.

"This will be the last time," she promised in a low voice. Impulsively, she pressed his hand. "You've been a good friend, Morely."

Standing beside the road, she watched the carriage recede toward the city, feeling abandoned and very alone. It was a grey day with storm clouds billowing over the mountains, and the rolling fields sloping away from the foothills seemed to wear their burden of snow with a resignation that suggested the land was as weary of winter as Lily was.

When she spotted a carriage bowling down the road toward her, she straightened her shoulders against the cold March breeze, lifted the hood of her cloak, then raised her hems and walked toward the path hidden by a tangle of bare willow branches. The gravel was muddy in places, but dry enough not to splatter her skirts.

Until she rounded a curve and saw Marshall Oliver jump up from the bench beneath the old cottonwood, she hadn't realized how much she'd hoped he would not be here, or how deeply she dreaded this encounter. And feared it. If anyone would recognize her as an impostor, surely it would be Miriam's lover.

Sweeping off his hat, he ran forward and enveloped her in a fierce embrace. He would have kissed her lips, but Lily turned her head at the last moment and his mouth grazed her cheek.

"Oh, my dearest. I feared you wouldn't come." Clasping her face between his hands, he examined her as if drinking in the sight. "I told myself you didn't come last week or the week before because it was impossible for you to get away, but I also feared Helene was correct and you refused to see me."

He would recognize the impersonation the minute she spoke. "I'm not the same person you knew, Marshall," she said slowly, watching his pale eyes for the instant of denouement.

"Helene told me you're trying to make changes." Pushing aside her hood, he pressed her head to the crook of his neck and held her against his body. "When I think of you coughing so violently that your voice . . . my poor brave darling." Assisting her as if she were an invalid, he guided her to the bench and sat facing her, holding her gloved hands. "Let me just look at you."

"I have many things to say and not much time." Helene had unwittingly paved the way for her, and for that she was thankful.

"And I have much to tell you, dearest." Closing his eyes, he released a breath. "You can't imagine the anguish I suffered when you vanished. I was certain the son of a bitch had murdered you in a rage of injured pride or because he feared a scandal that would destroy his precious campaign."

Lily stared and her hands jerked. "Quinn would never—"

"First there was the fire, and shortly afterward you vanished. Of course I thought he'd killed you." Lifting a hand. he caressed her cheek, her bottom lip. "I can't prove it, Miriam, but I'll never believe the fire was an accident. I believe he intended you and Susan to die that night. He and Kazinski must have been very disappointed when they realized they'd only succeeded in murdering our daughter but not you. I thank God every day that you survived."

Lily stared into his pale eyes and decided Marshall Oliver either hated Quinn enough to genuinely believe his accusation, or he was a very convincing actor.

Stalling to conceal her shock and redirect her thoughts, she pulled back and raised both hands to cover her face. "Oh please. I can't bear to think about Susan."

"Shh, darling. We'll have other children, I promise." Gently he lowered her hands. "Miriam, since you've returned I've done a lot of thinking. I know what we decided, but it isn't right that we should be apart. We've loved each other for a decade."

Lily lowered her eyes so he wouldn't see her disbelief. She didn't doubt that Miriam had loved this man. But if Marshall had returned her love, he'd had a strange way of showing it. He'd married another woman when he knew Miriam was waiting for him. And he hadn't cared enough to write and release her so she could marry someone else with a free mind and open heart.

"Miriam," he gripped her hands so tightly that her knuckles ached. "Come away with me. We'll elope to Chicago or New York City, if you like. We'll be together as we were meant to be."

They would have discussed this before, Lily thought, her mind racing. "We can't," she said, shaking her head. "You know the reasons."

"Hear me out, I beg you. I've come into some money recently."

From the Van Heusens? What would they pay to see Quinn's wife run off with another man mere weeks before the election?

"I'll leave some of it with Sara. If the sum isn't enough, then she and the girls can sell the farm." He peered into her face. "The important thing is, they won't suffer financial want if we seize our moment of happiness."

Did he really believe that his wife and daughters would not suffer if he turned his back and walked away from them? Did he believe his daughters could grow up fatherless and not feel a lack? Did he care so little for his own flesh and blood?

Rose rushed to the front of her mind. Rose, who would grow up fatherless. Heat flooded her throat, and she felt as if she were choking.

"And it won't matter about Quinn now, not after he tried to murder you, not after he did murder our daughter."

So Miriam *had* cared about the effect of her mistakes on Quinn.

"The important thing is, we'll finally be together. I can love you as you deserve to be loved and cherished."

Lily looked down at her hands clasped in his grip. "I did a lot of thinking while I was in the sanitarium."

She intended to tell him what she had told Helene. That she and Quinn were rebuilding their marriage. That they loved each other. But suddenly she understood Marshall would know this was a lie.

He had reappeared in Miriam's life, had seduced her and had reawakened her love for him. She had loved him enough to cast aside a lifetime of honor. And she must have justified her actions by painting Quinn as a villain. Perhaps Miriam had come to believe it herself. Whatever her private feelings, she had convinced Marshall that he was the man she loved, not Quinn.

"Dearest, your sweet nature and tender heart are things

I adore about you. But everything is different now. Westin has proved what he is. A murderer. And now I'm able to provide for Sara and the girls."

"Your wife is an invalid, Marshall. Your daughters are still children. Your family needs you."

"Miriam, darling, we've discussed this over and over. It's regrettable that others will suffer on our account, but we cannot live without each other. Don't we deserve to be happy? Why should we be the ones to suffer?"

Now she saw how to end this in a way that Marshall would believe and that would remove him as a threat to Quinn. This would be her gift to Quinn, although he would never know of it. And it was also a gift to Miriam, who had been badly used.

Jerking her hands out of his, she stood and stared down at him. "You are contemptible," she said in a low, shaking voice. Her tone carried the utter conviction of her emotions.

"I came here today to tell you that I've finally seen through you. You jilted me ten years ago. And now you're prepared to treat your wife and daughters in the same shabby, cowardly, and contemptible manner you treated me." If she could have been Lily in this situation, the air would have turned blue with the words she would have chosen. "You don't love me. You didn't seek me out. The Van Heusens found you and paid you to seduce me."

It was an informed guess, and when she saw his expression and the dull red flush that climbed his jaw, she knew she had guessed correctly.

"How did you . . . ? I can explain that. It isn't what it appears, I——"

"How much are the Van Heusens paying you now, Marshall? How long would you stay with me in Chicago? Until after the election? Once Quinn was defeated, would you have left me? If you can justify abandoning an invalid wife and three daughters, it wouldn't be too difficult for you to justify ruining my life, then walking away."

"Miriam, for God's sake! What's come over you? We love each other. We had a child together."

"Susan is a tragedy I will regret for the rest of my days. I made a terrible mistake, Marshall. I was unhappy in my marriage, so I convinced myself that I still loved you. But the man I thought I loved doesn't exist. That man would never accept payment to make love to a vulnerable woman. The man I thought I loved would never turn his back on his own children or abandon them. I thank heaven that I have come to my senses and see you for the scum that you are."

He stared in anger and astonishment. "I don't recognize you. I've never seen you like this."

"Leave me alone. If you contact me again, I'll tell Quinn. I won't beg him to spare you. I want nothing to do with you, Marshall. I don't want to see you, talk to you, have any further contact with you. And I can promise that I will never think of you again."

"Miriam!"

"You are despicable!"

Turning in a swirl of skirts, she set off down the gravel path secure in the knowledge that he would not follow. She had seen unpardonable offense in his light-colored eyes, and a flash of fear when she threatened him with Quinn. She had made it clear by tone and expression that she considered him an amoral bastard.

Miriam's sad affair was finally over. Lily's only regret

was that Miriam herself had never recognized that she loved a man who existed only in her imagination.

Lily hurried around the curve with her head down, so intent on her thoughts that she didn't see the man waiting on the path until Paul clamped a hand on her arm and spun her to face him.

"What the hell do you think you're doing!" he snarled, his voice shaking with fury.

Chapter 20

Paul practically flung her inside the carriage she had earlier seen approaching on the road.

"You followed me," Lily accused him, pulling herself up
on the seat and shoving her skirts down. Her face was
white with resentment. Months had passed since a man had
handled her so roughly.

"I've had you followed since you called on Helene Van
Heusen. And with good reason."

"Where is Morely?"

"By now Quinn has received my message. I doubt very
much that you'll see Morely again." Paul's voice was cold
enough to ice her blood. He stared at her, stony with hostility
as the carriage wheels spun then lurched forward. "I don't
know what your game is, Lily, but it ends here and now."

"Damn it, Paul. Whatever you're thinking, you're
wrong." She would talk to Quinn about Morely. Morely
shouldn't lose his post on her account.

"I'm thinking you've found a better offer," he said in a
voice raspy with rage. "I'm thinking you've joined forces
with the Van Heusens, and you've negotiated a deal. What
are they paying you to resume the affair with Oliver? Do
they know you aren't Miriam, or do they believe it's
Miriam who's willing to ruin Quinn?"

For a moment Lily was speechless. Shock widened her eyes and her hands began to shake. "My God! You can't believe that!" Speaking rapidly and earnestly, she explained how Marshall had approached her outside the cloak room at the ball, his notes, and why she had decided to meet him today. "And I succeeded. It's over. Marshall Oliver will not be a problem in the future."

"First, I was a member of the committee who drew up the guest list for the duke's ball. Marshall Oliver's name was not on the list."

"Are you saying . . . Paul, Marshall was there! So were the Van Heusens."

"The list was compiled by a bipartisan committee, so of course the Van Heusens received an invitation, but Oliver did not. He was not at the ball, and he did not approach you outside the cloak room. That's a clumsy lie, Lily. Second, when I almost stumbled into you and your lover, you were wrapped in each other's arms. That was no farewell scene."

"My lover? Paul, he believed I was Miriam! He embraced me, then we talked. Did you hear what I said to him?"

"You can be damned sure I wanted to, but I didn't have to hear the words. I saw enough to understand you were picking up where Miriam left off."

"If you'd been closer, you would have heard me tell him that he's despicable. You would have heard me end the affair and make certain Marshall knows it's ended! He won't pursue Miriam any farther. That's the truth!"

"Why should I believe anything you say?" Paul's face twisted. "You've been lying so long that you wouldn't recognize the truth if it spit on your skirts."

"Would you?" Tears of frustration scalded the back of her eyes. "You're so steeped in lies and half-truths that you can't recognize the truth when you hear it!"

He fell silent, studying her with hard flat eyes. "For the sake of discussion let us pretend for a moment that it happened exactly as you claim. Oliver wanted a meeting, and you agreed. Why, Lily? And don't give me that nonsense about ending the affair. The affair ended the day Miriam confessed her pregnancy."

"No it didn't. The boy I met on the path knew Miriam had had a child. He either saw her with Marshall while she was in a state of advanced pregnancy, or he saw them together after Susan's birth. I believe Miriam loved Marshall, and she was too weak to resist his persistence. She may have genuinely intended to end the liaison, but Marshall continued to pursue her, and she continued to see him."

"I don't give a damn what you believe. What I care about is Quinn and winning this election. And I'm not going to let you destroy everything we've worked for. You're finished, Lily. You've become a problem."

The ice in her blood congealed. She heard the unmistakable threat shaking his voice, read it in his stony expression. "This isn't fair, Paul." Wetting her lips, she cleared her throat and tried to speak above a whisper. "I beg you, please don't send me back to Yuma. I don't deserve that."

"If I could send you back to the hellhole where I found you, I'd do it right now," he snarled. "I'm angry enough to throw you out of this carriage in front of the sheriff's office and order him to shackle you and take you back to Arizona."

Bewilderment vied with the anguish draining the blood from her face. "What do you mean, if you could? The provisional pardon—"

"There's no such thing as a provisional pardon. Believe me, right now I wish there were," he hissed at her. "There's a pardon. Period."

"You son of a bitch!" Stunned, she fell backward on the seat as if he had shot her. "You made me believe I had no choices at all. And all the time, it was a goddamned lie. I could have said no and walked away. I could have gone home to Rose right then! Does Quinn know this?"

But she remembered him saying that he regretted forcing her to impersonate Miriam. That he had done things that were hard to live with. Of course he knew.

The lies and deceit had begun ten minutes after she met him. What had he called them? Necessary lies. Necessary lies that wrapped around her like invisible chains. Had he told her the truth about anything? Anything at all?

Numbed by the discovery of how badly she'd been deceived, Lily fell silent, focusing dulled eyes on the countryside. All this time she could have been with Rose. A cold weight settled on her shoulders.

Quinn opened the door as Paul was dismissing his carriage in front of the mansion. "I've given the servants the rest of the day off and instructed them not to return until tomorrow." He stared at Lily as if he'd never seen her before.

If he had cleared the house of servants, then they could speak freely. What Lily burned to express freely was her fury and devastation at being tricked into impersonating Miriam. But first, she had to dispose of the Marshall Oliver misunderstanding. "I can explain why I met Marshall today."

"You'll have that opportunity," he snapped, glaring at her hand on his sleeve until she removed it. The lines had deepened beside his mouth and set in granite. He must have looked this coldly furious and betrayed when he learned of Miriam's affair. Now it was Lily coming home after meeting Marshall Oliver. At this moment, Lily wished she had never heard of Miriam's lover.

Instead of choosing the informality of the family parlor, Quinn went directly to the library. It was a dark, chilly room, a masculine room designed for meetings rather than comfort. Lily dropped her cloak over the back of a chair and went to the window in time to watch the first snowflakes tumble out of a flinty twilight sky. The days were short now, and full darkness would descend in another thirty minutes. It was going to be a cold night.

Quinn placed three glasses and a decanter of brandy on the table, but none of them moved to pour a drink. "I doubt there is any explanation you could offer that I can accept," he said, his slate eyes hard. "But what in the hell did you think you were doing?"

Standing away from them beside the window, feeling the cold air leaking around the panes and chilling her back, she spoke for twenty minutes. To their credit, neither man interrupted. They sat at the table, watching with expressions as unyielding as the marble tiles beneath her boots.

"Quinn, I did this for you," she finished, her eyes pleading for understanding. She hated his hard, closed expression. "I ended it with Marshall once and for all."

Standing slowly, he placed his palms on the table and leaned forward. "What you did was dangerous and stupid, Lily. How do you know this wasn't a trap? Are you absolutely certain there was no journalist hidden in the willows listening to you admit to an affair? Did you and Marshall talk about Susan? Did either of you refer to the circumstances of Susan's birth? Were things said that would create a front-page scandal? Think about what the two of you said to each other and picture how your conversation will read in print."

She gaped at him. It hadn't occurred to her that Marshall, or more likely the Van Heusens, would alert a reporter and conceal him nearby to eavesdrop. At once she understood that she should have considered this possibility. "I don't think there was anyone else present," she stammered.

"But you don't know for certain."

"Marshall didn't know that I would come today," she said, thinking out loud and wringing her hands. Now that she understood the possible repercussions of today's impulse, she genuinely regretted having gone to the City Ditch. Morely had lost his post, and Quinn could lose the election. "If Marshall or the Van Heusens intended the meeting as a trap, surely they would have set it up immediately after the ball. But Quinn, I didn't go to the ditch then. Or the week after. So, I don't think——"

"That's right, Lily," Paul said sharply, his voice heavy with censure and disgust. "You didn't think."

Tears sprang into her eyes. "Please believe me. I wouldn't do anything to——"

But Quinn cut her off with a slashing gesture and turned to Paul. "I owe you an apology. You were right about following her. I was wrong."

When she heard his tone, her heart sank. Nothing she said would make him see what she'd done as anything but a betrayal.

Then Paul related what he had seen and how he interpreted it. Lily writhed inside. Surely Quinn would not believe that she'd fallen in with the Van Heusens. He couldn't believe that. But he listened to Paul as intently as he had listened to her. Her heart silently pleaded, imploring him to remember that she loved him and would never knowingly damage him.

But why would he trust that she loved him or that she wouldn't try to destroy him? From the very beginning everything about their relationship had been a lie or a deception.

Paul finished by staring at her. "I know she lied about Oliver being at the hotel the night of the ball. Someone would have seen him. On reflection, I don't know if she's lying about what happened between her and Oliver at the ditch. Maybe—maybe—it happened the way she says and for the reasons she claims. Maybe it didn't. I do know we can't trust her. Instead of a solution, she's become a problem."

It was dark now. Light from the wall sconces and the lamps did not reach the corners of the room. For several minutes after Paul stopped speaking, the only sound was the ticking of the mantel clock and the soft hiss of snow against the windowpanes. The sound of Quinn's heels pacing across the marble floor.

Anger exploded in Lily's chest and grew. She hadn't done anything wrong. She'd been trying to help. When she thought about Paul saying that *she* couldn't be trusted her hands shook with fury.

"There was never a provisional pardon, and you knew it," she said to Quinn, her voice husky with injury and reproach. "How do either of you dare speak of trust? You've used me and lied to me from the minute we met! Did you tell me anything that wasn't a lie? Anything at all?" She threw out her hands. "When this is over, will there be a home for Rose and me? Or was that a lie, too? Can I believe anything you've said?"

"Don't try to turn the tables. This is about you." Quinn stopped pacing and looked down the length of the long library table. "I don't believe you've joined forces with my political enemies," he said after a long moment, his voice frigid. "But you have consistently disobeyed my instructions, and you might well have destroyed everything I've worked for by doing so."

"I didn't—"

"If Marshall Oliver was at the ball as you say, then it's because Helene Van Heusen arranged it. You didn't stop Helene's involvement by calling on her after I ordered you not to. We'll know soon if a journalist was present during your meeting with Oliver. His article will make the front pages. And my campaign will be over."

"I truly believe Marshall and I were alone!"

"I hope you're right, Lily. But eventually there *will* be a witness to any trysts with Oliver."

"There won't be any further meetings!"

"This one shouldn't have happened," Quinn snapped, his eyes blazing cold fire. "When Oliver approached you, you should have informed me immediately. No one asked you to inject yourself into this situation. We never wanted you involved with Marshall Oliver. You should have told me, then Paul and I could have handled the problem!"

"Like you handled the Callihan problem?" she asked sharply, throwing the accusation at him.

Paul sat up straight, and his shoulders stiffened. "What are you implying?"

"I'm not as blind as you think I am!" Lifting her skirts, she ran out of the library and bolted up the staircase, stumbling in the darkness. When she reached her bedroom, she slammed the door and leaned against it, fighting the sting of tears and a confusing mix of emotions.

Quinn was furious, and after he'd pointed out the possibility of a trap, she understood why he would be. But she'd only been trying to help.

And learning there was no such thing as a provisional pardon had jolted her badly and made her furious. At the same time, she understood why they'd deceived her. Finding a dead ringer for Miriam must have seemed like a godsend, a solution to an enormous problem. And they had to make certain that Lily would agree to the impersonation.

Rubbing her temples, she paced across the chilly, dark room. With the servants gone, no fire had been laid in her bedroom grate, the lamps were not lit. Worse, knowing that she, Quinn, and Paul were the only people in the house made her acutely aware of the mansion's massive size and the myriad of dark, silent rooms.

She considered lighting a fire, but she was too upset, too drained from the day's events. Dropping into a chair next to the window, she gazed outside at the blackness beyond the falling snow and wrung her hands in her lap. Could the meeting with Marshall have been a trap? Was someone listening to everything they had said?

Casting back in her mind, she tried to reconstruct the conversation, examining every word for damaging content. And God help her, if a third party had been listening, the conversation would indeed be destructive to Quinn.

Marshall had revealed that Susan was his daughter. He'd revealed that he and Miriam had discussed eloping.

Moreover, he had repeatedly stated that Quinn was a murderer. There hadn't been a hint of doubt in his voice or expression. Marshall Oliver believed that Quinn had murdered his daughter and had attempted to murder Miriam.

At the time, Lily had dismissed the accusations as ridiculous. And they were.

Weren't they?

Frowning, she watched the snow collect on the windowsill. From the beginning, Quinn and Paul had insisted that Miriam was alive.

But Quinn and Paul had lied about everything.

Thoughts racing, Lily sat up straight and rubbed her cold hands together. It didn't make sense to insist that Miriam was alive if she was dead. If they'd told her that Miriam had died, so many of Lily's questions would have been answered. She wouldn't have wondered why they were not searching for Miriam. She wouldn't have asked herself time and again: Where is Miriam now? How is she supporting herself? And why did she flee?

But she would have demanded to know how Miriam had died. She would have been curious about Miriam's death and wondered why it had to be kept secret.

It was foolish and frightening to let these disturbing doubts enter her mind. At times, she had herself believed that Miriam must be dead. So why did the idea unnerve her now? Because she had assumed suicide. Murder had never occurred to her.

Marshall's words rang in her memory. "I was certain the son of a bitch had murdered you in a rage of injured pride or because he feared a scandal that would destroy his precious campaign."

Biting her lip, she stared out at the cold darkness. How far would Quinn go to prevent a scandal from ruining his political ambitions? Could he have weighed an image of himself as a bereaved husband against that of a cuckold and decided he preferred bereavement to being a laughingstock?

A chill shuddered down her spine as she imagined him and Paul discussing the Miriam problem. They would have speculated that Miriam's affair with Marshall Oliver might resume. They would have wondered how much the Van Heusens knew, would have worried if Marshall would keep silent. They would have discussed the possibility of Miriam deciding to elope with Marshall once Susan was old enough to travel. They would have decided Miriam's support of the campaign would certainly be halfhearted, considering she remained in the marriage only because she had no choice. The Miriam threat would have loomed very large.

Lily shook her head hard, desperately attempting to dislodge horrifying thoughts. No, no, no. Murder was not a solution. No.

But she could imagine the conclusion Quinn and Paul must have reached. The Miriam problem vanished if Miriam disappeared from Quinn's life. And the best solution would be a permanent solution. Eyes wide and horrified, Lily recalled Quinn's face when he'd told her there were things he could not undo, things he would have to live with for the rest of his life. He had looked soul-weary, angry, guilty. What awful things had he been remembering at that moment?

Standing abruptly, she crossed to the fireplace and knelt before it. She needed light and warmth to conquer the growing and unthinkable suspicions. But terrible thoughts poured into her mind like ice water, rushing with unstoppable force toward a horrifying conclusion.

Miriam had left her wedding rings behind.

She had left most of her clothing behind. Her furs, shoes, hats, undergarments, even her jewelry.

She had left Susan's grave, a place that would have been almost sacred to her.

And equally unbelievable, she had left Marshall Oliver behind.

Rocking back on her heels, Lily frowned at the small blaze she'd built in the grate and extended her shaking hands to the warmth. If Miriam had decided to run away from Quinn, why didn't she run away with her lover? Even if compassion for Marshall's wife and family prevented an elopement, wouldn't Miriam at least have sent him a message that she was alive? She had loved him, had borne his child. It didn't make sense that she wouldn't have opened some kind of contact with him. If she could.

All of these puzzling questions and situations could be explained by three words: Miriam is dead.

That's why Quinn had insisted it was pointless to search for her. That's why Quinn displayed no qualms about altering her portrait, and had no fear that Miriam might reappear. It explained why Quinn had stared at Lily so strangely in the beginning, as if he were seeing a ghost.

And if—she made herself think the words—if Quinn had agreed to Miriam's murder, then it explained the despair she occasionally glimpsed in his eyes, and the nights she heard him pacing in his bedroom long after the rest of the household slept.

Lily dropped her head in her hands and found tears on her cheeks. She loved him. Surely, if Quinn was the kind of man ruthless enough to murder his wife and her child, Lily would have sensed it. Or had love blinded her? Everything she was seeing now and thinking now had always been there. But she hadn't let herself really see. She hadn't pushed hard enough, hadn't fought hard enough to learn what had happened to Miriam Westin. Because she didn't want to face the truth?

Terrible thoughts continued to electrify her mind.

Quinn hadn't been home the night of the fire. An alibi? He'd said no one knew how the fire started. But maybe he did know. Maybe the fire had been what Marshall believed it was. A murder weapon. Quinn insisted that Miriam had survived the fire, but in all these months, none of Miriam's friends had mentioned seeing her afterward. When they made a remark about the fire, they usually added, "And then you seemed to vanish." Or, "And immediately afterward you departed for the sanitarium."

Quinn and Paul insisted Miriam was alive because they were covering up a murder.

Moaning softly, Lily hunched forward as horrifying images flamed in her mind. No, no. She desperately did not want to think these things.

But she did. And she also thought of Ephram Callihan.

Shuddering, she drew several deep breaths and tried to consider what she knew in a way to explain it differently.

But there was only one reasonable conclusion, Quinn's problems had a convenient way of disappearing or dying.

And now, she was a problem.

Lily stared into the flames with wide, frightened eyes. There would never be a home for her and Rose. The promises were lies. Quinn and Paul would not take the chance that someday she might tell the story of her impersonation to a reporter. They wouldn't risk an opportunity for blackmail. They would believe that as long as Lily was alive, Quinn's reputation and his place in the history books was in danger.

But the Lily problem vanished if, like Miriam, she disappeared forever.

"Oh my God." No one knew where she was. If Lily Dale disappeared, no one would search for her or even miss her. It would be ridiculously easy to dispose of the Lily problem.

If she hoped to see her daughter ever again, she had to escape. Tonight. Right now.

"Quinn you know what I'm saying is correct."

He stood at the window, staring out at the thickening snow. "She thought she was helping. She used poor judgment, but I can't believe she's in league with the Van Heusens. And I don't believe her intention is to ruin my chances in the election."

Paul poured a splash of brandy into one of the glasses and took a long swallow. "Now that I've had a chance to think more calmly, I agree. And I concede that it's possible Oliver was in the hotel the night of the ball, and we didn't spot him. This incident could have happened exactly as Lily claims it did. But that doesn't change my opinion. It's time to get rid of her."

"It's still four weeks until the election."

"That's four weeks of worrying every time she leaves the house. Four weeks of waiting for someone to recognize her or realize that she isn't Miriam. It's four weeks of anxiety over whether or not she'll make an embarrassing or revealing mistake." He paused. "Four more weeks of worrying that she'll learn about Miriam. It's time, Quinn. You've established yourself as a family man, we don't really need her anymore. If you lose your wife now, this close to the election . . . now, a sympathy vote could put you over the top."

Quinn lowered his head and rubbed the bridge of his nose. Paul was right. Lily had served her purpose. There was no urgent reason to keep her with him until after the election, and many good reasons to move to the resolution.

Except he loved her.

"She's willful and defiant, Quinn. She obeys instructions only when it suits her. The more I think about this, the more I think now is the time to get rid of her. Now is the time to play for the sympathy vote. Earlier, it wouldn't have worked. But this close to the election . . ."

Lifting his head, Quinn listened and frowned. Sound carried in the empty house. They were talking loudly, but he still thought he'd heard something. Moving to the library door, he peered into the darkness beyond. Had one of the servants returned?

"We've made our point with the family-man image," Paul continued. "Since it's in our best interests to dispose of Lily immediately, you need to know that I believe we can swing rather easily to a portrayal of you as a tragic figure. The fire, Susan's death, and then Miriam's death. In fact, I like this plan a lot."

"You're a ruthless bastard, Paul."

"We both are, my friend."

Now his eyes had adjusted to the darkness in the corridor, and he spotted movement in the foyer. Heard a sound like a muffled sob of pain or frustration.

Striding into the corridor, he moved swiftly toward the front door and the shadowy movement. The snowy light from the flanking windows was dim but enough for him to identify Lily pulling and jerking at the door handle.

"It's locked," he said, frowning at her coat and hat. "Where are you going?" Why would she run into a blizzard?

She spun toward him, gasping as if he'd startled her badly, and he saw a gleam of tears wetting her cheeks.

"I heard you talking about getting rid of me," she said in a thin, frightened voice. "Oh Quinn. How could you agree to kill me, too? I loved you."

Her movements frantic and jerky, she spun to the door latch again, swearing under her breath.

"Lily—"

But when he touched her shoulder, she screamed and wrenched backward. Lifting her skirts, her eyes wild, she spun toward the corridor in time to see Paul emerge. Gasping for breath, badly frightened, she dashed toward the staircase and ran up the stairs into the blackness above.

Chapter 21

Lily skidded to a halt in the long, dark corridor just beyond the landing and collapsed against the wall. Her heart slammed in her chest, beating as fast and furious as a hummingbird's. She couldn't breathe.

"Damn!" she muttered, dashing at the tears in her eyes. She should have run past Paul and tried to reach the back door. Except that door would be locked, too, and Paul would have grabbed her before she got past him.

"Damn, damn, damn!" The corridor before her was inky, the only light a faint flicker of firelight glowing beyond her bedroom door. Pressing a hand over her pounding heart, she tried to think what to do, where to go. Fear fogged her mind, she couldn't concentrate, couldn't focus.

"Lily? Lily!" Quinn's angry voice called up the staircase. "Come down here at once. We need to talk."

Lily cursed herself. She had badly bungled the encounter at the door. She shouldn't have blurted that she'd overheard them talking about disposing of her. She might have gained time to plan an escape if she'd been quicker-witted. Instead she had revealed that she knew they intended to kill her. Now they had to capture her; they couldn't let her leave the mansion tonight.

She had to elude them, but how?

"We have to find her. Paul, you take this staircase, I'll take the servants' stairs."

Struggling for breath, feeling as if she were strangling, Lily blinked hard and peered down the corridor. In the darkness she couldn't see the doorway to the servants' staircase, but in minutes that door would open, and Quinn would start down the corridor toward her; Paul would come up the stairs behind her. And she would be trapped. Gasping and wringing her hands, she tried to think. What to do, what to do? Jump out a window? The two-story fall could injure her badly, and she might freeze to death before someone found her. Besides, Quinn and Paul were likely to be the ones to find her.

Oh Quinn, my darling. How did this happen?

She had to hide. But where? Choking, a sob of fear burning her throat, she tried to think of a place where she could conceal herself. But that's what they would expect. They would search all the rooms on this floor.

A light flared behind her, and she sucked in a frightened breath, then slid along the wall, moving deeper into the dark corridor. Paul had lit the jets in the foyer.

"Lily? You're being a fool. Come downstairs right now," he shouted. Any second he would pursue her up the staircase.

She could lean out a window and scream for help. But the houses were too widely spaced and the nearest neighbors would have their windows closed on a night like this. The falling snow would muffle her cries in any case.

Quinn. Quinn.

Fear overcame reason. She couldn't think. She knew she was trapped in the locked house, and they would catch her. There was no way out. But by God she wouldn't make it easy. They'd have to work for their prize.

Lifting her skirts, and reacting instinctively, she ran down the black corridor. She had to find a place where she would be safe for a few minutes. She needed to think. The warm light and familiarity of her bedroom drew her, but that was a dead end, and she raced past it.

When she reached the door to the servants' staircase, she thought at first it was locked, but the difficulty was her shaking hands. Once she had fumbled the door open, she saw light shining up on the first landing and froze as she heard Quinn's boots on the stairs.

"Lily! For God's sake. This is insane. I love you!"

Fresh tears sprang to her eyes, and she swayed on her feet. She had longed to hear those words. Now they broke her heart.

There was only one direction to run. Up. Even as she gathered her skirts and whirled up the stairs, she knew there was no place to hide in the spare servants' rooms on the third floor. But it would gain her a few minutes while they searched the rooms below.

"Lily! Please. This is a terrible misunderstanding."

No, it wasn't. She knew what he planned for her. Holding her breath, she flattened herself against the wall of the second landing. Her heart was beating so hard and loud that she feared he would hear as he reached the second floor door and burst into the corridor.

Lowering her head, she touched violently shaking fingertips to her eyelids. Did he really believe she'd suddenly turn obedient and meekly emerge because he asked her to? Not when she knew he kept a pistol in the desk drawer in his bedroom. Undoubtedly, he was running to fetch the pistol right now.

She couldn't bear this. *Quinn.*

A soft whoosh caught her attention as gas jets flared and a spill of light poured through the stairway door. He'd lit the gas lamps in the corridor.

"She's not in the first two rooms," Paul called.

"Lily!" Quinn shouted. "Darling, no one is going to harm you. Please, Lily, come out. We have to talk."

She knew all about the talk, talk, talk, and where it would lead. Desperately trying to move quietly, she ran up the rest of the stairs and opened the door to the third floor. It was as black as pitch, and she was not familiar with this section of the house.

She stumbled over something, caught her balance, then sagged against the wall, shaking hard. It was hopeless. When they didn't find her on the second floor, they would move upstairs. They had all night. They would catch her.

They would kill her as they had killed Ephram Callihan and Miriam Westin.

Letting her head drop back against the wall, she closed her eyes, feeling hot tears slip down her cheeks. What hurt like a dagger to the heart was hearing him say he loved her. Using the words she had ached to hear as a lure, as bait.

"Oh Quinn." Agony lay in those two words.

There was nowhere else to run, nothing to do but stand here in the darkness and wait for them to close in on her. Sliding to the floor, she drew her knees up under her chin and opened her eyes, expecting to see nothing but blackness.

Instead, she discovered she was looking at a thin bar of light shining beneath a door. For an instant she didn't believe what she was seeing. Quinn had said all the servants were out of the house. Lies. So many lies.

Jumping to her feet, she ran to the door and frantically jerked at the handle, but it was locked. Banging her fists against the door and kicking at the bottom, she shouted. "Help me! Please! Open the door, please, please. I beg you! Help me!"

How many people would they sacrifice to the altar of Quinn's political ambition? Was she saving herself or endangering someone else?

Pounding on the door, knowing Quinn and Paul would hear her, she screamed. "Please! Let me inside! They're going to kill me! Please, please, help me!"

The door opened, and she stumbled inside, blinking and shielding her eyes against a sudden shine of light. Dimly she registered that she was inside the Blalocks' third-floor apartment. And Quinn and Paul were not far behind her. She heard them shouting on the servants' staircase.

"Please," she said wildly, lowering her hand to see James Blalock standing in his living room staring at her. The lines in his face sagged with astonishment and dismay. "I have to hide, I have to—"

"James? What's all the—" Mary Blalock stepped out of a bedroom and stopped abruptly. Her hands flew to her lips and her eyes widened. "Oh no!"

"Lily!"

She cast a desperate look behind her. They were on the third floor now. In seconds they would have her.

Tears blurring her vision, knowing it was hopeless, knowing it was over, Lily ran into the room Mary Blalock had stepped out of, whirled and fumbled her fingers over the latch, looking for a lock. Pushing the lock button, she exhaled a sharp breath of momentary relief. The lock would not hold against a determined assault, but she'd given herself a few more minutes.

There was only one thing left. She would crawl out onto

the snowy rooftop. If she didn't fall three floors to her death, she would scream and pray that someone heard her pleas.

Spinning, she cast a swift look around the bedroom, concentrating on the window.

Then her gaze swung back to the bed and her knees buckled. Throwing out a hand, she caught the back of a chair and held herself upright.

A woman sat propped against the pillows, holding a book in one hand and a china doll cradled in the crook of her arm. Blond wisps spilled from a charming coil wound on top of her head. She looked up at Lily with wide lavender-blue eyes and a smile of surprise and utter delight.

"Susan! Oh my dearest, at last you've come! I've been waiting so long!" Dropping the book, she stretched out a hand. Tears of happiness flooded her eyes. "I have so much to tell you!"

"Miriam," Lily whispered, gripping the chair back.

It was like gazing into a distorted mirror and seeing a slightly older, slightly altered version of herself. Miriam was heavier than she was, her cheeks rounder, the heart shape of her face more pronounced. Arizona's harsh sun had etched faint lines in Lily's forehead that lotions could not erase, but Miriam's face was as smooth as a child's. The childlike impression was further enhanced by the frilly white nightgown she wore and the doll in her arms.

Someone was shouting and pounding on the door, but Lily didn't hear. Drawn irresistibly forward, she approached the bed and sat on the edge when Miriam patted the coverlet beside her. Miriam clasped her in a long, emotional embrace, and the sweet scent of forget-me-nots reeled through Lily's senses.

"Oh my dearest, you look exactly as I knew you would," Miriam said, reaching a trembling hand to tuck a strand of hair behind Lily's ear. "I've missed you so much all these years." Her voice was sweet and high, slightly breathless.

Gently, Lily touched her cheek. "You're alive," she whispered.

Miriam laughed. "Of course I'm alive. And look. Look at my beautiful, wonderful baby." Pride glowed in her eyes. "I named her after you. Isn't she beautiful?"

"Beautiful," Lily murmured, blinking at the doll. Tears swam in her eyes. Miriam was alive. And hopelessly crazy.

"And so good. Aren't you, darling?" Tenderly, she kissed the doll's forehead. "Sleep now, my dearest, your auntie Susan and I have so much to talk about."

The door splintered around the handle, burst open, and Quinn ran into the room. He started forward, then stopped when he saw Lily sitting on the side of the bed, holding Miriam's hand. Shoulders sagging, he lifted a hand and covered his eyes.

"Richard! Is it Wednesday already? How wonderful. And look who's finally come. It's Susan, all grown-up." After kissing the doll again and gently placing her on the bed beside her, Miriam withdrew a handkerchief from the sleeve of her nightgown and wiped at the tears on her lashes. "I'm so happy that we're all together again. Marshall will be very pleased when he arrives home." She gripped Lily's hand. "I've told my husband all about you. He'll be so happy for me that you've finally come."

Richard and Susan. Miriam's brother and sister.

Lily met Quinn's gaze and held it. Silently, she begged his forgiveness for believing he had murdered his wife.

Shame and confusion heated her face. And deep, heart-aching sadness.

Rubbing the shoulder he'd used to break in the door, Quinn walked to the bed, drew a breath, then bent over Miriam and kissed her forehead.

"It's not Wednesday," he said softly, stroking her arm. "I came because Susan is here." One dark eyebrow lifted, and he gave Lily a weary, questioning look. She nodded.

Miriam covered his hand with hers and darted an eager glance toward the shattered door. "Is Marshall home yet?"

"Not yet," Quinn said, taking the chair beside the bed. "I'm sure he'll be here soon. How is the baby tonight?"

"Not as fussy as yesterday. Would you like to hold her?" She beamed at Lily. "Richard is such a dear brother. And he adores his niece. Baby Susan loves it when he rocks her."

Lily opened wet eyes when she felt a hand touch her shoulder. Looking up, she met Paul's steady gaze, and he beckoned her to her feet. Quietly, they walked to the door, where Lily paused. Miriam was talking softly to Quinn, who held the doll in his arms.

Miriam glanced toward them and her face fell. "Oh! Susan, please don't go! We have so much to catch up on, and Marshall will be home soon. I've told him all about you, and he wants to meet you."

Lily swallowed hard and blinked at the tears that swam in her eyes. "Dearest Miriam, I'll return when I can stay longer. We'll have a nice visit then."

"Do you promise?"

"Yes, my friend," she whispered, gazing at a mirror image of herself. "I promise."

"I love you, Susan. I'm so happy that you've come back to me."

"I love you too, Miriam. I always have."

Leaning on Paul, she entered the small living room. James Blalock sat on a horsehair sofa, his arms around his wife. Mary Blalock leaned forward, her face in her hands.

"It's all right," Lily murmured, hardly aware of what she was saying to the old couple. Gripping Paul's arm, still trembling, she gazed into his eyes. "I want a whiskey."

"So do I," he said, opening the apartment door for her. "This has been a hell of a day."

Paul related most of the story while they waited for Quinn in the family parlor.

Miriam had lost her senses the night baby Susan died in the fire. "She tried desperately to reach the nursery, but the blaze was too intense. Her hands and arms were burned, and she fell through the flaming gallery railing. The fall crippled one leg and severely damaged the other."

"Is she an invalid?" Lily asked in a choked voice. She fell into a chair and took another long swallow of whiskey, holding the glass with both hands as her fingers continued to shake.

"She might as well be. She never leaves her bed. In actuality?" He shrugged and gazed into his whiskey glass. "She could probably manage with a crutch or a wheelchair, but she won't. She knows Marshall Oliver's wife is an invalid. Since she believes that she is Oliver's wife, she also believes that she's an invalid."

"Is there any hope that she'll regain her sanity?"

"None. Quinn brought in the best doctors money can buy. One came all the way from Berlin to examine her. Their consensus is that Miriam cannot face surviving the fire when her baby died. The German doctor suggested she had two choices, suicide or insanity. Not much is known about these things, but he believes Miriam chose insanity without being aware she was making a choice. She's hidden a truth too terrible to confront by constructing an alternate world where she is safe and happy and everything in her world is the way she wants it to be. Miriam believes she is happily married to Marshall Oliver, she has a beautiful healthy baby, and her adored brother Richard visits her every Wednesday evening."

Lily gazed at the embers glowing in the hearth. "That breaks my heart," she said softly.

"We discussed placing her in an institution, but Quinn wouldn't hear of it after inspecting the appalling conditions in several asylums. More importantly, he wanted her close enough that he could visit regularly without arousing anyone's curiosity, and close enough that he could monitor her care and condition. Although Miriam does not leave the Blalocks' apartment, at least she is in her own home. If she did manage to wander out of the apartment, there's nothing in this house that would frighten her or be unfamiliar."

So many mysteries, large and small, were unraveling tonight. So many things were beginning to make sense. Lily met his gaze. "It seems ridiculous now, but I believed that you and Quinn had murdered Miriam."

"I know you did," Quinn said, walking into the room. He went directly to Lily and gently lifted her from the chair and wrapped his arms around her. He stroked her hair with a hand that lightly trembled. "Where do I begin?" he murmured looking deeply into her eyes. "Can you ever forgive me for frightening you so badly? By now you must know that when Paul spoke of getting rid of you, he meant sending you to Europe immediately instead of waiting until after the election."

"Given what you were thinking," Paul said drily, "it was an unfortunate choice of words."

Lily inhaled Quinn's clean outdoors scent and a faint sweet trace of forget-me-nots. Felt the solid strength of his body there for her to lean on. "I'm so sorry," she whispered. "I even believed you had Callihan killed."

"Callihan?" Paul's eyebrows rose. "If ever I wanted to murder someone, it was Ephram Callihan. And that son of a bitch, Marshall Oliver."

"Of course," Lily whispered, releasing a breath. "Why didn't I see it? If you were going to solve a problem by killing anyone, it should have been Marshall."

Paul patted his pockets, looking for his pipe. "Callihan died in a drunken brawl exactly as the newspapers reported. As far as I'm concerned, his death was a stroke of rare good luck. And good riddance. But Lily, it was also a surprise."

"I wanted to tell you about Miriam. I almost did a dozen times," Quinn said softly.

"If anyone is to blame for keeping Miriam a secret, it's me," Paul said, moving away from the fireplace. He sat heavily in the chair Lily had vacated and let his head fall back, closing his eyes. "No one in the party would have agreed to run a candidate with a crazy wife. There's too much shame and disgrace attached. As for you, in retrospect it seems foolish, but I thought the fewer secrets you knew, the less of a threat you would be in the future. I found you in prison, Lily. You'd shot a man, and the prosecutor believed you had lied on the stand. There was no reason to suppose we could trust you."

"Keeping Miriam locked away is something I'm deeply ashamed of," Quinn said in a voice rough with emotion.

"I'm not proud of anything connected with my marriage. I left Miriam alone too often. I didn't care for her the way she needed to be cared for. It's my fault that she was vulnerable to Oliver's seduction. And the night of the fire. I should have been here. Instead, I put the campaign first." Releasing Lily, he clenched his teeth and knots rippled up his jawline. "How does a man forgive himself for these things?" He shook his head.

Tonight would change things in ways Lily couldn't yet guess, but she knew nothing could be the same. "I was afraid of you," she said softly, marveling that such a thing could be true. She had seen him rocking a doll, and in that moment, if not before, she had known there was nothing whatever to fear in Quinn Westin. Not now, not ever. He was a good man with a good heart who had made a chain of unfortunate decisions.

"I will regret that I frightened you until the day I die," he said, leaning a hand against the mantelpiece and staring into the fireplace. Lifting his head, he frowned at her, bewilderment in his gaze. "What kind of monster have I become? That a woman I love could fear me?"

Lily ran to him and threw her arms around his waist. "That's behind us now." Pressing her forehead against his shoulder, she closed her eyes and drew a shaking breath. "Quinn? What happens next?"

After a moment he lifted her face and gazed into her eyes. "To a large extent, that depends on you."

Chapter 22

They drove through the snowstorm to the ranch, arriving near midnight. Both were exhausted but neither could sleep. They sat by the fire in the living room, holding each other, and beginning again, this time with the truth.

Quinn was harshly unsparing of himself. He spoke of his rage at discovering Miriam's affair with Marshall Oliver, spoke of his conflict regarding the fire. "I was deeply sorry that Miriam's child died that night but secretly relieved that I wouldn't have to live with a constant reminder of my wife's preference for another man." Tilting his head back, he stared at the ceiling. "I'll flog myself for the rest of my life for my selfishness and that small pang of relief."

Near dawn, he spoke of Miriam as she was now. "I couldn't give up my dreams, Lily, so I hid her away." He blinked at her with reddened eyes. "I think of it now and wonder how such a thing could ever have seemed reasonable."

"You're being too hard on yourself," she said softly, leaning to gently kiss him. "People fear insanity. The moment Miriam's condition became known, your campaign would have been over."

He nodded. "I know. I had to make a choice, and then

discovered how hard it was to live with that choice. There was the knowledge that once we announced Miriam's death, her confinement would become permanent, with no hope that she could be seen in public again. The constant fear that someone would learn of her insanity or discover her. And the crushing guilt of blame. If only I'd been a more attentive husband, maybe the affair wouldn't have happened. If only I'd been home the night of the fire. If only I'd been able to find a doctor who could have helped her."

"No one can help her," Lily said sadly.

"And all the lies. One on top of another. Especially the lies to you."

"It's over now, Quinn."

"Is it, Lily?" He stared at her in the flickering light of the embers. "The lies will go on. Lies to the voters about what I believe in. Lies to Miriam's friends and acquaintances when we announce that she has died. Lies to Miriam, supporting her delusion that I'm her brother. And the lies to myself that everything I've done is justified by ambition."

Lily didn't know what to say and turned her face to the window. A pale sun had chased the last of the night away.

"Good morning, Miss Dale," Quinn said after a period of silence. He ran a hand over the bristle on his jaw. "It's been a long night."

"It's a new day, cowboy."

"I promise you, Lily. There will never again be any lies between us," he said slowly, loving the look of her, the scent of her, the trust growing again in her lovely eyes.

She kissed him, her soft mouth clinging to his. Then she wrapped her arms around his neck and gazed into his eyes. "I think before you can be honest with me, you need to be honest with yourself. Perhaps that's one of the things you should think about, Quinn."

God, he loved this woman. Despite all the deceptions, she knew him so well, knew him better than he knew himself. Holding her, breathing her and feeling her heartbeat against his own, he asked how he could possibly let her go. Would anything in his life have meaning if she wasn't beside him to share it?

"Go," she said softly. "Ride your horse and do your thinking."

He rode across snowy fields, his head down, thinking about his life and the mistakes he had made. He thought about what he wanted and what he valued, what was possible and what was not, what was important. That evening he sat with Lily before the fire and again they talked deep into the night. They talked about Miriam and a failed marriage, discussed the prevailing attitudes toward insanity, and he spoke about the horrifying asylums he had visited. Lily related her growing-up years, her unhappiness with Cy Gardener, and talked about her prison experiences. They agreed there were many areas where an enlightened governor could make a significant and beneficial difference. Lily asked him to add these areas to his list of projected reforms. But he doubted the political system would permit him to inaugurate the reforms he wanted.

It wasn't until the next day that she raised the subject they had been avoiding, the future.

Tucking her cloak around her, she leaned against the corral fence, keeping her eyes on the horses. "I've read some books about your Italy, and I've decided that's where I'll go." She drew a deep breath and exhaled slowly, watching her breath plume before her. "And Quinn, I think

Paul is right. You'll gain a tremendous advantage if I leave immediately. You can say I died. A bereaved candidate is a sympathetic candidate."

Quinn rested his arms on the top rail and frowned at the distant snowcapped peaks. "I love you, Lily. I don't want you to leave."

"I know," she whispered, blinking rapidly. "But you and I both understand that I can't stay. Nothing has really changed. Since I must leave, we might as well do it in a way that gives you the greatest political advantage. That means immediately."

She was wrong. Since Lily had come into his life, everything had changed.

They turned back to the ranch house, and she took his arm, following a path in the snow. It occurred to Quinn that he would be glad to see spring. He'd never been fond of snow.

"I just thought of something," he said with a smile. So many conversations had begun this way during yesterday and today. "I have a surprise for you."

"I've had enough surprises for a lifetime," she said, hugging his arm close to her body.

He waited, knowing her well enough to know she would ask about the surprise, and he laughed when she did. "You'll know soon enough. Paul is bringing you something wonderful from town. It took a while to arrange."

"Speaking of town," she said, turning into his arms. "Shouldn't we go back? You have a speech the day after tomorrow. And I promised Miriam a long visit, which I'm looking forward to."

He couldn't speak. Standing in the snowy yard, he held her and couldn't let her go. But he felt everything else falling away. Ambitions—dreams that no longer mattered. She was a lovely, compassionate, and caring woman, and nothing else was important in his life except being with her.

When he could speak, he lifted her face and brushed his thumb across her lips. "Yesterday you told me that you'd learned the value of rules . . ."

She laughed, and her lovely eyes softened. "I'm afraid I'll never be completely reformed," she said, teasing him. "But I concede that society needs rules, and it's better if people obey them."

"Are you aware that different societies have different rules? Europe, for instance, views certain arrangements much differently than America does."

"Oh no," she said with an exaggerated groan. "Are you saying I'll have to learn new rules?"

"Lily?" It was all so clear. Framing her face between his hands, he examined her face. "Do you love me?"

"With all my heart and soul," she said simply.

"Come inside by the fire. We have a future to decide."

Hand in hand, they stood on the veranda, watching Paul's sleigh approach the ranch house. It reminded Lily of that long-ago day when she had stood outside the Yuma Women's Prison watching Paul's coach whirl toward her in a trail of dust. She had been a different woman then. Suspicious, bitter, finished with men, a woman with a past and no future.

She would never be a fine lady. She would always be a little too outspoken, a little too vivacious and boisterous, a little careless with the dictates of etiquette. She would always be a woman who liked her whiskey and an occasional cigar. Who dropped a cussword now and again. She would always be a woman better suited as a gentleman's mistress than a wife.

"Any last-minute regrets?" she asked softly, looking up at Quinn and squeezing his hand.

"None," he said firmly. His gaze was soft when he bent to kiss her lips.

The answer was written on his craggy face. He was more relaxed today than she had ever known him to be. The anxiety and anger had vanished from the back of his eyes. The lines framing his mouth seemed lighter. He looked younger, happier than she had ever seen him.

"I'll inform Paul that I'm withdrawing from the race while you enjoy your surprise," he said, turning her into his arms.

Lily wrapped her arms around his waist and smiled up at him. "Paul is not going to be happy. A Kingmaker needs a king."

"Paul will understand. In fact, I doubt he'll be surprised."

"You would have made a fine governor, Quinn."

"The system wouldn't have allowed me to accomplish the things I wanted, Lily. In the end, I would have betrayed my backers or myself. Paul knows that, too."

"I hope he'll understand and be happy for us." Shading her eyes against the glare of sunlight on snow, she peered toward the driveway and raised her brows in surprise. "He has someone with him."

"I believe he does," Quinn said, smiling. "Someone who's been waiting several days for this meeting." He touched her face. "I had planned to explain her as your niece."

Lily's heart stopped and a thrill of goose bumps lifted on her arms. "Quinn! Oh my God!" She would have crumpled if he hadn't gripped her arms and held her upright.

Shaking, clinging to him for support, she turned a white face toward the sleigh in time to see Paul lift a small girl to the ground.

She was blond like Lily, with huge anxious blue eyes and a rosy mouth. A small widow's peak made a valentine of her face. She wore a red-velvet cloak over a plaid dress and carried a white fur muff that matched her little hat. Tears ran down Lily's cheeks as she realized her Aunt Edna couldn't afford to dress Rose so exquisitely. That was Quinn's doing.

"I love you so much!" she whispered, her voice choked.

And then she ran down the stairs, dropped to her knees in the snow, and swept Rose into her arms. When she could bear to break away, she leaned back and smiled at her daughter with swimming eyes. "I have longed for you every day!"

Rose touched a shaking hand to her wet cheek. "I didn't believe I had a mama. I thought you were dead." Rose studied her with shining eyes. "You're so beautiful, Mama."

"So are you, darling, so are you! Come inside, I have so much to tell you!"

"I'm going to marry Uncle Paul when I grow up."

"This wonderful man," she said, speaking around tears of joy, "is your new papa."

Quinn dropped down beside them in the snow and smiled. "When I met your mama, she and I were strangers like you and I are now. But that will change. We're going to be friends, Rose, and I expect to love you as much as I love your mother. I hope one day you'll love me, too."

Blazing with happiness, Lily watched the two people she loved best solemnly shake hands. And then, she didn't know what came over her, but she filled her hands and pelted them both with snow. One of her snowballs struck Paul and he, too, jumped into the fray of flying snow.

At the end, she and Rose were wrapped in Quinn's arms and they were all laughing, loving, strangers no more.

April, 1881
My dearest Paul,

I love Italy in all seasons, but I think spring is my favorite time of year. The olive trees are in blossom now and the sweet fragrance drifts through the windows of the villa. The sky is a lovely bright blue that often reminds me of Colorado.

We were so sorry that you couldn't come to us this year, but we understand that you're guiding a new king through his first year on the throne. Do come as soon as you're able. We miss you.

Thank you for sending the crate of books. I adored the novels you chose for me. Quinn will write separately to tell you how helpful he found your selections. Unfortunately, his book on political reform progresses slowly and with many interruptions. Over the years, the trickle of villagers coming up the hill to seek legal advice has swollen to a stream, and eventually my darling will be forced to quit resisting and acknowledge that he has become the village counsel. Yes, I hear you laughing even from this distance.

The children are well and happy. At ten, Rose is quite a young lady, my treasure and joy. She asks that I remind you that you promised to marry her when she's all grown-up. Paul is four now and runs the governess a merry chase. Little Miriam is three and shows promise of being as lovely as her namesake.

Our sad news is that Miriam died shortly after the new year. To the end, she believed I was her sister and Quinn was her brother. And so it seemed to us. I loved her as if we were indeed the sisters she believed us to be. I miss her terribly.

I will close by telling you that Quinn and I were quietly married last month. I thought it didn't matter that we weren't married. But I have become the woman you set out to make me, my dear friend. I wept with joy when we said our vows. After all these years, the last deception is finally ended. Our joy could have been greater only if you had been with us.

Dear Paul, I think of you often, more frequently than you would imagine. I remember that first day and hear you telling me that I had so much to gain from becoming a stranger's wife. I didn't believe you then. But I look at my beloved husband and our children, and everything you promised came true. Thank you, my friend, for creating a lady and giving me this life. With love and gratitude.

Lily Westin